Heart of the Sea

ALSO BY NORA ROBERTS
FROM CLIPPER LARGE PRINT

JEWELS OF THE SUN

Heart of the Sea

Nora Roberts

W F HOWES LTD

This large print edition published in 2007 by
W F Howes Ltd
Unit 4, Rearsby Business Park, Gaddesby Lane,
Rearsby, Leicester LE7 4YH

1 3 5 7 9 10 8 6 4 2

First published in the United Kingdom in 2006
by Piatkus Books Ltd.

A CIP catalogue record for this book is available
from the British Library

ISBN 978 1 40740 938 2

Typeset by Palimpsest Book Production Limited,
Grangemouth, Stirlingshire
Printed and bound in Great Britain
by Antony Rowe Ltd, Chippenham, Wilts.

To Pat Gaffney
All references to Irish music are just for you

Her eyes they shone like diamonds, you'd think she was queen of the land.

—THE BLACK VELVET BAND

CHAPTER 1

The village of Ardmore sat snug on the south coast of Ireland, in the county of Waterford, with the Celtic Sea spread out at its feet. The stone seawall curved around, following the skirt of the golden-sand beach.

It boasted in its vicinity a pretty jut of cliffs upholstered with wild grass, and a hotel that clung to them. If one had a mind to, it was a pleasant if hearty walk on a narrow path around the headland, and at the top of the first hill were the ruins of the oratory and well of Saint Declan.

The view was worth the climb, with sky and sea and village spread out below. This was holy ground, and though dead were buried there, only one grave had its stone marked.

The village itself claimed neat streets and painted cottages, some with the traditional thatched roofs, and a number of steep hills as well. Flowers grew in abundance, spilling out of window boxes, baskets, and pots, and dooryards. It made a charming picture from above or below, and the villagers were proud to have won the Tidy Town award two years running.

Atop Tower Hill was a fine example of a round tower, with its conical top still in place, and the ruins of the twelfth-century cathedral built in honor of Saint Declan. Folks would tell you, in case you wondered, that Declan arrived thirty years before good Saint Patrick.

Not that they were bragging, they were just letting you know how things stood.

Those interested in such matters would find examples of ogham carving on the stones put for safekeeping inside the roofless cathedral, and Roman arcading faded with time and wind but still worth the study.

But the village itself made no attempt at such grandeur. It was merely a pleasant place with a shop or two and a scatter of cottages built back away from lovely sand beaches.

The sign for Ardmore said FAILTE, and that was 'welcome.'

It was that very combination of ancient history and simple character and hospitality that interested Trevor Magee.

His people had come from Ardmore and Old Parish. Indeed, his grandfather had been born here, in a small house very near Ardmore Bay, had lived the first years of his life breathing that moist sea air, had perhaps held his mother's hand as she'd walked to the shops or along the surf.

His grandfather had left his village and his country, taking his wife and young son with him to America. He had never been back, and so far as

Trevor knew, had never looked back either. There had been a distance and a bitter one, between the old man and the country of his birth. Ireland and Ardmore and the family Dennis Magee had left behind had rarely been spoken of.

So Trevor's image of Ardmore had a ripple of sentiment and curiosity through it, and his reasons for choosing it had a personal bent.

But he could afford personal bents.

He was a man who built, and who, as his grand-father and father before him, built cleverly and well.

His grandfather had made his living laying brick, and made his fortune speculating on properties during and after World War II, until the buying and selling of them was his business, and the building done by those he hired.

Old Magee had been no more sentimental about his laborer's beginnings than he had been about his homeland. To Trevor's recollection, the man had shown no sentiment about anything.

But Trevor had inherited the heart and hands of the builder as much as the cool, hard sense of the businessman, and he had learned to use both.

He would use them both here, and a dash of sentiment as well, to build his theater, a traditional structure for traditional music, with its entrance the already established pub known as Gallagher's.

The deal with the Gallaghers had been set, the ground broken for the project before he'd been able to hack through his schedule for the time he wanted to spend here. But he was here now, and he intended to do more than sign checks and watch.

He wanted his hands in it.

A man could work up a good sweat even in May in such a temperate climate when he spent a morning hauling concrete. That morning Trevor left the cottage he'd decided to rent for the duration of his stay wearing a denim jacket and carrying a steaming mug of coffee. Now, a handful of hours later, the jacket had been tossed aside, and a thin line of damp ran front and back down his shirt.

He'd have paid a hundred pounds for one cold beer.

The pub was only a short walk through the construction rubble. He knew from stopping in the day before that it did a brisk business midday. But a man could hardly quench his thirst with a chilly Harp when he forbade his employees to drink on the job.

He rolled his shoulders, circled his neck as he scanned the site. The concrete truck let out its continuous rumble, men shouted, relaying orders or acknowledging them. Job music, Trevor thought. He never tired of it.

That was a gift from his father. Learn from the ground up had been Dennis Junior's credo, and the third-generation Magee had done just that. For more than ten years – fifteen if he counted the summers he'd sweated on construction sites – he'd

4

learned just what went into the business of building.

The backaches and blood and aching muscles.

At thirty-two, he spent more time in boardrooms and meetings than on a scaffold, but he'd never lost the appreciation, or the satisfaction of swinging his own hammer.

He intended to indulge himself doing just that in Ardmore, in his theater.

He watched the small woman in a faded cap and battered boots circle around, gesture as the wet concrete slid down the chute. She scrambled over sand and stone, used her shovel to rap the chute and alert the operator to stop, then waded into the muck with the other laborers to shovel and smooth.

Brenna O'Toole, Trevor thought, and was glad he'd followed his instincts there. Hiring her and her father as foremen on the project had been the right course of action. Not just for their building skills, he decided – though they were impressive – but because they knew the village and the people in it, kept the job running smoothly and the men happy and productive.

Public relations on this sort of project were just as vital as a sturdy foundation.

Yes, indeed, they were working out well. His three days in Ardmore had shown him he'd made the right choice with O'Toole and O'Toole.

When Brenna climbed out again, Trevor stepped over, extended a hand to give her a final boost.

'Thanks.' She sliced her shovel into the ground, leaned on it, and despite her filthy boots and faded cap, looked like a pixie. Her skin was pure Irish cream, and a few curls of wild red escaped the cap.

'Tim Riley says we won't have rain for another day or two, and he has a way of being right about such things more than he's wrong. I think we'll have the slab set up for you before you have to worry about weather.'

'You made considerable progress before I got here.'

'Sure, and once you gave us the high sign there was no reason to wait. We'll have you a good, solid foundation, Mr Magee, and on schedule.'

'Trev.'

'Aye, Trev.' She tipped back her cap, then her head so she could meet his eyes. She figured him a good foot higher than her five-two, even wearing her boots. 'The men you sent along from America, they're a fine team.'

'As I handpicked them, I agree.'

She thought his voice faintly aloof, but not unfriendly. 'And do you never pick females then?'

He smiled slowly so it seemed that humor just moseyed over his face until it reached eyes the color of turf smoke. 'I do indeed and as often as possible. Both on and off the job. I've put one of my best carpenters on this project. She'll be here next week.'

'It's good to know my cousin Brian wasn't wrong

in that area. He said you hired by skill and not gender. It's a good morning's work here,' she added, nodding to the site. 'That noisy bastard of a truck will be our constant companion for a while yet. Darcy'll be back from her holiday tomorrow, and I can tell you she'll bitch our ears off about the din.'

'It's a good noise. Building.'

'I've always thought the same.'

They stood a moment in perfect accord while the truck vomited out the last yard of concrete.

'I'll buy you lunch,' Trevor said.

'I'll let you.' Brenna gave a whistle to catch her father's attention, then mimed spooning up food. Mick responded with a grin and a wave, then went back to work.

'He's in his heaven,' Brenna commented as they walked over to rinse off their boots. 'Nothing makes Mick O'Toole happier than finding himself in the middle of a job site, the muckier the better.'

Satisfied, Brenna gave her feet a couple of stomps, then headed around to the kitchen door. 'I hope you'll take some time to see the area while you're here, instead of locking yourself into the job at hand.'

'I plan to see what's around.' He had reports, of course – detailed reports on tourist draws, road conditions, routes to and from major cities. But he intended to see for himself.

Needed to see it, Trevor admitted to himself. Something had been pulling him toward Ireland, toward Ardmore, for more than a year. In dreams.

'Ah, now there's a fine-looking man doing what he does best,' Brenna said when she pushed open the kitchen door. 'What have you for us today, Shawn?'

He turned from the enormous old stove, a rangy man with shaggy black hair and eyes of misty blue. 'For the special we've sea spinach soup and the beef sandwich. Good day to you, Trevor. Is this one working you harder than she should?'

'She keeps things moving.'

'And so I must, for the man in my life is slow. I wonder, Shawn, if you've selected another tune or two for Trevor's consideration.'

'I've been busy catering to my new wife. She's a demanding creature.' So saying, he reached out to cradle Brenna's face and kiss her. 'Get out of my kitchen. It's confusing enough around here without Darcy.'

'She'll be back tomorrow, and by this time of the day you'll have cursed her a dozen times.'

'Why do you think I miss her? Give your order to Sinead,' he told Trevor. 'She's a good girl, and our Jude's been working with her. She just needs a bit more practice.'

'A friend of my sister Mary Kate is Sinead,' Brenna told Trevor as she pushed open the door that swung between kitchen and pub. 'A good-natured girl, if a bit scattered in the brain. She wants to marry Billy O'Hara, and that is the sum total of her ambitions at this time.'

'And what does Billy O'Hara have to say?'

8

'Being not quite so ambitious as Sinead, Billy keeps his mouth shut. Good day to you, Aidan.'

'And to you.' The oldest of the Gallaghers worked the bar and had his hands on the taps as he looked over. 'Will you be joining us for lunch, then?'

'That we will. We've caught you busy.'

'God bless the tour buses.' With a wink, Aidan slid two pints down the bar to waiting hands.

'Do you want us to take it in the kitchen?'

'No need for that unless you're in a great hurry.' His eyes, a deeper blue than his brother's, scanned the pub. 'Service is a mite slower than our usual. But there's a table or two left.'

'We'll leave it to the boss.' Brenna turned to Trevor. 'How will you have it?'

'Let's get a table.' The better to watch how the business ran.

He followed her out and sat with her at one of the mushroom-shaped tables. There was a buzz of conversation, a haze of smoke, and the yeasty scent of beer.

'Will you have a pint?' Brenna asked him.

'Not until after the workday.'

Her lips twitched as she kicked back in her chair. 'So I've heard from some of the men. Word is you're a tyrant on this particular matter.'

He didn't mind the term 'tyrant.' It meant he was in control. 'Word would be correct.'

'I'll tell you this, you may have a bit of a problem enforcing such a rule around here. Many who'll labor for you were nursed on Guinness and it's as natural to them as mother's milk.'

'I'm fond of it myself, but when a man or woman is on my clock, they stick with mother's milk.'

'Ah, you're a hard man, Trevor Magee.' But she said it with a laugh. 'So tell me, how are you liking Faerie Hill Cottage?'

'Very much. It's comfortable, efficient, quiet, and has a view that rips your heart into your throat. It's just what I was looking for, so I'm grateful you put me on to it.'

'That's not a problem, not a problem at all. It's in the family. I think Shawn misses the little kitchen there, as the house we're building's far from finished. More than livable,' she added, as it was one of their current sore points, 'but I figure to concentrate on the kitchen there on my off days so he'll be happier.'

'I'd like to see it.'

'Would you?' Surprised, she angled her head. 'Well, you're welcome any time. I'll give you the direction. Do you mind me saying I didn't expect you to be as friendly a sort of man as you seem to be?'

'What did you expect?'

'More of a shark, and I hope that doesn't offend you.'

'It doesn't. And it depends on the waters where I'm swimming.' He glanced over, and his face warmed as Aidan's wife came up to the table. But when he started to rise, Jude waved him down again.

'No, I'm not joining you, but thanks.' She rested a hand on her very pregnant belly. 'Hello, I'm Jude Frances and I'll be your server today.'

'You shouldn't be on your feet like this, carrying trays.'

Jude sighed as she took out her order pad. 'He sounds like Aidan. I put my feet up when I need to, and I don't carry anything heavy. Sinead can't handle things on her own.'

'Not to worry, Trevor. Why me own blessed mother dug potatoes on the day I was born, then went back to roast them after the delivery.' At Trevor's narrowed glance, Brenna chuckled. 'Well, maybe not, but I'll wager she could have. I'll have today's soup, if you don't mind, Jude, and a glass of milk,' she added with a wicked smile for Trevor.

'The same,' he said, 'plus the sandwich.'

'A fine choice. I'll be right back with it.'

'She's stronger than she looks,' Brenna told him when Jude moved to another table. 'And more stubborn. Now that she's found her direction, so to speak, she'll only work harder to prove she can do what you tell her she shouldn't. Aidan won't let her overdo, I promise you. The man adores her.'

'Yes, I've noticed. The Gallagher men seem to be devoted to their women.'

'So they'd better be, or their women will know why.' Relaxed, she kicked back, pulled off her cap. Those red curls tumbled down. 'So you aren't finding it, I guess we'd say "too rustic" for you – out

11

in the countryside here after being used to New York City?'

He thought of the job sites he'd experienced: mud slides, floods, blistering heat, petty vandalism, and sabotage. 'Not at all. The village is exactly what I expected after Finkle's reports.'

'Ah, yes, Finkle.' She remembered Trevor's scout very well. 'Now there's a man I believe prefers urban conveniences. But you're not so . . . particular, then.'

'I'm very particular, depending. That's why I incorporated most of your design into the theater project.'

'Now that's a fine and sneaky compliment.' And nothing could have pleased her more. 'I suppose I was angling more toward the personal. I have a special fondness for the cottage on Faerie Hill, and I wasn't sure you'd find the place to your liking. Thinking, I suppose, a man with your background and wherewithal would be more inclined to settle at the cliff hotel with maid service and the restaurant and so forth.'

'Hotel rooms become confining. And I find it interesting to stay in the house where the woman who was engaged to one of my ancestors was born, and lived, and died.'

'She was a fine woman, Old Maude. A wise woman.' Brenna kept her eyes on Trevor's face as she spoke. 'Her grave's up near the well of Saint Declan, and it's there you can feel her. She's not the one in the cottage now.'

12

'Who is?'

Brenna lifted her eyebrows. 'You don't know the legend, then? Your grandfather was born here, and your father as well, though he was a babe when they sailed to America. Still, he visited many years back. Did neither of them tell you the story of Lady Gwen and Prince Carrick?'

'No. So it would be Lady Gwen who haunts the cottage?'

'Have you seen her?'

'No.' Trevor hadn't been raised on legends and myths, but there was more than enough Irish in his blood to cause him to wonder about them. 'But there's a feminine feel to the place, almost a fragrance, so odds are for the lady.'

'You'd be right about that.'

'Who was she? I figure if I'm sharing quarters with a ghost, I should know something about her.'

No careless dismissal of the subject, no amused indulgence of the Irish and their legends, Brenna noted. Just cool interest. 'You surprise me again. Let me see to something first. I'll be right back.'

Fascinating, Trevor mused. He had himself a ghost.

He'd felt things before. In old buildings, empty lots, deserted fields. It wasn't the kind of thing a man generally talked about at a board meeting or over a cold one with the crew after a sweaty day's work. Not usually. But this was a different place, with a different tone. More, he wanted to know.

Everything to do with Ardmore and the area was

13

of interest to him now. A good ghost story could draw people in just as successfully as a well-run pub. It was all atmosphere.

Gallagher's was exactly the kind of atmosphere he'd been looking for as a segue into his theater. The old wood, blackened by time and smoke and grease, mated comfortably with the cream-colored walls, the stone hearth, the low tables and benches.

The bar itself was a beauty, an aged chestnut that he'd already noted the Gallaghers kept wiped and polished. The age of customers ranged from a baby in arms to the oldest man Trevor believed he'd ever seen, who was balanced on a stool at the far end of the bar.

There were several others he took as locals just from the way they sat or smoked or sipped, and three times that many who could be nothing other than tourists with their camera bags under their tables and their maps and guidebooks out.

The conversations were a mix of accents, but predominant was that lovely lilt he'd heard in his grandparents' voices until the day they died.

He wondered if they hadn't missed hearing it themselves, and why they'd never had a driving urge to come to Ireland again. What were the bitter memories that had kept them away? Whatever, curiosity about them had skipped over a generation and now had caused him to come back and see for himself.

More, he wondered why he should have *recognized* Ardmore and the view from the cottage and even now know what he would see when he climbed the cliffs. It was as if he carried a picture in his mind of this place, one someone else had taken and tucked away for him.

They'd had no pictures to show him. His father had visited once, when he'd been younger than Trevor was now, but his descriptions had been sketchy at best.

The reports, of course. There had been detailed photographs and descriptions in the reports Finkle had brought back to New York. But he'd known – before he'd opened the first file, he'd already known.

Inherited memory? he mused, though he didn't put much stock in that sort of thing. Inheriting his father's eyes, the clear gray color, the long-lidded shape of them, was one matter. And he was told he had his grandfather's hands, and his mind for business. But how did a memory pass down through the blood?

He toyed with the idea as he continued to scan the room. It didn't occur to him that he looked more the local than the tourist as he sat there in his work clothes, his dark blond hair tousled from the morning's labor. He had a narrow, rawboned face that would put most in mind of a warrior, or perhaps a scholar, rather than a businessman. The woman he'd nearly married had said it looked to be honed and sculpted by some wild genius. The faintest of scars marred his chin, a result of a storm of flying glass during a tornado in Houston, and added to the overall impression of toughness.

It was a face that rarely gave anything away. Unless it was to Trevor Magee's advantage.

At the moment it held a cool and remote expression, but it shifted into easy friendliness when Brenna came back toward the table with Jude. Brenna, he noted, carried the tray.

'I've asked Jude to take a few moments to sit and tell you about Lady Gwen,' Brenna began and was already unloading the order. 'She's a *seanachais*.'

At Trevor's raised eyebrow, Jude shook her head. 'It's Gaelic for storyteller. I'm not really, I'm just—'

'And who has a book being published, and another she's writing. Jude's book'll be out at the end of this very summer,' Brenna went on. 'It'll make a lovely gift, so I'd keep it in mind when you're out shopping.'

'Brenna.' Jude rolled her eyes.

'I'll look for it. Some of Shawn's song lyrics are stories. It's an old and honored tradition.'

'Oh, he'll like that one.' Beaming now, Brenna scooped up the tray. 'I'll deal with this, Jude, and give Sinead a bit of a goose for you. Go ahead and get started. I've heard it often enough before.'

'She has enough energy for twenty people.' A little tired now, Jude picked up her cup of tea.

'I'm glad I found her for this project. Or that she found me.'

'I'd say it was a bit of both, since you're both

16

operators.' She caught herself, winced. 'I didn't mean that in a negative way.'

'Wasn't taken in one. Baby kicking? It puts a look in your eye,' Trevor explained. 'My sister just had her third.'

'Third?' Jude blew out a breath. 'There are moments I wonder how I'm going to manage the one. He's active. But he's just going to have to wait another couple of months.' She ran a hand in slow circles over the mound of her belly, soothing as she sipped. 'You may not know it, but I lived in Chicago until just over a year ago.'

He made a noncommittal sound. Of course he knew, he had extensive reports.

'My plan was to come here for six months, to live in the cottage where my grandmother lived after she lost her parents. She'd inherited it from her cousin Maude, who'd died shortly before I came here.'

'The woman my great-uncle was engaged to.'

'Yes. The day I arrived, it was raining. I thought I was lost. I had been lost, and not just geographically. Everything unnerved me.'

'You came alone, to another country?' Trevor cocked his head. 'That doesn't sound like a woman easily unnerved.'

'That's something Aidan would say.' And because it was, she found herself very comfortable. 'I suppose it's more that I didn't know my own nerve at that point. In any case, I pulled into the street, the driveway actually, of this little thatched-roof cottage. And in the upstairs window I saw a woman. She had a lovely, sad face and pale blond hair that fell around her shoulders. She looked at me, our eyes connected. Then Brenna drove up. It seemed I'd stumbled across my own cottage, and the woman I'd seen in the window was Lady Gwen.'

'The ghost?'

'That's right, yes. It sounds impossible, doesn't it? Or certainly unreasonable. But I can tell you exactly what she looked like. I've sketched her. And I knew no more of the legend when I came here than you appear to know now.'

'I'd like to hear it.'

'Then I'll tell you.' Jude paused as Brenna came back, sat, and tucked into her meal.

She had an easy way with a story, Trevor noted. A smooth and natural rhythm that put the listener into the tale. She told him of a young maid who'd lived in the cottage on the faerie hill. A woman who cared for her father, as her mother had been lost in childbirth, who tended the cottage and its gardens and who carried herself with pride.

Beneath the green slope of the hill was the silver glory of the faerie raft, the palace where Carrick ruled as prince. He was also proud, and he was handsome, with a flowing mane of raven-black hair and eyes of burning blue. Those eyes fell upon the maid Gwen, and hers upon him.

They plunged into love, faerie and mortal, and at night when others slept, he would take her flying on his great winged horse. Never did they speak of that love, for pride blocked the words. One night Gwen's father woke to see her with Carrick as they dismounted from his horse. And in fear for her, he betrothed her to another and ordered her to marry without delay.

Carrick flew on his horse to the sun, and gathered its burning sparks in his silver pouch. When Gwen came out of the cottage to meet him before her wedding, he opened the bag and poured diamonds, jewels of the sun, at her feet. 'Take them and me,' he said, 'for they are my passion for you.' He promised her immortality, and a life of riches and glory. But never once did he speak, even then, of love.

So she refused him, and turned from him. The diamonds that lay on the grass became flowers.

Twice more he came to her, the next time when she carried her first child in her womb. From his silver pouch he poured pearls, tears of the moon that he'd gathered for her. And these, he told her, were his longing for her. But longing is not love, and she had pledged herself to another.

When she turned away, the pearls became flowers.

Many years passed before he came the last time, years during which Gwen raised her children, nursed her husband through his illness, and buried him when she was an old woman. Years during which Carrick brooded in his palace and swept through the sky on his horse.

He dived into the sea to wring from its heart the last of his gifts to her. These he poured at her feet, shimmering sapphires that blazed in the grass. His constancy for her. When now, finally, he spoke of love, she could only weep bitter tears, for her life was over. She told him it was too late, that she had never needed riches or promises of glory, but only to know that he loved her, loved her enough that she could have set aside her fear of giving up her world for his. And as she turned to leave him this time, as the sapphires bloomed into flowers in the grass, his hurt and his temper lashed out in the spell he cast. She would find no peace without him, nor would they see each other again until three times lovers met and, accepting each other, risking hearts, dared to choose love over all else.

Three hundred years. Trevor thought later as he let himself into the house where Gwen had lived and died. A long time to wait. He'd listened to Jude tell the tale in her quiet, storyteller's voice, without interrupting. Not even to tell her that he knew parts of the story. Somehow he knew.

He'd dreamed them.

He hadn't told her that he, too, could have described Gwen, down to the sea green of her eyes and the curve of her cheek. He'd dreamed her as well.

And had, he realized, nearly married Sylvia because she'd reminded him of that dream image.

A soft woman with simple ways. It should have been right between them, he thought as he headed upstairs to shower off the day's dirt. It still irritated him that it hadn't been. In the end, it just hadn't been right.

She'd known it first, and had gently let him go before he'd admitted he already had his eye on the door. Maybe that was what bothered him most of all. He hadn't had the courtesy to do the ending. Though she'd forgiven him for it, he'd yet to forgive himself.

He caught the scent the minute he stepped into the bedroom. Delicate, female, like rose petals freshly fallen onto dewy grass.

'A ghost who wears perfume,' he murmured, oddly amused. 'Well, if you're modest turn your back.' So saying, he stripped where he stood, then walked into the bath.

He spent the rest of his evening alone, catching up on paperwork, scanning the faxes that had come in on the machine he'd brought with him, shooting off replies. He treated himself to a beer and stood outside with it in the last of the dying light listening to the aching silence and watching stars pulse to life.

Tim Riley, whoever the hell he was, looked to be right. There was no rain coming yet. The foundation he was building would set clean.

As he turned to go back in, a streak of movement overhead caught his eye. A blur of white and silver across the darkening sky. But when he looked back for it, narrowing his eyes to scan, he saw nothing but stars and the rise of the quarter moon.

A falling star, he decided. A ghost was one thing, but a flying horse ridden by the prince of the faeries was another entirely.

But he thought he heard the cheerful lilt of pipes and flutes dance across the silence as he shut the door of the cottage for the night.

CHAPTER 2

Darcy Gallagher dreamed of Paris. Strolling along the Left Bank on a perfect spring afternoon with the scent of flowers ripe in the air and the cloudless blue sky soaring overhead.

And perhaps best of all, the weight of shopping bags heavy in her hands.

In her dreams she *owned* Paris, not for a brief week's holiday, but for as long as it contented her. She could stop to while away an hour or two at a sidewalk café, sipping lovely wine and watching the world – for it seemed the whole of the world – wander by.

Long-legged women in smart dresses, and the darkeyed men who watched them. The old woman on her red bicycle with her baguettes spearing up out of her bakery sack, and the tidy children in their straight rows marching along in their prim school uniforms.

They belonged to her, just as the wild and noisy traffic was hers, and the cart on the corner bursting with flowers. She didn't need to ride to the top of the Eiffel Tower to have Paris at her feet.

As she sat sampling wine and cheese that had been aged to perfection, she listened to the city that was hers for the taking. There was music all around her, in the cooing of the ubiquitous pigeons and the swirling *whoosh* when they took wing, in the steady beep of horns, the click of high, thin heels on sidewalks, the laughter of lovers.

Even as she sighed, blissfully happy, the thunder rolled in. At the rumble of it, she glanced skyward. Clouds spewed in from the west, dark and thick. The brilliant sunlight fell into that false twilight that precedes a storm. The rumble became a roar that had her leaping to her feet even while those around her continued to sit, to chat, to stroll as if they heard or saw nothing amiss.

Snatching up her bags, she started to dash away, to safety, to shelter. And a bolt of lightning, sizzling blue at the edges, lanced into the ground at her feet.

She woke with a start, the blood pounding in her ears and her own gasp echoing.

She was in her own rooms over the pub, not in some freakish thunderstorm in Paris. She found some comfort in that, in the familiar walls and quiet light. Found more comfort when she sat up and saw the clothes and trinkets she'd treated herself to in Paris strewn around the room.

Well, she was back to reality, she thought, but at least she'd bagged a few trophies to bring home with her.

It had been a lovely week, the perfect birthday

present to give herself. Indulgent, she admitted, taking such a big chunk of her savings that way. But what were savings for if a woman couldn't use them to celebrate in a spectacular way her first quarter century of living.

She would earn it back. Now that she'd had her first good taste of real travel, she intended to experience it on a more regular basis. Next year, Rome, or Florence. Or perhaps New York City. Wherever it was, it would be someplace wonderful. She would start her Darcy Gallagher holiday fund this very day.

She'd been desperate to get away. To *see* something, almost anything that wasn't what she saw every day of her life. Restlessness was a sensation she was accustomed to, even appreciated about herself. But this had been like a panther inside her, pacing and snarling and ready to claw its way out of her and leap on the people she loved best.

Going away had been the best thing she could have done for herself and, she was sure, for those closest to her. The restlessness was still there, would always stir a bit inside her. But that pacing and snarling had stopped.

The fact was, she was glad to be home, and looking forward to seeing her family, her friends, and all that was dear. And she looked forward to telling them all she'd seen and done during that glorious seven days to herself.

But now she'd best get up and put things back in order. She'd gotten in too late the night before to do more than throw open her bags and admire her new things. She needed to put them away proper, and stack up the gifts she'd bought, for she was a woman who couldn't abide untidiness for long.

She'd missed her family. Even through the giddy rush of seeing, doing, just *being* in Paris, she'd missed having them around. She wondered if it was shameful of her not to have expected to.

She couldn't say she missed the work, the hefting of trays and serving yet another pint. It had been glorious to *be* served for a change. But she was eager to go down and see how the pub had fared without her. Even if it did mean spending the rest of the day on her feet.

She stretched, lifting her arms high, letting her head roll back, focusing on the pleasure the movement gave her body. She was a woman who didn't believe in wasting her senses any more than she would waste her pounds.

It wasn't until she'd climbed out of bed that she realized the constant rumble outside wasn't thunder.

The construction, she remembered. Now wasn't it going to be lovely hearing that din every blessed morning? Gathering up a robe, she walked to the window to see what progress had been made in her absence.

She didn't know anything about the business of building, but what she saw out her window looked to be a terrible mess created by a team of half-wit pranksters. Piles of rubble, scars in the soil,

26

a large concrete floor bottoming out a hole in the ground. Squat towers of cinder block were being erected at the corners with spears of metal poking out of the tops, and a great ugly truck was grinding away with an awful noise.

Most of the workmen, in their rough clothes and filthy boots, were going about the business of making a bigger mess altogether.

She spotted Brenna, her cap perched on her head, her boots mucked nearly to the knee. Seeing her, this forever friend who was now her sister, brought Darcy a warm flood of pure pleasure.

It had shamed her, and did still, to know that part of the reason she'd been wild to get away had been Brenna and Shawn's wedding, as well as her older brother Aidan and his wife Jude's happy planning for the baby they'd have by end of summer. Oh, she was thrilled for them all, couldn't be more delighted with what they'd found together. But the more content and settled they were, the more discontent and unsettled she found herself.

She'd wanted to ball her fists, shake them in the air, and demand, Where's mine? When will I have mine?

It was selfish, she thought, and it was sinful, but she couldn't help it.

Well, now she was back and, she hoped, better.

Darcy watched her friend stride around and give one of the laborers a hand with the blocks. She's in her element here, Darcy mused. Pleased as a puppy with a teat all to herself. She considered opening the window, leaning out to call a hello, and further considered just what having a woman leaning out a window in her robe would do to the rhythm of the work crew.

Because the thought of causing a stir amused her, Darcy reached down. She had the window open the first inch when she spotted the man watching her watching.

He was a tall one, she noted. She'd always had a particular fondness for tall men. He was hatless, and his burnt-honey hair was tousled by the breeze. He wore the rough clothes of a laborer and in her opinion wore them better than most. The long, lanky build had something to do with that, but she thought it was also a matter of confidence. Or arrogance, she mused as he coolly kept his eyes on her face.

She didn't have a problem with arrogance, as she had plenty of her own.

Well, now, you might be an interesting diversion, she thought. A handsome face, a bold eye. If you can string words into a decent conversation, you might be worth a bit of my time. Providing you're not married, of course.

Married or not, she decided, there was no harm in a bit of a flirt, since she intended to have no more than that with a man who likely lived from one payday to the next.

So she smiled at him. Slowly, warmly, deliberately. Then, touching a finger to her lips, she blew him a saucy kiss. She watched his teeth flash in appreciation, then eased out of sight.

It was always best, in Darcy's opinion, to leave a man not only wanting more, but wondering.

Now there was a woman who packed a punch, Trevor thought. And he still felt the impact. If that was Darcy Gallagher, and he assumed it was, he had a good idea why the characteristically dour Finkle had become tongue-tied and bright-eyed whenever her name had come up.

She was a stunner, all right, and he was going to appreciate a closer look. What she'd left him with now was the impression of sleepy beauty, of dark and tumbled hair, white skin, and delicate features. No false modesty there, he decided. She'd met his open stare equally, had taken his measure even as he took hers. The carelessly blown kiss had definitely scored a point.

He thought Darcy Gallagher would be a very interesting pastime while he was in Ardmore.

Casually he hefted some blocks, transferring them to Brenna's work area. 'The mix suit you?' he asked, nodding toward the trough that held fresh mortar.

'It does, yes. Good consistency. We're going through it fairly quickly, but I think we've enough to do us.'

'If you see us running low, order what you think we need. I think your friend's back from her vacation.'

'Hmm.' Distracted, she knocked loose mortar from her trowel, glanced up. 'Darcy?' Pleased, Brenna looked toward the window.

'Lots of black hair, wicked smile. Gorgeous.'

'That would be Darcy.'

'I . . . caught a glimpse of her in the window there. If you want to go in and see her, you can take a break.'

'Well, I would.' But she scooped up more mortar. 'Except that she'd take one look at me as I am at the moment and bolt the door. Darcy's very particular about her living quarters. She wouldn't appreciate me trailing in dirt. I'll see her midday.'

Brenna spread her mortar with the quick efficiency of the experienced and hauled up the next block. 'I can tell you this, Trevor, your men are about to have their hearts broken. It's a rare one who brushes up near our Darcy and walks away unaffected.'

'As long as we stay on schedule, the crew's hearts are their own concern.'

'Oh, I'll keep them on schedule for you, and Darcy will give them happy, if impossible, dreams. Speaking of schedules, I'm thinking we could have the plumbing roughed in on this section by end of week. The pipe didn't arrive this morning as expected. Do you want me or Dad to check on it when we're done here?'

'No, I'll deal with it now.'

'Then I hope you give them a good boot in the ass. You can use the phone in the pub's kitchen.

I unlocked the back when I got here this morning. I've the number in my book.'

'No, I have it. You'll have the pipe today.'

'I've no doubt of that,' Brenna murmured as he strode toward the kitchen door.

The kitchen was spotless. It was one of the things Trevor noticed, and demanded, when it came to any business he had a part in. He imagined the Gallaghers wouldn't think of him as having a part in their pub, but from his viewpoint their business was now very much his concern.

He dug his book out of his pocket. In New York his assistant would have located the number, made the call. She would have worked her way through the various steps until she'd reached the person in charge. Only then, if it was necessary, would the matter have passed into Trevor's hands.

He had to admit, though that saved time and frustration, he rather enjoyed wading in at the bottom and administering that good boot in the ass.

In the five minutes it took him to reach the top level, he spied the biscuit tin. In the few days he'd been in and around Gallagher's he'd come to know that when there were cookies, they were homemade. And they were spectacular.

He helped himself to a honey and oatmeal cookie as big as his fist as he annihilated the supply supervisor without ever raising his voice. He jotted down the name, in case retribution should become necessary, and was given a personal guarantee that the pipe in question would be delivered to the site by noon.

Satisfied with that, he broke the connection and was considering a second cookie when he heard the footsteps on the stairs. Selecting peanut butter this time, Trevor leaned back against the counter and prepared for his first real eyeful of Darcy Gallagher.

Like Shawn's cookies, she was spectacular.

She stopped at the base of the stairs, lifted one slim eyebrow. Her eyes were blue, like her brothers', a brilliant color against flawlessly white skin. She left her hair loose so that it waved beguilingly over her shoulders.

She was dressed with a tailored smartness that seemed more suited to Madison Avenue than Ardmore.

'Good morning to you. Having a tea break?'

'Phone call.' He took a bite of the cookie as he watched her. The voice, Irish and smoky as a turf fire, was as straight-out sexy as the rest of her.

'Well I'm making some tea here, as I've run out upstairs and don't like to start my day without. Makes me cross.' She skimmed her gaze over him as she moved to the stove. 'Will you have a cup to wash down the biscuit? Or must you go straight back to work?'

'I can take a minute.'

'You're fortunate your employer's not so strict. I've heard that Magee runs a very tight ship.'

'So he does.'

While the kettle heated, Darcy dealt with the pot. The man was better up close. She liked the sharp angles of his face, the little scar on his chin. It gave him a dangerous look, and she was so bloody weary of safe men. No wedding ring, she noted, though that didn't always tell the tale.

'You've come all the way from America,' she continued, 'to work on his theater?'

'That's right.'

'A long way from home. I hope you were able to bring your family with you.'

'If you mean wife, I'm not married.' He broke the cookie in half, offered her a share.

Amused, she took it. 'That leaves you free to travel for your work, doesn't it? And what is it you do?'

'Whatever's necessary.'

Oh, yes, she thought and nibbled on the cookie. Just dangerous enough. 'I'd say that makes you a handy man to have around and about.'

'I'm going to be around and about here for some time yet.' He waited while she lifted the sputtering kettle, poured the boiling water into the pot. 'Would you like to have dinner?'

She sent him a long sidelong glance, added a hint of a smile. 'Sure I like a good meal now and then, and interesting company with it. But I'm just back from my holiday and won't have time off for a bit. My brother Aidan's a hard man with a schedule.'

'How about breakfast?'

She set the kettle down. 'I might enjoy that. Perhaps you'll ask me again in a day or two, once I've settled back in.'

'Perhaps I will.'

She was vaguely surprised, and a little disappointed that he hadn't pursued the invitation then and there. She was used to men pleading a bit. But she turned, took out a thick mug for his tea. 'What part of America are you from, then?'

'New York.'

'New York City?' Her eyes sparkled as she turned back. 'Oh, is it wonderful?'

'A lot of it is.'

'It has to be the most exciting city in the world.' She cupped the mug in both hands as she imagined it, as she'd imagined it countless times before. 'Maybe not the most beautiful. I thought Paris so beautiful – female and sly and sexual. I think of New York as a man – demanding and reckless and so full of energy you have to run to keep up.'

Amused at herself, she set down his mug. 'It probably doesn't strike you that way since you're used to being there your whole life.'

'I doubt you think of Ardmore, or this area, as magic.' He saw her eyebrow arch up again at his words. 'As a small and nearly perfect corner of the world where you can reach back or forward in time as suits you. And while there's energy here, it comes with patience so you don't have to run to keep up.'

'It's interesting, isn't it, how people see what's the everyday to someone else?' She poured out his tea. 'I'd think a man who can philosophize so easily over tea and biscuits might be wasting his talents hauling bricks.'

'I'll keep that in mind. Thanks for the tea.' He moved toward the door, passing close enough to appreciate that she smelled every bit as good as she looked. 'I'll bring back the mug.'

'Mind you do. Shawn knows his kitchen supplies down to the last spoon.'

'Come to the window again sometime,' he added as he opened the door. 'I liked looking at you.'

She smiled to herself when he left. 'Well, now, that goes both ways, New York City.'

Debating how she would answer him the next time he asked her out, she picked up the pot of tea to carry it upstairs. The back door flew open.

'You're back.'

Brenna took one leap inside. Little pellets of drying cement flew.

'Keep your distance.' Darcy held up the pot like a shield. 'Christ Jesus, Brenna, you have as much of that muck on your person as you do on the brick.'

'Block, and not by any means. Don't worry, I won't hug you.'

'Damn right you won't.'

'But I missed you.'

Though she was touched, Darcy let out a snort. 'You're too busy being a newlywed to have missed me.'

'I can do both. Can you spare a cup of that? I've ten minutes coming.'

'All right, then, but get some old newspaper to put on the chair before you sit down. I missed you too,' Darcy admitted as she took out another mug.

'I knew you would. I still say it was adventurous of you to go off to Paris like that by yourself. Did you love it?' Brenna asked as she dutifully laid out newspaper. 'Was it everything you wanted it to be?'

'It was, yes. Everything about it: the sounds and the scents, the buildings, the shops and cafés. I could've spent a month just looking. Now if they'd just learn to make a decent cup of tea.' She sipped at her own. 'But I made out fine with wine. Everyone dresses so smart, even when they aren't trying to. I got some marvelous clothes. The shopkeepers are very aloof and act as if they're doing you a great favor in taking your money. I found it added to the overall experience.'

'I'm glad you had a good holiday. You look rested.'

'Rested? I barely slept the whole week. I'm . . . energized,' Darcy decided. 'Of course, I'd planned to lay like a slug until I had to get up for work this morning, but that noise outside's enough to keep the dead alert.'

'You'll have to get used to that. We're making fine progress.'

36

'Not from my window. It looks like a rubble heap, with ditches.'

'We'll have the foundation finished and the plumbing roughed in by the end of the week. It's a good crew, the ones from New York are well trained, and the ones from here Dad and I picked ourselves. Magee doesn't tolerate slackers. And he knows every step of putting a building up, so you'd better be on your toes.'

'Which tells me you're enjoying yourself.'

'Tremendously. And I'd best get back to it.'

'Wait. I got you a present.'

'I was counting on it.'

'I'll go up and get it. I don't want you tracking through my rooms.'

'I was counting on that, too,' Brenna commented as Darcy hurried up the stairs.

'It's not boxed,' Darcy called down. 'It was easier to pack just keeping it in a bag. Jude was wise in telling me to take an extra suitcase as it was. But yours didn't take up much room.'

She came back with a small shopping bag, then narrowed her eyes at Brenna's hand. 'I'll take it out for you.' She slid out a thin bundle wrapped in tissue, carefully uncovered it, then held it up.

Brenna's mouth fell open.

'Shawn's going to love it,' Darcy decided.

It was a short, narrow-strapped nightgown in a shimmering green that was nearly transparent. 'He'd have to be a complete dunderhead not to,' Brenna agreed once she had her voice back. 'I'm

37

trying to imagine wearing that.' Slowly wicked amusement brightened her eyes. 'I think I'll love it, too. It's beautiful, Darcy.'

'I'll keep it for you until you're cleaned up and ready to go home.'

'Thanks.' Brenna kissed Darcy on the cheek, mindful not to transfer any dirt. 'I won't say I'll think of you when I'm wearing it, nor do I think you'd want me to.'

'That I don't.'

'Don't let Shawn see it,' Brenna added as she started out. 'I've a mind to surprise him.'

It was almost too easy to fall back into routine. Though Shawn refused to bicker with her because she'd bought him a fancy French cookbook in Paris, everything else just slipped right into place. As if, she thought, she'd never been away.

For the life of her, Darcy wasn't sure if that pleased or annoyed her.

The lunch shift kept her busy. Added to the regulars were the tourists who were beginning to come in packs for the season, and added to them were the men hired to work on the theater.

Only half-twelve, Darcy thought, and not a single empty table in the place. She was grateful Aidan had hired Sinead on for an extra pair of hands. But Mother of God, the girl was slower than a snail with a limp.

'Miss! We're still waiting to order.'

Darcy caught the tone, British, public school,

38

annoyed, and put her best smile on her face. It was Sinead's station, but the girl was off God knew where. 'I'm so sorry. What would you like to have today?'

'We'll both have today's special, and a glass of Smithwick's.'

'I'll have your drinks right back to you.' She wove her way to the bar, taking three more orders as she went. Moving fast, she scooted under the pass-through, called out the drinks to Aidan, and swung straight into the kitchen.

Grace under pressure, Trevor noted. He'd slipped in and joined some of his crew at a back table. The perfect vantage point, he decided, to watch the very attractive Miss Gallagher at work.

There was a light of battle in her eye when she came back out of the kitchen, and there it remained no matter how brightly she chatted up the customers. She served drinks and food, showering goodwill over the patrons. But Trevor noted that those sharp blue eyes were scanning. And when they lit on Sinead as the girl wandered back in from the direction of the rest rooms, they fired.

Oh, honey, Trevor thought, you are meat. She's going to chew you up and spit you out.

Which, he thought, was precisely how he would have dealt with a lazy employee.

He gave Darcy full marks for holding her temper and doing no more than giving the new waitress a fulminating look and a quick order to tend to her stations. A busy lunch hour wasn't the time for a dressing-down. He imagined Sinead's ears would be burned off after shift.

And he figured it was his lucky day, as Darcy was even now working her way back to his table.

'And what can I get you fine, handsome men this afternoon?' She got out her pad, then focused those glorious eyes on Trevor. 'You look hungry.'

'You can't go wrong with the special at Gallagher's,' Trevor said.

'That you can't. Will you have a pint to go with it?'

'Tea. Iced.'

Now she rolled her eyes. 'That's a Yank's way of ruining a perfectly good pot of tea. But we'll accommodate you. And for you gentlemen?'

'I sure like the way y'all do fish and chips.'

Darcy smiled at the scrawny man with a pleasantly homely face. 'My brother will appreciate that. And where are you from, if you don't mind my asking, for that's a lovely accent.'

'Georgia, ma'am. Donny Brime from Macon, Georgia. But I've never heard anyone talk prettier than you. And I'd love some of that iced tea like the boss here.'

'And just when I was thinking you must have some Irish in you. And for you, sir?'

'I'll have the meat pie, fries – I mean chips – on the side, and . . .' The burly man with a scraggly dark beard slid a sorrowful glance at Trevor. 'Make it iced tea all around.'

'I'll be back with your drinks quick as I can.'

'Now, that,' Donny said with a long sigh as Darcy walked away, 'is the most beautiful thing I've seen in my entire life. Makes you glad to be a man, doesn't it, Lou?'

Lou stroked his beard. 'I've got a fifteen-year-old daughter, and if I caught a man looking at her the way I figure I just looked at that tasty little dish there, I'd have to kill him.'

'Your wife and daughter still planning on coming over?' Trevor asked him.

'As soon as Josie's out of school. 'Nother couple of weeks.'

Trevor settled back while his two men talked of family. There was no one waiting for him at home, or looking forward to the day she could fly over and join him. It wasn't something that troubled him. It was better to live alone than to make a mistake, as he'd nearly done.

Living alone meant he could come and go as he needed to, as his business demanded. And without the guilt or tension that regular travel could add to a relationship. No matter how much his mother might pine for him to settle down and give her grandchildren, the simple fact was that his life ran more efficiently solo.

He glanced at a nearby table where a young family was crowded together. The woman was doing her best to distract a fussy infant while the man frantically mopped up the soft drink their whining toddler had just managed to spill all over everything.

41

Nothing efficient about it, Trevor mused.

Darcy delivered their tea, apparently unaffected by the fact that the toddler had gone from whine to wail. 'Your meals will be out directly, and if you've a need for more tea, just give me a sign.' Still smiling, she turned to the next table and handed the young father a stack of napkins, all the while waving away his apologies.

'Oh, it's not so much of a thing, is it, little man?' She crouched down to the little boy's level. 'Wipes up, doesn't it, but such things scare off the faeries. You might lure them back if they weren't afraid your tears would flood them out again.'

'Where are the faeries?' he demanded in the testy voice of a child who desperately needs a nap.

'Oh, they're hiding now, but they'll come back when they're sure you mean them no harm. Could be they'll be dancing around your bed next time you lay your head on your pillow. I bet your sister's seeing them now.' Darcy nodded toward the baby, who had drifted off to sleep. 'That's why she's smiling.'

The boy subsided into sniffles and watched his sister sleep with both suspicion and interest.

That, Trevor thought as she moved on to the next table, was efficient.

CHAPTER 3

'Now, Sinead, can we go over the things we talked about when I hired you?'

With the pub cleared between shifts, and her brothers ordered out, Darcy sat across from her new waitress. Aidan ran the pub, it was true, and Shawn ruled the kitchen, but it was understood that when it came to the serving, Darcy held the controls.

Sinead shifted her skinny butt on the stool and tried to concentrate. 'Well, you said as to how I was to take the orders in a friendly manner.'

'Aye, that's true.' Darcy sipped her soft drink and waited. 'And what else do you remember?'

'Ah . . .'

Jesus God, Darcy thought, can the girl do anything faster than the pace of a turtle?

'Well.' Sinead chewed her lip and drew little patterns on the table with her fingertips. 'That I was to make certain that the right food and drink was served, again in a friendly manner, to the proper customers.'

'And do you remember, Sinead, anything about

43

the taking and serving of those orders in an efficient and timely manner as well?'

'I do, yes.' Sinead dropped her gaze to her own glass, all but pinned her eyes to it. 'It's all so confusing, Darcy, with everyone wanting something, and at the same time.'

'That may be, but you see, the thing with a pub is people tend to come in wanting something, and our job is to see they get it. You can't do your job if you hide in the loo half your shift.'

'Jude said I was coming along.' Sinead raised her eyes now, and they brimmed with tears.

'That won't work with me.' Darcy leaned forward. 'Filling your eyes up and letting tears shimmer only works on men and soft hearts, and that's not what you're dealing with here. So sniff them back, girl, and listen.'

The sniff was more of a wet snuffle, but Darcy nodded. 'You came to me asking for work and promising that you'd work hard. Now, it's barely three weeks since that day, and you're already slacking. I'm asking you straight out, and you answer in the same manner. Do you want this job?'

Sinead dabbed at her eyes. The new mascara she'd purchased out of her first week's pay smeared. Some might have found the look pitiful and softened. Darcy only thought the girl needed to practice shedding tears with more grace.

'I do. I need the work.'

'Needing work and doing work are two different matters.' As you're about to discover, Darcy decided.

'I want you back here in two hours for the evening shift.'

Tears dried up quickly with sheer shock. 'But I've the night off.'

'Not anymore, you don't. You'll come back prepared to do the job you're paid to do if you want to keep it. I want you moving smartly from table to table, from table to kitchen and back again. If something confuses you or there's something you don't remember or understand, you can come to me and I'll help you out. But . . .'

She paused, waiting until Sinead met her eyes again. 'I won't tolerate you leaving your stations. You've got to pee, that's fine, but each time I note you sliding into the back and staying over five minutes at it, I'm docking you a pound.'

'I've . . . got a bladder problem.'

Darcy would have laughed if it hadn't been so pathetic. 'Now that's bullshit and the both of us know it. If you had any problems with your plumbing I'd've heard, as your mother would have told Brenna's mother and so it would have come to my ears.'

Trapped, Sinead shifted from apologetic to pout. 'But a pound, Darcy!'

'Aye, a pound, so consider before you nip off what it's costing you.' Which, she already decided, would go into her own wish jar, as she'd be the one taking up the slack.

'We've a reputation here at Gallagher's that's generations in the making,' she continued. 'You work for us, you meet the standards we set. If you can't or won't, you get the boot. This is your second chance, Sinead. You won't get a third.'

'Aidan's not so hard as you.'

Darcy lifted a brow as Sinead's bottom lip trembled.

'Well, now, you're not dealing with Aidan, are you? You've two hours. Be on time, or I'll assume you've decided this isn't the job for you.'

'I'll be here.' Obviously irked, Sinead got to her feet. 'I can handle the work. It's nothing but hauling trays about. Doesn't take any brains.'

Darcy sent her the most pleasant of smiles. 'There you are, then.'

'When I save enough money so I can marry Billy, I'm leaving all of this behind me.'

'That's a fine ambition. But this is today. Go on now and walk off your temper before you say something you'll be sorry for later.'

Darcy sat where she was as Sinead strode across the room. Since she'd expected the girl to slam the door, she only rolled her eyes at the bullet crack of it. 'If she used half that energy for the job, we wouldn't have had this pleasant little chat.'

She shrugged her shoulders to relieve some of the tension, curled her toes in her shoes to work out some of the ache, then got to her feet. Gathering the glasses, she turned to carry them to the bar. And Trevor came through the kitchen door.

That, she thought, was a fine example of what God had intended when he'd designed man. He might

46

look a tad rough and dirty from the day's work, but it didn't mar the appeal.

'We're closed at the moment,' she told him.

'The back door was unlocked.'

'We're a friendly sort of place.' She carried the glasses to the bar. 'But I'm afraid I can't sell you a pint right now.'

'I didn't come in for a pint.'

'Didn't you now?' She knew what a man was after when he had his eyes on her that way, but the game required playing. 'What are you looking for, then?'

'I wasn't looking for anything when I got up this morning.' He leaned on the bar. They both knew what they were about, he thought. It made the dance simpler when both people knew the steps. 'Then I saw you.'

'You're a smooth one, aren't you, Mr New York City?'

'Trev. Since you've got a couple hours free, why don't you spend them with me?'

'And how would you know I have free time?'

'I came in on the end of your employer directive. She's wrong, you know.'

'About what?'

'It does take brains, and knowing how to use them. You do.'

It surprised her. It was a rare man who noticed she had a mind, and a rarer one who commented on it. 'So you're attracted to my brain, are you?'

'No.' At the quick humor in his eyes and a flash

47

of grin a nice little ripple moved up her spine. 'I'm attracted to the package, but I'm interested in your brain.'

'I like an honest man under most circumstances.' She considered him another moment. He wouldn't do, of course, for more than a pleasant flirtation. No, wouldn't do, she thought and was surprised by a very real tug of regret.

But he was right about one thing. Time she had. 'I wouldn't mind a walk on the beach. But aren't you supposed to be working?'

'My hours are flexible.'

'Lucky for you.' She moved down the bar, lifted the pass-through. 'And maybe for me as well.'

He came through the opening, then stopped so they stood close and face-to-face. 'One question.'

'I'll try to give you one answer.'

'Why isn't there someone I have to kill before I do this?' He leaned down and brushed his lips very lightly over hers.

She dropped the pass-through back in place. 'I'm choosy,' she said. She walked to the door, then sent him a level and amused look over her shoulder. 'And I'll let you know if I choose to have you try that again, Trev of New York. With a bit more enthusiasm.'

'Fair enough.' He stepped outside with her, waiting while she locked the front door.

The air smelled of sea and flowers. It was something she loved about Ardmore. The scents and sounds, and the wonderful spread of the water.

There were such possibilities in that vast sea. Sooner or later it would bump into land again, another place with new people, different things. There was wonder in that.

And comfort here, she supposed, raising a hand in greeting as Kathy Duffy called out to her from her door-yard.

'Is this your first time in Ireland?' Darcy asked him as they walked toward the beach.

'No, I've been to Dublin several times.'

'One of my favorite cities.' She scanned the beach, noting the pockets of tourists. Automatically she angled away and toward the cliffs. 'The shops and restaurants are wonderful. You can't find that in Ardmore.'

'Why aren't you in Dublin?'

'My family's here – well, part of them. Our parents are settled in Boston now. And I don't have a burning desire to live in Dublin when there are so many places in the world and I haven't seen nearly enough of them yet.'

'What have you seen?'

She looked up at him. A rare one indeed, she thought. Most of the men of her acquaintance wanted to talk about themselves. But they'd play it his way for now. 'Paris, just recently. Dublin, of course, and a great deal of my own country. But the pub hampers traveling.'

She turned, walking backward for a bit with her hand up to shield her eyes. 'I wonder what it'll look like when he's done with it.'

Trevor stopped, studied the pub as she was. 'The theater?'

'Yes. I've looked at the drawings, but I don't have an eye for such things.' She lifted her face to the breeze of salt and sea. 'The family's pleased with it, and they're very particular.'

'So is Magee Enterprise.'

'I imagine so, though it's difficult to understand why the man would pick a small village in the south of Ireland for his project. Jude, she says part of it's sentiment.'

It surprised and nearly disconcerted him to have the truth spoken so casually. 'Does she?'

'Do you know the story of Johnnie Magee and Maude Fitzgerald?'

'I've heard it. They were engaged to be married, and he went off to war and was killed in France.'

'And she never married, but lived alone in her cottage on Faerie Hill all her days. Long days, as Old Maude was one hundred and one years when she passed. The boy's mother, Johnnie Magee's mother, grieved herself to death within a few years. They said she favored him and could find no comfort in her husband, her other children, or her faith.'

It was odd to walk here and discuss these pieces of his family, pieces he had never met, with a woman he barely knew. Odder still that he was learning more of them from her than he'd learned from anyone else.

'I'd think losing a child has to be the biggest grief.'

50

'I'm sure it is, but what of those who were alive yet and needed her? When you forget what you have for what you've lost, grieving's an indulgence.'

'You're right. What happened to them?'

'The story is that her husband finally took to the drink, excessively. Wallowing in whiskey's no better or worse than wallowing in grief, I suppose. And her daughters, I think there were three, married as soon as they could and scattered. Her other son, he who was more than ten years younger than Johnnie, eventually took his wife and his little boy away from Ireland to America, where he made his fortune. Never did he come back nor, they say, contact those left here of family and friends.'

She turned and looked back at the pub again. 'It takes a hard heart never to look back, even once.'

'Yeah,' Trevor murmured. 'It does.'

'But so the seeds of Magee Enterprise were sowed first in Ardmore. It seems the Magee running matters now is willing to put his time and money into seeing those seeds grow here.'

'Do you have a problem with that?'

'No, indeed. It'll be good for us, and for him as well most likely. Business is business, but there's room for a bit of sentiment as long as it doesn't cloud the bottom line.'

'Which is?'

'Profit.'

'Just profit?'

51

She angled back, gestured out to the bay. 'There's Tim Riley's boat coming in for the day. He's been out with his crew since before first light. It's a hard life, that of a fisherman. Tim and those like him go out day after day, casting their nets, fighting weather, and breaking their backs. Why do you suppose they do it?'

'Why don't you tell me?'

'They love it.' She tossed her hair back, watching the boat ride a crest. 'No matter how they bitch and complain, they love the life. And Tim, he cares for his boat like a mother her firstborn. He sells his catch fair so there's no one would say Riley, he's not to be trusted. So there's love of the work, tradition, reputation, but at the bottom of it all is profit. Without an eye on making a living, it's only a hobby, isn't it?'

He caught a curl of her hair as it flew in the wind. 'Maybe I'm attracted to your mind after all.'

She laughed at that and began walking again. 'Do you love what you do?'

'Yes. Yes, I do.'

'What is it appeals to you most?'

'What did you see when you looked out your window this morning?'

'Well, I saw you, didn't I?' She was rewarded by the humor that moved warmly over his face. 'And other than that, I saw a mess.'

'Exactly. I enjoy most an empty lot, or an old building in disrepair. The possibilities of what can be done about them.'

'Possibilities,' she murmured, looking out to sea again. 'I understand about that. So you enjoy building something out of nothing, or out of what's been neglected.'

'Yes. Changing it without damaging it. If you cut down a tree, is what you're putting in its place worth the sacrifice? Does it matter in the long run, or is it only short-term ego?'

'Again the philosopher.' His face suited that, even while the windblown hair and little scar spoke another, less quiet side. 'Are you the conscience of Magee, then?'

'I like to think so.'

An odd sentiment for a laborer, she thought, but it appealed to her. The fact was, she couldn't at the moment find one thing about him that didn't appeal. 'Up on the cliffs there, beyond the big hotel, men once built grandly. The structures are ruins now, but the heart remains and many who go there feel that. The Irish understand sacrifice, and why and when it matters. You'll have to find time to walk there.'

'I'll plan on it. I'd like it better if you found time to show me the way.'

'That's another possibility.' Judging the hour, she turned to walk back.

'Let's build on it.' He took her hand to stop her, enjoyed the faint hint of irritation that came into her eyes. 'I want to see you.'

'I know.' Because it was the simplest angle, and never failed her, she tilted her head and allowed a teasing smile to play on her lips. 'I haven't made up my mind about you as yet. A woman has to be careful when dealing with strange and handsome men.'

'Sweetheart, a woman with your arsenal uses men for target practice.'

Irritated, she tugged her hand free. 'Only if they ask for it. Having a pleasing face doesn't make me heartless.'

'No, but having a pleasing face and a sharp mind is a potent combination, and it'd be a waste if you didn't know how to use both.'

She considered flicking him off and walking away, but damned if he didn't intrigue her. 'Sure and this is the strangest of conversations. I don't know if I like you or not, but maybe I'm interested enough to take some time to find out. But at the moment, I have to head back into work. It wouldn't do for me to be late after I've lectured Sinead.'

'She underestimates you.'

'I beg your pardon?'

'She underestimates you,' Trevor repeated as they walked back across the sand. 'She sees the surface – a beautiful woman with a keen sense of fashion who's passing the time working in her family business. One her brothers run. A woman who in her mind holds the lowest position on the ladder and doesn't do much more than take orders.'

Darcy's eyes narrowed now, but not against the sun. 'Oh, is that how you see it?'

'No, that's how your Sinead sees it. But she's young, inexperienced. So she doesn't see that you have as much to do with the running of Gallagher's as your brothers. The way you look doesn't hurt a thing when it comes to setting the atmosphere, but I watched you today.' He glanced down at her. 'You never missed a step, even when you were pissed off you never broke rhythm.'

'If you're trying to get 'round me with compliments . . . it's in the way of working. Though I have to say I can't remember having any like these from a man before.'

'No, they all tell you you're the most beautiful woman they've ever seen. It's a waste of time to state the obvious, and it must get tedious for you.'

She stopped as they reached the street, stared at him a moment, then laughed. 'You're a rare one, Trev from New York. I think I like you, and wouldn't mind spending a bit of time here and there in your company. Now if you were just rich, I'd marry you on the spot so you could keep me entertained and indulged all my days.'

'Is that what you're looking for, Darcy? Indulgence?'

'And why not? I've expensive tastes that I want to feed. Until I meet a man who's willing and able to fill my plate, I'll go on filling my own.' She reached up to touch his cheek. 'Doesn't mean I can't have a meal or two with another along the way.'

'Honesty, too.'

'When it suits me. And since I have a feeling you'd cut through even a well-crafted lie quick enough, why waste the effort?'

'There it is again.'

She sent him a puzzled look as they crossed the street. 'What?'

'Efficiency. I find that very arousing in a woman.'

'Christ, you're the oddest of ducks. Since I find it amusing to arouse you so easily, I'll take you up on that breakfast offer.'

'Tomorrow?'

She jingled her keys in her pocket and wondered why the idea was so appealing. 'Eight o'clock. I'll meet you in the restaurant at the hotel.'

'I'm not staying at the hotel.'

'Oh, well, if you're at the B and B, we can—'

'There you are, Darcy.' Aidan came up behind, his keys already in his hand. 'Jude thought you were coming down the house to visit.'

'I was distracted.'

'I see you met my sister,' he said to Trevor. 'Why don't you come in for a pint on the house?'

'Actually, I have some work. I was also distracted,' Trevor said with a glance at Darcy. 'But I'll take you up on the offer later.'

'Always welcome. Your men are keeping us busy. Now with Darcy back, I'm wagering they'll keep us busier yet.' He winked and shot the key into the lock. 'Likely we'll have a *seinsiun* going later tonight. Come in if you've the chance and you'll get a small idea of what we'll be offering

56

those who come through on the way to your theater.'

'I'll look forward to it.'

'Darcy, did you have that chat with Sinead?'

She kept her eyes on Trevor's. 'It's dealt with. I'll be coming in to tell you about it in just a minute.'

'That's fine, then. Good evening to you, Trevor.'

'I'll see you later.'

'Your men,' Darcy said when the door closed. 'Your theater.'

'That's right.'

'And that would make you Magee.' She took a careful breath, knowing it would only keep her calm for the short term. 'Why didn't you tell me?'

'You didn't ask. What difference does it make?'

'I think it makes a difference in how you presented yourself to me. I don't care to be deceived and toyed with.'

He slapped a hand on the door before she could wrench it open. 'We've had a couple of conversations,' he said evenly. 'There was nothing deceptive about them.'

'Then we have different standards in that area.'

'Maybe you're just ticked off that I'm rich after all, and now you'll have to marry me.'

He sent her a smile designed to charm, and got nothing but a withering stare in return. 'I don't find your humor appropriate. Now step back from the door. We're not yet open to the public.'

'Is this our first fight?'

'No.' She did manage to yank open the door now, nearly bashing his face with it. 'It's our last.' She didn't slam it, but he clearly heard the click of the lock through the thick wood.

'I don't think so,' he said with a great deal more cheer than another man might have felt under the circumstances. 'Nope, I don't think so.' He strolled down to his car and thought it might be a good opportunity to wander up to the cliffs and take a look at the ruins everyone had told him about.

This was the Ireland he'd come to see. The ancient and the sacred, the wild and the mystic. He was surprised to find himself alone, as it seemed to him that any who were drawn to this area would be compelled to come here, high on the cliffs where the ruins brooded.

He circled the steep stone gables of the oratory that had been built in the saint's name. It stood on the rough and uneven ground and was guarded, he supposed, by the souls who rested there. Three stone crosses stood guard as well, with the fresh water quiet in the well beneath them.

He'd been told it was a lovely walk from here around the headland, but he found himself more inclined to linger where he was.

Darcy was right, he decided, the structure might have tumbled, but the heart of it lived.

He stepped back, respectful enough, or just

superstitious enough, not to step on graves. He assumed the small, pitted stones were graves.

And glancing down, he saw the marker for Maude Fitzgerald.

Wise Woman

'So here you are,' he murmured. 'There's a picture of you with my great-uncle in one of the old albums my mother salvaged when my grandfather died. He didn't keep many pictures from here. Isn't it odd that he had one of you?'

He hunkered down, touched and gently amused to see that flowers had been planted over her in a soft blanket of color. 'You must have had a fondness for flowers. Your garden at the cottage is lovely.'

'Had a way with growing things, did Maude.'

At the comment, Trevor looked back toward the well, then rose. The man who stood there was oddly dressed, all in silver that sparkled in the sun. A costume, Trevor assumed, for some event at the hotel. He was certainly the theatrical sort, with his long flow of black hair, wicked smile, and lightning-blue eyes.

'Don't startle easily, do you? Well, that's to your favor.'

'A man who startles easily shouldn't pass the time here. Great spot,' Trevor added, glancing around again.

'I favor it. You'd be the Magee come from America to build dreams and find answers.'

'More or less. And you'd be?'

'Carrick, prince of the faeries. Pleased to make your acquaintance.'

'Uh-huh.'

The bland amusement in Trevor's tone had Carrick's brows beetling. 'You'd have heard of me, even over in your America.'

'Sure.' Either the man was a lunatic or he wasn't willing to step out of character. Probably both, Trevor decided. 'It so happens I'm staying in the cottage over the hill.'

'I know where the devil you're staying, and I don't care for that indulgent tone you're using. I didn't bring you here to have you make sport of me.'

'*You* brought me here?'

'Mortals,' Carrick grumbled. 'They like to think everything's their own doing. Your destiny's here, tied with mine. If I planted a few seeds to get you moving on it, who has a better right?'

'Pal, if you're going to drink this early in the day, you ought to stay out of the sun. Why don't I give you a hand back down to the hotel?'

'Drunk? You're thinking I'm drunk?' Carrick threw back his head and laughed until he was forced to hold his sides. 'Bloody bonehead. Drunk. We'll show you drunk. Just give me a moment here to recover myself.'

After several long breaths, Carrick continued. 'Let's see here, something not so subtle. I'm thinking, for I see already you're the cynical sort. Ah, I've got it!'

His eyes went dark as cobalt, and Trevor would have sworn the tips of the man's fingers began to glow gold, then in his hands was a sphere, clear as water. Swimming in it was the image of Trevor himself and Darcy, standing together on the beach while the Celtic Sea charged the shore beside them.

'Have a look at your destiny. She's fair of face and strong of will and hungry of heart. Are you clever enough to win what the fates offer you?'

He flicked his wrist, sent the globe flying toward Trevor. Instinctively he reached out, felt his fingers pass through something cool and soft. Then the globe burst like a bubble.

'Hell of a trick,' Trevor managed, then looked over at the well. He was alone again, with just the stir of the grass in the wind for company. 'Hell of a trick,' he repeated, and more shaken than he cared to admit, he stared down at his empty hands.

CHAPTER 4

Dreams haunted him through the night. Trevor had always dreamed in broad and vivid strokes, but since coming to Faerie Hill Cottage his dreams had taken on a finite, crystalline quality. As if someone had sharpened a lens on a camera.

The odd man from the cemetery rode a white, winged horse over a wide blue sea. And Trevor felt the broad back and bunching muscles of the mythic steed beneath him. In the distance, the sky and water were separated clearly, like a thin pencil stroke drawn with a ruler.

The water was sapphire, the sky gray as smoke.

The horse plunged, its powerful forelegs cutting through the surface, spewing up water that Trevor could see, could *feel* in individual drops. He could taste the salt of it on his lips.

Then they were in that swirling underworld. Cold, so cold, with the dark underlit with some eerie glow. There were flickers of iridescent light, like faerie wings fluttering, and the music playing through the pulse beat of water was pipes.

Deeper, still deeper, flying down in this element

as smoothly as they had flown in the air. The thrill of it coursed through him like blood.

There, on the soft floor of the seabed a hillock of darker, wilder blue throbbed, like a waiting heart. Into this, the man who called himself a prince thrust his arm to the shoulder. And Trevor felt the slick texture of the mass on his own flesh, the vibration ripple up his own arm. His hand flexed, closed, twisted, and he wrenched free the heart of the sea.

For her, he thought, clutching it tight. This is my constancy. Only for her.

When he woke, his hand was still fisted, but the only heart that pounded was his own.

As baffled as he was shaken, Trevor opened his hand. It was empty, of course it was empty, but he felt the charge of power fading from his palm.

The heart of the sea.

It was ridiculous. He didn't have to be a marine biologist to know there was no shimmering blue mass, no organic life beating away on the floor of the Celtic Sea. It was all nothing more than an entertaining scene played by the subconscious, he told himself. Full of symbolism, he was sure, that he could analyze to death if he were so inclined.

Which he wasn't.

He got out of bed, heading for the bath. Absently he pushed a hand through his hair. And found it damp.

He stopped short, lowering his hand slowly, staring at it. Cautious, he brought his hand to his face, sniffed. Sea water?

Naked, he lowered himself to the side of the bed again. He'd never considered himself a particularly fanciful man. In fact, he liked to think he was more grounded in reality than most. But there was no denying that he'd dreamed of flying through the sea on a winged horse and had awakened with his hair damp from sea water.

How did a rational man explain that?

Explanations required information. It was time he started gathering it.

It was too early to call New York, but it was never too early to fax. After he'd dressed for the day, Trevor settled into the little office across from his bedroom and composed the first message to his parents.

Mom and Dad:

Hope you're both well. The project's on schedule and remains on budget as well. Though after a couple of days' observation, I've concluded the O'Tooles could handle the job without me, I prefer staying, at least for the present, to supervise. There's also the matter of community relations. Most of the village and the surrounding parish seem to be in favor of the theater. But the construction disturbs the general tranquility of the area. I think it's wise for me to remain visible and involved.

I also intend to continue the preliminary publicity from here.

Meanwhile, I'm enjoying the area. It's as beautiful as you told me, Dad. And you're remembered fondly here. The two of you should take some time and come over.

Gallagher's is as you remembered and Finkle reported, a well-run, friendly, and popular business. Connecting the theater to it was a brilliant concept, Dad. I'm going to spend more time there, getting a clearer feel for just how it all runs and what changes or improvements we might want to implement to benefit the theater.

Mom, you'd particularly like the cottage where I'm staying. It's a postcard – and better yet is reputed to have its own ghost. You and Aunt Maggie would get a kick out of it. No unearthly visitation to report, I'm afraid, but since I'm trying to drench myself in local color, I wonder if the two of you can pass on any information you might have on the legend based here. It's something about star-crossed lovers, of course. A maid and a faerie prince.

I'll call when I get a chance.
Love, Trev

He read it over to be sure he'd kept his request casual, then shot it off to his parents' private line.

The next fax was to his assistant and was much more to the point.

Angela, I need you to research and relay any and all information available on a legend local to Ardmore. References: Carrick, prince of faeries, Gwen Fitzgerald, Faerie Hill Cottage, Old Parish, Waterford. Sixteenth century.
Trevor Magee

Once he'd transmitted, he checked his watch. Though it was just past eight, it was too early to tap his other source. He'd wait an hour before he paid a visit to Jude Gallagher.

With the business completed, the sudden and desperate urge for coffee broke through. It was strong enough to have him abandoning everything else. The one thing he missed was his automatic coffeemaker and its timer. It was something he intended to purchase at the first opportunity.

There was, in Trevor's mind, little more civilized in this world than waking up to the scent of coffee just brewed.

As he came to the base of the steps, a knock sounded on the door. With his mind already in the kitchen, his system already focused on that first jolting sip, he opened the door.

And concluded there was perhaps one thing more civilized than waking up to coffee. She was standing on his little stoop.

A smart man, a wise man, would forgo a life-time of coffee for a beautiful blue-eyed woman wearing a snug scoop-necked sweater and a come-

66

get-me smile. And he was a very smart man.

'Good morning. Do you wake up looking like that?'

'You'll have to do more than offer me breakfast before you get the chance to find out for yourself.'

'Breakfast?'

'I believe that was the nature of the invitation.'

'Right.' His mind wasn't clicking rapidly along without its daily dose of caffeine. 'You surprise me, Darcy.'

She'd intended to. 'Are you feeding me or aren't you?'

'Come in.' He opened the door wider. 'We'll see what we can do.' She stepped inside with a light brush of her body against his. She smelled like candy-coated sin.

She wandered by to glance in the front parlor. It was very much as Maude had left it, with its pretty fancies set out here and there, the shelf thick with books, and the soft old throw tossed over the faded fabric of the sofa.

'You're a tidy one, aren't you?' She turned back. 'I approve of a tidy man. Or perhaps you consider it efficiency.'

'Efficiency is tidy – and it's my life.' With his eyes on hers he laid a hand on her shoulder, pleased when she simply stared back at him with that same mild amusement on her face. 'I was just wondering why it's not cold.'

'Cold shoulders are a predictable reaction, and predictability is tedious.'

'I bet you're never tedious.'

'Perhaps on the rare occasion. I'm annoyed with you, but I still want my breakfast.' She skirted around him, then glanced over her shoulder. 'Are you cooking, or are we going out?'

'Cooking.'

'Now I'm surprised. Intrigued. A man in your position knowing his way around a kitchen.'

'I make a world-famous cheddar-and-mushroom omelette.'

'I'll be the judge of that – and I'm very . . . particular about my tastes.' She walked back toward the kitchen and left him blowing out one long, appreciative breath before he followed.

She sat at the little table in the center of the room, draping her arm over the back of her chair and looking very much like a woman accustomed to being served. Though his system no longer needed a jump-start, Trevor made coffee first.

'While I'm sitting here watching you deal with some homey chores,' Darcy began, 'why don't you tell me why you let me babble on yesterday about your family and ancestors and seemed so interested in information that would be already familiar to you.'

'Because it wasn't familiar to me.'

She'd suspected that, after she'd calmed down. He didn't strike her as a man who'd waste time asking questions when he already had the answers. 'Why is that, if you don't mind me asking?'

He would mind. Usually. But he felt he owed her

an explanation. 'My grandfather had very little to say about his family here, or Ardmore. Or Ireland, for that matter.'

While he waited for the coffee to brew – please, God, soon – he got out what he needed for the omelette. 'He was a difficult man, with a very hard shell. My impression was that whatever he'd left here made him bitter. So it wasn't discussed.'

'I see.' Not clearly, Darcy mused, as it was hard to understand a family that didn't discuss every-thing. At the top of their lungs as often as not. 'Your grandmother also came from here.'

'Yes. And my grandmother abided by his wishes.' He glanced at Darcy, his eyes cool and remote. 'In everything.'

'I imagine he was a powerful man, and powerful men are often difficult and intimidating.'

'My father would be viewed as a powerful man. I wouldn't consider him difficult or intimidating.'

'So you've come back in part, have you, to see for yourself where those Magee seeds were first sown?'

'In part.'

She did not fail to notice the dismissive tone. A sore spot here, she decided, and though she'd have dearly loved to poke a bit, she left it alone. For now. 'Well, then, since here's where you are, why don't you tell me what you think of the cottage?'

Tension, tension that irritated him, eased a bit. He poured his first cup of coffee as he dealt with the eggs. 'I just sent my mother a fax telling her it was a postcard.'

'A fax? Is that the way mother and son communicate?'

'Mother and son use technology where it's useful.' Remembering manners, he poured her a cup, brought it to the table. 'Best of all worlds, isn't it? A thatched-roof cottage in the Irish countryside and the conveniences of modern times.'

'You left out your ghost.'

He had a steady hand, but nearly bobbled the skillet. 'I wouldn't say she's mine.'

'While you're living here she is. A tragic figure is Lady Gwen, and while I sympathize and appreciate the romance of it all, I find it hard to understand anyone who would pine, even for love, over the centuries, beyond death. Life's the point, isn't it, and making it work for you.'

'How much more do you know about her?'

'As much as any in these parts, I suppose.' She enjoyed watching his long fingers and competent hands do their work. 'Though Jude's done more of a study on the matter for her book. Several I know have seen her.'

He glanced back. It wasn't surprise in his eyes, but caution. 'Have you?'

'I don't think I'm the type a ghost spends time with. Perhaps you will, as she walks here.'

'You're vision enough for me. What about the second half of the legend? This Carrick.'

'Oh, he's a clever one, and tricky with it. Stubborn

pride and poor temper put him in the fix he's in and he's not above using his wiles to repair it now that the time's up. You may not have noticed, but Brenna wears her rings, her engagement and wedding rings, on a chain around her neck when she's working.'

'I saw a man come close to losing his finger on a job once when his wedding ring caught in a skill saw. She's smart to avoid that.' He took out plates, divvied up the egg dish, all with a smooth efficiency that she appreciated. 'What do Brenna's rings have to do with the legend?'

'Her engagement ring is a pearl, the second of the jewels Carrick offered Gwen. Those tears of the moon he gathered into his magic bag. Carrick gave the pearl to Shawn.'

Trevor's eyebrows lifted, but he turned back for flat-ware. 'A generous sort.'

'I don't know about that, but the pearl was given to him by Carrick at Old Maude's grave, and now it's Brenna's. The first offered was diamonds. Jewels of the sun. Ask Jude about that if you have an interest. The third and last he offered were sapphires. From the heart of the sea.'

'The heart of the sea.' His dream came back to him, fast and clear so that he once again stared down at his own hand.

'A pretty story, you're thinking, and so I would myself if those I know hadn't become part of it. There's one more step that has to be taken, one more pair of hearts that have to meet and promise

71

to each other.' She sipped her coffee, watching him over the rim. 'The others who lived here in this cottage since Old Maude passed were step one and step two.'

He said nothing for a moment, just retrieved the toast that had popped up. 'Are you warning me that I've been selected as step three?'

'It follows smoothly, doesn't it? Now, however practical-minded a man you might be, Magee, you've Irish blood in your veins, and you share that blood with a man who once loved the woman who lived in the place. As candidates go for the breaking of spells, you'd be my pick.'

Considering, he took out the butter and jam. 'And a practical-minded woman like you believes in spells.'

'Believe in them?' She leaned toward him as he sat. 'Darling, I cast them.'

The way she looked at the moment, her eyes hot and bright, her smile just the other side of wicked, he'd have believed her a witch without hesitation. 'Setting aside your considerable powers, are you going to tell me you believe this story, and all its parts, as reality?'

'I do, yes.' She picked up her fork. 'And if I were you, and living here, I'd take great care with my heart.' She lifted a forkful of creamy egg and cheese, slid it between her lips. 'There are those who also believe if one loses that heart here, it's forever pledged.'

'Like Maude's.' The idea of it worried him more

than he wanted to admit. 'Why are you telling me this?'

'Well, I wondered if you'd ask. You're an attractive man, and I like the look of you. Added to that – and I'm not ashamed to say it's a big 'added to that' to me – you're rich. I think there's a good possibility I might enjoy your company as well.'

'Are you proposing?'

She shot a grin at him, wide and gorgeous. 'Not quite yet. I'm telling you this because I've the impression you're a man who sees through pretenses as easy as a knife slides through butter.'

She picked up her own knife and demonstrated on the stick he'd taken from the refrigerator. 'I'm not a woman who falls in love. I've tried,' she said, and for a moment the light in her eyes clouded. Then she shrugged and spread the butter on a slice of toast. 'It's just not in me. And it may be that we're not what destiny has in store for each other, but if we are, I think we might come to an arrangement that pleases both of us.'

Under the circumstances, he decided, another refill of coffee couldn't hurt. He got up to top off the cups. 'I've met a lot of people in my business, sampled a lot of cultures, and I have to say this is the strangest breakfast conversation I've ever had.'

'I believe in fate, Trevor, in the meeting of like minds, in comfort and in honesty when it serves its purpose.' She took another bite of omelette. 'Do you?'

'I believe in like minds, comfort and honesty when it serves its purpose. As to fate, that's a different matter.'

'There's too much Irish in your blood for you not to be a fatalist,' she told him.

'Is that the nature of the beast?'

'Of course. And at the same time, we manage to be optimistically sentimental and full of dark and exciting superstition. As for honesty.' Her eyes twinkled at him. 'Now that's a matter of degrees and viewpoints, for what's better, all in all, than a well-told tale embroidered with colorful exaggerations? However, honesty is something I think you appreciate, so what's wrong with letting you know that if you fall in love with me, I'll likely let you?'

He enjoyed the rest of his coffee. And her. 'I've tried to fall in love. It didn't take for me, either.'

For the first time sympathy moved over her face, and she reached out to touch his hand. 'It's as painful not being able to stumble, I think, as the fall would be.'

He looked down at their joined hands. 'What a sad pair we are, Darcy.'

'Best, isn't it, to know yourself, and your limitations? It could be that some pretty young woman will catch your eye and your heart will pop right out of your chest and plop at her feet.' She shrugged her shoulders. 'But meanwhile, I wouldn't mind having you spend some of your time, and your not inconsiderable funds, on me.'

'Mercenary, are we?'

'Yes, I am.' She gave his hand a friendly pat, then went back to her breakfast. 'You've never had to count your pennies, have you?'

'Got me there.'

'But if you ever have to earn a few extra, you make a very fine omelette.' She rose, taking both of the plates to the sink. 'I appreciate a decent cook, as it's not a skill I have, nor one I care to develop.'

He came up behind her, ran his hands over her shoulders, down her arms and back again in one long stroke. 'Going to wash my dishes?'

'No.' She wanted to stretch like a satisfied cat, but thought it wiser not to. 'But I might be persuaded to dry them for you.'

She let him turn her around, kept her eyes on his as he lowered his head. Then, with not a little regret, placed her fingers on his lips before they touched hers. 'Here's what I'm thinking. Either of us could seduce the other with considerable style if not much effort.'

'Okay. Let me go first.'

Her laugh was low and smooth. 'And however satisfied we might be after, it's early days yet. Let's keep that adventure for another time.'

He gathered her a little closer. 'Why wait? You're the fatalist.'

'Clever. But we'll wait because I've a mind to. I've a very strong mind.' She tapped his lips with her finger once, then drew back.

'Me, too.' Deliberately, he lifted her hand to his lips again, brushed them over her palm, then her knuckles.

'I like that. I might just come back for more, another time. And as things are, I believe I'll leave the dishes to you after all. Now, will you walk me out like a proper gentleman?'

'Tell me,' he said as they started out of the kitchen, 'how many men have you wrapped around your finger to date?'

'Oh, I've lost count. But none of them seemed to mind it.' She glanced back as the phone began to ring. 'Do you need to answer?'

'The machine'll get it.'

'Answering machines and faxes. I wonder what Old Maude would think.' She stepped outside and off the stoop to where the flowers were dancing in the breeze. 'You look suited to this place,' she said after a moment's study of him. 'And I imagine you look just as suited to some lofty boardroom.'

He reached down to snap off a spray of verbena and handed it to her. 'Come back.'

'Oh, I imagine I'll wander your way again.' She tucked the flower into her hair as she turned to the garden gate.

He saw then why he hadn't heard her drive up. She'd ridden a bike. 'Darcy, if you'll wait a minute, I'll drive you back down.'

'No need. Good day to you, Trevor Magee.'

She straddled the bike and steered down the narrow drive and into the bumps and ditches the locals claimed was a road. And managed, Trevor noted, to look outrageously sexy doing it.

Since he stopped by the site after going into the village, it was after noon when he walked to the Gallagher house. His knock was answered by the barking of a dog, a throaty, excitable sound that made him take a cautious step in reverse. He was an urbanite and had a healthy respect for anything capable of making that kind of noise.

The barking stopped seconds before the door opened, but the dog itself sat beside Jude, madly thumping its tail. Trevor had seen the dog a time or two, but at a distance. He hadn't realized the thing was quite so large.

'Hello, Trevor. How nice. Come in.'

'Ah . . .' He glanced meaningfully at the dog, and Jude laughed.

'Finn's harmless. I promise. He just likes to make a racket so I'll think he's protecting me. Say good day to Mr Magee,' Jude ordered, and Finn obediently lifted a huge paw.

'I'd like to stay on his good side.' Hoping the dog would let him keep all his fingers, Trevor shook, hand to paw.

'I can put him out back if he worries you.'

'No, no, it's fine.' He hoped. 'I'm sorry to interrupt your day. I was hoping you had a minute.'

'I've several minutes. Come in and sit down. Can I get you some tea? Have you had lunch? Shawn sent down a lovely casserole.'

'No, nothing, thanks, I'm fine. Don't go to any trouble.'

'It's not a bit of trouble,' she began, but she pressed one hand to the small of her back and the other to her belly as she stepped back.

'You sit down.' Trevor took her arm and steered her to the living room. 'I'll confess, large dogs and pregnant women unnerve me.'

It wasn't true. Large dogs might have unnerved him, but pregnant women melted him. But the statement got her to a chair.

'I promise neither of us will bite.' But she sat, gratefully. 'I swore I was going to stay calm and graceful through this experience. I'm pretty calm yet, but I said good-bye to grace at the six-month point.'

'You look like you're handling it well. Do you know if you're having a boy or a girl?'

'No, we want to be surprised.' She laid a hand on Finn's head when he came to sit by her chair. Trevor noted she didn't have to reach far. 'I took a walk last evening and looked at your site. You're making progress.'

'Steady. This time next year you'll be able to walk down and take in a show.'

'I'm looking forward to it, very much. It must be satisfying to turn your visions into reality.'

'Isn't that what you're doing? With your books, with your baby?'

'I like you. Are you comfortable enough to tell me what's on your mind?'

He waited a beat. 'I forgot you're a psychologist.'

'I *taught* psychology.' In a gesture of apology, she lifted her hands, let them fall again. 'In the last year or so I've cured myself of being too shy to say what I'm thinking. The result has pros and cons. I don't mean to be pushy.'

'I came here to ask you something, talk to you about something. You figured it out. That's not pushy, that's . . . efficient,' he said after a moment. 'One of my favorite words lately. Carrick and Gwen.'

'Yes?' Now she folded her hands, looking serene and easy. 'What about them?'

'You believe they exist? Existed?' he corrected.

'I know they exist.' She saw the doubt in his eyes and took a moment to gather her thoughts. 'We're from a different place, you and I. New York, Chicago. Urban, sophisticated, our lives based on facts and the tangible of the everyday.'

He saw where she was going and nodded. 'We're not there anymore.'

'No, we're not there anymore. This is a place that . . . "thrives" isn't the word I want, because it doesn't need to thrive. It just is. This place that's home for me now, this place that's drawn you to build one of your dreams here, isn't just apart from where we came from because of history or geography. It understands things we've forgotten.'

'Reality is reality, whatever part of the world you're standing in.'

'I thought that once. If you still do, why do Carrick and Gwen worry you?'

'Interest me.'

'Have you seen her?'

'No.'

'Him, then.'

Trevor hesitated, remembering the man who'd appeared near Saint Declan's Well. 'I don't believe in faeries.'

'I imagine Carrick believes in you,' Jude murmured. 'I want to show you something.' She started to rise, cursed under her breath, then held up a hand, waving it testily when Trevor got to his feet. 'No, damn it, I'm not ready to be hauled up every time I sit down. Just a minute.' She shifted, then boosted herself out, belly first, by pushing her hands against the arms of the chair. 'Relax. It'll take me a minute. I'm not as light on my feet as I used to be.'

As she walked out, Trevor sat back down. He and Finn eyed each other with interest and suspicion. 'I'm not going to steal the silverware, so let's both just stay in our respective corners.'

As if it had been an invitation, Finn sauntered over and planted both forepaws in Trevor's lap.

'Christ.' Gingerly, Trevor lifted the dog's feet out of his crotch. 'Perfect aim. Now I know why my father never let me have that puppy. Down!'

At the command Finn's butt hit the floor, then he lovingly licked Trevor's hand.

'There, you've made friends.'

Trevor glanced up at Jude and barely resisted squirming to relieve the throbbing in his balls. 'You bet.'

'Go lie down, Finn.' Jude gave the dog an absent pat before sitting on the hassock at Trevor's feet. 'Do you know what this is?' She opened her hand, held it out. Centered in her palm was a clear and brilliant stone.

'At a glance it looks like a diamond, and given the size, I'd say it's a very nicely faceted piece of glass.'

'A diamond, first water, between eighteen and twenty carats. I got a book, a loupe, and figured it out. I didn't want to take it to a jeweler. Go ahead,' she invited, 'take a closer look.'

Trevor took it out of her hand, held it to the light streaming through the front window. 'Why didn't you want to take it to a jeweler?'

'It seemed rude, as it was a gift. I visited cousin Maude's grave last year, and I watched Carrick pour a flood of these out of the silver bag he wears at his belt. I watched them bloom into flowers, except for this one that lay sparkling in the blossoms.'

Trevor turned the stone over in his hand, and wondered. 'Jewels of the sun.'

'My life changed when I came here. This is a symbol. Whether it's pretty glass or a priceless gem doesn't matter really. It's all how you look at things. I saw magic, and it opened my world.'

'I like my world.'

'Whether you change it or not is your choice. You came here for a reason. To Ardmore.'

'To build a theater.'

'To build,' Jude said quietly. 'How much, is up to you.'

CHAPTER 5

Trevor's decision to spend the evening in the pub was a logical one. A professional one. He preferred thinking of it that way, as it was just a little too hard on the ego to admit he was there largely to look at Darcy. He wasn't a horny teenager, he was a businessman. Gallagher's Pub was now very much part of his interests.

And it appeared to be a thriving one.

Most of the tables were full – families, couples, tour groups huddled together over pints and glasses and conversations. A young boy who couldn't have been more than fifteen sat in a corner playing a weepy tune on a concertina. A fire had been lit, as with evening the weather had gone chilly and damp, and around the red glow of the simmering turf a trio of old men with windraw faces sat smoking contemplatively and tapping booted feet to the music.

Nearby, a child who couldn't have seen his first birthday bounced and giggled on his mother's knee.

His own mother, Trevor thought, would have

loved this. Carolyn Ryan Magee was fourth-generation Irish, born of parents who'd never set foot on Irish soil, any more than their parents before them had. And she was unabashedly sentimental over what she considered her roots.

She was, he understood, the only reason he knew as much as he did about family history on his father's side. Family, no matter if they'd been dead and buried for generations, meant something to her. When something mattered to his mother, she made certain it mattered to her men. Neither of whom, Trevor mused, could resist her.

It was she who'd played Irish music in the house while his father had rolled his eyes and tolerated it. It was she who had told her son stories at bedtime of the Good People and silkies and pookas.

And it had been she, Trevor knew, who had smoothed over in her fiercely determined way whatever hurts and resentments his father had felt toward his parents. Even with her powers, she hadn't been able to add warmth, but at least she'd built a shaky bridge that had allowed for civility and respect on both sides.

In fact, Trevor wondered if he'd have noticed the distance between his father and his father's parents if it hadn't been for the love and openness of his own home.

Of all the couples he knew, he'd never known any as cheerfully devoted to each other as the one who'd created him. It was a marvelously intimate miracle, and one he never took for granted.

He imagined his mother would sit here, as he was now, and soak it all up, join in the songs, chat with all the strangers. Thinking of it, he scanned the room through the pale blue haze of smoke, and thought of ventilation systems. Then he shook his head and headed to the bar. Whatever the health hazards, he supposed this was precisely the atmosphere those who came here were looking for.

He saw Brenna at the far end of the bar, working the taps and having what appeared to be the most serious of discussions with a man who had to be a hundred and six.

The only stool left was at the opposite end, and sliding on, Trevor waited while Aidan passed out glasses and made change.

'Well, how's it all going, then?' Aidan asked, and added the next layers to a pair of Guinnesses he was building.

'Fine. You're busy tonight.'

'And busy we should be most nights from now till winter. Can I quench your thirst for you?'

'You can. I'll have a pint of Guinness.'

'That's the way. Jude said you were by to see her today, and having some concerns about our local color.'

'Not concerns. Curiosity.'

'Curiosity, to be sure.' Aidan began the slow, intricate process of building Trevor's pint while he finished off the two in progress. 'A man's bound to have some curiosity about the matter when he

85

finds himself plunked down in the middle of it. Jude's publisher has the notion that when her book comes out, it could stir more interest in our little corner of the world. Good business that, for both of us.'

'Then we'll have to be ready for it.' He glanced around, noted that Sinead was moving with a great deal more energy tonight. But Darcy was nowhere to be seen. 'You're going to need more help in here, Aidan.'

'I've given that some thought.' He filled a basket with crisps and set them on the counter. 'Darcy'll be talking to some people when the time comes.'

As if hitting the cue, Darcy's voice rang through the kitchen doorway in a peal of heartfelt and inventive curses.

'You're a miserable excuse for a blind donkey's ass, and why you require a head hard as rock when you've nothing inside it needing protection, I'll never know, for you're brainless as a turnip and twice as disagreeable.'

When Trevor cocked his head in question, Aidan merely continued to work his taps. 'It's a bit of a temper our sister has, and Shawn needs only to exist to provoke it.'

'A shrew is it? I'll give you a shrew, you slant-eyed, toothless toad.'

There was an audible thud, a yelp, more cursing, then Darcy, face flushed, eyes lightning-hot, swung through the door with a large and loaded tray on her hip.

'Brenna, I brained your husband with a stewpot – though why an intelligent woman such as yourself would choose to wed a baboon like that escapes me.'

'I hope it wasn't full, as he makes a fine stew.'

'It was empty. You get a better ring that way.' She tossed her head, drew in a long breath, and let it out again with a satisfied huff. Shifting the tray, she turned toward the pass-through, and spotted Trevor.

Temper vanished from her face like magic. Though her eyes remained hot, they took on an unmistakable sexual edge. 'Well, now, look who's come in out of the rainy evening.' Her tone went to purr as she sauntered to the end of the bar. 'Would you mind flipping up the pass-through, darling? I've my hands a bit full at the moment.'

She'd been balancing trays one-handed more than half her life, but she liked to see him move. The hum in her throat was a sound of pure appreciation when he slid off the stool and walked over to do as she'd asked.

'It's nice to be rescued by a strong, handsome man.'

'Mind yourself, Trev, there's a viper under that comely face.' This was Shawn's opinion, and he gave it a bit testily as he came out to serve another pair of orders at the bar.

'Pay no attention to the babblings of our pet monkey.' She sent one steely stare over her shoulder. 'Our parents, being kindhearted, bought him from a traveler family – gypsies, you'd say. A waste of two pounds and ten, if you're asking me.'

With a twitch of hip she walked off to deliver her orders.

'That was a good one,' Shawn murmured. 'She must've been saving it up. Good evening to you, Trev. Are you looking for a meal?'

'I guess I'll try the stew. I've heard it's good tonight.'

'Aye.' With a rueful smile, Shawn rubbed the bump on his head. His gaze drifted to the side where the young boy teased out a livelier tune. 'You've come on a good evening. Connor there can play like an angel or a demon, depending on the mood.'

'I've yet to hear you play.' Trevor settled on his stool again. 'I'm told that, like the stew, it's good.'

'Oh, I've a bit of a hand with it. We all do. Music's part of the Gallagher way.'

'Just a bit of advice, on your music. Get an agent.'

'Oh, well.' Shawn looked back, met Trevor's eyes. 'You're paying me a good price for the songs you've bought so far. I trust you to be fair. You've an honest face.'

'A good agent would squeeze out more.'

'I've no need for more.' He glanced over at Brenna. 'I've everything already.'

With a baffled shake of his head, Trevor picked up the beer Aidan set in front of him. 'Finkle said you weren't a business-minded man. But I have to say you're not anywhere near as dim as he led me to believe. No offense.'

'None taken.'

Trevor watched Shawn over the rim of his mug. 'Finkle said you kept getting him confused with another investor, a restaurateur from London.'

'Did he now?' Amusement twinkled in Shawn's eyes. 'Imagine that. Aidan, do we know anything about a restaurant man from London who'd have been interested in connecting to the pub here?'

Aidan tucked his tongue in his cheek. 'I seem to recall Mr Finkle bringing that matter to my attention, though I assured him there was no such person at t'all. Fact is,' Aidan continued after a weighty pause, 'we, all of us, went to great pains to assure him of it.'

'That's what I thought.' Impressed, Trevor took a deep gulp of Guinness. 'Very slick.'

Then he heard Darcy laugh, quick and bright, and turned to see her rub her hand over the boy Connor's head. She left it there, her eyes sparkling on his as she began to sing.

It was a fast tune, with lyrics tumbling into each other. He'd heard it before, in the pubs of New York or when his mother was in the mood to listen to Irish music, but he'd never heard it like this. Not in a voice that seemed soaked in rich wine with gold at the edges.

He'd had the report from Finkle, and there had been mention of Darcy's singing voice. In fact, the man had rhapsodized about it. Trevor hadn't put any stock in that issue. As his pet business was a recording company, he knew how often voices were praised through the roof when they deserved no more than polite applause.

Listening now, watching now, Trevor admitted he should have given his scout more credit.

When she came back into the chorus, Shawn leaned on the bar and matched his voice to hers. There was a laugh in the music of it as she wandered back toward the bar, and laying a casual hand on Trevor's shoulder, sang straight to her brother.

'I'll tell me ma when I go home the boys won't leave the girls alone.'

No, Trevor imagined, the boys had never left this one alone. He had an urge to pull her hair himself, but not in the playful manner the song indicated. No, to fill his hands with it, pull it back, and feast on her.

Thousands of men, he imagined, would react the same way. The notion appealed to his business side even as it irked on a personal level. Since jealousy made him feel ridiculous, he concentrated on the business angle.

When the song was over, she reached over the bar to grab Shawn by the collar and haul him halfway across it for a loud kiss. 'Moron,' she said, with obvious affection.

'Shrew.'

'Three fish and chips, two stews, and two portions of your porter cake. Now back into the kitchen

90

where you belong.' She ran her hand absently across Trevor's shoulder as she turned to Aidan. 'Three pints each Guinness and Harp, a glass of Smithwick's, and a pair of Cokes. The one Coke's for Connor, so there's no charge. Do you mind?' she said to Trevor, and picked up his pint for a small sip.

'So, do you take requests?'

'Hmm. I'm here to do nothing but.'

'Sing another.'

'Oh, it's likely I will before the evening's done.' She transferred the drinks that were poured onto her tray.

'No, now.' He pulled a twenty-pound note out of his pocket, held it up between two fingers. 'A ballad this time.'

Her gaze shifted from his face to the bill, then back again. 'That's a considerable tip for a bit of a tune.'

'I'm rich, remember?'

'That's something I haven't forgotten.' She reached out for the twenty, narrowed her eyes when he jerked it away.

'Sing it first.'

She considered ignoring him on principle and perhaps a little spite. But it was twenty pounds, and singing wasn't a trial to her. So she smiled at him, then lifted her voice as she lifted her tray.

Come all ye maidens young and fair / All you that are blooming in your prime / Always

*beware and keep your garden fair / Let no man
steal away your thyme.*

Connor picked up the melody, flushing a bit
when she winked at him and served his soft drink.
She served the others as well, singing as she did
a song of regret and the loss of innocence.
Conversations hushed, and more than a few hearts
sighed. Because he was paying for it, she looked
at Trevor as she walked back to the bar. She gave
the last lines to him.

Satisfaction warmed her eyes when applause
broke out. It gleamed there as she nipped the
bill from his hand. 'At twenty each, I'll sing as
many tunes as you like.' Then taking the
Guinnesses Aidan had finished, she moved off to
serve them.

'Hell, I'll do one for half that,' someone called
out, and over a roar of laughter, began on 'Biddy
Mulligan.'

'There's formal music over the weekend,' Aidan
told Trevor. 'And Gallagher's pays the band.'

'I'll check it out.' He watched Darcy go back
behind the bar, into the kitchen. 'Do the three of
you ever play together?'

'Shawn and Darcy and myself? At *ceilis* now and
again, or in here for a bit of fun. I sang for my
supper a time or two when I was traveling. It can
be a hard life.'

'Depends on the booking.'

Trevor stayed another hour, nursing his pint,

enjoying his stew, and listening to the apparently tireless Connor play tune after tune.

He got up once to open the door for a couple who each had a sleeping child over a shoulder. It was families, he noted, who left for home, and a couple of men with weather-beaten faces. Fishermen, he imagined, who would be up before dawn to head out to sea.

Food orders began to taper off after nine o'clock, but the taps ran steadily as he rose to go.

'Are you calling it a night, boss?' Brenna called out.

'Yeah. Until I find out what vitamins you're taking that keep you going strong for fifteen hours' work.'

'Ah, it's not vitamins.' She leaned over to pat the gnarled hand of the old man who'd sat on the same stool for hours. 'It's being near my true love, Mr Riley, here that keeps me going.'

Riley let out a cackle. 'Come give us a last pint, then, my darling, and a kiss to go with it.'

'Well, the pint will cost you, but the kiss is free.' She glanced back at Trevor as she drew it. 'I'll see you in the morning.'

'I need to borrow your sister a minute,' Trevor told Aidan, then took Darcy's hand before she could move past him. 'It's your turn to walk me out.'

'I suppose I can spare you a minute.' She set down her tray and, ignoring Aidan's frown, strolled to the door.

The rain was a fine mist that drenched the air. Smoky drifts of fog crept in from the sea to crawl along the ground. Through it came the steady beat of the water, and the far-off call of a horn as a boat passed in the night.

'Ah, it's cool.' Closing her eyes, Darcy lifted her face to the thin rain. 'It gets stuffy in there by this time of night.'

'Your feet must be killing you.'

'I won't deny they could use a good hard rub.'

'Come back with me, and I'll give them my attention.'

She opened her eyes at that. 'Now, sure and that's a tempting offer, but I've work yet, then I need my sleep.'

He lifted her hand to his lips as he had once before. 'Come to the window in the morning.'

She didn't mind the way her heart gave one hard thud, or the tingle low in her belly. She was a woman who believed in enjoying sensations, in savoring every one of them. But she had to think past that and remember how the game was played.

'I might.' Slowly, she ran a fingertip along his jaw. 'If the thought of you comes into my mind.'

'Let's make sure it does.' His arms slid around her, but the forward motion stopped when she laid a hand against his chest.

Her pulse was beating fast, an exciting feeling of anticipation. She liked the smell of the rain, and wet skin, the strong band of his arms around her. It had been some time since she'd allowed a man to put his arms around her.

That was the key, after all. The allowing. Her choice, her move, her mood. It was important, always, to stay in charge of those parts, and of the man she allowed to touch her.

Once you turned the reins over, you could forget that sensations, however lovely, were only fleeting after all.

It was safe enough here to have a sample of him, she decided. And to see if she really wanted more. So she slid her hand up his chest, around the back of his neck, and with her eyes open brought his mouth down to hers.

He took his time, she had to give him that, and didn't go grabbing and fumbling and trying to extract her tonsils with his tongue. He had a nice style about him, firm, confident, with just a hint of bite. Not so dangerous as she'd thought, which was rather a shame all in all.

Then he shifted the angle of his body, his hands running up her back, his lips slanting over hers.

The edges of her mind blurred, and she thought, Oh, God! Then didn't think at all.

He wanted to eat her alive, in fast, greedy bites. And imagined that was just what she expected from a man. Greed and heat and desperation. She had them all churning inside him. He'd seen it in a kind of mild disdain in her eyes when he'd reached for her.

So he moved slow, watched as he tasted, seen

the shift to approval, even pleasure. Along with a measuring that annoyed him even as the flavor of her poured into him. Then he needed more, just needed more, and took it.

He felt the change register dimly in some far corner of his mind. A tension in her mixed with a soft and slow yielding that was as quiet as the rain around him.

His eyes closed even as hers did, and all calculation between them was lost.

The hand at his neck skimmed into his hair. Her body lifted, pressed against his, seemed to flow into him as he moved until her back was pressed to the stone wall of the pub. Heart thundered against heart.

He drew back, wanting to clear his head, catch his breath. Think. She stayed against the wall, then gave one long, feline sigh and opened her eyes.

'I liked that.' A little more, she was sure, than was good for her. Still, she ran her tongue over her bottom lip, as if to steal a bit more taste, and had his blood swimming again. 'Why don't you do it again?'

'Why don't I?'

This time he framed her face in his hands, combed his fingers through her hair until they fisted in it. Then hesitated, waited, suffered, with his mouth a whisper from hers until her breath, and his, quickened.

'We'll drive each other crazy.'

The sound she made was more gasp than laugh.

'I've come to the same conclusion. Let's start right now.' She closed the distance by catching his bottom lip between her teeth, tugging lightly, then not so lightly before soothing the nip with her tongue.

'Good start,' he managed and crushed his mouth to hers.

Her head went spinning, quick, dancing circles that left her giddy and dizzy and delighted. Every sensation was a burst through her system – the taste, the hard lines of him, the damp stone at her back, the shimmer of rain on her skin.

She wanted to push him to urgency, to make him weak, to hear him beg – before she did. She threw herself into the kiss, into the moment, and as a result gave him more than she'd intended.

Again, it was he who drew back. It was either that or drag her off to the car and tumble her in the backseat with all the finesse and control of a kid on prom night. She'd taken him right to the edge with a kiss on a wet sidewalk outside of a crowded pub.

'We're going to need more privacy,' he decided.

'Eventually.' She needed to get her legs back under her. 'But at the moment we've stirred each other up enough. I don't think we'll get much sleep tonight, but I don't mind that.' Steadier, she brushed a hand through her hair, scattering fine drops of rain. 'You know, the last time I kissed a Yank, I slept like a baby after.'

'That would be a compliment.'

'Oh, indeed it would. I'll enjoy thinking about kissing you again at the next opportunity, but for now I have to go back inside, and you should go home.'

She turned to go, stopping when he took her arm. She wasn't quite steady enough to resist if he recognized his advantage and pressed it. So she sent him a bright and sassy look over her shoulder. 'Behave yourself, Trevor. If I'm any longer out here, Aidan will lecture me and spoil my nice mood.'

'I want your next evening off.'

'And I've a mind to give it to you.' She gave his hand a friendly pat, then slipped quickly inside again.

It was a surprise and an annoyance to find himself shaken. He had to sit in the car, listening to the rain, waiting for his blood to cool and his hands to steady. He knew what it was to want a woman, even to crave the feel of one under his hands, under his body. Just as he knew, and accepted, that the need brought with it certain vulnerabilities and risks.

But whatever it was he wanted, needed, craved from Darcy Gallagher was on a different level than anything that had come before.

She was different, he admitted, frowning at the pub for a moment before starting his car. Sexy, selfish, seductive. There were other women he knew with those attributes, but they were rarely so unapologetic and honest about it.

She was toying with him, and doing nothing to hide the fact. And by God, he had to admire her for it. Just as he had to admire her for being perfectly aware that he was playing the same game.

It was going to be fascinating to see who won, and how many rounds it took.

Relaxing since he was confident he'd handle her, he bumped along the track toward home and found himself smiling. Christ, he liked her. He couldn't remember another woman who'd heated his blood, engaged his mind, and sparked his humor in quite the way she managed to do all three. Often at the same time.

If there'd been no physical spark between them, he would still have enjoyed being with her, picking his way through that marvelous and straightforward brain of hers. As it was, he thought he was about to explore the best of all possible worlds, romantically speaking. And what a relief it was to head toward intimacy knowing that both parties looked for nothing more than mutual gratification and interesting companionship.

The business end of their relationship was relatively uncomplicated. The pub belonged to her, as much as to her brothers, but it was Aidan Trevor had dealt with, and would continue to deal with in that area.

There was that voice of hers, which was a separate and intriguing matter. He had a couple of ideas he wanted to let simmer before he discussed them with her. In that area he was confident that she'd be guided by his experience. And lured by what he could, and would, offer her.

She appreciated money and wanted enough to live stylishly. Well, he had a feeling he was going to be able to help her out there.

Profit was the bottom line, she'd told him that day on the beach. He had some ideas how that bottom line could be reached by both of them. For a song.

He turned into his street next to his cottage, very satisfied at how well his time in Ireland was being spent, and how successful the results were to date.

He got out of the car, locking it out of habit, then used the light he'd left burning to guide him through the mist to the garden gate.

He didn't know why he looked up, why he was compelled to lift his eyes to the window. The jolt that went through him was like a lightning bolt through the center of his body, one hard sizzle from head to foot.

At first he thought of Darcy, of the way she'd stood framed in her bedroom window the first time he'd seen her. A similar jolt then, not of recognition but of desire.

This woman stood framed in the window as well, was lovely as well. But her hair was pale, like the mists around him. Her eyes he knew, though it was too dark to see their color, were a haunted sea green.

This woman had been dead for three centuries.

He kept his eyes on her face as he pushed open the gate. Saw a single tear shimmer as it slipped slowly down her cheek. His heart was a trip-hammer in his chest as he walked quickly along the path through drenched flowers, through the faint music that was the wind chimes dancing in the breeze. The air was ripe, almost overpowering, with the wet perfume, the tinkling notes.

He unlocked the door, shoved it open.

There wasn't a sound. The single light he'd left burning caused long shadows to slant into corners, over the old wooden floor. With the keys still in his hand, forgotten, he started up the stairs. As he stepped to the bedroom doorway, Trevor took a breath, held it, then flipped on the light.

He hadn't expected her to be there. Illusions faded in the light. When it flashed on, flooded the room, he let out the breath he'd been holding in one short whoosh.

She stood facing him, her hands folded neatly at her waist. Her hair, delicately gold, spilled over the shoulders of a simple gray dress that flowed down to her feet. The tear, bright as silver, was drying on her cheek.

'Why do we waste what's inside us? Why do we wait so long to embrace it?'

Her voice lifted and fell, the rhythm of Ireland, and stunned him more than the vision of her.

'Who—' But of course he knew who she was, and asking was a waste of time. 'What are you doing here?'

'It's always more comforting to wait at home. I've waited a long time. He thinks you're the last. I wonder, could he be right when you don't wish to be, and wish it so strongly?'

It was impossible. A man didn't hold a conversation with a ghost. Someone, for some reason, was playing games, and it was time to put a stop to it. He strode forward, reached out to take her arm. And his hand passed through her as it would through smoke.

The keys slipped out of his numb fingers and clattered on the floor at her feet.

'Is it so difficult to believe that more exists than what you can touch?' She said it kindly, because she understood what it was to fight beliefs. She could have allowed him to touch an illusion of what she had been, but it would have meant less to him. 'You already know it in your heart, in your blood. It's only a matter of letting your mind follow.'

'I'm going to sit down.' He did so, abruptly, on the side of the bed. 'I dreamed of you.'

And for the first time, she smiled. Mixed with gentle humor was compassion. 'I know it. Your coming here to this place at this time was determined long ago.'

'Fate?'

'It's a word you don't like, one that makes you want to brace for battle.' She shook her head at him. 'Such a thing as fate takes us to certain points along a path. What you do here and now is up to you. The choice at the end of a path. I made mine.'

'Did you?'

'Aye. I did what I thought right.' Annoyance filtered into the musical voice. 'It doesn't make it right, but only what I thought, and what I felt needed to be done. My husband was a good man, a kind one. We had children together who were the joy of my life, a home that contented us.'

'Did you love him?'

'I did, oh, aye, I did after a time. A warm and settled love we had, and he would have asked no more of that from me. 'Twasn't the flash and burn I felt for another. Do you see that's what I believed it was I felt for Carrick? A fire that would flame hot and high, then die away to nothing but ash. And there I was wrong.'

She turned, as if looking out the window, beyond the glass, beyond the rain. 'I was wrong,' she repeated. 'I've bided in this place a long time, a long and lonely time, and still the burn of that love, the ache and the joy of it's inside me. It's so easy for love to hide itself under passion and not be recognized.'

'Most would say it's easy to mistake passion for love.'

'Both are true enough. But for me, I feared the fire, even as I longed for it. And fearing, and longing, never looked into the flames for the jewels that waited there for me.'

'I know about passion, but I don't know about love. And still, I've looked for you in other women.'

Her eyes met his again. 'You haven't realized

what you look for, and I hope you will. We're coming to the end of it, one way or the other. Look hard at what you want to build, then make your choices.'

'I know what—' But she was fading away. He leaped to his feet, reached out again. 'Wait. Damn it!' Alone, he tried to pace off nerves, but they stretched and snapped inside him.

How the hell was he supposed to handle this? Dreams and magic and ghosts. There was nothing solid there, nothing tangible. Nothing believable, if it came to that.

But he did believe, and that was what worried him.

CHAPTER 6

'You're looking a bit the worse for wear this morning.'

Trevor took another gulp of the coffee he'd brought to the site with him and sent Brenna a murderous look. 'Shut up.'

She didn't bother to disguise her snort of amusement. She was used to him now and didn't worry overmuch about his bark. When the likes of him meant to bite, they didn't warn you first.

'And cross as well. There now, I can have someone bring out a nice rocking chair and you can sit under an umbrella and have a bit of a nap.'

He sipped again. 'Have you ever seen a cement mixer from the inside?'

'As rough as you look 'round the edges this morning, I could take you one-handed. Seriously, you can go into the kitchen and have your coffee in peace and in quiet.'

'Construction zones cheer me up.'

'And me.' She glanced around at the tacks of equipment, the hulking machines, the men hefting pipe and cheerfully insulting each other. 'Odd creatures, aren't we? Dad's off this morning doing a spot of repair jobs here and there, so I'm glad you're here and in the mood for working off your sulks.'

'I'm not sulking. I don't sulk.'

'Ah, well, brooding, then. I enjoy a good brood myself, though most often I prefer just punching something and being done with it.'

'Shawn must lead an interesting life.'

'He's a darling man, and the love of my life, so I do my best to keep him from tedium.'

'Tedium,' Trevor muttered, 'kills.'

She nodded. He didn't look cool and reserved this morning, nor did his voice hold that faint tint of distance. She judged him to be a man that put all of that up as a barrier until the one he dealt with proved trustworthy.

She was glad to have passed the mark.

'I should tell you the lines from the new well and those from the septic are to be inspected this morning. All goes okay, we'll be burying them by end of day.'

She headed over to show Trevor the progress. The ground was muddy from the night's rain, which continued to fall steadily. It dripped off the brim of Brenna's cap, glimmered on the little silver faerie she had pinned on it, as she hunkered down beside a trench.

The smell of mud and men and gasoline pleased her enormously.

'As you see, we've used the grade of material you specified, and a pretty job it is, too. Dad and I dealt with a busted septic line during the flood last winter, and it's not an experience I'm after repeating any time in the near future.'

'This'll hold.' He crouched where he was, scanned the area. He could see it perfectly, the long, low sweep of the theater, faced with stone to blend with the existing pub, the trim of dark, distressed wood. Charming and simple, but what it was built of, and built on, would be the best that modern technology offered.

That was the dream, after all. Taking what was here, respecting it, even showcasing it, while using the material and ingenuity man had devised along the way. That's why he was here, to put the Magee mark on the place they'd come from. It had nothing to do with old legends and lovely ghosts.

Tuning back to the present, he glanced back and saw Brenna patiently watching him. 'Sorry, mind wandered.'

He looked perplexed and not a little angry. She hesitated. After all, they'd only known each other in the face-to-face manner for a handful of days. 'If it's something to do with the job that's troubling you, I hope you'll tell me so I can do what I can to smooth it out. That's part of what you're paying me for. If it's a personal matter, I'll be glad to listen if it's something you feel the need to talk through.'

'I guess it's a combination. I appreciate it, but I'll mull a while.'

'I find I mull most successfully when my hands are busy.'

'Good point.' He straightened. 'Let's get to work.'

It was rough and messy work, and most wouldn't find it pleasant. Trevor did. Large sheets of plywood were spread over the mud to give barrows and boots traction as material was transported. He hauled lumber for studs and joists, stood under the tarp where the plumbers worked and listened to rain patter on canvas. He drank a gallon of coffee and began to feel marginally human again.

Brenna was right, he decided. Busy hands kept the mind occupied so what was troubling it could stew and turn in the corners. He would figure out what was happening and what to do about it while he dealt with the business at hand.

That, he thought, amused at himself, was a great deal more efficient than brooding.

Drenched and muddy and in a much happier frame of mind, he hefted another board. And nerves danced in his belly, up his spine, over the back of his neck. He was compelled, as he had been the night before, to look up.

Darcy stood in the window, watching him through the thin curtain of rain.

She didn't smile, nor did he. In that meeting of eyes was an acute awareness that was primitive, sexual, erotic as the slide of naked flesh on naked flesh. There was nothing of the casual flirtation that had passed between them that first morning.

Nothing of the clever, seductive game they'd played since.

The flash and burn. Yes, he understood that exactly as he stood in the chilly rain staring at a woman he barely knew.

Barely knew, he thought, but had to have. And he didn't give a damn how quickly the fire died. Annoyed that he could be so easily manipulated by his own desires, he shifted the lumber on his shoulder and carried it to the team of carpenters.

When, unable to do otherwise, he looked back, she was gone.

She acted as if nothing had happened, as if that bolt of knowledge hadn't flashed between them. When Trevor came in out of the wet for lunch, she sent him a casual glance and continued to take the orders at one of her stations without a single hitch of rhythm.

It was admirable, and infuriating. He'd never had a woman stir both emotions in him so effortlessly.

The lunch crowd was thinner today. He supposed the weather kept some of the tourists within the confines of the hotel. Knowing it was perverse, he deliberately chose a table in Sinead's section. It would be interesting to see what move Darcy made in this little chess match they appeared to be playing.

Clever, was Darcy's opinion when she noticed his strategy. Though it would cost him in speed of service, he'd made his point. It was her turn to take a step ahead or back. Then again, she pondered as she scooped up the tip from a table that had just cleared, there was always sideways.

'A bit wet out today, is it, Trevor?' She called across the room while she gathered dirty dishes.

'More than a bit.'

'Ah, well, it's what makes us what we are. A day like this I imagine you'd rather be tucked into your fancy office in New York City.'

Enjoying himself, he propped a booted foot on his knee. 'I like it fine where I am. How about you?'

'Oh, when I'm here I think about being there, and vice versa. I'm a fickle creature.' Pulling out her pad, she moved to the next table, beamed smiles. 'And what is it I can get for you today?'

She took their orders, and those of another table besides, delivered them in to Shawn, and served drinks before Sinead managed to make her way to Trevor. Out of the corner of his eye, he saw Darcy smirk.

He kept it simple, a bowl of soup, and waited until Darcy was serving the next batch of meals. 'I need to do some research in the area, and this seems like a good day for it. Why don't you play guide for me?'

'It's kind of you to think of me, but I wouldn't have time to do it justice.'

'I can only spare a couple of hours myself. How about it, Aidan, can I borrow your sister between shifts?'

'Her time's her own until five.'

'Borrow, is it?' Darcy let out a short laugh. 'I think not. But if you've a mind to hire me for the service of guiding you here and about, we could negotiate a reasonable fee.'

'Five pounds an hour.'

Her eyes were sharp and somehow sweet. 'I said reasonable. Ten, and I'll spare you the time.'

'Greedy.'

'Piker,' she shot back and had several customers chuckling.

'Ten it is, and you'd better be good.'

'Darling' – she fluttered her lashes – 'no man's ever told me otherwise.'

She headed toward the kitchen, and Trevor dipped into the soup Sinead set in front of him. Both of them were completely satisfied with the arrangement.

She had to fuss a bit. It would have gone against both nature and habit for Darcy not to take time to put on fresh lipstick, dab on some perfume, rearrange her hair, debate about changing her clothes. In the end she decided the sage green shirt and black weskit and trousers were more than adequate for a daytime tour.

Yanks, as far as she could tell, were mad keen on driving around Irish roads, rain or shine, as if they'd never seen a field of grass in their lives.

Mindful of the weather, she tied back her hair with a black ribbon and tossed on a jacket before meandering back downstairs.

She was used to men waiting for her.

Shawn was whistling over the last of the lunch shift cleanup. It surprised her that Trevor wasn't, as she'd expected, cooling his heels in the kitchen and drinking a cup of the coffee he seemed to live on.

'Trevor out in the pub, then?'

'Couldn't say. I heard him mention to Brenna he had some calls to make. That was before you went upstairs to redo your war paint.'

Since that remark didn't rate a response, she sailed out into the pub, only to find Aidan alone, and preparing to lock up.

'Did you kick the man out and make him wait in the car?'

'Hmm? Oh, Trevor? No, I think he said he had someone to ring up.'

Shock ran straight down to her pretty painted toenails. 'He left?'

'I imagine he'll be back directly. Since you're waiting, I'll leave you to lock up. And see that you're back on time, Darcy.'

'But—' She could barely stutter out the single syllable, which didn't matter in the least, as Aidan was already out the door.

She *never* did the waiting. It was just wrong somehow to be ready and not have the man pacing about and looking at his watch for the second or third time. It set the wrong tone entirely.

More baffled than annoyed she turned to go back up to her rooms and forget the entire arrangement. The door opened, letting in a damp chill and Trevor.

'Good, you're ready to go. Sorry, I got hung up.' He stood, holding the door, smiling easily. The puzzled irritation on her face was very close to what he'd expected. He was certain that every man she'd ever dealt with had waited, panting, for her to finally make her entrance.

Your move, gorgeous, he thought.

'My time's worth considerable, even if yours isn't.' She strode past him, flashing him an annoyed look before she stepped outside.

'Time's part of the problem.' He stood, shielding her from the worst of the wet as she locked the pub doors. 'Everybody wants a piece of it. What I want is a couple of hours away from phones and demands for answers.'

'Then I won't ask you any questions.'

He led her to the car, held her door until she was settled. And wondering how long she was going to steam, rounded the hood to the driver's side.

'I thought we'd head north for a while. Maybe hook up with the coast road, then just . . . see.'

'You've the wheel, and the wallet.'

He pulled away from the curb. 'Everyone says getting lost in Ireland is part of its charm.'

'I don't imagine those with a destination in mind would find it charming.'

'Fortunately I don't have one at the moment.'

Darcy shifted, settled comfortably. It was a fine

vehicle, roomy and with an expensive smell to it, even if it was leased. It wasn't such a hardship, she supposed, to ride around in a classy car with a handsome man. Who was, when it came down to it, paying for the privilege.

'I imagine you always have your destination firmly in mind before taking the first step.'

'The purpose,' he corrected. 'That's a different matter.'

'And your purpose today is to see the near area, to put a picture in your mind of what people might be coming to your theater, and how they'd go about getting there.'

'Yes, that's one purpose. The other is to have some time with you.'

'So it's clever you are to find a way to do both now. Traveling this way,' she continued, 'you'll go to Dungarvan. If you take the coast road, you'll go to Waterford City; go north instead and you come to the mountains.'

'Which way would you like to go?'

'Oh, I'm just along for the ride, aren't I? The tourists often enjoy a stop by An Rinn, between here and Dungarvan. It's a little fishing village where they still speak Gaelic. There's nothing much otherwise, but a fine view of cliffs or the mountains, but the tourists often go there, finding it quaint to hear the old language spoken routinely.'

'Do you speak any Gaelic?'

'A bit, but not enough for any real conversation.'

'It's a pity such things are lost.'

'You think so because you've a sentimental view of the matter. When the simple fact is, English is easier all around. When I was in Paris, I could always find someone who knew enough English so I could be understood. I wouldn't have found anyone who'd've understood the Gaelic.'

'No sentiment about things Irish, Darcy?'

'Are you sentimental about things American?'

'No,' he said after a moment. 'I take them for granted.'

'There you have it.' She watched the rain patter, and the shift of light that brought a pearly gleam to the edges of the gray. 'It's going to clear. You might spot a rainbow if you enjoy such things.'

'I do. Tell me, what do you enjoy best about Ardmore, about where you are? The place itself.'

'The place?' She couldn't remember ever being asked such a question, and was surprised that the answer was right there. 'The sea. The moods of it, and smell of it, the feel of it in the air. There's a softness to it on a quiet morning, and a fury about it during a storm.'

'The sound of it,' Trevor murmured. 'Like a heart beating.'

'That's poetic. More something I'd expect Shawn to say than you.'

'The third stage of the legend. Jewels from the heart of the sea.'

'Ah, yes.' She liked it that he thought of the legend. She'd been giving it considerable thought herself just lately. 'And she let them go to flowers, which wouldn't buy her family supper. I've a great deal of respect for pride, but not when it's so costly.'

'You'd trade your pride for pretty stones.'

'That I wouldn't.' She sent him a sly and confident look. 'I'd find a way to keep both.'

If anyone could, he thought, it would be Darcy. He wondered why that annoyed him.

Sunshine streamed through the clouds, sparkled off the still falling rain and turned the light into something found inside a polished seashell. Those luminous, magical colors streaked across the sky in three distinct rainbows. It seemed to Trevor that the air simply bloomed, a simple and delicate flower unfurling petal by petal.

Enchanted, he stopped the car right in the middle of the road and watched those three arcs of color shimmer against the fragile blue canvas of the sky.

Darcy was more interested in watching him. It was like seeing a shield drop. And under it, hidden under that toughness, the sophistication, was a core of sweetness she'd never imagined. It touched her the way he could stare at those pretty tricks of light and wet, with the pure pleasure of it gleaming in his eyes.

When he turned his head and flashed a blinding grin in her direction, she gave in to impulse. Leaning toward him, she caught his face in her hands and kissed him quick and light and friendly, as his grin had been.

'For luck,' she said when she sat back again. 'There must be something about rainbows and kisses and luck.'

'If there isn't, there should be. Let's see where they take us – the rainbows,' he said when her eyebrow lifted. 'I like to think I know where the kisses are leading, and my luck's been pretty good lately.'

He turned down a narrow, poorly marked road. Away from the coast, and still distant from the mountains, the land rolled wet and green. Lines of gray from stone walls, deeper green from rough trees, ran through the fields and turned function into charm. He spotted a cottage, much like the one on Faerie Hill, with its creamy walls and thatched roof. A scatter of sheep, little white blobs wandering over the postcard.

And above it all, those three smears of color on a pale sky.

He opened the sunroof, chuckling when Darcy cursed as the water that had pooled on the glass showered in. It smelled fresh, gloriously clean, and added something elemental to the scent of her skin.

Then, as the road climbed, he saw it. Dull and gray and forbidding against the seashell sky. Only three walls of the structure were standing, the fourth long fallen into a tumble of stones. But what was left was defiant, spearing up out of the quiet country field as a monument to blood, to power, to vision.

He swung off the road, stopped the car. 'Let's go see it.'

'See what? Trevor, it's only a ruin. You can find one by doing hardly more than turning a corner in Ireland. There are far better ones than this if such things interest you. You've the oratory or the cathedral in Ardmore, for that matter.'

'This one's here, and so are we.' He reached across her to open her door. 'This is just the sort of thing that draws people to an area.'

'Those who haven't the sense to take holiday where there's a nice pool and a collection of five-star restaurants.' Grumbling a bit, she climbed out, then sighed and followed after him. 'Just one of the many ruined castles or forts, probably sacked by the Cromwellians – they seemed to like nothing so much as sacking and burning.'

The grass was damp, which made her glad she'd thought to wear boots. Knowing just what sheep and cows did in fields, she watched her step.

'No sign, no marker, nothing. It just stands here.'

Darcy cocked her head, deciding it was more productive to be amused than annoyed. 'And what do you think it should do but stand here?'

He only laid a hand on the stone and looked up. 'How many men, I wonder, did it take to build this? How long? Who ordered it built here, and why? Shelter and defense.'

He stepped inside and, humoring him, Darcy followed.

Grass had grown up, wild and tough, through

fallen stones. The walls, open to the elements, dripped with wet from the recent storms. His builder's eyes could make out where the separate stories had been, and he marveled at the sheer size of the broken wooden beams.

'It would've been drafty, smelly as well,' Darcy commented.

The light was shifting again, growing, and he could still see the rainbows overhead. 'Where's your romance?'

'Ha. I doubt many of the women who had to cook and clean between having their babies thought it was very romantic. Survival would have been the point.'

'Then they made their point. This survived. The people survived. The country survived. That's the magic that draws people here, the magic you miss because it's all around you.'

'It's history, not magic.'

'It's both. That's what I'm building here, that's why I came.'

'That's a large ambition.'

'Why have small ones?'

'Now that's a sentiment I can agree with. And as that ambition includes Gallagher's, I'll do my best to help you realize it.'

'That's something else I want to talk to you about. Another time.'

'What's wrong with now?'

'Because now I need a little more luck.'

He took her hands, threading his fingers through

hers. This time instead of drawing her toward him, he stepped to her. 'In an ancient castle, under a trio of rainbows, I think this ought to be worth big pots of luck.'

'You've your myths confused. The pot's at the end of the rainbow.'

'I'll take my chances right here.' He touched his lips to hers, light and friendly, as she had to his. He liked the glint of amusement it brought to her eyes and did it again, a little firmer this time, a little warmer.

'I've also heard it said, third time's the charm,' he murmured, and took her mouth again. Fast and deep and hot. The change deliberately abrupt to test both of them.

She answered as if she'd known, as if she'd only waited. Her lips parted for his. No surrender, but demand. Equal to equal, hunger to hunger. Together their fingers curled until they formed taut fists, held as if it was understood that if either let go they'd rush blindly to the next step.

Her heart leaped against his, a quick kick of excitement that sent his own racing.

It thrilled and it stunned her that it should be as wild, as near to feral as it had before. A storm brewed inside her, wanted to whip high and free. And God, she wanted to ride it, even at the risk of finding herself battered and wrecked at the end.

Here, now, what did it matter where they were, or who they were or why it seemed so desperately right?

When his lips left hers to trail to her temple, into her hair, to rest quietly there, the sweetness of the gesture after the passion left her shaken and weak. And allowed caution to return.

'If such activities under rainbows bring luck,' Darcy began, 'the pair of us are set for life.'

He couldn't laugh, nor come up with a joke in return. Something was churning inside him, something complicated, folding itself cannily in with simple desire. 'How many times have you felt like that?'

Before she could answer he released her hands, put his own on her shoulders to draw her away enough for their eyes to meet. 'Give me a straight answer. How many times have you felt the way you felt just now?'

She could have lied. She knew herself skilled at the careless and casual lie. But only when it didn't matter. His eyes were intense, direct, and, she thought, just a little angry. She found she couldn't blame him for it. 'I can't say I ever have, excepting last night.'

'Neither have I. Neither have I,' he repeated, and let her go so he could pace. 'That's something to think about.'

'Trevor, I think we both know that the hotter the flame, the quicker it flashes, and the sooner it goes cold.'

'Maybe.' He thought of Gwen, the words she'd spoken to him. 'We'd both know that going in.'

'We would.' Just as they both accepted they

weren't capable of falling in love. He was right, she thought. They were a sad pair. 'We'd know,' she agreed. 'Just as we both know we'll sleep together before we're done, but there are matters that tangle it up. Business matters.'

'Business isn't involved in this.'

'No, and it shouldn't be. But since we have a business relationship – mutual professional interests that involve my family, there are things to be discussed and agreed upon before we roll ourselves into bed. I want you, and having you is my intention, but I have terms.'

'What do you want, a goddamn contract?'

'Nothing so formal – and don't take that tone with me. You're just annoyed that the blood's still in your lap and you didn't think of it first.'

He opened his mouth, then closed it again and turned away. She had a point, damn it. 'So we work out what we want and expect out of our personal relationship and agree to keep it separate, entirely, from the business one.'

'We do, yes. And, as you said, that's something to think about. You might think that I sleep with anyone I find appealing or even handy.' She kept her voice cool as he turned back. 'But the fact is, I don't. I'm careful and selective, and I have to have some affection for a man, some understanding of him, before I take him to bed.'

'Darcy, I understood that after an hour in your company. I'm also selective.' He walked back to her. 'I like you, and I'm beginning to understand you. And when the time comes, we'll take each other to bed.'

She relaxed into a smile. 'I think we've just had a serious conversation. We'll have to be careful not to get in the habit of it and frighten ourselves. Now, I'm sorry to say, you have to take me back.'

She held out a hand.

'Next time we'll drive along the coast.'

'Next time, you'll be taking me out to a candle-light dinner, buying me champagne, and kissing my hand in that way you have.' She glanced up, caught another glimpse of the fading rainbows as they crossed the wet grass. 'But we can drive along the coast road to get there.'

'Sounds like a deal. Get a night off.'

'I'll start working on that.'

CHAPTER 7

Warm, dry weather returned to paint both sky and sea the vivid blue of coming summer. Clouds that hovered were white and harmless, and the flowers of Ardmore drank in the sun as they had the rain. The round tower cast its long and slender shadow over the graves it guarded. And high on the cliffs the wind blew gentle ripples over the water in the well of the saint.

In the village, men worked in shirtsleeves, and arms turned ruddy in the sun. Trevor watched the skeleton of his building take shape, the beams and block that were the solid bones of his dream.

As the work progressed, the audience grew. Old Mr Riley stopped by the site every day at ten until you could set your watch by him. He brought along a folding chair and sat with his cap shielding his eyes and a thermos of tea for company. There he would sit and watch, sit and nap until, sharply at one, he would stand up, fold his chair, and toddle off to his great-granddaughter's for his midday meal.

As often as not, one of his cronies would join

124

him, and they would chat about the construction while playing at checkers or gin rummy.

Trevor began to think of him as the job mascot.

Children came by now and again and sat in a half circle by Riley's chair. Their big eyes would track the sway of a steel beam as it was lifted into place.

This event was sometimes followed by a round of appreciative applause.

'Mr Riley's great-great-grandchildren and some friends,' Brenna told Trevor when he expressed some concern about them being near the site. 'They won't go wandering closer than his chair.'

'Great-*great*-grandchildren? Then he must be as old as he looks.'

'One hundred and two last winter. The Rileys are long-lived, though his father died at the tender age of ninety-six, God rest him.'

'Amazing. How many of those double greats does he have?'

'Oh, well, let me think. Fifteen. No, sixteen, as there was a new one last winter, if memory serves. Not all of them live in the area.'

'Sixteen? Good God!'

'Well, now, he had eight children, six still living. And between them I believe they made him near to thirty grandchildren, and I don't have count on how many children they made. So there you have it. You've two of his great-grandsons on your crew, and the husband of one of his grand-daughters as well.'

'How could I avoid it?'

'Every Sunday after Mass, he goes to visit his wife's grave, she that was Lizzie Riley. Fifty years they were married. He takes with him that same old ratty chair there and sits by her for two hours so he can tell her all the village gossip and family news.'

'How long has she been gone?'

'Oh, twenty years, give or take.'

Seventy years, give or take, devoted to one woman. It was flabbergasting and, Trevor thought, heartening. For some, it worked.

'He's a darling man, is Mr Riley,' Brenna added. 'Hey, there, Declan Fitzgerald, have a care there with that board before you bash someone in the face with it.'

With a shake of her head, Brenna strode over to heft the far end of the board herself.

Trevor nearly followed. It had been his intention to spend most of his afternoon lifting, hauling, hammering. The sound of air guns and compressors whooshing and rumbling along with the constant rattle of the cement mixer had the young audience enthralled. Beside them in his chair, Riley sipped tea. Going with impulse, Trevor walked over to him.

'What do you think?'

Riley watched Brenna place her board. 'I'm thinking you build strong and hire well. Mick O'Toole and his pretty Brenna, they know what they're about.' Riley shifted his faded eyes to Trevor's face. 'And so, I think, do you, young Magee.'

126

'If the weather holds, we'll be under roof ahead of schedule.'

Riley's weathered face creased into smiles. It was like watching thin white paper stretch over rock. 'You'll be there when you get there, lad. That's the way of things. You've the look of your great-uncle.'

As he'd been told so once, hesitantly, by his grandmother, Trevor considered, then crouched down so Riley wouldn't have to crane his neck.

It's just that you look so like John, Trevor, his brother who died young. It makes it hard for your grandfather to . . . It makes it hard for him.

'Do I?'

'Oh, aye. Johnnie Magee, I knew him, and your grandfather as well. A fine-looking young lad was Johnnie, with his gray eyes and slow smile. Built like a whip, as you are yourself.'

'What was he like?'

'Oh, quiet, he was, and deep. Full of thoughts and feelings, and most of them for Maude Fitzgerald. He wanted her, and little else.'

'And what he got was war.'

'Aye, that's the way it was. Many young men fell in 1916, on those fields of France. And here as well, in our own little war for Ireland's independence. Elsewhere, for that matter, at any time you can pick. Men go to battle, and women wait and weep.'

He laid a bony hand on the head of one of the children who sat at his side. 'The Irish know it comes 'round again. And so do the old. I'm both old and Irish.'

'You said you knew my grandfather.'

'I did.' Riley sat back with his tea, crossed his thin legs at the ankles. 'Dennis, now, he was a brawnier type than his brother, and more apt to look a mile down the road instead of where he was standing. A discontented sort was Dennis Magee, if you don't mind me saying. Ardmore wasn't the place for him, and he shook off the sand of it as soon as he was able. Did he, I wonder, find what he was looking for there, and contentment with it?'

'I don't know,' Trevor answered frankly. 'I wouldn't say he was a particularly happy man.'

'I'm sorry for that, for it's often hard for those around the unhappy to be happy themselves. His bride, as I recall, was a quiet-mannered lass. She was Mary Clooney, whose family farmed in Old Parish, and one of a family of ten, if my memory can be trusted.'

'It seems sharp enough to me.'

Riley cackled. 'Oh, the brain's stayed with me well enough. Just takes the body a mite longer to get up and running these days.' The boy wanted to know what had been and where he'd come from, Riley decided. And why shouldn't he? 'I'll tell you, the babe, the boy who grew to be your father, was a handsome one. Many's the time I saw him toddling along the roads holding his ma's hand.'

'And his father's?'

'Well, perhaps not so often, but now and again. Dennis was after making a living and putting by for his journey to America. I hope they had a good life there.'

'They did. My grandfather wanted to build, and that's what he did.'

'Then that was enough for him. I remember your father, the younger Dennis, coming back here when he was old enough to have grown a few whiskers.' Riley paused to pour himself more tea from his thermos. 'He seemed to've grown fine, had a pleasing way about him, and set some of the local lasses fluttering.' He winked. 'As you've done yourself. Still, he didn't choose, at that time, to leave anything behind him here but the memory. You've chosen different.'

Riley gestured toward the construction with his cup. 'Building something here's what you're about, isn't it?'

'It seems to be, at the moment.'

'Well, Johnnie, he wanted nothing more than a cottage and his girl, but the war took him. His mother died not five years after, heartbroken. It's a hard thing, don't you think, for a man to live always in the shadow of a dead brother?'

Trevor glanced up again, met the faded and shrewd eyes. Clever old man, he thought, and supposed if you lived past the century mark, you had to be clever. 'I imagine it is, even if you go three thousand miles to escape it.'

'That's the truth. Better by far to stand and build your own.' He nodded, this time with a kind of approval. 'Well, as I said, you've the look of him,

129

long-dead John Magee, in the bones of your face and around the eyes. Once they landed on Maude Fitzgerald, she was his heart. Do you believe in romance and ever after, young Magee?'

Trevor glanced away, up toward Darcy's window, then back again. 'For some.'

'You have to believe in it to get it.' Riley winked and passed his cup to Trevor. 'What's built isn't always of wood and stone, and still it lasts.' Reaching out, he once again laid one of his gnarled hands on the head of the child nearest his chair. 'Ever after.'

'Some of us do better with wood and stone,' Trevor commented, then absently drank the tea. He lost his breath, his vision blurred. 'Jesus,' he managed as the heavy lacing of whiskey scored his throat.

Riley laughed so hard he fell to wheezing, and his wrinkled face went pink with humor. 'There now, lad, what's a cup of tea without a shot of the Irish in it, I'd like to know? Never say they've diluted your blood so over there in Amerikay you can't handle your own.'

'I don't usually handle it at eleven in the morning.'

'What's the clock got to do with a bloody thing?'

The man, Trevor thought, seemed old as Moses and had been steadily sipping the spiked tea for an hour. Compelled to save face, Trevor downed the rest of the cup and was rewarded by a wide, rubbery grin.

'You're all right, young Magee. You're all right. Since you are, I'll tell you this. That lovely lass inside Gallagher's won't settle for less in a man than hot blood, a strong backbone, and a clever brain. I'm considering you have all three.'

Trevor handed Riley back his cup. 'I'm just here to build a theater.'

'If that's the truth, then I'll say this as well: It goes that youth is wasted on the young, but I'm of a mind that the young waste youth.' He poured another cup of tea. 'And I'll just have to marry her meself.' Amusement danced in his eyes as he sipped. 'Step lively, boyo, for I've a world of experience with the female of the species.'

'I'll keep that in mind.' Trevor got to his feet. 'What did John Magee do before he went to war?'

'For a living, you're meaning.' If Riley thought it was odd that Trevor wouldn't know he didn't say so. 'He was for the sea. His heart belonged to it, and to Maude, and to nothing else.'

Trevor nodded. 'Thanks for the tea,' he said and went back to join his crew.

He skipped lunch. There were too many calls to make, faxes expected, to take time for an hour in the pub and his afternoon dose of Darcy. He hoped she looked for him, wondered a little. If he understood her as he thought he did, she would expect him to come in, to *have* to come in. And it would annoy her when he didn't.

Good, Trevor mused as he let himself into the

cottage. He wanted to keep her a little off-balance. That careless confidence of hers was a formidable weapon. Her arrogance played right along with it. And damned if he didn't find them both attractive.

Amused at himself, he went directly up to his office and spent thirty minutes immersed in business. It was one of his skills, this ability to tune out every other thought and zero in on the deal of the moment. With Riley's memories fresh in his own mind, and Darcy dancing at the edges of it, he needed that skill now more than ever.

Once current projects were handled, faxes zipped off, E-mail answered and sent, he gave his thoughts to a future project he was formulating.

Time, he thought, to lay the groundwork. Picking up the phone, he called Gallagher's. He was pleased that Aidan answered. Trevor made it a point to go straight to the head of a company. Or in this case, a family.

'It's Trev.'

'Well, now, I thought I'd see you sitting at one of my tables by this time of day.'

Aidan raised his voice over the lunchtime clatter, and Trevor imagined him pulling pints one-handed while he talked. In the background he heard Darcy's laugh.

'I had some business to do. I'd like to have a meeting with you and your family, when it's convenient for you.'

'A meeting? About the theater?'

'Partly. Do you have an hour to spare, maybe between shifts?'

'Oh, I imagine we can accommodate you. Today?'

'Sooner the better.'

'Fine. Come on by the house then. We tend to hold our family meetings 'round the kitchen table.'

'I appreciate it. Would you ask Brenna to come by?'

'I will, yes.' Taking her off the job, Aidan thought, but made no comment. 'I'll see you a bit later, then.'

Around the kitchen table. Trevor recalled several of his own family meetings in the same venue. Before his first day of school, when he was going off to baseball camp, about to take his driver's test, and so on. All of his rites of passage, and his sister's, had been discussed there. Serious punishments, serious praise had warranted the kitchen table.

Odd, he remembered now, when he had broken his engagement, he'd told his parents as they sat in the kitchen. That's where he'd told them of his plans for the Ardmore theater, and his intention of coming to Ireland.

And, he realized as he calculated the time in New York, that was where his parents most likely were at this moment. He picked up the phone again and called home.

'Good morning, Magee residence.'

'Hello, Rhonda, it's Trev.'

'Mister Trevor.' The Magee housekeeper had

never called him anything else, even when she'd threatened to swat him. 'How are you enjoying Ireland?'

'Very much. Did you get my postcard?'

'I did. You know how much I love to get them. I was telling Cook just yesterday that Mister Trevor never forgets how I like postcards for my album. Is it as green as that, really?'

'Greener. You should come over, Rhonda.'

'Oh, now you know I'm not getting on an airplane unless somebody holds a gun to my head. Your folks are having breakfast. They're going to be thrilled to hear from you. Just hold on a minute. You take care of yourself, Mister Trevor, and come back soon.'

'I will. Thanks.'

He waited, enjoying the picture of the rail-thin black woman in her ruthlessly starched apron hurrying over the rich white marble floor, past the art, the antiques, the flowers, to the back of the elegant brownstone. She wouldn't use the intercom to announce his call. Such family dealings could only be delivered in person.

The kitchen would smell of coffee, fresh bread, and the violets his mother was most fond of. His father would have the paper open to the financial section. His mother would be reading the editorials and getting worked up about the state of the world and narrow minds.

There would be none of that uneasy quiet, that under-the-polish tension that had lived in his grandparents' home. Somehow his father had escaped that, just as his own father had escaped Ardmore. But the younger Dennis had indeed stood and built his own.

'Trev! Baby, how are you?'

'I'm good. Nearly as good as you sound. I thought I'd catch you and Dad at breakfast.'

'Creatures of habit. But this is an even lovelier way to start the day. Tell me what you see.'

It was an old request, an old habit. Automatically he rose to go to the window. 'The cottage has a front garden. An amazing one for such a small place. Whoever designed it knew just what they wanted. It's like a . . . a witch's garden. One of the good witches who helps maidens break evil spells. The flowers tumble together, color, shape, and scent. Beyond it are hedges of wild fuchsia, deep red on green and taller than I am. The road they line is narrow as a ditch and full of ruts. Your teeth rattle if you go over thirty. Then the hills slope down, impossibly green, toward the village. There are rooftops and white cottages and tidy streets. The church steeple, and well off is a round tower I have to visit. It's all edged by the sea. It's sunny today, so the light flashes off the blue. It's really very beautiful.'

'Yes, it is. You sound happy.'

'Why wouldn't I be?'

'You haven't been, not really, for too long. Now I'll let you talk to your father, who's rolling his eyes at me, as I imagine you have business to discuss.'

135

'Mom.' There was so much, so much that his morning conversation with an old man and his horde of progeny had set to swirling inside him. He said what he felt the most. 'I miss you.'

'Oh. Oh, now look what you've done.' She sniffled. 'You can just talk to your father while I cry a little.'

'Well, you got her mind off the editorial on handguns.' Dennis Magee's voice boomed over the wire. 'How's the job going?'

'On schedule, on budget.'

'Good to hear. Going to keep it there?'

'Close to there, anyway. You, Mom, Doro, and her family better keep a week next summer open. The Magees should all be here for the first show.'

'Back to Ardmore. I have to say, I never figured on it. From the reports, it hasn't changed much.'

'It's not meant to. I'll send you a written update on the project, but that's not why I called. Dad, did you ever visit Faerie Hill Cottage?'

There was a pause, a sigh. 'Yes. I had some curiosity about the woman who'd been engaged to my uncle. Maybe because my father so rarely spoke of him.'

'What did you find out?'

'That John Magee died a hero before he ever had the chance to live.'

'And Grandfather resented that.'

'That's a hard way to put it, Trev.'

'He was a hard man.'

'What he felt about his brother, his family, he

kept to himself. I never tried to get through. What was the point? I knew I would never get through to him about what he felt about anything, much less what he'd left behind in Ireland.'

'Sorry.' He could hear it, that weariness, that vague tone of frustration in his father's voice. 'I shouldn't have brought it up.'

'No, that's foolish. It would be on your mind. You're there. I think – looking back, I think he was determined to be an American, to raise me as an American. Here is where he wanted to make his mark. In New York he could be his own man. He was his own man.'

A cold, hard man who paid more attention to his ledgers than his family. But Trevor saw no point in saying so when his father knew that better than anyone.

'What did you find, for yourself, when you came back here?' he asked instead.

'Charm, some sentiment, more of a link than I'd expected.'

'Yeah, exactly. That's exactly it.'

'I meant to go back, but something else always seemed to come up. And truth is, I'm a city boy. A week in the country and I'm itchy. You and your mother never minded roughing it, but the Hamptons is about as rural as I can manage and stay sane. Don't snicker, Carolyn,' Dennis said mildly. 'It's rude.'

Trevor scanned his view again. 'It's a long way from the Hamptons to here.'

'Absolutely. A couple of weeks in that cottage you're renting and I'd be babbling. I don't do quaint for long.'

'But you visited, saw Maude Fitzgerald.'

'Yes. Jesus, must be thirty-five years ago. She didn't seem old to me, but I guess she was well into her seventies. I remember her being graceful, not creaky the way I, being callow, expected an old woman to be. She gave me tea and cake. Showed me an old photograph of my uncle. She kept it in a brown leather frame. I remember that because it reminded me of the song – what is it – 'Willie MacBride.' Then she walked with me to his grave. He's buried on the hill by the ruins and the round tower.'

'I haven't been there yet. I'll go by.'

'I don't remember what we talked about exactly. It was all so long ago. But I do remember this because it seemed odd at the time. We were standing over his grave and she took my hand. She said what came from me would journey back and make a difference. I would be proud. I suppose she was talking about you. People said she had the sight, if you believe in such things.'

'You start to believe in all sorts of things once you're here.'

'Can't argue with that. One night while I was there I took a walk on the beach. I could swear I heard flutes playing and saw a man flying over-head on a white horse. Of course, I'd had a few pints at Gallagher's Pub.'

Even as his father laughed, Trevor felt a chill skate down his spine. 'What did he look like?'

'Gallagher?'

'No, the man on the horse.'

'A drunken delusion. Well, that set your mother off,' Dennis muttered, and through the line Trevor could hear his mother's delighted laugh.

'I'll let you get back to breakfast.'

'Take some time to enjoy yourself while you're there. Get me the report when you can, Trev, and we'll all keep next summer in mind. Stay in touch.'

'I will.'

He hung up, then continued to stare thoughtfully out the window. Delusions, illusions, reality. There didn't seem to be very much space between them in Ardmore.

He finished up what business could be done before New York opened, then took a walk to John Magee's grave.

The wind was high and the graves were old. The shifting of ground had tipped and tilted many of the markers so they leaned and slanted toward the bumpy grass to cast their shadows over their dead. John Magee's stood straight, like the soldier he'd been. The stone was simple, weathered by wind and time, but still the carving was deep and clear.

JOHN DONALD MAGEE
1898–1916
Too young to die a soldier

139

'His mother had that carved in her grief,' Carrick said as he stepped up to stand beside Trevor. 'In my estimation, one is always too young to die a soldier.'

'How would you know why she had it carved?'

'Oh, there's little I don't know and less I can't find out. You mortals make your monuments to the dead. I find it an interesting habit. A peculiarly human one. Stones and flowers, symbols, aren't they, of what lasts and what passes away? And why do you come here, Trevor Magee, to visit those you never knew in life?'

'Blood and bonds, I suppose. I don't know.' Frustrated, he turned to face Carrick. 'What the hell is this?'

'By that you're meaning me. You've more of your mother in you than ever your grandfather, so you know by now the answer to that, even if your diluted Yank blood doesn't accept what's in front of your face. You're a traveled man, aren't you? You've been more places and seen more things than most who are your age. Have you never found magic on your journeys till now?'

He wanted to think he had more of his mother in him, much more than he had of his grandfather. But there was nothing in Carolyn Magee of the easy mark. 'I've never had conversations with ghosts and faeries till now.'

'You talked with Gwen?' The amusement died out of Carrick's eyes, turning the bright blue dark and with an edge. He gripped Trevor's arm with a hand that transferred a jolt of heat and energy. 'What did she say to you?'

'I thought you knew or could find out.'

Abruptly, Carrick released him and turned away. He began to pace through the grass, around the stones in quick, almost jerky movements. The air around him sizzled with a visible color and spark. 'She's the only thing that matters, and the only thing I can't see clear. Can you know, Magee, what it is to want one person with all your heart, with all that you have in you, and for her to be just out of your reach?'

'No.'

'I blundered with her. Now that's a deep score to the pride, make no mistake. Not that it was only my fault. She blundered as well. It hardly matters who holds the heaviest weight of the blame at this point.'

He stopped, turned back. The air grew still again. 'Will you tell me what she said to you?'

'She spoke of you and regrets, of passions that flash and burn, and love that lasts. She misses you.'

Emotions swirled in Carrick's eyes. 'If she – should you speak with her again, would you tell her I'm waiting, and I've loved no other since last we met?'

For some reason it no longer seemed odd to be asked to deliver a message to a ghost. 'I'll tell her.'

'She's beautiful, isn't she?'

'Yes, very.'

'A man can forget to look past beauty and into the heart. I did, and it's cost me dear. You won't make that mistake. It's why you're here.'

'I'm here to build a theater, and to acquaint myself with my roots.'

His humor restored, Carrick strolled back to Trevor. 'You'll do both, and more. Your ancestor here was a fine young man, a bit of a dreamer, with a heart too soft for soldiering and what war makes men do to men. But he went out of duty and left his love behind.'

'You knew him?'

'Aye, both of them, though only Maude knew me. She gave him a charm before he marched off, for protection.'

He snapped his fingers and from them dangled a chain with a little silver disk. 'I expect she'd want you to have it now.'

Too curious for caution, Trevor reached out and took the object. The silver was warm, as if it had been worn against flesh, and on it the carving was faint.

'What does it say?'

'It's in old Irish, and says simply "Forever Love." She gave it to him, and he wore it faithful. But war was stronger than the charm in the end, if not stronger than the love. He wanted a simple life, unlike his brother, who went off to America. Your father's father wanted something more, and he worked for it and brought it to be. That's an admirable thing. What do you want, Trevor Magee?'

'To build.'

'That's an admirable thing as well. What will you call your theater?'

'I haven't thought of it. Why?'

'I have an idea you'll choose correctly because you're a man who chooses carefully. That's why you're still living alone.'

Trevor's fingers curled around the disk. 'I like living alone.'

'That may be, but it's making mistakes you dislike most of all.'

'True enough. I have to go now. I have a meeting.'

'I'll walk with you a ways. 'Tis a fine summer we have in store. You'll hear the cuckoo call if you listen. It's a good omen of things to come. I'm wishing you luck on your meeting, and with Darcy.'

'Thanks, but I know how to handle both.'

'Oh, well, now, I believe you do, or I wouldn't be in so cheerful a mood. She'll be handling you as well. It helps the last of this waiting, if you don't mind me saying, to be entertained by the pair of you.'

'I'm not part of your plan.'

'It's not a matter of planning. It's a matter of what is, and what will be. You've more say in it than I, and you've little enough.'

Carrick stopped. He could see the cottage now, the creamy walls, the sunny thatched roof, the rainbow spread of flowers. 'Once she would have come out to meet me, her heart pounding, her eyes bright. Fear and love so mixed together neither of us could untangle them. And me so sure I could dazzle her with gifts and promises that I never held out to her the single thing that mattered.'

'No second chance?'

A wry smile twisted Carrick's lips. 'There might have been, had I not waited so long to take it. I'll go no farther than this, until the waiting's done. Handle Darcy, Magee, before she handles you.'

'My life,' Trevor said briefly. 'My business.' He strode down the slope toward the house and his car. But he couldn't resist a glance back.

It barely surprised him that Carrick had vanished. All that was left was the green hill, and sweetly, brightly, the two-tone call of a bird.

The cuckoo, Trevor supposed. He couldn't think of anything more apt.

Put it aside, he ordered himself and continued to walk. Tuck away the sentiment over long-dead relatives and their sweethearts, visits with faerie princes, and messages for beautiful ghosts.

He had business to attend to.

But he slipped the chain around his neck, and tucked the silver disk under his shirt, where it lay to warm against his heart.

CHAPTER 8

The home team always had the edge. Trevor knew it going in, but didn't see a way around it. Not only was the house Gallagher turf, but the village, the county, the whole damn country was theirs. Unless he found a way to shift the meeting to New York, he would just have to play it as underdog.

Added to that, they outnumbered him. It couldn't be helped.

Not that he minded working a deal when the odds were against him. The challenge of it only made the satisfaction of success sweeter.

He'd already worked out his approach. The questions, the doubts, the general unease of what he supposed would be termed his paranormal experiences would just have to wait until after business hours.

The minute he knocked on the door of the Gallagher house, he was representing Magee Enterprises. It was a responsibility, and a privilege, that he took very seriously.

Darcy opened the door, a sassy smile on her

face, her head tilted at the perfect angle to display both arrogance and humor.

Jesus, he'd like to take her in one quick gulp and be done with it. Instead he greeted her with an easy grin. 'Afternoon, Miss Gallagher.'

'And a good day to you, Mr Magee.' Deliberately provocative, she stepped toward him rather than back. 'Don't you want to kiss me?'

He wanted to swallow her whole. 'Later.'

She gave her head a little toss that sent her clouds of dark hair tumbling back. 'I might not be in the mood later.'

'You will be, if I kiss you.'

She shrugged, though she was faintly irritated, then moved back to let him in. 'I like confidence in a man. Mostly. The rest of us are in the kitchen, awaiting your presence. Is this to do with your theater?'

'Partly.'

Irritation clicked up another level, but she spoke coolly as she led him toward the rear of the house. 'And a mysterious man as well. Now I'm in love for certain.'

'How many times would this make?'

'Oh, I stopped counting years ago. I've such a fickle heart. How many is that for you?'

'Still batting zero here.'

'That's a pity. Here's himself come to call,' Darcy announced over what seemed to Trevor to be a heated conversation around the table.

'If I'm interrupting . . .'

'Not at all.' Aidan rose and waved a hand toward Brenna and Shawn, who sat scowling at each other. 'If these two don't snap at each other six times a week, we're worried enough to ring up the doctor.'

'You said you'd leave the details of the house to me,' Brenna reminded her husband.

'You're talking about the materials and colors of the kitchen counters and such. Who does the bloody cooking?'

'The blue laminate's pretty and sensible.'

'The granite's subtle and strong. It'll last two lifetimes.'

'Well, we've only this one to concern us at present, don't we? Trevor—'

Even as she turned to him, Trevor held up a hand. 'No, absolutely no. Don't even think of asking me for an opinion. I have no opinion when it comes to arguments between husband and wife.'

''Tisn't an argument.' Sulking, Brenna sat back, folded her arms. 'But a discussion. I can have the laminate done in a wink. Do you know how long it'll take to do the damn business in granite?'

'When it's right you wait.' Shawn leaned over, kissed her softly. 'And then you treasure.'

'You think you'll get around me that way?'

'I do, yes.'

She sucked in a breath, then let it out on a huff. 'Bastard,' she said, with great affection.

'Well, now that we've settled that vital and thorny matter . . .' Aidan gestured Trevor to a chair. 'Can we get you a beer, then, or some tea?'

147

Their turf, Trevor reminded himself as he sat. 'A beer'd be great, thanks.' He glanced at Jude. 'How are you doing?'

'Good.' She didn't think he'd want her to mention she felt as if she had a semi parked on her bladder. 'Aidan said you didn't stop in the pub for lunch today. Why don't I fix you a sandwich?'

'I'm fine.' He reached over, laid his hand on hers. 'Sit. I appreciate you all taking the time to meet with me on such short notice.'

'It's not a problem.' Aidan put the beer in front of Trevor, then sat. Head of the table. Advantage, Gallagher. And they all knew it. 'Not a problem at all. Brenna tells us the building's going up right on schedule, and I have to say that's a bit of a surprise in these parts.'

'I have a good foreman.' He toasted Brenna, then sipped. 'I think we'll be ready by next May.'

'So long?' Darcy looked both shocked and horrified. 'And will that noise be part of the whole for a year?'

'What noise?' he replied nonchalantly. When she sputtered, he simply rolled over her. 'I hope to scatter in a few performances, primarily for the locals, by next spring. Warm things up. But I'm aiming for the third week in June for the grand opening.'

'Midsummer,' Darcy commented.

'The middle of summer is July.'

'Don't you know your pagan calendar? Midsummer's June twenty-second, and a fine choice.

A night for celebrating. Jude had her first *ceili* on that night last year, and it turned out well, didn't it, darling?'

'Eventually. Why the month delay?' Jude asked him.

'Basically to cover our asses, to build anticipation, to book acts, generate press. My plan is to have a small, intimate opening in May. Exclusive. Invited guests, which would include the village, family, and a select number of VIP's.'

'That's very clever,' Darcy murmured.

'It's part of my job. It'll generate interest, and publicity, in the official June opening. And give us time to tweak any details that need tweaking.'

'Like a dress rehearsal.'

He nodded at Darcy. 'Exactly. I'd like your help with the guest list for the area.'

'That's as easily done as said,' Aidan told him.

'And I'd like you to perform. The three of you.'

Aidan reached for his own beer. 'In the pub.'

'Onstage,' Trevor corrected. 'The main stage.'

'In the theater?' Aidan set his beer down again without drinking. 'Why?'

'Because I've heard you, and you're perfect.'

'Well, now, Trev, that's flattering to be sure.' Thoughtfully, Shawn reached for one of the tea biscuits Jude had set out. 'But all you've heard from us is a bit of fun. It's not as if we're a professional act or anything of that nature. The kind you're looking to have in your theater.'

'You're exactly what I'm looking for.' His gaze

skimmed to Darcy, lingered a moment, then moved on. She'd yet to say a word. 'Showcasing local talent is part of what this project is about. Mixing that, together with new and established acts. I can't think of anything more appropriate than having the Gallaghers perform, and perform a selection of Shawn Gallagher's music, at the first showing.'

'Mine.' Shawn went very pale. 'At such a time? I don't mean to tell you your business, Trev, but that's surely a mistake.'

'It's not.' Brenna rapped a fist on his shoulder. 'It's brilliant. It's perfect. But you've only bought three of his tunes so far, Trev.'

Trevor angled his head. 'He's only shown me three so far.'

'There.' Brenna socked Shawn again, with more enthusiasm. 'You moron. He's dozens more. If you come by the house you can have a look. He can play them for you. He's got his piano crammed in what there is of our front room already. And his fiddle and—'

'Quiet,' Shawn muttered.

'Don't tell me to be quiet when—'

'Quiet.' This time the order was sharp, and Brenna seethed, but subsided. 'I have to think about it.' Flustered, he dragged a hand through his hair. 'It's a lot to think about.' At his wife's annoyed hiss he simply looked at her. 'Brenna.'

She quieted. His look was a plea for patience and understanding. How could she refuse? 'I'll just say this. You've so much to give, Shawn, and it shouldn't worry you. But the fact that it does is likely part of why you're brilliant in the first place. Make a bargain with me.'

He made a restless movement with his shoulders. 'What bargain?'

'Let me pick the next, just one, to show Trev. I had fine luck with the first, didn't I?'

'You did. That you did. All right, then. Brenna'll bring you a song tomorrow so you can see what you think of it.'

'I'll look forward to it.' Trevor hesitated. The trouble was, he realized, he *liked* these people. 'I wish to God you'd get an agent.'

'Isn't she bad enough?' Shawn countered, jerking a thumb at Brenna. 'Hounds me day and night as it is, and read every word in the contract you sent twice over. My eyes would have bled. We'll just go on as we are.'

'It keeps my end of it less complicated.' Trevor set the subject aside and turned back to Aidan. Businessman now to businessman. 'The three of you are Gallagher's, and Gallagher's is Ardmore. The theater's going to be part of that, and because of it will benefit all of us here. The two are linked, for the very practical reason that your business is already established, already considered a center for music. Bringing the three of you forward as the first act to perform will get us a lot of press. Press means tickets, and tickets mean profit. For Gallagher's and for the theater.'

'I follow that well enough. But that we are Gallagher's is another point. Running the pub is what we do.'

'And how much will it add to Gallagher's reputation when the three of you perform, and record, Shawn's music?'

'Record?'

'For Celtic Records. We'll have the CD's available at the theater,' Trevor went on smoothly. 'And we have a reputation of our own – artists, packaging, promotion, distribution. You can't manufacture this kind of hook. The three of you were born into it.'

'But we're not performers, we're publicans.'

'You're wrong. You're natural performers. I understand the pub's your priority. I'm counting on that. But this could be, would be, a very interesting, profitable, and satisfying sideline.'

'Why does it matter to you?'

It was the first question Darcy had asked, and Trevor shifted his attention to her. 'Because the theater matters to me, and I never settle for less than the best. It means profit,' he added. 'Isn't that the bottom line?'

Aidan said nothing for a moment, then nodded. 'You'll appreciate that this is a bit of a surprise to us all, and is something we need to think over and discuss. The five of us have to be agreed, one way or another, on the matter. The overall picture, so to speak, before we can even consider discussing details. Of which I can only imagine there are many.'

'Understood.' Knowing it was time to step back and let the idea percolate, Trevor got to his feet. 'If you have any questions you know where to find me. Brenna, take your time coming back. I'm going to the site.'

'Thanks. I'll be right along.'

Darcy tapped a finger on Aidan's arm to keep him in place. 'I'll walk you out,' she said to Trevor.

There were so many thoughts whirling through her mind. She knew it was important, vital, to snatch the most significant of them and get a firm hold. So she kept all those thoughts to herself until they walked outside again.

'Sure and it's quite the surprise you've brought us today, Trevor.'

'So I see, but I wonder why it's such a surprise. You've got ears and brains. You've heard how the three of you are together.'

'Maybe it's that I've already heard it.' She glanced back, knowing her family was already discussing the matter. Still, she wanted her own thoughts and feelings settled before she added them to the mix. 'You're not the impulsive sort, not with business.'

'No.'

'So this isn't something that just popped wild into your head.'

'I've been playing the angles since the first time I heard you sing. You've got a voice that goes straight to the gut, right after it's broken the heart. It's quite a talent.'

'Hmm.' She strolled by, down the narrow path through Jude's garden. 'And this notion you've come to us with today, you're thinking it'll enhance our mutual concerns.'

'Not think, Darcy. I know. It's my business to know.'

She turned her head, studied him over her shoulder. 'Aye, I suppose so. And how much would you be paying for this enhancement?'

Now he smiled. Trust her to get right down to the sharpest point in the quill. 'It's negotiable.'

'And what would be the floor of that negotiation?'

'Five thousand for the performance. The recording rights are a separate issue.'

Her eyebrows arched. One evening singing, and more than she'd earn waitressing for weeks in the pub. 'Pounds or dollars?'

He hooked his thumbs in the front pockets of his jeans. 'Pounds.'

She made a little humming sound again. 'Well, if we decide we're interested, Aidan will haggle with you over that pitiful amount, to be sure.'

'I'm looking forward to it. Aidan's the businessman.' Keeping his eyes on hers, Trevor moved to her. 'Shawn's the artist.'

'And what would I be?'

'The ambition. Put the three parts together, and you've got a hell of a team.'

'As I said before, you're a clever man.' She looked away from him and out to sea, where the waves rolled in slow and smooth. 'I've ambitions, right enough. And I'll be honest with you here, Trevor, and tell you this particular idea has never occurred to me. The singing for anything but my own enjoyment.'

He surprised her by trailing a finger down the line of her throat. 'What you've got in there can make you rich. Famous. I can help that happen.'

'That's quite an offer, and appeals to my basest of egos and desires.' She walked on a little farther, until she stood near the street of the village where she'd lived all her life. 'How rich?'

His laugh was easy and full of pure pleasure. 'I like you.'

'I'm growing fonder of you by the minute. I've a yen to be rich, and I'm not ashamed to say so.'

He jerked his head toward the house. 'Talk them into it.'

'No, that I won't. I'll put in my thoughts, and I'll shout if I need to be heard, and exchange the usual insults when they're warranted, but I won't pressure them to do anything that doesn't sit comfortably. It'll come from all of us, or not at all. It's the Gallagher way.'

'Does it sit comfortably with you?'

'I haven't decided, but I'm enjoying the trying of it on, so to speak. I have to get back in there, as the discussion's hot and heavy by this time. But . . .'

'What?'

'I wanted to ask, as you're in the way of being

an expert on such things.' She laid a hand on his arm, looked into his eyes. She wanted to see her answer there before she heard it. 'Shawn. He's brilliant, isn't he?'

'Yes.'

It was a simple answer, almost casually given. And perfect. 'I knew it.' Tears swam into her eyes, shimmered beautifully against the blue. 'I have to get over this before I go back in or his head'll swell up so I won't be able to connect with his brain next time I cosh him. I'm so proud of him.' A tear spilled over, made her sniffle. 'Damn it.'

Caught off guard, Trevor stared at her, then dug in his back pocket for his bandanna. 'Here.'

'Is it clean?'

'Christ, you're a maze, Darcy. Here.' He dabbed at her cheeks himself, then handed the cloth to her. 'You'd do it for him, wouldn't you?'

She blew her nose. 'What?'

'The performance, the recording. You'd do it for Shawn even if you hated the idea.'

'It's not going to hurt me any, is it?'

'Stop it.' He took her arms, his eyes narrowed. 'It wouldn't matter what it cost you, you'd do it for him.'

'He's my brother. There's nothing I wouldn't do for him.' She let out a steadying breath, eased back, then handed him the bandanna. 'But damned if I'll do it for free.'

When she turned to walk away, he fought a little war with himself. Pride against need. And need

156

won. 'Get a night off. Damn it, Darcy, get a night off.'

The thrill of the rough demand shivered straight up the center of her body. But the look she shot over her shoulder was designed to taunt. 'We'll see.'

The minute she was inside, she leaned back against the front door, shut her eyes. Weak, something about the man left her weak. And it was an odd sensation when tangled with the burst of energy that his offer and his promises had spurting through her.

Her knees wanted to shake, her feet wanted to dance.

And despite it all, she hadn't a clue what it was she wanted in her heart.

She opened her eyes, nearly smiled. From the raised voices coming from the kitchen it was clear that her family hadn't a clue either.

She started back, then stopped in the parlor doorway and looked at the old piano. Music had been as much a part of her life as the pub. For always. But the music had always been for the fun, for the pleasure of it, never for money. One of her earliest memories was of that piano, of sitting on her mother's lap there on that same stool while the music and the laughter ran all around.

She had a good strong voice. She wasn't a bubble-head – she knew her voice was fine enough. But to pin her hopes on it, and on Trevor Magee's making something of it, that was a different matter entirely.

Wiser, she decided, to consider taking that first step without any real expectations. That way there couldn't be any real disappointments.

She headed back in time to hear Brenna's furious disgust.

'A potato's got more sense than you, Shawn. The man's giving you the opportunity of a lifetime, and you're worrying it to pieces.'

'It's my lifetime, isn't it?'

'I think this gives me some say in your lifetime.' She held up the chain that held her rings.

'It's my music, and even you can't hammer it out of me.'

'You've agreed to show him another tune,' Aidan put in, playing peacemaker. 'Let's see where it goes once you have. As for the other, we have to look at all the angles of it.' He looked up, gestured to Darcy. 'And we haven't heard what Darcy thinks about it.'

'If it'll put her in a spotlight and cash in her pocket,' Shawn said, 'we already know what she thinks.'

Darcy merely smiled sourly. 'As I'm not a pea-brained idiot like some at this table, I've no objection to either of those things. But . . .' She trailed off until Shawn narrowed his eyes. 'I'm also thinking that a man the likes of Magee isn't after thinking in one-shot sorts of deals, or in small numbers. I'm not sure any of us are prepared for what he really has in his mind.'

'He wants Shawn's music, and he wants the

three of you to sing it.' Brenna threw up her hands. 'It makes good, strong sense to me.'

'There are three of us.' Aidan spoke quietly, looking from face to face. 'Each of us has different needs. Jude, the baby, the pub, this house. They're my center. I won't change that. Shawn has the new home and new life he's building with Brenna, the pub as well, and his music. But the music is made in his own time and his own way. Do I have the right of that?'

'You do, yes.'

'And Darcy, I'm thinking that what was under the idea we've heard today, what was between the lines, which I caught as you did, might be just the sort of thing you need.'

'I haven't decided. Music has always been a personal thing to us, something shared with family and friends. I understand what Brenna's saying, as the simple part of the notion – just the singing that night to cement the link between the pub and the theater does make good, strong sense. And it's not as if the three of us screech like cats at the moon and would embarrass the family name by doing it. But he's a canny individual is Trevor Magee. So we'll have to be cannier, and see that whatever we do or don't is precisely what we intend.'

Aidan nodded, then turned to his wife. 'You've said nothing, Jude Frances. Don't you have thoughts on the subject?'

'Several.' Now that the shouting was over, she

judged everyone ready to hear them. She folded her hands on her belly. 'First, the practicalities. I don't know anything about publicity or entertainment, but it seems to me the scenario Trevor outlined is simple and smart and would be effective. That benefits all of us.'

'That's true,' Aidan agreed. 'But if we take our music into the theater, what does that leave us in the pub?'

'The informality. A bigger impact because you *have* performed onstage, because you've recorded. And then anyone coming in for a pint might catch you in the mood to do a song while you're at the bar or coming out of the kitchen. The tourists, in particular, will love it.'

'Well, now, that's bloody brilliant,' Darcy murmured.

'Not really. It's just that I've sat in the pub, and I've watched and I know how lovely it is. So has Trevor. He's very much aware of how one will affect the other. Next . . .' She took a deep breath. 'Individually. Aidan, it won't change your center. Nothing could. It isn't a matter of either/or. Whatever you decide will be right, because you have that center and it matters most to you.'

He picked up her hand, kissed it. 'Isn't she wonderful? Have you ever seen the like of her?'

Jude merely kept her hand in his and laid them both over their baby. 'Shawn. You have a beautiful talent. The more Brenna loves you, and admires that, the more impatient she is with you for hesitating to share it.'

'Then she must love me a hell of a lot.'

'Which is my cross to bear.' Brenna bit into a biscuit and glared at him.

'I would think,' Jude continued, 'having your family perform and record your music would be the perfect solution. You trust them, and they understand you. Won't it be easier for you to take that step when you have that bond?'

'It shouldn't be because of me.'

'Oh, just answer the question,' Darcy snapped. 'You fish-faced jackass.'

'Of course it'd be easier, but—'

'Now shut up.' Darcy nodded smugly. 'And let Jude finish. Because I think she's about to come to me, and I love the attention.'

'You don't shrink from attention.' Jude picked up her tea to sip. She couldn't sit much longer in one spot. Her back was starting to ache. 'Performing would be second nature to you. You'd enjoy the stage, the lights, the applause.'

Shawn snorted. 'She'll lap it up like cream. Vanity is our Darcy's middle name.'

'Can I help it if all the good looks in the family waited for me?'

'I don't know, as I haven't seen your face without a layer of paint since you were thirteen.'

'The pity of it is I have to see yours every time I turn around.'

'Since looking at each other is the next thing to

161

looking in a mirror, you could find something else to argue over.' Aidan held up a finger before either of his siblings could snipe. 'Let Jude finish.'

'I nearly am.' Amazing, she thought, how quickly she'd become used to the rhythm of this family. 'I imagine you'd enjoy being onstage, playing to the audience. But, if the idea of it terrified you, if you hated the very thought of it, you'd do it anyway. You'd do anything for these two.'

Though the statement was perilously close to the end of her conversation with Trevor, Darcy let out an amused snort. 'I do to please myself.'

'In a great many things,' Jude agreed. 'This you'd do for Aidan, and Aidan's the pub. You'd do it for Shawn, and Shawn's the music. Last of all you'd do it for yourself. For the fun.'

'The fun's a factor, isn't it?' Darcy rose, started to move casually to the stove, but Aidan caught her hand as she went by.

He tugged, she resisted. He tugged again. With a little sigh, she went into his lap. 'Tell me what you want, Darcy darling.'

'A chance, I suppose.'

He nodded, met Shawn's eyes across the table. 'Let's give it a day or two to simmer. Then I'll talk to Magee again and see just what's up his sleeve.'

CHAPTER 9

The hums and grumbles and thuds outside her window drove Darcy out of bed early every morning. Whenever she thought about it going on for nearly another year, she was tempted to bury her head under the pillow and smother herself.

Since suicide wasn't in her makeup, though, she tried to make the best of it. She could turn up her music loud, or just lie there and pretend she was in a big, noisy city.

New York, Chicago. All that noise was really traffic, and people bustling under her lovely, lofty penthouse flat.

Most of the time that worked. When it didn't, she got up and spent quite a bit of time in the shower cursing.

Otherwise, if she was in the mood, she'd wander over to look down and watch the work for a while. And look for Trevor. She didn't allow herself to do it daily – or allow herself to be seen daily.

That would be predictable.

She liked looking at him, seeing what he was up to that morning. Some days he was standing on the edge of things, his hair blowing in the wind, discussing something or other with Brenna or Mick O'Toole in the way men did, with thumbs tucked into pockets and wise, sober expressions on their faces.

And others – and she liked the others best – he was in the middle of the thing, hammering or hauling or drilling, stripped down to his shirt-sleeves, and if the angle was right she could watch a ripple of muscle.

It was odd. Not that she hadn't always enjoyed taking a good, long look at men, but she couldn't remember ever being so interested in the look of one man before. Or being so fascinated by studying him as he went about manual labor.

He had a fine build, she mused as she stood framed in the window. That was part of it. A woman who didn't appreciate a long and wiry build on a man, well, she had a problem, as far as Darcy was concerned. It was the way he moved, too. Light on his feet, confident and in control.

She imagined, and why wouldn't she imagine, that he would be just as confident and in control with a female in bed. Control would make a man thorough, and a thorough loving was no small matter to a woman.

Still, she had to wonder what it would take to snap that control. A loving wild and fierce was no small matter either.

It concerned her in a mild sort of way that she thought of him as often as she did. Looked for him as often as she did. In the mornings like this, at midday, in the evening.

Sometimes he came into the pub. Sometimes he didn't. She was certain it was purposeful on his part. That lack of predictability. They were gaming with each other, and both knew it perfectly well.

And damn, but didn't she like that about him! The man was every bit as arrogant as she was herself.

She hadn't arranged for a night off. That was purposeful on her part. It was true enough that she liked keeping him waiting. But she was keeping herself waiting as well, with a delicious sort of tension inside her. She understood that when they spent the evening together, it wouldn't be just a matter of having dinner.

Dinner wasn't what either of them wanted.

It had been a long time since she'd had an urge for a man. A particular man. She missed the feel of one against her, that was true. The strength and the heat, that flash of fire in the belly that came just before release.

She was a woman who enjoyed sex, Darcy admitted, the problem being there'd been no one to tempt her for more than a year.

Sure and she was tempted now, she thought when Trevor looked up and their eyes met. She enjoyed, absorbed, the edgy little thrill that whipped down her spine. The man tempted her in all manner of ways. So . . . it was time to arrange for that night off.

She smiled down at him, slow and sly, then deliberately stepped back. Let him do some thinking about that, she decided.

Restless, not ready to face the long day, or even dress for it as yet, she wandered her rooms. She put on the kettle for tea more out of habit than desire. The rooms, such as they were, were the first she'd had all to herself in all of her life. It had been a shocking surprise to realize she missed the company of her brothers. Even their untidiness.

She'd always liked things just so, and her rooms reflected it. She'd painted the walls a quiet rose. Well, she'd browbeaten Shawn into doing most of the work, but the results were pleasing to her. From her bedroom at home, she'd taken her favorite framed posters. Monet's water lilies and a forest scene she'd found in a bookshop. She liked the dreaminess of them.

She'd made the curtains herself, as she had a fine hand with a needle when she wanted to. The pillows she piled on the ancient sofa were from her hand as well. A practical woman who preferred nice things understood it was cheaper by far to buy a length of satin or velvet and put in the time than to plunk down the cost for ready-made.

And it left more spending money for shoes or earrings.

Standing on a table was her wish jar, full of coins that came from tips. And one day, she thought, one fine day, there would be enough for her to take the next trip. An extravagant trip next time, to anywhere.

A tropical island, maybe. Where she could wear an excuse for a bikini and drink something foolish and fruity out of a coconut shell. Or Italy, to sit on some sunbaked terrace and look out over red-tiled roofs and grand cathedrals.

Or New York, where she would stroll along Fifth Avenue and gaze at all the treasures behind the forest of shop windows and pick out what was waiting just for her.

One day, she thought, and wished whenever she imagined it that she didn't see herself alone.

It didn't matter. She had enjoyed her week in Paris alone, so she would enjoy the others, in their time. Meanwhile, she was here, and so was the work.

She brewed the tea first, and told herself that since she was up early she'd lounge on the sofa, page through one of her glossy magazines and enjoy a quiet morning.

Before she settled in, her gaze landed on the violin she kept on a stand, more for decoration than convenience. Frowning, she set her cup aside and picked up the instrument. It was old, but had a clear voice. Would it be this, she wondered? Would it be the music that had always been part of her life that finally opened the doors for her, that took her into those places she dreamed of and rolled out the red carpet she was dying to walk on?

'Wouldn't that be odd,' she murmured. 'Something you never think twice about because it's always been there.'

Idly, she rosined the bow, tucked the violin under her chin, and played what came first to mind.

He'd expected her to come down. Trevor left the site, slipped into the kitchen with the excuse of making a phone call. But she wasn't there.

He heard the music, the aching, romantic notes of a violin. The kind of music, he thought, that belonged to moonlight.

He followed it.

Her door was at the head of the stairs, and the music seemed to swell against it, rising up like hope, sliding down like tears.

He didn't even think to knock.

He saw her, half turned away, eyes closed. Lost. Her hair was loose, still tumbled from sleep to rain down the back of a long blue robe. One narrow bare foot tapped the time.

The look of her clogged his lungs. The music she made had his throat burning. She played for herself, and the quiet pleasure of it glowed on that remarkable face.

Everything he wanted, had planned for, dreamed of, seemed to melt together in that one woman, that one moment. And left him shaken to the bone.

The music soared, note echoing against note, then slid away to silence.

Still drifting, she sighed, opened her eyes. And saw him. Her heart stuttered, an almost painful sensation. Before she could recover, before she could slip on the mask of a knowing smile, he crossed to her.

She felt her breath catch, as if someone had squeezed a hand over her throat. Or her heart. Then his mouth was on hers, hot, fierce. Glorious.

Her arms fell weakly to her sides, as if the fiddle and bow had taken on great weight. His hands were on her face, in her hair, and need pumped like heat from his body into hers. She took, had no choice but to take, that hard slap of desire.

She gave, finally; he felt her give. That slow, somehow liquid surrender of the female that made every man feel like a king. Because she did, because it brought the ache inside him toward something like a tremble, he gentled – lips, hands – cruising now, caressing. Savoring.

When he drew away, she fought off a shudder, forced a smile to her lips. 'Well, now, good morning to you.'

'Just shut up a minute.' He pulled her back, but this time simply rested his cheek on top of her head.

She wanted to step back. This embrace was more intimate than the kiss, and just as stirring. Just, she realized as she relaxed against him, as irresistible.

'Trevor.'

'Ssh.'

For some reason, that made her laugh. 'Aren't you the bossy one!'

The tension he'd worried would blow off the top of his head faded away. 'I don't know why I bother. You don't listen anyway.'

'Why should I?'

He held her another moment, steady enough now to appreciate that her robe was very thin. 'Do you ever lock that door?'

'Why should I?' Now she did step back. 'No one comes in and stays in unless I want them to.'

'I'll remember that.' He lifted a hand, brushed at her hair. 'I didn't know you could play.'

'Oh, music is the Gallagher way.' She gestured with the violin, then set it back on its stand. 'I was in the mood for some, that's all.'

'What was it you were playing?'

'One of Shawn's tunes. There aren't any words to it.'

'It doesn't need any.' He saw it, the way her eyes warmed with pride. 'Play something else.'

She only moved her shoulders, laid the bow aside. 'I'm not in the mood now.' She picked up her tea, and now her eyes were sharp with both humor and calculation. 'And I'm thinking I might start saving my songs for those who pay.'

'Would you sign a recording contract? Solo?'

She nearly jolted, but recovered neatly. 'Why, that would depend on the terms.'

'What do you want?'

'Oh, I want this and that. And all of the other

things.' She walked to the sofa, sat, crossed her legs. 'I'm a selfish and greedy creature, Magee. I want lavish luxury and pampering and slavish admiration. I don't quibble about working for them, but I want them at the end of the day.'

Considering her, he sat on the arm of the couch beside her and, testing, trailed a fingertip over her collarbone, paused just above the rise of her breast. 'I can get them for you.'

Her eyes went cold, shot out a blast of air so frigid it could have frozen blood. 'I've no doubt you can.' With one sharp move, she knocked his hand aside. 'But that's not the sort of work I have in mind.'

'Good. Then we keep one separate from the other.'

Ice turned to fire in the blink of an eye. 'Was that a little experiment, then? And what would you have done if I'd laid back for you?'

'Can't say.' He took her cup and helped himself to her tea. 'You're a delectable package, Darcy. But you'd have disappointed me.' He placed a hand on her shoulder when she started to spring up, felt the temper vibrating like a plucked bow string. 'I'll apologize for it.'

'I don't trade myself for profit.'

'I didn't think you did.' But there had been other women who'd offered. It had, and did, leave a nasty taste in his mouth. 'I want you on two levels, one as a business, one as a man. I'd like you to understand the first has nothing to do with the second.'

She eased back, struggling with the temper she knew could be an ugly thing. 'And you'd like reassurance of the same from me.'

'I just got it.'

'You could have done so with more style.'

'Agreed.' It had been cold, calculated – something, he thought, that his grandfather might have done. 'I'm sorry,' he said, and meant it.

'And which level would that apology come from?'

Touché, he thought. 'One from each, as each was out of line.'

She took her tea back from him. 'Then I'll accept each.'

'Let's put the business aside for now. I need to go to London for a couple of days.' He'd intended to put it off, but . . . she wanted things, why not give her a taste? 'Come with me.'

She'd clicked her temper back to simmer, but this sudden twist blanked it out and left her puzzled. Wary. 'You want me to go to London with you? Why?'

'First, because I want to take you to bed.' He took the mug back again, thinking as he did that the tea had become a kind of prop between them.

'That we've established already. There are beds in Ardmore.'

'Our schedules haven't been meshing in Ardmore. And second, I enjoy your company. Have you been to London?'

'No.'

'You'll like it.'

'Most probably I would.' She took the mug when he held it out, sipped the tea to give herself time to think. He was offering her something she'd always wanted. To travel in style. To see London, and not to see it alone.

He would expect sex, naturally. But then, so would she. What point was there pretending to be coy about something they both knew was bound to happen anyway?

'When do you go?'

'I'm flexible.'

She let out a short laugh. 'No, that you are not. But if your schedule is, I might be able to work it out. I need to speak with Aidan and arrange for a replacement. He won't be pleased with me, but I can get 'round him.'

'I'm sure you can. Let me know what days work for you, and I'll take care of the rest.'

That practiced feline smile was back. 'Oh, I like that. Having a man take care of the rest. You run along now.' She rose, then deliberately trailed her fingers over his jaw. 'I'll get back to you when I can.'

He caught her wrist, his grip just hard enough to show her he was serious. 'You won't play me, Darcy. I'm not like the others.'

She stood where she was as he released her, as he walked out and shut the door. Yes, indeed, she could agree with that. He wasn't anything like anyone she'd known. And wasn't it going to be interesting to find out just what and who he was?

'You've had your holiday.'

She'd wanted to catch Aidan at home rather than wait for him to come into the pub. She'd had to rush to manage it, and was pleased to find him finishing up his breakfast. His first response was exactly what she'd expected and didn't discourage her in the least.

'I know, and a lovely one it was.' All cheer, she topped off his tea. Then snuck Finn a corner of toast under the table. 'Just as I know it's a lot to ask of you so soon after, but this is an opportunity I don't want to miss. You've traveled, Aidan.'

She kept her voice soft and sweet. It was the tack she'd decided on. Just as effective would have been demands, curses, and tempers, but she was certain that this tone would work more quickly.

'You've already seen so much and been so many places. You know what it is to yearn for that. It's in our blood.'

'So's the pub, and high season's starting.' He added more jam to his bread. Finn, knowing the routine, shifted so Aidan could sneak him a bite in turn. 'I can't have Jude filling in for you now when she's only weeks till term.'

'I wouldn't think of it. If I see her carrying a tray I'll knock you upside the head with it.'

Because he knew the sentiment, and the threat,

were completely sincere, Aidan sighed. 'Darcy, I count on you to keep the service running smooth.'

'I know, and that's what I do, day in and day out. I've worked with Sinead, though there were times I wanted to bash the girl's brains on the bar. She's improved considerable over the last couple weeks.'

'She has.' But Aidan continued to brood over his breakfast.

'I was going to ask Betsy Clooney if she'd do me the favor of covering for me, for the two days. She's worked the pub before, and she knows the routine.'

'Christ, Darcy, Betsy's got herself a brood of kids now. She hasn't worked the pub for ten years.'

'It hasn't changed overmuch, and I'll wager Betsy'd enjoy it. She's reliable, Adian, as you know.'

'She is, but—'

'And there's another thing I wanted to put to you. Young Alice Mae could use a summer job.'

'Alice Mae?' Aidan stopped brooding to goggle. 'She's barely fifteen.'

'And all three of us were working before that, without harm. Brenna mentioned her baby sister wanted to earn some spending money. I'd like to give her a chance. She's a bright girl, and being an O'Toole she'll work hard. I'd start her on the one shift, the midday. Today, so I can have her trained before I leave for London.'

'Christ, she was in nappies yesterday.'

'Getting old, aren't you?' She rose just long enough to kiss his cheek. 'I want to go, Aidan, and I'll see the service is handled smooth while I'm gone.'

'Was a time only Gallaghers worked Gallagher's. But for Brenna now and again, but that was practically the same thing.'

'We can't stay with that.' And because she understood some of the sentiment, even a twinge of the regret, she rose again and standing behind him, wrapped her arms around his neck. 'We've already made the changes. I guess we started when Ma and Dad moved to Boston. We'll be bigger now, but we'll still be Gallagher's.'

'Aye, and it's what I want for us. Still, there are moments I remember and wonder if I've done right.'

'You're the worrier, and bless you for it. Of course you've done right. Well and right, Aidan, by Gallagher's and all of us. I'm proud of you.'

He lifted a hand, patted hers, sliding a bit of bacon to Finn with the other. 'Now you're trying to get 'round me that way.'

'I would if I'd thought of it.' She gave him a last squeeze. 'I need to go. I need to see.'

He knew how it was, precisely. The deep, churning need to go and to see. He'd taken five years to work it out of his system. She was asking for two days.

But . . .

'I'm going to say it out plain. I don't care for the notion of you going off with Magee.'

Darcy rounded her eyes, pursed her lips. When Jude came in at that moment, she decided it was perfect timing and turned to her sister-in-law. 'Did you hear that?'

'No, I'm sorry. What?'

'Aidan's taken a sudden and avid interest in my sex life.'

'I've not. Damn it.' He wasn't easily fuddled, but she'd managed it. 'I didn't say anything about sex.' He hissed out a breath when Darcy only stared at him. 'I implied it,' he said with some dignity.

'Oh, implied, is it?'

'I think I'll go back upstairs,' Jude began.

'No, you don't.' Darcy waved her to a chair. Finn immediately bellied over, prepared for the next covert treat. 'Sit down, for this should be interesting. Your husband here, my darling brother, is *implying* that he disapproves of my having sex with Magee.'

'Christ Jesus.' Aidan put his head in his hands. 'I'll go upstairs.'

'That you won't. Would you like some tea, Jude, darling?' Without waiting for an answer, Darcy got a cup and poured out. 'First we should establish whether your husband, my brother, objects to me having sex altogether or just in this particular case.' She sat again, and her smile was sugar-sweet. 'And which would it be, Aidan, my dear?'

'You're pissing me off.'

'Oh, now, temper, temper.'

'I didn't say anything about sex. I said I didn't care for the idea of you going off to London with him.'

'You're going to London?' Jude asked and decided to relax and have some toast.

'Trevor asked me to accompany him on a short business trip. But it appears Aidan would prefer I had sex with Trevor here rather than there. Is that correct?'

'I don't want you having sex with him at all, as it's a tangle.' Frustration pumped through him, causing him to roar it as both women sat quietly staring at him. 'And I don't want to know about it one way or the other.'

'Then I'll be sure to spare you the details.' She spoke coolly now, which only rattled the sabers of his own temper.

'Mind your step.'

'Mind your own,' she shot back. 'My personal life, particularly this area of it, is no one's business but mine. Trevor and I understand the tangle you've referred to and, as sensible people, will be careful enough not to trip up in it.'

Eyes still frosty, she rose. 'I'm going to ring up Brenna's mother and ask about Alice Mae. And I'll talk to Betsy Clooney as well. The details will be seen to before I go. Good day to you, Jude,' she added, and kissed her sister-in-law on the cheek before she flounced out.

The air hummed in the Gallagher kitchen for several moments, as Jude casually nibbled her toast.

178

'Well, what have you to say about it?' Aidan demanded.

'Not a thing.'

'Hah.' He stewed, drummed his fingers, scowled. 'But you're thinking of saying something about it.'

She decided to try the jam. 'Not really. I think Darcy covered it all.'

'There!' He jabbed an accusing finger. 'You're on her side.'

'Of course.' She smiled now. 'So are you.'

He shoved back from the table and began to pace. In sympathy, Finn came out from under the table to pace with him. 'She thinks she can handle this, handle him. The girl sees herself as sophisticated and worldly. Christ, Jude, she's been sheltered all her life. She hasn't had the time or opportunities to know.'

Jude set her toast aside. 'Aidan, some are born knowing.'

'Be that as it may, she's never come up against a man like Magee. He's a slick one. I think he's a good man, an honest one, but slick all the same. I don't want him using my sister.'

'Is that how you see it?'

'I can't see it, and that's the problem. But I know he's handsome and he's rich and however much Darcy's always joked about landing herself just that, he could dazzle her. And dazzled, how can she see where she's going?'

'Aidan,' Jude said softly, 'how can you?'

'I don't want her hurt.'

'I do.'

Shock simply robbed him of speech. He stared at his wife, laid a hand on the back of his chair, and managed to find his voice. 'How could you say such a thing? How could you want Darcy hurt?'

'If he can hurt her, he matters. Aidan, no man's ever really mattered to her. They've been, well, toys, amusements, diversions. Don't you want her to find someone who matters?'

'Of course I do. But I can't see it being Magee.' Annoyed, he began to pace again. 'Not when both of them are thinking with their glands.' He shook his head. 'Trips to London. Barely know each other and it's trips to London.'

'I walked into a smoky pub on a rainy night, and there you were. My life changed, and I didn't even know who you were.'

He stopped pacing. Love too huge to measure swelled in his heart. 'A one in a million for us.' He sat, reached across the table for her hands. 'And fate played a part.'

'Maybe it's playing one now.'

His eyes narrowed. 'You're thinking this has something to do with the legend? The last part of it?'

'I think there's one Gallagher left. One heart not yet touched or offered or given. And I think it's interesting – no, it's fascinating – that Trevor Magee is in Ardmore. As a writer . . .' She paused a moment, because it was still thrilling to know she was a writer. 'I'd have trouble believing it's just coincidence. The old family connection, Darcy's a Fitzgerald on your mother's side, and cousin to Maude. Trevor's great-uncle was Maude's one and only love. They lost each other, just as Gwen and Carrick lost each other.'

'That's just your imagination, and your romantic side taking over, Jude Frances.'

'Is it?' She shrugged. 'We'll have to wait and see, won't we?'

She wasn't waiting for anything. Alice Mae was already on her way in, and Betsy had been delighted at the offer of two days' work. Pleased with herself, Darcy breezed through the kitchen and straight out the back door.

It was a bit of a shock to step out and into the solid gray block walls and lumber bones of the breezeway that would connect the two structures. Already, she thought, there was some form to it, recognizable even to her untutored eye. Men stood on scaffolding, hammering or drilling or riveting. How could she tell through all the noise?

Someone, a very optimistic someone, to her mind, was playing a radio. All she could hear from it was a tinkle and squawk that might have been music.

She saw the way the roof would curve in a kind of arch, the rafters thick to echo the feel of those that had held the pub for generations.

Unexpectedly, she felt a twinge, and recognized it as pride. Gallagher's was the root, and the theater a branch on the tree.

She walked through, mindful of the cables and cords that snaked over the subflooring. She'd already spotted Trevor, up on the scaffolding platform at the far end where the breezeway widened. His tool belt was slung at his waist, and there was some clever power tool buzzing in his hand. He wore tinted glasses, as much for protection from flying wood and concrete dust, she supposed, as a shield against the mild sunlight.

He looked rough and ready and exactly right for her mood.

She stopped beneath him, waiting, aware that many of the men were looking at her rather than going safely about their business. Mick O'Toole sauntered by, a bundle of rebar balanced over his shoulder.

'You're distracting our crew, pretty Darcy.'

'I won't be but a minute. How's it all going, then, Mr O'Toole?'

'Himself knows what he wants and how he wants it. As I'm in agreement with him, it couldn't be going better.'

'Will it be wonderful?'

'It will. A credit to Ardmore. Watch your step here now, darling. Lots to trip over hereabouts.'

'I've thought of that,' she murmured. There was a great deal to trip over when it came to Trevor Magee.

When Mick headed off, she looked back up and saw it was Trevor who waited now. That was more like it.

'A word with you, Mr Magee?' she shouted up.

'What can I do for you, Miss Gallagher?'

So, he wouldn't trouble to come down. That was fine. She skimmed her hair back from her shoulder. 'I need today and tomorrow to train a new part-time waitress. But I'm at your disposal come Thursday if that suits you.'

Anticipation curled in his gut, but he merely nodded. 'We'll leave Thursday morning, then. I'll pick you up at six.'

'That's a very early start.'

'Why waste time?'

For a beat, they only watched each other. 'Why, indeed?'

She turned, strolled back into the kitchen. And when the door was closed did a quick victory dance.

CHAPTER 10

After considerable debate and weighing of the pros and cons, Darcy decided to be on time. Her reasons for breaking precedent were purely selfish, and she didn't mind admitting it. She wanted to enjoy every minute of her two days off.

She'd packed light, which hadn't been an easy feat for her, and because of it the chore had taken her hours. Planning, debating, discarding. She'd raided her wish jar, something she did only for the most important of events. But she needed to buy something wonderful to commemorate the trip, didn't she?

For two days she'd worked like a mule to be certain her responsibilities at the pub were well covered. In lieu of sleep she'd given herself a manicure, a pedicure, and a facial to make certain she presented as polished an image as she could manage.

She'd selected her lingerie with the canniness and foresight of a general preparing for battle.

Trevor Magee wouldn't know what hit him – once she allowed him to seduce her.

The idea had odd little nerves fluttering in her stomach. And she wanted to be, had to be, calm, cool, cosmopolitan. She had no intention of playing the *culchie* – country bumpkin – in London or in bed. Part of the problem was Trevor was exactly as Aidan had described him.

Slick.

It didn't matter if he dressed in work clothes and sweated along with his crew or waded through the mud hauling supplies. Still, beneath the sweat and dirt was a gloss that came from privilege, education, and wealth.

She'd met other men from privilege. The fact was, she'd honed the skill of recognizing, and separating from the pack, those trust fund babies on tour or holiday.

But, a trust fund babe Trevor was not, and she thought never had been. With all his wealth he worked, and the power of both the rewards and the labor sat well on him. That earned her respect, and Darcy gave her respect sparingly.

She'd never known anyone quite like him. And while that intrigued her, it also made her wary.

Added to it all, layered through the observations and the interest, was the not so simple fact that she wanted him. She'd never wanted a man with quite so much focus and intensity. She wanted his hands on her, his mouth on hers. His body on hers.

In the few hours she'd slept the night before, she'd dreamed of him. Strange, confused dreams.

In them he'd come to her on a white winged horse, and together they'd flown over a sea as blue as sapphire, over the damp green fields of home, through pearly light toward a silver palace where trees had dripped with golden apples and silver pears, and the music that rose into the air was enough to break the heart.

In the dream, for that short, misty time, she was in love. In a way she'd never thought she could be, had never been certain she wanted to be. So completely, blindly, joyfully in love that nothing seemed to matter but those moments with him.

He'd said only one thing to her as they'd flown through sunlight, moonlight, faerie light.

Everything. And more.

All she could say, all she could feel as she turned her body to his, laid her cheek upon his was, *You. You're everything, and more.*

She'd meant it, with everything she had inside her, all she would ever have, would ever be. And waking, she'd wished she could feel that again, so much power of emotion. But she'd lost it in dreams and could only smile at her own fancies.

Neither she nor Trevor wanted fancies.

At six on the dot, she carried her bag downstairs, and her heart thumped with anticipation. What would she see and do and taste over the next forty-eight hours?

Everything. The thought elated her. *And more.*

She took one last scan of the pub, tidy and scrubbed. Sinead, Betsy, and Alice Mae should surely be able to handle what she often did alone. She'd drummed the routine into their heads and had left a written list as a backup. Satisfied, she let herself out and promised not to give the pub a single thought until she stepped foot in it again.

It was the dot of six.

It pleased her to see Trevor pull up to the curb as she walked out. They were of a mind, then, she thought. Things would go smoother because of it.

It surprised her to see he was wearing a suit. Italian, she imagined when he got out of the car to take her luggage. Blisteringly pricey, she was sure, but not a bit flashy. The stone gray matched his eyes well, and the shirt and tie were all of a hue, so the look was smartly European.

Power, she thought again. Yes, he wore it very well.

'Well, now, look at you.' Deliberately she fingered his sleeve as he loaded her luggage into the boot. 'Aren't you pretty this morning?'

'I have a meeting.' He closed the boot, then went around to open her door. 'The timing's a little tight.' He got a whiff of her as she slid past him and wished the meeting and all its participants straight to hell.

She waited until he was in the driver's seat. 'I'd think a man in your position could call his own time.'

'You do that and you bring one more thing into a meeting that usually bogs things up. Ego.'

'But I've noticed you've got one.'

He swung away from the curb. 'The trick's recognizing it. I've arranged for a car and driver to meet us at Heathrow. He'll take you to the house so you can settle in. He'll be at your disposal through the day if you want to sightsee or shop.'

'Will he?' Imagine that. 'Well, that's considerate of you.'

'I'll have more free time tomorrow, but today's packed.' He glanced at her. 'I should be done by six this evening. We have dinner reservations at eight. Does that suit you?'

'Perfectly.'

'Good. My assistant faxed over several points of interest. I have the file in my briefcase. You can take a look during the flight to help you plan what you'd like to do today.'

'That's a lovely thought, and I'll do just that. But you needn't worry that I'll have trouble entertaining myself.'

He glanced over. She wore a trim jacket and slacks of slate blue, and had matched them with a soft, faintly shimmering blouse the color of roses drenched in cream. The choice was more than stylish. It was cleverly, completely female.

'No, I don't imagine you will.'

Inexplicably miffed that she wouldn't be wandering aimlessly, missing him, waiting for him, he fell into silence.

More like a business arrangement than a . . . what the hell was it, anyway? An assignation? He didn't care for the word. But he didn't suppose 'romance' fit the situation either. Neither of them was the starry-eyed type. They wanted what they wanted. Better to be up front and systematic about it.

But it irritated him nonetheless.

They arrived at Waterford's airport on schedule. And it was there Darcy got her first taste of what a man who walked in wealth could command. Their luggage was whisked away, and they were guided through security with a great deal of 'This way, Mr Magee' and 'I hope you enjoy your trip, Mr Magee.'

Remembering the hassles and glitches in her recent travel to Paris, Darcy reaffirmed her determination to travel first class or not to travel at all. But even her imagining of top drawer took a bump when Trevor led her out on the tarmac toward a sleek little plane.

'Is this yours?'

'The company's,' he told her, taking her arm for the short trip up the steps. 'I do a lot of traveling, so it's more convenient to have my own transportation.'

She stepped inside and had to struggle not to gasp. 'I bet it is.'

The seats were done in rich navy leather and were sized generously. Crystal vases were tucked into silver holders on the cream-colored walls between the windows. Each held a dewy bouquet of fresh yellow rosebuds. Her feet sank into the carpet.

A uniformed flight attendant with a polite smile

and flawless skin greeted her by name, then asked if she would care for a mimosa before takeoff.

Champagne for breakfast, she thought. Just imagine that. 'That would be lovely, thank you.'

'Coffee for me, Monica. Want a tour?' he asked Darcy.

'I would, yes.' Hoping she wasn't gawking, Darcy set down her purse.

'Galley's through here.'

She peeked in and saw that the efficient Monica already had coffee brewing and was popping the cork on a bottle of champagne. The small space seemed to use every inch resourcefully, and stainless-steel surfaces gleamed.

'Cockpit.' Trevor gestured through the already open door. The man sitting at a panel of complicated-looking controls swiveled in his chair. 'Ready when you are, Mr Magee. Good morning, Miss Gallagher. You can look forward to a short but smooth flight into Heathrow.'

'Thank you. Do you fly this plane all by yourself? With no copilot?'

'It's a one-man operation,' he told her. 'But I don't need a copilot when Mr Magee's on board.'

'Is that so? Do you fly, then, Trevor?'

'Occasionally. Give us ten minutes, Donald, then clear with the tower.'

'Yes, sir.'

'We have a lot of interests in Europe,' Trevor began as he led Darcy back through the main cabin. 'We use this equipment primarily for the short-range flights over here.'

'And for the longer flights?'

'We have larger equipment.' He opened a door. Inside was an office complete with what looked to be a trim antique desk, a computer console, a wall screen for viewing videos, and a bed. She caught a glimpse of the bath through a side door. Everything gleamed.

'All the creature comforts and the business ones as well.'

'You do better with the second if you have the first. Celtic's relatively young at six years, but it's growing, and it's profitable.'

'Ah, so the London business has to do with Celtic Records, then.'

'For the most part, yes. If you need something and don't see it, just ask.'

She turned back to him. 'I see everything I need.'

He lifted a hand to toy with the ends of her hair. 'Good. Let's get started.'

'Haven't we already?' she murmured as they walked back to their seats.

Darcy settled in, accepted the glinting flute holding her mimosa, and prepared to have the time of her life.

The pilot was a man of his word. The flight was short and smooth. As far as Darcy was concerned, she could have flown for hours and been thrilled. She'd made casual small talk until she'd realized

Trevor was distracted. About his upcoming meetings, she imagined, and left him to his planning while she looked over the list of suggestions from his assistant.

God, yes, she wanted to see it. All of it. Hyde Park and Harrods, Buckingham Palace and Chelsea. She wanted to experience the wild traffic of the streets and the grand shade of the great parks.

The trip through Heathrow was hardly more complex than the airport at home. Money paves the way, she thought as they slid through customs. Still, she hadn't expected the car and driver he'd arranged for her to be a limo and a chauffeur. Words stuttered into her throat and were ruthlessly swallowed down again until she could smile up at Trevor easily.

'Are we dropping you at your meeting, then?'

'No, opposite directions. I'll see you this evening.'

'Good luck with your work.' She started to take the driver's offered hand, to slip into the limo as she'd practiced doing in her mind. Smoothly, gracefully, as if she'd done it all her life.

But Trevor took her arm, said her name, and had her looking back up at him, lips just curved.

Then she was yanked up on her toes, her hands clutching at his shoulders for balance, her mouth gloriously assaulted. The swift change of mood from coolheaded businessman to hot-blooded lover was so swift, so complete, so erotic.

Before the moan could slither from heart to throat

to lips, he released her. After one smoldering look, he nodded in what might have been satisfaction.

'Enjoy your day,' he told her, and left her standing, nearly swaying, beside the discreetly blank-eyed driver and the open limo door.

She managed to slide in. The fact was, her bones were so loose it felt as though she was pouring herself into the rarefied air inside the limo, scented with roses and leather.

It took every ounce of will to click herself back, to absorb and appreciate her first ride in a long, quiet car. She trailed her fingers along the seat. Butter-smooth and the color of storm clouds. Like his eyes just moments before, she thought.

The driver seemed to be a full block away behind the smoked-glass privacy screen. Determined to remember every detail, Darcy noted the television, the crystal glasses, the shimmer of lights along the roof, and the window in it. She relaxed to the romantic sweep of classical music already playing over the stereo. And as she started to stretch out her legs and purr, she finally spotted the slim box on the seat beside her.

It was wrapped in gold with a silver ribbon. She snatched at it, then, wincing, glanced toward the driver. A woman of the world would hardly dive into a gift. She'd be so used to them as to nearly be bored.

Chuckling to herself, Darcy opened the small envelope.

Welcome to London. Trev.

'Doesn't miss a trick, does he?' Darcy said to herself. 'Well, good for me.' Assured that the driver wasn't paying attention, she picked at the tape with her fingernail. She didn't want to tear the paper. Wallowing in anticipation, she tucked both the ribbon and the gift wrap, carefully folded, into her purse, then took a breath, held it.

Opened the long velvet box.

'Oh, Mother of God.' She yelped it, forgot about the driver, about sophistication. About everything but the outrageous sparkle currently dazzling her eyes.

Gaping, she held the bracelet up, letting the glinting stones stream down like water. It was slim, and might have been delicate if not for all those bold colors. Surely that was emerald and ruby and sapphire and all framed by diamonds as brilliant as the sun.

Never in her life had she touched anything so beautiful, so fine, so ridiculously expensive. She really shouldn't accept it. She'd only just try it on. See how it looked. How it felt.

It looked gorgeous and felt even better.

As she turned her wrist, watched it wink, felt that almost liquid slide of gold over her skin, she decided she'd rather cut off her hand than give the bracelet back.

Her conscience would just have to adjust.

She spent so much time admiring the bracelet she nearly missed the thrill of the drive through London. When she snapped back she had to struggle with the urge to roll down the window and lean out. To take in everything all at once.

What to see first, she wondered, what to do? It was all so much to squeeze into two short days. She would unpack her things quickly and dive straight in.

She began outlining her stops as she watched London sweep by. When the limo stopped in front of a dignified town house she frowned and searched for the hotel.

No, she remembered with a jolt. Trevor had said 'house,' not 'hotel.' The man lived three thousand miles away in New York City and had a house in London.

Would wonders never cease?

Composing herself, she took the driver's hand when he came around to her door.

'I'll bring your bags straight in, Miss Gallagher.'

'Thank you very much.' She crossed over and started up the short set of steps between rigorously formal hedges, hoping she looked as though she knew what she was doing.

The door opened before she'd worked out whether she should knock or just go inside. A tall, slim man with a fringe of white hair bowed to her. 'Miss Gallagher. I hope your trip was pleasant. I'm Stiles, Mr Magee's butler. We're pleased to welcome you.'

'Thank you.' She started to offer her hand, stopped. That probably wasn't done, particularly with British butlers.

'Would you care to see your room, or may we offer you some refreshment?'

'Ah, I'd like to see my room, if that's convenient.'

'Of course. I'll see to your luggage. Winthrup will show you upstairs.'

Winthrup moved forward with barely a sound, a wisp of a woman in the same formal black as the butler. Her hair was a colorless ash, quietly styled, her eyes pale as water behind thick lenses.

'Good morning, Miss Gallagher. If you'll follow me, I'll see you settled.'

Don't gawk, you idiot. Trying desperately for casual, Darcy crossed the gleaming golden wood of the foyer, walked under the magnificence of the central chandelier, and started up the grandeur of the staircase.

She couldn't say it was like a palace. It was too ruthlessly dignified for that. Like a museum, she thought, all polished and hushed and intimidating.

There was art on the walls, but she didn't dare take time to study it. The walls themselves must have been papered in silk, so smooth and rich did they appear. She had to curl her fingers to keep them from touching.

The housekeeper, as she imagined Winthrup was the housekeeper, led the way down a corridor wainscoted in deep, rich wood. Darcy wondered how many rooms there were, how they were furnished, what she would see from the windows. Then Winthrup opened a deeply carved door onto luxury.

The bed was big as a lake, its four posters spearing toward the deeply coved ceiling. Darcy didn't know what sort of rugs were spread over the polished floor, but she could tell they were old and magnificent.

Everything – chest of drawers, bureaus, mirrors, tables – was polished to mirror gleams. Dozens of white roses bloomed out of a crystal vase that she imagined weighed ten pounds if it weighed an ounce.

Draperies of deep forest green were tied back with gold tassels, framing the glinting glass.

There was a fireplace fashioned out of white marble veined with rose, and towering candlesticks flanked the mantel. More flowers, lilies this time, in that same blinding white stood in the center.

A cozy arrangement, plush chairs, polished tables, was set in a way that invited her to settle in.

'The sitting room is to the right and the master bath to the left.' Winthrup folded her thin hands. 'Would you like me to unpack for you now, or would you prefer to rest a bit first?'

'I . . .' Darcy feared she might swallow her tongue. 'Actually, I . . . no, I don't need to rest, thank you just the same.'

'I'll be happy to show you around the house if you like.'

'Do you think I might just wander about a bit?'

'Of course. Mr Magee hopes you'll make yourself at home here. You've only to push nine on the house phone to reach me, and eight to reach Stiles. Perhaps you'd like to freshen up.'

'I would, thank you very much.' On rubbery legs, Darcy started toward the bath. The hell with it, she thought, turned back. 'Miss Winthrup, it's a lovely room.'

Winthrup's smile was as wispy as the rest of her, but it managed to soften her face a little. 'Yes, it is.'

Darcy walked into the bath, deliberately shut her eyes and leaned back on the door. She felt as though she were in a play, or one of her own more creative dreams. But she wasn't. It was real. She could feel her heart beating in her chest, and little thrills of sheer pleasure dancing over her skin.

She sighed once, then opened her eyes to simply grin at the bathroom.

They must've taken out another room to make it so large, she imagined. More flowers graced the long counter between two oval sinks. The tiles, floor, and walls were of a soft seafoam green, so it seemed you were in some lovely underwater fantasy.

The tub, with its wide ledge covered with lush, ferny plants, was surely big enough for three. The shower was separate, a room in itself, she thought as she moved closer to investigate. Behind the waving glass were a half a dozen nozzles. She imagined it was like bathing in a waterfall and nearly stripped down to the skin then and there to see if she was right.

More crystal was set about, little bowls and

dishes holding fragrant soaps or rose petals, pretty bottles holding bath oils and bath salts and creams. She sat on a padded bench at a separate counter obviously designed for milady and studied her own flushed and delighted face in the mirror.

'You've arrived, haven't you?'

Throughout his first meeting, and his second, Trevor kept Darcy tucked away. Or nearly. She had a baffling habit of popping out of the corner where he wanted her. Sliding out was more like it, he mused. Sneakily, sinuously sliding into his mind when it needed to be focused elsewhere.

He glanced at his watch, again. There were hours yet before he could afford to focus on her. But when he did, by God, he'd make sure the wait was worth it.

'Trev?'

'Hmm?' When he realized he was scowling, he smoothed out his features, waved a hand in apology. 'Sorry, Nigel. My mind wandered.'

'That's a new one.'

Nigel Kelsey, the head of the London arm of Celtic Records, had a sharp eye, and sharper ears. He'd been with Trevor at Oxford, where they'd clicked. When the time had come to expand his personal baby into the international arena, Trevor had put the responsibility into Nigel's trusted hands.

'Just shuffling items in my head. Let's flip Shawn Gallagher to the top of the list.'

'Happy to.' Nigel sat back in his chair. He rarely used his desk, thought of it primarily as a prop.

He'd been earmarked to follow his father, and his father's father, into law, a fate that even now caused him to shudder. He hadn't wanted to thumb his nose at family tradition, precisely, but he was much happier putting what education he had to use doing something entertaining. Celtic Records was vastly entertaining, even if his old friend did run a tight ship. A tight ship, and a profitable one, Nigel thought now.

A ship that visited such fascinating ports. Part of his responsibilities, and he took them seriously, included attending parties, events, entertaining the talent. And doing it all on expense account.

'I'm negotiating with him one on one,' Trevor continued. 'Two on one, if we count his wife. And we should. I've advised him to get an agent.' Nigel seemed a bit surprised, but Trevor only shrugged. 'I like him, Nigel. And I intend to deal straight with him, since he won't go through a representative.'

'You deal straight in any case, Trev. I'm the one who doesn't mind slipping a card from the bottom of the deck now and again. Just to liven things up.'

'Not with him. Instinct tells me we've got a prize here, one that if left to his own pace will pay off for years.'

'I agree with you. His work's brilliant, and very marketable.'

'There's more.'

'Is there?' Nigel puzzled again when Trevor rose to wander the office. It was a rare thing to see Trevor restless, to have the man let any restlessness show. Even to him. 'I thought there might be when you scheduled this meeting in the middle of your other project.'

'He has a brother and a sister. I want the three of them to record his stuff, for the first release.'

Nigel frowned, drummed his hand, which was studded with rings. 'Must be some brother and sister.'

'Believe me.'

'Still, Trev, you know it would be easier to market this package using an established artist.'

'I'm leaving it to you to find a way around that.' With a faint smile, Trevor turned back. 'I've heard them. I want you to come to Ardmore for a couple of days. You listen, and if you think I'm wrong about this, we'll talk again.'

'Ardmore.' Nigel winced, then twisted the tiny gold hoop in his earlobe. 'Jesus, Trev, what's an avowed urbanite like myself going to do in a barely-on-the-map Irish seaside village?'

'Listen,' Trevor said simply. 'There's something about the Gallaghers, but before I push the point with them or with you, I want you to see and hear for yourself. I want an objective opinion.'

'And when hasn't your own been objective?'

'There's something about the Gallaghers,' Trevor said again. 'Something about Ardmore, the area.'

Unconsciously, he fingered the silver disk resting under his shirt. 'Maybe it's the goddamn air, I don't know. I want you to come over. I want your take on it.'

Nigel lifted his hands, let them fall. 'You're the boss. I suppose I should see what there is about this place that's caused you to sink so much time, money, and effort into your theater brainstorm.'

'It wasn't a brainstorm. It's a very solid business concept. Don't snort,' Trevor warned, anticipating him.

'I never snort. I do occasionally guffaw, but I'll resist.'

'Good. I have a new piece from Shawn Gallagher.' Trevor walked over, retrieved the sheet music from his briefcase. 'Take a look.'

Nigel only smiled. 'Rather hear it,' he said and gestured to the piano across the room.

'All right, but he's orchestrated it for guitar, violin, and flute.'

'I'll get the idea.' Nigel closed his eyes as Trevor walked to the piano. He himself couldn't play a note, but he had an uncanny sense of music nonetheless.

And his antenna began to quiver as Trevor played the opening bars.

Quick, Nigel thought, lively, subtly sexy, and fun. Yes, Trevor was right, as always. They had a gold mine in Shawn Gallagher. And it wouldn't hurt to meet the man face-to-face, he supposed, even if it did mean traveling to Ireland. God help him.

He listened, nodding to himself, then grinning when Trevor sang the lyrics. His friend had a strong voice, and still an easy one. But the words needed a female. Nigel recognized it at once.

I'll have your hand
I'll have your heart
I'll have them all together.
For if you think I'll settle for part,
Prepare for stormy weather.

Yes, a woman's song, confident, even arrogant and sexy.

He opened his eyes again, and grinned as Trevor played it out. He wasn't an easy sell, but his foot was tapping before the song was done.

'The man's a fucking genius,' Nigel declared. 'Simple, straightforward lyrics in a tangle of complicated notes. Not everyone can sing that one and punch it.'

'No, but I have someone in mind who can. Make arrangements for Ardmore, Nigel.'

Nigel took a pull on the designer water that was never beyond arm's reach. 'If I must, I must. Now, is that the bulk of the business on our slate this afternoon?'

'The bulk, yes. Why?'

'Because I'd like to know, as an old and trusted friend, just what's crawling around under your skin. You're nervy, Trev, and it's not usual for you.'

He didn't like that it showed, was going to make damn sure it didn't before he saw Darcy again. 'There's a woman.'

'Son, there's always a woman.'

'Not like this one. I brought her with me.'

'Oh, did you now? That's a new one.' Each word was stretched long and full of meaning. 'And when do I get to have a look at her?'

Trevor sat again, ordered himself to relax. 'Come to Ardmore,' he said and directed the conversation back to business.

CHAPTER 11

She wasn't quite sure how to play it, and it did seem like being onstage. Should she be sitting in the splendor of the parlor having tea or a cocktail when Trevor returned? Or would it be more casual and sophisticated if she were up in the sitting room, passing the time with a book?

Perhaps she should take a walk and not be there at all.

In the end, not being sure of the lines or motivations of the character she appeared to be playing, Darcy prepared to dress for the evening. She took her time about it, and that was a luxury itself. Having buckets of time to loll in the bath, to make use of the lovely scented creams that were set about in antique bottles.

Better to be ready, she decided as she smoothed the silky lotion on her legs, and avoid any awkwardness of just how and where the two of them were going to dress for dinner. Sex, as she saw it, was the final act in today's play, and she had to admit she was both eager for and nervous about the performance.

Yes, much wiser to meet him in the sophisticated mode, wearing the little black dress. She would indeed go down, have a cocktail, so when he came in she would be sitting in that almost terrifyingly formal parlor, all sort of lady-of-the-manorish.

Winthrup would probably serve little canapés – or did the butler do that? Well, no matter. She could offer him one as if she did such things every day.

That was just how to play the part.

When scented and polished, she stepped out of the bath to the bedroom just as Trevor stepped in from the hall, her stomach did a shaky flip. Time to ad-lib, she thought and put on her best smile.

'Well, hello, there. I thought you'd be another hour or more.'

'I finished up early today.' He kept his eyes on hers as he closed the door behind him. 'And how was your day?'

'Lovely, thank you.' Why couldn't she get her legs to move? It would be far better if she could just stroll across the room. 'I hope yours was successful.'

'It was worth the trip.'

As he stepped forward, she managed to shove herself away from the door, moved to the little table where she'd laid the bracelet. 'I want to thank you for this. It's beautiful, and extravagant, which is nearly as important. We both know I shouldn't accept it.'

He closed the distance between them and, taking

the bracelet, circled it around her wrist. 'And we both know you will.' He fastened it with a quiet click that echoed in her head.

'I suppose we do. I've a hard time resisting the beautiful and extravagant.'

'Why resist?' Firmly, possessively, he laid his hands on her shoulders, ran them down the arms of her robe. 'I don't intend to.'

It wasn't the way he'd planned it. He'd imagined it all very civilized. Drinks, then the sort of elegant dinner she'd enjoy, a quiet ride home, then a smooth, practiced seduction that would please them both.

But here she was, in that long robe, her skin warm and fragrant from her bath, her eyes wary and watchful.

Why resist?

His gaze held hers as he loosened the tie of her robe. He watched the heat flicker in that deep, deep blue, heard the quick and quiet catch of her breath. Lowering his mouth to hers, he captured that breath, skimmed his hands under the thin material to trail his fingers up and down her sides.

'Now.' He murmured it, surprised that he had to fight off a shudder at just the touch of his fingertips to her flesh.

'Well, then.' She let her body have its way, lifted her arms around him.

He meant to go slowly, to savor, to take them both up level by level. But the moment her mouth answered his, the instant her body pressed to his, greed swallowed him. It was as if he'd been waiting his whole life to taste this, to touch this, to have this.

He jerked the robe off her shoulders and set his teeth on her.

She gave a muffled cry, both pleasure and shock. In that flash of heat, she forgot all about role playing, motivation, consequences. Desperate for more, she tugged at his jacket, yanked and pulled until it was in a heap on the floor. His mouth was savaging hers, her hands dragging at his tie as they stumbled to the bed.

Light going dim with evening poured through the windows, and the busy sounds of London traffic swished and coughed on the street below. The grand clock in the hall struck the hour of five. Then the only sound in the room were gasps and murmurs.

She rolled with him over the luxurious duvet, sinking in, sliding over. Her fingers fought with the buttons of his shirt, and his pulled her robe aside. The weight of him pushed her deep into the covers, like sinking into clouds of silk, she thought, then he took her breast in his mouth and she didn't think at all.

Fire and light and the sharp saber points of desire, the wild, unsteady roll of sheer lust. It filled her, and burned in the blood, and pushed a raw cry of delight from her throat.

'Hurry.' She all but chanted it. 'Hurry, hurry,

hurry.' She'd die without him inside her. Frantically she struggled with the hook of his trousers.

His fingers shook. The roar in his head was a thousand waves pounding on a thousand rocks. All he knew was that to wait a moment longer would destroy him.

Her hips arched toward him, and he drove into her in one violent thrust.

Their twin groans rippled the air, and their eyes met – shock mirroring shock. For a heartbeat, then two, they stared at each other.

Then it was all movement, a frantic mating driven by hot blood. Flesh against flesh, the ragged strain of quickened breath, the low cry of a woman at peak. Bodies plunged together in a slick and sensuous dance.

She came again, staggered that there could be so much, so very much. As her hands slid limply onto the rumpled covers, she felt him fall with her. And thought he said her name.

She lay still, wrecked, wonderfully wrecked, with his face buried in her hair and his long, lovely body pressing hers into the bed. Now she knew, she thought, just what happened when his control snapped. And oh, it was a wild and marvelous thing.

His heart still hammered, she could feel it knocking against hers. Drifting on that gilded plateau of contentment, she turned her head and skimmed her lips over his shoulder.

That one gesture had him opening his eyes,

struggling to clear his head again. She seemed soft as water under him, limp as melted wax and nothing like the frenzied woman who'd urged him to hurry. He knew he'd have taken her fast and hard in any case. He'd never needed anything, anyone, the way he'd needed Darcy at that moment. As if his very survival depended upon it.

A dangerous woman, he thought. And found he didn't give a damn. He wanted her again. And again.

'Don't go to sleep,' he murmured.

'I'm not.' But her voice was thick and rough and at the sound of it his blood heated once more. 'I'm just considerably relaxed.' She opened her eyes and pondered the plasterwork of scrolls and stars on the ceiling. 'And enjoying the view.'

'Late eighteenth century.'

'Isn't that interesting?' Amused, she stretched under him like a cat, then ran her hands over his back, more for her pleasure than his. 'Would that be Georgian or rococo? I never can keep my historical periods straight.'

It made him grin and lift his head to look down at her. 'I'll give you the full tour with a lesson later if you like. But just now . . .' He began to move inside her again.

'Oh, well, now,' she murmured. 'You're a healthy one, aren't you?'

'If you don't have your health' – he lowered his head, bit her lip – 'you don't have anything.'

★   ★   ★

210

He was a man of his word and took her to dinner. French food served elegantly enough to soothe, fussily enough to amuse, with wine designed to turn golden on the tongue. The surroundings – gilt mirrors, quiet colors, candlelight glowing in crystal – suited her, Trevor thought. No one looking at the stunning woman in the sleek and simple black dress would imagine her waiting tables in an Irish pub.

Another skill of hers, he decided, a chameleon's ability to alter her image at will. The sassy barmaid, the heartbreaking singer, the sexy delight, the breezy sophisticate.

And which, he wondered, was Darcy Gallagher, at the heart?

He waited until she was sipping champagne with her elaborate dessert before he touched on business.

'One of my meetings today involved you.'

She glanced over, momentarily distracted from her debate of whether eating every bite of that fancy and extraordinary concoction on her plate would be bourgeois.

'Me? Oh, you mean the theater?'

'No, though I had some dealings regarding that, too.'

She decided she could safely eat half of it without looking like a complete bumpkin, and spooned up a glorious combination of cream and chocolate. 'What other business might I be a part of?'

'Celtic Records.' He gauged his rhythm. One

more aspect of her was the businesswoman, and he didn't underestimate that side of her.

She frowned a little, lifted her glass. 'For the recording of Shawn's music, and the performance at the opening. That's a family decision and a family enterprise, I suppose you'd call it. I think we'll be willing to come to terms on that.'

'I hope you will.' Casually, he sampled a bite of her dessert. 'But that isn't what I meant. I'm speaking of you, Darcy, specifically, exclusively.'

Her pulse jumped, so she set the champagne down again. 'Exclusively, in what way exactly?'

'I want your voice.'

'Ah.' She squashed the hard jolt of disappointment. It had no place here, she told herself. 'Is that why you brought me here, Trevor?'

'In part. And that part is totally separate from what happened this evening.'

When his hand covered hers, she glanced down, studied the way they fit. Then, because that was too romantic a notion for comfort, she looked back up at him. 'Naturally such matters must remain separate, or they're altogether a mess, aren't they? You wouldn't be a man who usually pursues, what would it be, clients, in this sort of way.'

He drew back from her, his eyes going hard as stone. 'I don't use sex as a lever, if that's what you mean. Being lovers has nothing whatsoever to do with any of our business dealings.'

'Of course not. And if we could only have one or the other, which would it be?'

'That,' he said stiffly, 'would be up to you.'

'I see.' She managed a faint smile. 'That's good to know. You'll excuse me a moment, won't you?'

She needed to gather herself, to give her head and heart a chance to settle. Leaving him frowning after her, she walked to the ladies' room, where she could lean on the pretty tiled counter and get hold of herself.

What was *wrong* with her? The man was offering her a once-in-a-lifetime opportunity, one that was hers to take or discard as she pleased. Why should it hurt? Why did it leave her feeling not just unsettled but unhappy as well?

Somehow she had come to weave romantic notions around Trevor Magee without even being aware of doing so. And those notions, those imaginings, had him caring for her. Caring for who she was, with all her many flaws. Caring with no strings attached, no outside interests connected. Just caring, she thought, and closing her eyes, she lowered herself to sit on the padded stool in front of the mirror.

Her own fault, of course. He stirred something in her that no one else ever had. And he'd come very close, dangerously close, to touching something so deep in her heart that she had trouble recognizing just what it was.

But she thought she could fall in love with him, with very little effort. And perhaps no encouragement at all. Then what?

Steadying herself, she looked in the mirror. Face

the facts, Darcy. A man like Trevor didn't tie himself permanently to a woman of her background and limitations. Sure, she could present herself well, play the game skillfully, but under it all she was and would forever be Darcy Gallagher of Ardmore, who worked the family pub.

Another type of man she could twist around her finger and make him forget such mundane matters. And hadn't she always planned to? Hadn't she hoped to find a fine, wealthy man one day who would fall under her spell and give her a life full of luxury? She'd have been willing to fall in love, or at least to have a great fondness for the man who fit the bill. She'd have wanted to respect him and enjoy him and would have given him all her affection and her loyalty in return.

That wasn't shameful.

But Trevor wasn't a man who would see only a pleasing face. He'd just given her proof of that. Business was very much a part of what he wanted from her, and a deal for mutual profit marched alongside the attraction.

Passion, she thought, such as they'd found in each other, would flame high and fizzle out. She didn't have to be a romantic like Jude to know that passion without love was short-lived.

So . . . it was best to be sensible and to take as much of both parts he offered her as she pleased. She rose, squared her shoulders, and went out to join him.

He'd ordered coffee and was brooding into it. He wasn't sure whether to be relieved or baffled that the sorrow he was certain had been in her eyes when she'd risen wasn't there as she sat across from him again.

'I'm not sure I made myself clear,' he began, but she shook her head, smiled easily.

'No, you did. But I wanted a moment to think.' She picked up her spoon, had another taste of dessert. 'First, tell me about Celtic Records. You said, on the plane, the company is six years old.'

'That's right. I had an interest in music, traditional in particular. My mother's fond of it.'

'Is she?'

'She's fourth generation. You'd think she'd been born in a crofter's cottage in County Mayo. She's fiercely Irish.'

'So you started the company for your mother.'

'No.' Then he found himself fumbling, frowning. Of course he had, in a very real way. Why hadn't he realized that before? For God's sake, he'd even named it for her. 'Partly. I suppose.'

'I think that's a lovely thing.' And made her want to stroke his hair. 'Why does it befuddle you?'

'It's business.'

'So's the pub, but it's family as well. I like your Celtic Records more for knowing it's both. It's more important to you, and you'll take more care of it, because it's both. I prefer considering dealings with a company that's well cared for.'

'This one is. And so are the artists we sign. We're

based in New York, but we've cracked the inter-national market, so we have an office here. And we'll open one in Dublin within the year.'

We, thought Darcy, almost never did he say *I* when speaking of it. She doubted it was modesty, but more a keen sense and appreciation of team-work. It made her think of the pub again, and she nodded. 'What kind of arrangement are you looking for? Business-wise,' she added, pleased when his eyes narrowed.

'A standard recording contract.'

'Well, now, I wouldn't know what that entails, having no experience in the area.' She studied him over the rim of her champagne flute, and went with impulse. 'But it seems wise for me to engage an agent to discuss the matter with you if I decide it interests me. To be frank, Trevor, I don't know as I want to make a living singing, but I'll listen to your offer.'

He should have left it at that. Every business instinct ordered him to simply nod and move on to some other topic. But he leaned forward. 'I'll make you rich.'

'That's a particular ambition of mine.' She scooped up more dessert, offered it to him. 'And it may be, in the end, that I'll let you help me achieve it.'

He took her wrist. 'You'll have everything you've ever wanted. A hell of a lot more than you've ever dreamed of.' And felt her pulse scramble.

'Christ, you know how to make the mouth water. But I'm not one to leap without looking.'

Relaxed again, he nodded. 'No, you're not. I like that about you. I like damn near everything about you.'

'Are you speaking to a potential client, or to your lover?'

He cupped the back of her neck and brought his mouth to hers, lingering long enough to make a few heads turn. 'Clear enough?'

'I'd say that was crystal. Why don't you take me back and make love with me until neither of us can think about anything at all?'

'Why don't I?' he agreed, and signaled for the check.

In the morning he rose while she was sleeping. He wanted to clear away the rest of his business as quickly as possible and spend the remainder of the day with her.

Shopping, he thought as he dressed. She'd enjoy that. He'd turn her loose in one of the boutiques and buy her whatever caught her fancy. Take her to tea at the Ritz, then seduce her into a private dinner at home.

If it made him a little uncomfortable, even a little ashamed to realize that he was showing off, trying to dazzle her with what he had at his disposal, he'd just have to live with it.

Damn it, he wanted another day with her. Two. A week. Somewhere they could be alone, without any distractions, any interruptions, any thought of business.

They'd burn each other out, he supposed, but Jesus, it would be a hell of a ride before they crashed.

On a whim, he pulled one of the white roses from the vase, scribbled a quick note and laid it on the pillow beside her. Then he found himself sitting on the side of the bed watching her. That perfect face, serene in sleep. All that glorious hair tumbled from his own hand in the night. The bracelet he'd given her flashed and blinked on her wrist, and he knew she wore nothing else.

But his blood didn't leap with lust. Rather it ran warm. Affection, he told himself. It was just affection, running alongside the desire he felt for her. He hadn't been glib when he'd told her he liked almost everything about her. She was a woman who attracted, entertained, challenged, annoyed, and amused. He understood her materialistic streak and didn't blame her for it.

But for a moment, just one foolish moment, he wished they'd met and clicked just as they had without her knowing the generosity of his bank balance.

She'd told him her mind right at the beginning. She wanted money, she wanted luxury. And she was willing to slide into a union with the right man, as long as he was willing and able to provide them.

He didn't intend to be taken for his money. Not now, not ever. Even if he was willing to use it to entertain them both in the short-term.

Shrugging that off, he leaned over to brush a kiss across her cheek, then left her sleeping.

She didn't stir for more than an hour after he'd gone, then rolled over lazily. The first thing she saw when she blinked her eyes open was the rose.

It made her smile, and it made her yearn. She reached for it, stroking its petals as she sat up and read his note.

I'll be done by two, and pick you up. I'm hoping you'll put yourself in my hands for the rest of the afternoon. Trev.

She'd certainly put herself in his hands the night before, she thought now and contentedly settled back against the pillows. What a lovely, lovely way to wake, she mused and stroked the rosebud against her cheek. She considered wandering down for breakfast, or being completely indulgent and ordering it up so she could have it in bed like royalty.

The second picture had such appeal that she reached for the phone. When it rang, she jerked back, then laughed at herself.

She didn't think she was supposed to answer it, so she climbed out of bed for her robe. The knock on her door came as she was belting it.

'Yes, come in.'

'Excuse me, Miss Gallagher, but Mr Magee's on the telephone and would like to speak with you.'

'Of course, thank you.' Darcy picked up the rose again and feeling blissfully romantic and lazy, lifted the receiver. 'Trevor, hello. I've just read your note, and I'd be happy to put myself in your hands.'

'I'm on my way back now.'

'This minute? It's a while till two.'

219

'Darcy, I have to get back to Ardmore right away. Mick O'Toole's been injured on the job.'

'Injured?' She leaped to her feet. 'How? Is he all right? What happened?'

'He took a fall. He's in the hospital. I just heard and I don't have all the details.'

'I'll be ready to go when you get here. Hurry.'

She hung up without another word, dragged out her suitcase, and began throwing clothes inside.

The trip back seemed hideously long. Darcy alternated between praying and listening to Trevor as he gathered more details about the accident.

'He was up on the scaffolding,' Trevor told her. 'One of the crew tripped, as far as we can tell, and Mick was knocked off or slipped off. He was unconscious when the ambulance came for him.'

'But alive.' Her knuckles went white as she locked her hands together.

'Yes, Darcy.' He took her hands, soothing them apart. 'They think concussion and a broken arm. They'll have to check for internal injuries.'

'Internal injuries.' Her stomach rolled, then went to slippery knots. 'That always sounds so dire, so mysterious.' When her voice broke, she shook her head. 'No, I'm not going to fall apart on you. Don't worry.'

'I didn't realize you were so close.'

'He's like family.' Tears rushed into her eyes and were viciously willed away. 'The closest thing to my own father. Brenna . . . all of them, they must be frantic. I should be there.'

'You will be.'

'I want to go straight to the hospital. Can you arrange for a car to take me there?'

'We'll both go straight there.'

'Oh, I thought you'd need to go to the job. All right.' She pressed her fingers to her eyes, took several breaths. 'I'm scared. I'm so awfully scared.'

He put his arm around her and held her until they landed.

And he watched her gather herself, steady herself on the drive from the airport. Her eyes were dry and calm, her hands quiet in her lap. By the time they arrived and walked down the corridor where they were directed, she was completely composed.

'Mrs O'Toole.'

Mollie looked over, rose from where she sat with all five of her daughters. 'Oh, Darcy, there you are – and had to cut your lovely trip short.'

'Tell me how he is, won't you?' She took Mollie's hands, held fast and tried not to think that both Maureen and Mary Kate were crying.

'Well, now, he took a bump. They're doing some tests on his head and so forth. You know the man has a mighty strong head, so we're not going to worry about that.'

'Of course not.' She gave Mollie's chilled hands a squeeze. 'Why don't I see about getting us all some fresh tea? You just sit down now, darling, while I organize that for you. Brenna, why don't you give me a hand with it and we'll get us all a nice hot cup.'

'Bless you, Darcy, that would be a godsend. Mr Magee.' Mollie worked up a tremulous smile. 'It's so kind of you to be here.'

He met Brenna's eyes as she rose, nodded, then took Mollie's hand and led her back to a chair.

'Tell me what happened,' Darcy demanded the minute they were out of earshot. 'And how bad it is.'

'I didn't see it, exactly.' Because her voice felt rusty, Brenna cleared her throat. 'It seems Bobby Fitzgerald lost his footing while he was hauling block up on the scaffold. Dad turned, I think, to steady him, but they were both off their balance and the floor of it was a little slick from a spot of rain. He just tumbled off. I'm thinking the brace of block Bobby was hauling up knocked him, and he went over the safety bar. God!'

She stopped, pressed her hands to her face. 'I saw him fall. I heard a shout and turned round, and I saw him hit the ground. He just lay there. He just lay there, Darcy, with his head bleeding.'

She sniffled, rubbed her fingers over her eyes. 'It wasn't such a terrible long fall, really, but he landed so hard. They stopped me from moving him. I wasn't thinking and just wanted to turn him over, but thank God, cooler heads were there in case there were spinal or neck injuries. Poor Bobby . . . Bobby's beside himself. I just had Shawn take him out for a walk around outside.'

'It's going to be all right.' She took Brenna's shoulders. 'We'll make it be all right.'

'I'm glad you're here. I can't tell them how scared I am. Mary Kate's prone to hysteria in any case, and Maureen's pregnant, and Alice Mae's so young. Patty can hold on, and God knows Ma can, but I can't tell them how it was to see him hit the ground, and how scared I am he won't wake up again.'

'Of course he will.' When Brenna broke, Darcy just gathered her in. 'They'll let you see him soon, I'll wager, then you'll feel better.'

Over Brenna's head she watched Trevor come down the hall. He paused, laid a hand on her shoulder. 'I'll see to the tea. Go sit with your family.'

'Thanks for that. Let's go wash your face,' she said briskly to Brenna. 'Then we'll have some tea and wait for the doctor.'

'I'm all right.' Brenna scrubbed at her face as she drew back. 'Go be with Ma. I'll go wash up and be right along.'

Back in the little waiting room, Darcy sat on the arm of Mollie's chair. 'Tea will be right along.'

'That's fine, then.' Mollie reached up to pat her knee, then left her hand there for her own comfort as well. 'That's a fine man, Trevor is. To break off his business and come back because my Mick's hurt.'

'Of course he came back.'

Mollie only shook her head. 'Not everyone

would. That he did says something about what kind of person he is. And just now, he sat here and he told me I wasn't to worry about anything but concentrating on helping Mick get better. He'll see to all the hospital charges and doctors. He says Mick'll get full pay even though he's off the job for a while. He expects it'll only be a bit of a while,' she continued, then stopped when her voice trembled. 'He expects Mick to be back to work, as both O'Tooles are required to do the job right.'

'He's right, of course.' Tears, this time of gratitude, filled Darcy's throat. How had he known just the right things to say to people he barely knew?

Darcy got to her feet when Trevor came to the doorway and, leading only with her heart, walked to him. She cupped his face in her hands and kissed him, soft and warm on the lips. 'Come sit with the family,' she told him, and brought him in.

Even as she resigned herself to waiting, the doctor stepped in. 'Mrs O'Toole.'

'Yes. My husband?' Mollie was on her feet, her hand clenching Alice Mae's, as it was closest.

'He's a tough one.' With a reassuring smile, the doctor stepped over as Brenna raced up. 'Let me tell you first, he'll be fine.'

'Thank God.' Mollie reached out to grip Brenna's shoulder. 'Thank God for that.'

'He has a concussion and a broken arm. The bone . . .' He demonstrated, putting his own hand on his forearm. 'Snapped rather than shattered, and that's fortunate. Some of the lacerations were

224

deep, and there's considerable bruising at the ribs, but no breaks there. We've run tests and haven't found any internal damage. We want to keep him for a day or two, of course.'

'Is he awake?'

'He is, yes. And considerably alert. He asked for you – and a pint, though you came first.'

Her voice broke in a laughing sob. 'I damn well better. Then I can see him?'

'I'll take you into recovery, then the lot of you can have a minute with him once we've got him settled in a room. He looks a bit fierce with the bruises and the cuts, and I don't want you to be alarmed by it.'

'You don't raise five children without seeing plenty of bruises and cuts.'

'That you don't.'

'You wait here now,' she said, turning to her family, 'while I go see your father. And when it's your turn, I don't want any weeping and wailing, so get it all out of your system now. And we'll all of us have a good cry if need be after we're home again.'

Darcy waited until Mollie walked away with the doctor before she turned to Brenna. 'All right, how do we go about sneaking him in a pint of Guinness?'

CHAPTER 12

'**D**arcy, there's my girl. You've come to spring me from this place, haven't you?' Twenty-four hours after he'd taken a hard tumble and landed for the most part on his head, Mick O'Toole looked pink and alert, bruised and battered, and just a little desperate. Darcy leaned over the bed rail and kissed his forehead fondly.

'I have not. You've one more day to go, if all's as it should be in that rock you call a brain. So I've brought you flowers.'

One of his eyes was blackened, there was a gouge in his cheek held together by a trio of butterfly bandages, and the forehead she'd kissed was a symphony of raw bruises and rawer scrapes.

All in all it gave him the look, Darcy thought, of a brawler who'd come out on the wrong side of fists.

When his big, hopeful smile faded immediately into a long, put-upon sigh, she wanted to cuddle him. 'There's nothing wrong with me head or the rest of me, save this busted wing here, and that's hardly enough to keep a man chained in hospital, now is it?'

226

'The doctors think different. But I've brought you something to cheer you up.'

'The flowers are very nice indeed.' But he said it with a pout, very much like a twelve-year-old who hadn't gotten his way.

'They are, yeah, and right out of Jude's own garden. The rest of it's from somewhere else altogether.' Slipping the flowers out of the bag she carried, Darcy set them aside and pulled out a plastic tumbler with a sealed lid. 'It's Guinness – only a half pint, as that's all I could manage, but it'll have to do you.'

'You're a princess.'

'I am, and expect to be treated as such.' After popping off the lid, she passed the contraband to him, then lowered the rail to sit on the side of the bed. 'Do you feel as well as you look?'

'I'm fit and fine, I promise. My arm pains me a bit, but nothing to speak of.' He took his first sip, then closed his eyes in pure pleasure. 'It was sorry I was to hear you and Trev rushed all the way back from London. It was nothing but a false step and a bit of a tumble.'

'You scared us all to pieces.' Affectionately, she brushed at the hair on his brow. 'And now I suppose you'll have all your ladies fussing over you.'

His eyes twinkled. 'It's hard to mind it, as I've such pretty ladies, though they've been in and out of here since I got my senses back. I'm ready to get back on the job, but Trev won't hear of it. A week, he's telling me, minimum, before I can so much as show me face, and then only with the doctor's say-so.'

Mick's tone turned wheedling. 'Maybe you could have a word with him, darling, tell him how much better off I'd be working than lying about. A man's bound to listen to a beautiful woman such as yourself.'

'You won't get 'round me, Mister Michael O'Toole. A week's a short enough time. Now, you rest and stop fussing about work. The theater won't be built before you're back to it.'

'I don't like taking a wage while I'm flat on my back.'

'It's right he's paying you, as you were hurt on his job, and he can well afford it. Doing so shows his character, just as fretting over it shows yours.'

'That may be, and I'll admit it's put Mollie's mind at rest even if she doesn't say so.' Still his fingers worried the edge of the sheet. 'He's a good man and a fair boss, but I need to know he's got his money's worth from me.'

'Since when haven't you given full shot for the pound? The sooner you're healed through, the sooner you'll be working again. And I'll tell you my plumbing needs another look.'

She'd made that one up, but saw it brightened him.

'I'll take a look-see the minute they let me on my feet again. 'Course, if it's urgent you can have Brenna see to it.'

'It'll wait for you, and so will I.'

'That's fine, then.' He settled back, and the sparkle on her wrist caught his eye. 'Well, now, what's this?' He took her hand, turned it so the bracelet shimmered. 'That's quite the little bauble, isn't it?'

'It is. Trevor gave it to me.' And she watched Mick's wicked smile.

'Did he now?'

'He did, and I shouldn't have taken it, but I decided not to refuse such a generous gesture.'

'Why should you? He's got his eye on you, and has since you first came into view. The man has fine taste if you're asking me, and you, my girl, could hardly do better than with the likes of Trevor Magee.'

'It won't do to get those sorts of notions, Mr O'Toole. It's no more than a bit of a frolic for both of us, with neither looking for seriousness.'

'Is it?' Mick questioned, then seeing Darcy set her chin, as he'd seen her set it all her life, he let it lie. 'Well, sure and we'll see about that, won't we?'

And to Mick's pleasure, it was barely more than an hour after Darcy left his bedside when Trevor came to it. He brought a pint of Guinness with him, and Mick appreciated his boldness in not troubling to hide it, just as he'd admired the neatness with which Darcy had delivered hers under cover.

'Now, that's a man after me own heart.'

'Oh, did you want one too?' With an easy smile, Trevor passed the glass and sat. 'I figured you'd be feeling restless by now.'

'That I am. If you'd get me some pants I'd walk out of here with you.'

'Tomorrow. I've just had a word with your doctor, and he says they'll release you in the morning.'

'Well, that's better than a jab in the eye with a sharp stick. I was thinking, I could be on the job straightaway, in a kind of supervisory capacity. No lifting.' He hurried on as Trevor merely stared blandly. 'No actual labor, just what you'd call keeping an eye on things.'

'In a week.'

'Bloody hell, man, I'll go mad in a week. Do you know what it is to be laid low this way and have a brood of hens clucking about you?'

'Only in my cherished fantasies.'

Mick gave a short laugh and settled into his pint. 'Darcy left hardly an hour ago.'

'She loves you.'

'That feeling's very mutual between us. I happened to notice the trinket you gave her, the wrist bauble.'

'It suits her.'

'It does indeed, being bright and rich and shiny. Some see the girl and think, now that's a flighty one only looking for fun and the easy way. They'd be wrong.'

'I wouldn't disagree with you.'

'As her father, and my good friend, Patrick Gallagher is across the pond, I'm taking it upon myself to say this to you in plain speech. Don't toy with that girl, Trevor. She's not a bauble like that pretty bracelet you picked out of a glass case somewhere. She's a big and seeking heart in her, even if she doesn't like to let it show. And for all she may tell you, and herself for that matter, that it's all fun and games, she'll bruise like any other woman with rough handling.'

'I don't intend to handle her roughly.' His voice was cool now, just a step away from aloof.

Not the sort of man who's accustomed to being given orders, Mick thought, or advice, or even warnings about his behavior. 'Maybe the word I should use is "careless." And a man can be careless with a woman even without intending it, especially if the woman expects it.'

'I'll make a point of being careful, whatever she expects.'

Mick nodded, and again let it lie. But he wondered just what Trevor himself expected.

Mick was right about one thing. Trevor wasn't a man who particularly cared for advice, and certainly not when it pertained to a woman. He knew what he was doing with Darcy. They were both clear-sighted adults, adults who had a very elemental attraction to each other. Mixed with it was simple affection and respect. What more could anyone want from a relationship, and a temporary one at that?

But Mick's words troubled him, and followed him on the drive back to Ardmore. Rather than head back to the job as he'd intended, he turned up Tower Hill. He'd yet to return to his ancestor's gravesite, or even to explore the ruins. He could spare another half hour.

The round tower loomed over the village and could be seen from below from almost every vantage point. He passed it often enough on his way to and from the cottage, but had never followed the urge to take real time to study it. This time he pulled to the shoulder of the narrow road and stepped out of the car. And into the wind.

When he walked through the little gate, he saw a scatter of tourists climbing over the hilly ground between the old stones and crosses, over toward the roofless stone building that had been the church built in the name of the saint. His first reaction surprised him, as it was mild resentment that anyone should be there, with their cameras and backpacks and guidebooks.

Stupid, he thought. These were just the people he hoped to appeal to with his theater. These, and more who would come for the beaches when the summer spread warmth along the coast.

So he joined them, picking his way down the slope to the church, taking the time he'd yet to allow himself to study the Roman arcading, the carving going weak from time and wind.

Inside with the rubble and graves, two ogham

stones had been placed for safekeeping. And how, he wondered, had those lines dug into stone been read as words? A kind of Morse code, he imagined, devised by ancients and left at crossroads for a traveler.

He heard a woman call out for her children in the flat accent that said States to him, East Coast, North. And seemed so out of place here. Did his voice have that same slightly-out-of-tune sound to it? Here voices should lilt and flow and have old music under each word.

He stepped out again, looking up now at the tower. The old defense had its conical roof still attached and seemed even now as if it could withstand any attack.

What had they come for, all the invaders? Romans, Vikings, Saxons, Normans, Britons. What fascination did this simple little island hold for them that they would war and die to take it?

And turning, he looked out and away, and thought he saw part of the answer.

The village below was neat and pretty as a painting, with the broad beach a sweep of sand glittering golden in the fitful sunlight. The sea spread, blue as summer, shimmering in that same restless light, foaming white at the edges.

The hills stretched back and back, green and lush with patches of rich brown, muted gold to complete the quilt of land. Just the shadow of dark mountain peaks rose behind them.

Even while he watched, the light changed,

shifted, grew, and he could see the shadows of clouds swim over the land as the sunlight beat through them.

The air smelled of grass, fading flowers, and sea.

He doubted it was the beauty of the country that brought those who wanted to land here. But he was sure it was part of the reason they had fought to stay.

'We're a land that absorbs our invaders, and makes them one of us.'

Trevor glanced around, expecting to see an Irish tourist or one of the locals behind him. Instead he looked into Carrick's wild blue eyes.

'You get around.' With some surprise, Trevor saw that they were alone, when only moments before there had been at least half a dozen people exploring the hill.

'I prefer a bit of privacy.' Carrick winked at him. 'Don't you?'

'It's difficult for me to be private when you pop up at will.'

'I've been wanting to have a word with you. How goes your theater, then?'

'We're on schedule.'

'Ah, you Yanks are big on schedules. I can't tell you how many come through here, checking their watches and their maps and figuring out how to do this and that and the other all with staying on schedule. You'd think they'd toss such things aside when they're about a flaming holiday, but habits die hard in some.'

With his hair blowing in the wind, Trevor tucked his hands in his pockets. 'So, you wanted to have a word with me about the American habit of clock watching?'

'Just a bit of a conversational gambit. If you're after seeing your uncle's resting place again, it's this way.' Carrick turned, walking gracefully over the rough ground with his silver doublet sparkling.

'John Magee,' Carrick began when Trevor joined him by the marker. 'Beloved son and brother. Died a soldier, far from home.'

Trevor felt an ache around his heart, a kind of distant grief. 'Beloved son, undoubtedly. Beloved brother is debatable.'

'You're thinking of your granda. He came here rarely, but he came.'

'Did he?'

'Aye, to stand as you are, with a scowl most often on his face and his thoughts dark and confused. Because it troubled him, he closed his heart. A deliberate click of a lock.'

'Yes.' Trevor murmured. 'I can believe that. He did nothing, as I can remember, that wasn't deliberate.'

'You're a deliberate man yourself, in some ways.' Carrick waited until Trevor's head lifted, until their eyes met again. 'But isn't it an interesting thing, that when he whose seed started your father stood on this hill, looked down at what was home, he didn't see what you do. Not a lovely spot, edged with magic and welcome. He saw a trap, and would have gnawed his leg off at the ankle to escape it.'

Carrick turned to study Ardmore again. His black hair streamed back, like a cape. 'Perhaps in a way, he did. And hobbled with the loss of some part of himself, he went to America. If not for his doing that, you wouldn't stand here today, looking down and seeing what he couldn't.'

'Wouldn't,' Trevor corrected. 'But you're right. I wouldn't be here without him. Tell me, who puts the flowers here on John Magee's grave, after all this time?'

'I do.' Carrick gestured to the little pot of wild fuchsia. 'As Maude no longer can, and it was the one thing she asked of me. Never did she forget him, and never did her love waver in all the years between his death and her own. Constancy is the finest of your mortal virtues.'

'Not everyone can claim it.'

'No, but those who do know a joy in it. Is your heart a constant one, Trevor Magee?'

Trevor looked up again. 'It's not something I've given a lot of thought to.'

'That's shading close to a lie, but we'll shift the question for you. You've had a taste of fair Darcy now. Do you think you can push back from the banquet and walk away?'

'What's between us is private.'

'Hah. Your privacy means nothing to me. Three times a century I've waited for you – you, I'm sure now, and no other. You're the last of it. You stand there, worrying about being taken for a fool, which is only another kind of pride, your granda's sort, when you've only to take what's already been given. Your blood's hot for her. Your mind's clouded with her, but you stop short of exploring what's in your heart for her.'

'Hot blood and a clouded mind have very little to do with the heart.'

'That's foolishness. Isn't the first step toward love the passion, the second the longing? And you're past the first step, already on to the second, and too stubborn to admit it. I'll wait.' Impatience shot into his eyes, and they seemed to burn. 'But I've a bloody schedule of me own, so make lively, Yank.'

He snapped his fingers, a kind of lightning shot. And vanished.

It put him in a foul mood. A rash and foul mood. As if it wasn't irritating enough to have Mick O'Toole handing him advice on his personal life, he'd been given a potful from someone who shouldn't even exist. Both mortal and mystic were pressuring him to take some sort of definitive step with Darcy, and he'd be damned if he'd be cornered that way.

His life was his own, and so was hers.

To make a point of it, he waved off the calls when he crossed the job site and went straight into the pub's kitchen door.

Shawn glanced up from scrubbing pots. 'Hello,

Trev. You're late for lunch, but I'll fix you up if you're hungry.'

'No, thanks. Darcy out there?'

'She just went up to her little palace. I've fish stew still on the . . .' Shawn trailed off, as Trevor was already climbing the stairs. 'Well, I suppose he's not hungry for what I can serve him.'

He didn't knock. It was rude, he knew it, and got some perverse satisfaction from it. Just as he got satisfaction from seeing Darcy's surprise when she walked out of the bedroom with a little shopping bag in her hand.

'Sure, you're at home, aren't you?' However mild the words, there was the unmistakable whip of irritation through them. He enjoyed it. 'It's sorry I am I can't entertain you at the moment, but I'm just off to Jude's to take her the little stuffed lamb I bought for the baby.'

His response was to stride to her, first her hair in his hand, and drag her head back even as his mouth swooped down to crush hers. Shock stabbed into her, fused with an instant and molten lust so it was like one slice from a burning sword.

She shoved at him first, and meant it. Then gripped him hard, and meant that as well. He paid no attention to either reaction until he was good and finished. And when he was, he pulled her back, and his eyes were steel bright.

'Is that enough for you?'

She struggled to find her balance, her wit. 'As kisses go, it was—'

'No, damn it.' Temper roughened his voice and at that her own eyes slitted. 'Is what that does to you, what you know it does to me, enough for you?'

'Have I said differently?'

'No.' But even as he struggled with his straining temper, he cupped her chin. 'Would you?'

However set off he was, she was sure his study of her was cool, calculated, and thorough. A man with that measure of control was an irritant, she thought. And a challenge. 'You can be sure you'll be the first to know if I'm dissatisfied.'

'Good.'

'And as a woman of my word, I'm telling you now I don't appreciate you bursting into my home uninvited and manhandling me because some bug's crawled up your arse.'

With a half laugh, he shook his head, stepped back. 'Point taken. I'm sorry.' He bent down, picked up the bag she'd dropped, and handed it to her. 'I was just up on Tower Hill, at my uncle's grave.'

She angled her head. 'Are you grieving, Trevor, for someone who died long before you were born?'

He opened his mouth to deny it, but the truth simply slid out. 'Yes.'

Everything about her softened. She reached out to touch his arm. 'Come sit down now, and I'll make you some tea.'

'No, thanks.' He took her hand, lifted it to his lips in an absent gesture that made something inside her stretch and yearn. Then he turned away and paced restlessly to the window to look out at the work in progress.

Was he the invader here, he wondered, staking his claim? Or a son returning to dig in roots? 'My grandfather wouldn't speak of this place, and being a slavishly dutiful wife, my grandmother wouldn't either. As a result—'

'Your curiosity was whetted.'

'Yes. Exactly. I thought about coming here for a long time. On and off, even made half-baked plans a couple of times. But I never seriously committed to it. Then the idea for the theater jumped into my head, full blown, as if I'd been building it there, stage by stage, for years.'

'Isn't that the way it is sometimes with ideas?' She crossed to him, looked out with him. 'They simmer around without you really being aware of it, until they're cooked proper.'

'I suppose.' Hardly aware of it, he took her hand. Just held it. 'Since the deal's done, there's no harm in telling you I'd have paid more for the lease, given you a higher percentage. I had to have it.'

'Well, then, there's no harm in telling you we'd have taken less all around. But we very much enjoyed the horse trading and winding up your man Finkle.'

This time he did laugh, and most of the tension drained. 'My great-uncle would have come here, and my grandfather. To Gallagher's.'

'Oh, to be sure. Is it what they'd think of what you're doing here that's worrying you?'

'I don't worry what my grandfather would have thought. Not anymore.'

There, she thought, that sore spot again. This time she probed, but gently. 'Was he so hard a man?'

He hesitated, but it seemed he was in the mood to speak of it. 'What did you think of the house in London?'

Puzzled, she shook her head. 'It was very elegant.'

'Fucking museum.'

She blinked at that, there was such undiluted anger in his voice. 'Well, I'll say the museum part of that statement occurred to me, but it was lovely.'

'After he died, my parents gave me clearance to change a few things in it. Things that hadn't been changed in thirty years. Opened it up a bit, softened some edges, but it's still his place underneath. Rigid and formal, as he was. That's how my father was raised. Rigidly, and without affection.'

'I'm sorry.' She stroked a hand in circles over his back. 'It has to be sad, hard and sad, to have a father who doesn't show he loves you.'

'I never had that problem. Somehow, through some miracle, my father was – is – caring, open and full of humor. Though his father wasn't. He still doesn't speak of it much, the way he was raised, except to my mother.'

'And she to you,' Darcy murmured, 'because she knows you'd need to understand it.'

'He wanted to make a family, a life, that was the opposite of the way he'd been raised. That's what he did. They kept us in line, my sister and me, but we always knew they loved us.'

'I think it shows the beauty of the gift they gave you that you don't take it for granted.'

'No, I don't.' He turned back to her. Odd, he hadn't really expected her to understand, nor had he expected to feel such relief that she did. 'That's why I don't worry what my grandfather would think of what I'm doing here. But I do think of how my parents will feel when it's done.'

'Then I'll say this. To my way of thinking, they'll be proud. Ireland's art is at its core, and you're bringing more of it here. Along with it the practicality of jobs and revenue. It's a good thing you're doing, and a credit to your father, your mother, and your heritage.'

A nagging little weight fell off his shoulder. 'Thanks. It matters, more than I anticipated. It was one of the things that hit me when I was standing up on the hill. It matters. What I do here, and leave here. And while I was coming to that conclusion, I had a conversation with Carrick.'

Her fingers jerked in his. When he looked down, he saw the surprise clearly on her face before she closed her mouth and made a quiet humming sound.

'Do you think I'm hallucinating?'

'No.' She paused, then shook her head. 'I don't, no. Others whose sanity I'm sure of claim to have done the same. We've broad minds around here.'

But she knew the legend, and it unnerved her enough that she took a step back and sat on the arm of a chair. 'And what did you converse about?'

'A number of things. My grandfather. Old Maude and Johnnie Magee. Schedules, virtues, the theater. You.'

'Myself.' Now she rubbed her suddenly damp hands on her trousers. 'And what would that be about?'

'You know the legend, probably better than I. It takes three couples, as I understand it, falling in love, accepting each other, taking vows.'

'So it's said.'

'And in the past year or so, your two brothers have fallen in love, accepted it, and taken vows.'

'I'm aware of that, as I was at their weddings.'

'Then, given the quickness of your mind, I assume you've considered the fact that there are three Gallaghers.' He took a step closer. 'You look a little pale.'

'I'd appreciate it if you'd get to the point you're dancing around.'

'All right, direct. He's pegged us as his third and final step.'

Her chest seemed to fill all at once with heat and pressure, making her want to knock her fist against it to loosen it again. But she kept her hands still and her eyes level. 'That wouldn't sit well with you.'

243

'Would it with you?'

She was too flustered to catch the evasion. 'I'm not the one having conversation with faerie princes, am I? And no, I don't particularly care to have my fate and future dictated by another's wants or needs.'

'Neither do I. Neither,' he added, 'will I.'

She thought she understood now why he'd told her of his grandfather. To show her he had cold blood in him.

Slowly she got to her feet. 'I see what put you in such a rare mood. The very idea of the remote possibility that I might be your fate and future set you right off, didn't it? The very thought that a man of your education and consequence should tumble heart-first for a barmaid.'

He was so genuinely baffled it took him a moment to answer. 'Where the hell did that come from?'

'Who could blame you for being angry and frustrated when such a suggestion was made? It's a fortunate thing for both of us that love has nothing to do with the matter.'

He'd seen angry women before, but he wasn't certain he'd ever faced one who looked so capable of inflicting real physical harm. To ward it off, he held up his hands palms out. 'In the first place, what you do for a living has nothing to do with . . . anything. In the second, you're hardly a barmaid, though it wouldn't matter if you were.'

'I serve drinks in a pub, so what's that if not a barmaid?'

'Aidan runs the bar, Shawn runs the kitchen, and you run the service,' Trevor said patiently. 'And I imagine if you wanted, you could run the whole shot – or any other pub in your country or mine. But that's hardly an issue.'

'It happens to be of some particular issue with me.' But she yanked back her anger and let it vibrate on the end of its tether.

'Darcy, I told you this because it concerns both of us, because we're lovers and it's only right we both know where we stand. Now we do, and we're agreed we don't intend to let ourselves get tangled up in some ancient legend.'

He took her hand again, rubbing his thumb over the knuckles to soothe out the stiffness. 'Separate from that – entirely separate from that – I like who you are, I enjoy being with you, and I want you in a way . . . I've never wanted anyone else in the same way,' he finished.

She ordered herself to relax, to accept, even to be pleased. But there was a hole somewhere inside her that wouldn't close up again. 'All right. Separate from that, I feel the same. So there's no problem at all.' Flashing a smile, she rose to her toes and kissed him warmly, then waved him toward the door.

'Now go on with you, as I've got to be on my way.'

'Will you come to the cottage tonight?'

She shot him a look from under her lashes. 'I'd be pleased to. You can look for me around midnight, and I wouldn't mind if you had a glass of wine poured and waiting.'

'Later, then.' He would have kissed her again, but she was already shutting the door in his face.

On the other side of it she counted to ten three full times. Then exhaled. So, they were to be reasonable and sensible and do it all exactly the Magee way, were they? He was too removed to tumble into legend, or into love.

Well, by God, she'd have him begging on his knees for her before she was done with him. He'd promise her the world and everything in it.

And when he had, well, she might just take it. That would teach the man not to shrug off the notion of loving Darcy Gallagher.

CHAPTER 13

All in all, Trevor found himself very satisfied by the way things were going. The project was moving along on schedule. The townspeople were supportive and interested. Never a day went by without at least some of them wandering by to watch the work, make comments, give suggestions, or tell him some story or other about his relations.

He'd met a few who were cousins. In fact, he had two of them employed as laborers.

With Mick out of commission for the next few days, he'd have to spend more time at the site. But he didn't mind. It would keep his mind focused on what it needed to be focused on. And give him less time to let it wander around Darcy.

He felt he'd straightened things out in that area as well. Both of them were too sensible to be influenced by legends, or self-interested faeries. Or dreams of a blue heart that beat steady and strong deep in the sea.

He had business to see to, he reminded himself as he carried coffee up to his office in the cottage. Calls to make, contracts to negotiate, supplies to order. He couldn't waste time thinking about what he did or didn't see, did or didn't believe. Responsibilities wouldn't wait while he pondered just how much of Irish myth was real and how much was imagined.

He touched the disk under his shirt. Real, he thought. As real as it gets. But he was handling it.

He glanced at his watch, and thought he might just catch his father at home in New York. And stepping into the bedroom, he jerked and spilled hot coffee over the back of his hand.

'Goddamn it!'

'Oh, there's no need to profane.' With a quiet cluck of her tongue, Gwen continued to ply her needle. She sat in the chair in front of the tidy hearth, her hair neatly bound back, her face composed, her hands quick and clever as she embroidered a white cloth.

'You'll want salve on that burn,' she told him.

'It's nothing.' What was a little discomfort compared to seeing ghosts? Much less to conversing with one. 'I'd nearly convinced myself not to believe in you.'

'Sure and you need to do what makes you most comfortable. Would you rather I let you be?'

'I don't know what I'd rather.' He set the coffee down on the table, turned his desk chair around to face her. And sitting, he sucked absently at the sting on his hand. 'I had dreams about you. I told you that. I didn't tell you I halfway believed I'd find you when I came here. Not you,' he corrected, fumbling just enough to annoy himself. 'Someone . . .' the word 'alive' seemed rude somehow. 'Real. A woman.'

Her gaze when it lifted to his was gentle and full of understanding. 'You thought perhaps you'd find the woman you'd dreamed of, and that she would be for you?'

'Maybe. Not that I'm looking particularly,' he added. 'But maybe.'

'A man can fall in love with a dream if he lets himself. It's a simple matter with no effort, no work, no troubles. And no real joy, when it comes down to it. You prefer working for something, don't you? It's part of who you are.'

'I suppose so.'

'The woman you did meet is a great deal of effort and work and trouble. Tell me, Trevor, does she bring you joy as well?'

'You mean Darcy?'

'And who else have you been walking with?' Gwen questioned. 'Of course I'm speaking of Darcy Gallagher. A beautiful and complicated woman that, with a voice like . . .' She trailed off, shaking her head and lightly laughing. 'I was going to say like an angel, but there's little of the angels about that one. No, she's a voice like a woman, full and rich and tempting to a man. She's tempted you.'

'She could tempt the dead. No offense.'

'None taken. I wonder, Trevor, don't you think she's what you're looking for?'

'I'm not looking for anything. Anyone.'

'We all look. The lucky find.' Her hands, stilled, lay on the cloth with bright patterns of thread. 'The wise accept. I was lucky, but not wise. Could you not learn something from my mistake?'

'I don't love her.'

'Maybe you do and maybe you don't.' Gwen picked up her needle again. 'But you haven't opened your heart to the risk of it. You guard that part of yourself so fierce, Trevor.'

'It may be that part of myself doesn't exist.' Chewed off at the knee in Ardmore, he thought, before I was even born. 'That I'm just not capable of loving someone the way you mean.'

'That's foolishness.'

'I hurt another woman because I couldn't love her.'

'And, I think, hurt yourself in the process. It puts doubts about yourself in your mind. Both of you, I can promise, will not only survive it, but be better off for the experience. Once you stop thinking of your heart as a weapon instead of a gift, you'll find what you're looking for.'

'My heart isn't the priority here. The theater is.'

She made a sound that might have been agreement. ''Tis a grand thing to be able to build, and build to last. This cottage, simple as it is, has lasted lifetime and lifetime. Oh, sure a few changes here, another room there, but the core of it remains. As does the faerie raft beneath it, with its silver towers and blue river.'

'You chose the cottage over the castle,' he pointed out.

'I did. Aye, I did. For the wrong reasons, but in spite of it, I won't regret my children or the man who gave them to me. Perhaps Carrick will never understand that part of my heart. I've come to understand it would be wrong to ask him to do so. Hearts can merge and the people who hold them still stand as they are. Love accepts that. It accepts everything.'

He saw now what pattern she worked into the cloth. It was the silver palace, its towers bright, its river blue as gemstones, its trees heavy with golden fruit. And on a bridge that spanned the water were two figures, not yet finished.

Herself, Trevor realized, with her hands held out toward Carrick's.

'You're lonely without him.'

'I have . . .' She brushed a finger gently over the threads that formed a silver doublet. 'An emptiness in me. A place that waits. As I wait.'

'What happens to you if the spell isn't broken?'

She lifted her head again, her eyes dark and soft and quiet. 'I'll bide here, and see him only in my heart.'

'For how long?'

'For as long as there is. You have choices, Trevor Magee, as once I had. You have only to make them.'

'It's not the same,' he began, but she faded away, like mist. 'It's not the same,' he said again, to the

251

empty room. Though he turned the chair around, it was some time before he picked up the phone and managed to get on with the business at hand.

He called his father first, and that connection of voice to voice soothed his nerves. With his rhythm back, he fell into routine, contacted Nigel in London, and his counterpart in Los Angeles. He checked the time again, noted it was closing in on midnight. Seven in New York, he thought, and called the ever reliable Finkle at home.

Notes were piled on his desk, his computer up and running, and the phone tucked on his shoulder with Finkle's voice droning through when he heard the sound of a car pulling in. Trevor shifted, angled so he could see through the window.

And watched Darcy walk toward the garden gate.

He'd forgotten the wine.

She considered knocking, but she'd seen the light in his office window. Working, are you? With a sly glint in her eye she let herself in the front door. She thought they'd soon put a stop to that, and walked straight up the stairs.

She paused at the door to his office, finding herself both irritated and pleased when he continued with his phone call and waved her in with a little finger crook.

Irritated that he didn't appear to have been anxiously awaiting her. And pleased because she imagined she would shortly have him panting like an eager pup.

'I'll need that report before New York closes tomorrow.' Trevor scribbled something down, nodded. 'Yeah, well, they've got till end of day to accept the offer or it's off the table. Yes, that's exactly how I want you to put it. Next item. I'm not satisfied with the bids on the Dressler project. Make it clear that if our usual lumber supplier can't do better, we'll look to alternate sources.'

He glanced over absently, took a sip of his coffee as Darcy unbuttoned her coat. Then inhaled caffeine like air – and choked on it.

The coat dropped to the floor, and he saw she wore nothing beneath it but his bracelet, high heels, and a very feline smile.

'Perfect,' he managed. 'Jesus, you're perfect.' As Finkle's voice buzzed in his ear, he simply hung up, got to his feet.

'I take it business hours are over.'

'They are.'

She looked around the room, angled her head. 'I don't see my glass of wine.'

He discovered it was just possible to speak when a man's heart was in his throat. 'I forgot it.' His breath already ragged, he crossed to her. 'I'll get it later.'

She tipped her head back to keep her eyes on his, and saw what she'd wanted to see. Desire, raw as a fresh wound. 'I've a powerful thirst.'

'Later' was all he could say before his mouth came down on hers.

He possessed. With quick, hard hands, restless lips, he took what she'd offered. Gave her what she'd wanted. Desperation was what she'd wanted from him, that jagged edge of need as dangerous as it was primitive. She'd come to him naked and shameless to lure the animal.

He was rough, and his recklessness added a slick layer of excitement. No control now, nor the need for it. So she lost herself in the wicked spell of her own brewing.

He shoved her against the wall, feasting on her throat, drugged on that sharply sexual taste of perfumed female flesh. And his hands streaked over her, bruised over her, greedy for the curves, the swells, the secrets of woman.

Hot, wet, vibrant.

His fingers slid over her, into her, driving her up. Even as he felt her body shudder, felt the violence of the orgasm rip through her, he looked into her eyes. In the dark and clouded blue, he thought he saw the flash of triumph.

He might have been able to pull back then, to clear his head enough to find his finesse, but she moved against him, one lazy, stretching arch, and her arms twined around him like chains wrapped in velvet.

'More.' She purred it. 'Give me more, and take more as well. Right here.' She nipped her teeth into his lip. 'Right now.'

If she'd been a witch murmuring the darkest of incantations, he'd have been no less spellbound.

He'd have sworn he caught the scent of hellfire as her mouth once again captured his.

Then there was madness, fevered and glorious. In her own triumph she found it, that wild pleasure, the terror-laced delight of having a man turn savage. And allowing it. Craving it.

Her blood beat as frantically as his, her hands raced, as urgent and as rough as those that raced over her.

She tore his shirt, and reveled in the harsh sound of cotton rending at the seam. And her teeth dug into his shoulder when he pushed her over the edge again.

A haze filled his vision, thick and red. Her nails bit into his back, glorious little points of pain. His blood was a drumbeat, a primitive tattoo in his head, heart, loins. He plunged into her where they stood, greedily swallowing her ragged cry.

Each thrust was like another step on a thin wire stretched over both heaven and hell. Whichever way they fell, it couldn't be stopped. Knowing it, he dragged her head back, kept his hand fisted in her hair, his eyes on her face.

'I want to see you.' He panted it out. 'I want to see you feel me.'

'I can't feel anything but you, Trevor.'

She tumbled off the wire, clasping him against her on the fall. And flying out with her, he didn't give a damn where they landed.

He stayed where he was, fighting for air, for his

sanity. The press of his body kept her upright as he braced a hand on the wall for balance.

She'd gone limp, as he knew now she did after loving. He told himself he'd find the energy, in just a minute, to get them both into bed.

'I can't stay like this,' she murmured against his shoulder.

'I know. Just a second.'

'Maybe we could just slide down to the floor here for a bit of a while. I can't feel me legs, anyway. You make me dizzy, Trevor.'

It made him laugh, and he turned his head, buried his face in her hair. 'I'd say I'd carry you to bed, but I'd never make it and it would ruin the image of manly prowess. You make me weak, Darcy.'

'It'd take quite a bit to spoil the image after this.'

'Well, in that case.' He slipped an arm behind her knees, lifted her. His hair was tousled, his eyes sleepy and satisfied.

She toyed with the silver disk dangling from the chain, closed her fingers around it. She started to answer his grin, then could only stare as her heart landed right at his feet.

'What is it?' Alarmed by the shock in her eyes and the quick paling of her cheeks, he crossed quickly to the bed to set her down. 'Did I hurt you?'

'No.' Oh, Jesus, oh, God. Holy Mother of God. 'Just dizzy for a minute, as I said. I'm better now, but I still have that powerful thirst. I could dearly use that wine, if you don't mind.'

'Sure.' Not quite convinced, he skimmed his knuckles over her cheek. 'Just sit there. I'll be right back.'

The minute he was out of the room, she grabbed a bed pillow and pummeled it viciously with her fists. Damn it all to hell and back again, she'd gotten caught in a web of her own spinning. The man was supposed to be bewitched by her, intrigued, frustrated, satisfied, stupefied, and willing to be her slave before she was done.

And now she'd kicked her own self in the ass and gone and fallen in love with him.

It wasn't supposed to be this way. She pounded the pillow again, then hugged it against her as her stomach took a deep, diving dip. How was she supposed to wrap the man around her finger when she was already wrapped around his?

It had been such a good plan, too: She would use her wiles, her lures, her charm, her temper, everything at her disposal. Then when he was caught, as surely he would have been, she'd have been free to snip him loose or keep him. There would have been time to decide which suited her best by then.

Well, this was God's punishment, she supposed. Fate's little joke. She'd been so certain she could keep her heart in check until she decided if she should love him or not. Now she had no choice at all.

For the first time in her life, her heart wasn't her own. And a terrifying sensation it was.

She bit her knuckles, worrying over it. What did she do now? How could she think just now?

It had been all right when it was a kind of game. It hadn't done more than nip at her temper to think that the manner of man Trevor was wouldn't be serious about a woman such as herself. Now, well, it was a great deal more important.

And more infuriating.

Because, she thought as that temper began to bubble and burn away panic, if the likes of him thought he could toss her aside just because he had a fancy education and property and money to burn, he was very much mistaken in the matter.

The bastard.

She was in love with him, so she would have him. As soon as she figured out the best way to get him.

Her head came up, a she-wolf prepared to bare fangs, when she heard him coming up the stairs. It took all her control, and all her skill, to bury that instinct, force that temper back, and greet him with a silky smile.

'Okay now?' He came to her, held out a glass of white wine.

She took it, sipped delicately. 'Never better,' she said and patted the bed beside her. 'Come sit by me, darling, and tell me all about your day.'

Her sugary tone had him wary, but he sat, tapped his glass against hers. 'The end of it was the best part.'

She laughed and walked her fingers up his thigh. 'And who said it was over?'

Brenna wasn't the least bit pleased about being hauled off the job at nine in the morning. She'd argued, cursed, and sulked while Darcy dragged her up the hill to the Gallagher house through a drizzling rain that sent puffs of mist creeping behind them.

'Trevor's a right to give me the boot for this.'

'He won't.' Darcy took a firmer hold on Brenna's arm. 'And you're entitled to a morning break, aren't you? Been on the job already since half-six. I need twenty minutes of your precious time.'

'You could have had it while I was working.'

'It's a private matter, and I could hardly ask Jude to waddle her way down there, could I, in the wet.'

'At least tell me what this is about, then.'

'I'm doing it all at once, so you'll just have to wait five more flaming minutes.' Puffing a bit – Brenna was small, but it wasn't an easy matter to pull a reluctant woman of any size up that steep hill – Darcy continued down the little walkway between Jude's wet flowers.

She didn't knock, and as the door was never locked, she hauled Brenna inside, where her work boots, unwiped, tracked mud down the hallway to the kitchen.

They looked so cozy there, Jude and Aidan, sharing breakfast at the old table, and the big dog sprawled hopefully under it. The smell of toast and tea and flowers hung in the air. It gave Darcy a little jolt in the center, made her wonder why she'd never before realized how satisfying such quiet moments could be. How intimate they were.

'Good morning.' Jude glanced over, and in a credit to friendship, said nothing about the mud. 'Do you want some breakfast?'

'No,' Darcy said just as Brenna moved forward to snag a piece of toast from the rack. 'We didn't come to eat,' she continued, aiming a lowering look at her friend. 'I need a word with you, Jude. In private. Go away, Aidan.'

'I haven't finished my breakfast.'

'Finish it at the pub.' Neat and deft, Darcy slapped the remainder of his bacon on toast, scooped the bit of egg left on his plate on top of it, and held it out. 'There. Now off with you. This is women's business here.'

'A fine thing this is, a fine thing for a man to be shoved from his own table, out of his own house.' He may have grumbled, but he got up and shrugged into his jacket. 'Females are rarely worth the trouble they take. Except this one,' he added and leaned down to kiss Jude.

'Bill and coo later,' Darcy ordered. 'Brenna only has a few minutes as it is.'

'You might as well go.' Resigned now, Brenna got herself a cup, brought it back to the table to enjoy some tea with her toast. 'She's on a tear.'

'I'm going. I'll expect you to be on time,' he said

260

to Darcy. He kissed Jude again, lingering over it as much to please himself as to annoy his sister.

He snapped his fingers at Finn, waiting while the dog happily scrambled out. 'Come along with me, lad. They don't want our kind here.' He strode out, Finn prancing behind him. 'Take a lie-down,' Aidan shouted, then the door slammed.

'You look a little tired,' Brenna commented, pursing her lips as she studied Jude. 'Aren't you sleeping well these nights?'

'The baby was feeling frisky last night.' Jude ran her hands in slow circles over her belly, thrilled at the impatient ripple under her palms. 'Kept me awake. I don't mind, really. It's a lovely feeling.'

'You need to nap when he naps.' Brenna decided to have another piece of toast, and began to load this one with jam. 'That's what I've heard, and do the same once he pops out as well. Sleep becomes a precious thing. How are the childbirth classes going?'

'Oh, they're fascinating. Wonderful. Terrifying. The last one—'

'If you don't mind,' Darcy interrupted, 'I've something I need to discuss. I'd hope my two closest friends in the world would have some interest.'

Brenna only rolled her eyes, but Jude tucked her tongue in her cheek, folded her hands on the table. 'Of course we're interested. What is it?'

'It's—' She found the words stuck in her throat. Hissing, she grabbed Brenna's tea and gulped it down over her friend's annoyed protest. 'I'm in love with Trevor.'

'Christ Jesus!' Brenna snatched her cup back. 'You've dragged me up here for that?'

'Brenna.' Jude spoke softly, her eyes on Darcy's face. 'She means it.'

'The girl's always making a stage production out of . . .' But Brenna trailed off, getting a good look at Darcy herself. 'Oh. Oh, well, then.' With a laugh, she leaped to her feet and gave Darcy a smacking kiss on the mouth. 'Congratulations.'

'I didn't win a bloody raffle.' Disgusted, she dropped into a chair. 'Why did it happen this way?' Dismissing Brenna as useless, she appealed to Jude. 'Without me having time to prepare or figure on it. It's like a punch in the face, and I have to keep my balance here, as I'll not be knocked on my ass by any man.'

'You've knocked more than your share of them on theirs,' Brenna pointed out. 'Seems you're due for some of the same. I like him.' She took a huge bite of toast and jam. 'I think he suits you.'

'Why?'

'Hold that thought.' Jude lifted a finger. 'Darcy, does he make you happy?'

'How do I know?' She threw up her hands, then pushed back from the table. 'I'm feeling too many things at the moment to know if happy is one of them. Oh, don't give me those smug, married-ladies' smiles. I like his company. I've never known a man I like being with so much as Trevor. Just

262

being with him. I'd look forward to seeing him even without the sex, and that's saying quite a bit, as the sex is fantastic.'

She hesitated for a moment, then continued. 'And last night, after we'd made love it just happened. It's like a slamming into you, so you can't get your air proper and the blood drains right out of your head and your joints go weak. I've never been so furious. What business does he have making me fall in love with him before I'm damn good and ready and have decided it's what I want?'

'Oh, he's a bounder all right,' Brenna said cheerfully. 'Why, the nerve of that man.'

'Oh, shut up. I should've known you'd take his part.'

'Darcy.' Brenna took her hand, and though the humor still brightened her eyes, there was an understanding in them that blew away Darcy's resentment. 'He's what you've always wanted. He's handsome and clever and rich.'

'That's part of the problem, isn't it?' Jude laid a hand over theirs, formed a unit. 'He's what you've always wanted, or told yourself you did. Now that you've found him, you wonder if it's real. And if it is, will he believe it?'

'I didn't know it would be this way.' The tears wanted to come, and here, with friends, she let them. 'I thought it would be fun, a lark. And easy. But it's not. I've always been able to tell what's going on inside a man, but I can't with him. He's a slick one, Trevor is, and slippery. God, I love that about him.'

That made her cry harder and reach for a napkin to wipe her face. 'Oh, if he knew what a mess he'd made out of me, he'd be so pleased about it.'

'You may be right, but not,' Jude added, 'for the reasons you might think. He has feelings for you. They show.'

'He has feelings, all right.' Some of the bitterness came through now, and she savored the taste of it on her tongue, as she might a medicine that cured madness. 'He's talked to Carrick.'

'I knew it.' Triumphant, Brenna slapped a hand on the table. 'I knew you'd be the third. You knew, didn't you, Jude?'

'Logically, it followed.' But Jude was watching Darcy again. 'You haven't seen Carrick, or Gwen, have you?'

'Apparently neither of them has time to chat with the likes of me.' And she wasn't sure if she was relieved or annoyed by the fact. 'However, they've time for Magee. He told me that Carrick's aiming toward the two of us, and wanted me to know – made it very clear – that he's no intention of falling in love with the legend. He's not looking for love and vows of forever from me, no indeed. He wants me,' she muttered, her eyes going dark, narrowing, sparking. 'In bed, and for his recording label. I've accommodated him on the first, to our mutual enjoyment, and I may just accommodate him on the second. But he's going to find Darcy Gallagher doesn't come cheap.'

Jude felt a twinge of apprehension. 'What do you have in mind?'

Her eyes might have been wet, but determination flashed through them. 'I'll have him crawling, belly down, before I'm done with him.'

'I don't suppose you considered meeting on equal ground?'

'Hah.' Darcy sat again. 'If I'm to be miserable and confused and scared to the bone, then by God, he'll be the same before I'm finished. When he's blind in love with me, I'll get a ring on my finger before he gets his vision back.'

'And then?' Jude murmured.

That part of the business was murky, so Darcy dismissed it with a shrug. 'Then the rest takes care of itself. It's the now I have to deal with.'

CHAPTER 14

For Darcy, the now had already started, and she didn't intend to fall behind. Back at the pub, she went directly to the kitchen. Irritated that Shawn wasn't in yet, as he made better coffee than she, she began to measure and brew. Once it was on, she checked her appearance in the mirror she'd hung by the door.

A little damp and windswept, she decided. Perfect.

She poured a mugful, gave her cheeks a quick slap to be sure her color was up, then stepped back out into the thin rain.

She had to pick her way over rubble and debris, skirting the thick block wall. Trevor wasn't up on the scaffold, which pleased her. She could hardly climb up herself and deliver the coffee. Still, she paused for a moment, looking up at the men who scrambled around. With timber now, which she could only suppose was for the roof. If she concentrated, she could almost see how it was to slope up into a gentle rise as if it had grown somehow out of Gallagher's rather than been added on.

It was a clever design, and clever of Trevor, she

thought, to have seen that in Brenna's drawing. But he'd be a man of vision, one who could see the potential of things and had the skill to turn a supposing into reality.

Oh, she admired that. It was just one more side of him she'd found herself loving.

There was the side of him for his family as well, the love he so obviously felt for his parents. And the hurt, not so obvious, from his grandfather's lack of affection. It touched her, the loyalty and the vulnerability. It made him so much more the man.

The bastard would make a simpering fool of her if she wasn't careful.

She could see where windows and doors would go from the rough openings in the dull gray block. That block, she knew, would be faced with stone and the stone would weather until it was impossible to tell where the new began and the old left off.

A merging, she thought as she began to walk again, of tradition with change. Of Gallagher and Magee. Well, the man might have vision, but she wasn't ready for him to see just how complete she intended that merger to be.

She stepped through one of the openings. There was activity inside the walls as well. Planking had already been set over the concrete she'd watched them pour that first day. Pipes and wires and rough boards were pocking out here and there. And the din as more were drilled and set into the block was amazing.

She saw him now, crouched down beside one of his crew, eyeballing a pipe that jutted out of the wall. He was covered with a fine gray dust that she supposed came from drilling into the block. Why that, and the tool belt slung at his hips, should have set her mouth to watering was just another part of her dilemma.

Still, she wasn't so dazzled she didn't know to bide her time, and wait until he rose, grunting in answer to something his man said, and turned. Saw her.

She watched his eyes change, and it was perfect. That instant of awareness, the connection that was like a hot spark flying dangerously. It wouldn't have surprised her a bit to see it land and leave a burn mark in the floor at her feet. Delighted, she stepped toward it, and him.

'I wanted a look at what's what before I got to work.' She smiled, held out the mug. 'And I thought you could use this to ward off the damp.'

It only pleased her more that it was suspicion more than surprise that crossed his face. 'Thanks.'

'You're very welcome, indeed. I suppose I'm in the way here.' But she turned a little circle, looking. 'But it's interesting, and it's moving along so fast.'

'It's a good crew.' He knew at the first sip she'd made the coffee. It was good and strong, but she didn't have the same touch as Shawn. Suspicion grew. Just what, he wondered, did she want?

'Sometime when you're not so busy, perhaps you'd show me how it'll be.'

'I can show you now.'

'Can you? That would be lovely.'

'We'll come through the pub there.' He pointed toward the back wall of the pub that was snugged now between the new block. 'We won't cut through for a while yet. You can see the levels are different. We've sloped the breezeway down. That'll give us more height without taking the roofline out of proportion. The breezeway widens.'

'Like an open fan, I remember.'

'That's right, so it becomes the lobby rather than having it a separate area.'

'What are all these pipes stabbing out here?'

'Rest rooms, either side of the lobby area. Brenna thinks we should use the Gaelic for "Men" and "Women," the way you have in the pub. I want dark wood, planked, for the doors.' He narrowed his eyes, brought the image into his head. 'Under it all, everything will be modern, slick. But what people will see is age.'

What he saw, among the work and supplies and equipment, was the whole of it, shining and complete. 'Bare floors,' he continued. 'We'll match them to what you already have. Soft, faded colors, nothing bright or vivid. We'll have some seating in the lobby, but keep it small, intimate. Benches, I think. We'll get some art for the walls, but keep it spare and all of it Celtic.'

He glanced at her, lifted his brow when he saw her staring at him. 'What?'

'I suppose I thought you'd go for the modern and slick, outside as well as in.'

'Would you?'

She started to speak, then shook her head. 'Not here,' she realized. 'No, not here, not for this. Here you want *duachais*.'

'Okay. Since I want it, why don't you tell me what it is?'

'Oh, it's Gaelic for . . .' She waved her hand as she tried to find the right translation. 'For "tradition." No, not just that. It has to do with a place most particularly, and its roots and its lore. With, well, with what and why it is.'

His eyes narrowed, focused. 'Say it again.'

'It's *duachais*.'

'Yeah, that's it. That's just exactly it.'

'You're very right about wanting that here, and I'm glad of it.'

'And considerably surprised by it.'

'A bit anyway, yes. I shouldn't be.' Because his perception unsettled her, she moved away. 'And into the theater?'

'Yeah, doors again, two across.' He took her hand, an absentminded gesture that neither of them noticed. But others did.

'The audience area, three sections, two aisles. Full house is two hundred and forty. Small again, and intimate. The stage is the star here. I can see you there.'

She said nothing, only studied the empty space ahead of her.

He waited a beat. 'Are you afraid of performing?'

'I've performed all my life.' One way or another, she thought. 'No, I've no stage fright, if that's what you mean. Maybe I need to build that image in my head, as you're building your theater, and see if it stands as sturdy. You're proud of what you've done and what you're doing. I intend to be the same.'

It wasn't why she'd come out. She'd meant to surprise him, to flirt with him, to make certain he thought of her through the day. Wanted her through the day.

'I like your theater, Trevor, and I'll be pleased to sing in it with my brothers, as discussed. As for the rest' – she moved her shoulders, took his empty mug – 'I need a bit more convincing. We'll likely have a session tonight.' She'd make sure of it. 'Why don't you have your supper here, stay for it. Then after, you can come into my parlor. This time I'll pour the wine.'

Rather than wait for his answer, she slid her free hand into his hair, lifted her mouth to his. And with the promise of more, should he care for it, in her eyes, she turned and walked away.

The minute she opened the kitchen door she smelled the baking. Apples, cinnamon, brown sugar. Shawn must have come in just behind her, and had been busy since. There was a pot already simmering on the stove, and he was chopping whatever else he intended to put in it on the thick board.

He barely glanced at her. 'You can put apple crumble as the sweet on the daily, and Mexican chile as well. We have some fresh plaice, for frying.'

Rather than spring into action, she wandered to the refrigerator and got herself a bottle of ginger ale. Here, she thought, sipping it and eyeing her brother, was a source that would be brutally honest and one she trusted completely.

'What do you think of my voice?' she demanded.

'I could do with hearing a good deal less of it.'

'It's my singing voice I'm referring to, you bonehead.'

'Well, thus far, it's cracked no glass that I'm aware of.'

She considered heaving the bottle at him, but she wasn't done with it. 'I'm asking you a serious question, and you could do me the courtesy of answering in kind.'

Because her tone had been stiff rather than hot as expected, he lowered his knife and gave her his full attention. The broody look she was wearing he was well accustomed to, but not when there was real worry in her eyes.

'You've a beautiful voice, strong and true. You know that as well as I do.'

'No one hears themselves as others do.'

'I like hearing you sing my music.'

That, she thought, was the most simple and most perfect of answers. Her eyes warmed and rather than throw the bottle, she set it aside to hug him.

'What's all this now?' He rubbed a hand over

her back, patted when she sighed and rested her head on his shoulder.

'What does it feel like, Shawn, to have sold your music? To know people will hear it, people who don't know you? Is it grand?'

'In part, aye, in part it's the grandest thing. And it's scary and befuddling all at the same time.'

'And still, deep down, it was what you always wanted.'

'It was. Keeping it deep down meant it didn't have to be scary and befuddling.'

'I like singing, but not as my life's ambition. It's just what we do, when the mood strikes. The Gallagher way.' She drew back. 'Tell me this, then, now that you are selling your music, does it take any of the joy out of it, or make it seem like no more than a job?'

'I thought it might, but no. When I sit down and there's a tune in my head, it's just the tune as it always was.' He stroked a finger under her chin. 'What is it, darling? Tell me the trouble.'

'Trevor wants to record me. Like a contract. Like a career. He thinks my voice will sell.'

There were a dozen things he could say, jokes that any brother might spring to out of habit and that odd affection. Instead, because he sensed she needed it, he gave her the easy truth. 'You'll be wonderful, and send us all mad with pride.'

She let out a sound that ended in a shaky laugh. 'But it wouldn't be like a session or a *ceili*. It would be real.'

'You'll travel, and get rich, which is what you've always wanted. And it'll come from what's inside you, which is the only way it'll make you happy.'

She picked up the ginger ale again. 'You're awfully smart all of a sudden.'

'I've always been smart. You only admit it when I agree with you.'

'Hmm.' She sipped again, her mind working quickly now, picking its way through obstacles and traps. 'You and Brenna are working together in a sort of way. I mean you write the music, but she pushes it. She's the one who arranged for Trevor to hear it. She's in a way of being your business agent, or partner, or whatever you might call it.'

Shawn's answer was a grunt as he picked up his knife and began chopping again. 'She can get on her bossy side about it, let me tell you.'

That had Darcy biting her lip. 'Does it cause problems between you?'

'None that wouldn't pass if she'd mind her own.' But when he glanced up again and saw Darcy's face, he laughed. 'Well, for heaven's sake, why the worry? I'm just winding you up a bit. It's true enough she pushes, and I can dig in when she shoves too fast and too hard. But I know it's that she believes in me. It matters, nearly as much as it does that she loves me.'

The pang inside her heart came hard and unwelcome. 'The believing in could be as important, as satisfying, to some. As a start, anyway. As a start,' she repeated in a murmur. 'You can't finish until you start.'

Determined to believe it, she took her apron off the hook and went into the pub, leaving Shawn frowning after her.

It was never hard to arrange for a session at Gallagher's. A word here, a word there. What better way was there, after all, to spend a rainy spring evening than with music and drink, with strangers and friends?

By eight, the pub was packed and pints were flowing. Brenna had already moved behind the bar to lend a hand, and Darcy felt she herself had served enough stew to make an ocean.

And Trevor Magee had yet to darken the door.

The devil take him, she decided, and had a table of tourists glancing around uneasily as she served their drinks with a smile that glittered sharp and bright as a blade.

If he couldn't be bothered to accept her invitation for supper, music, and sex, what was the man made of? Stone? Ice? Steel? She slammed empties on the counter and had Aidan's full attention.

'Mind the glassware, Darcy. We've hardly one to spare with the crowd we have tonight.'

'Bugger them,' she said under her breath. 'Two pints Guinness, one Smitty's, half of Harp, and two brandy and gingers.'

'Take a water to Jude, would you, while the Guinness is settling, and see if you can talk her into having some stew. Her appetite's been off the last day or so.'

She wanted to snap, just on principle, but it wasn't possible to take a bite out of a man who looked so concerned over his wife. Instead she simply went back to the kitchen herself, ladled out stew, added a basket of bread and butter. She carried them, with water and a glass of ice, to Jude's table.

'Now, you're to eat,' Darcy said as she set down the food. 'Else Aidan'll be worried, Shawn insulted, and I'll just be mad.'

'But I—'

'I mean it, Jude Frances. You've my niece or nephew to take care of, and I won't have him or her, as the case may be, going hungry.'

'It's just that . . .' She glanced around, motioned Darcy to lean down. 'The last couple of days, about five or so, I've had this terrible craving. I can't do anything about it, can't seem to stop myself. Ice cream,' she whispered. 'Chocolate ice cream. I swear I've eaten two gallons of it this week, bought the market out of it.'

Darcy snorted out a laugh. 'Well, what's wrong with that? You're entitled.'

'It's so clichéd. I'm not eating pickles with it or anything ridiculous, but just the same. I feel so stupid about it, I haven't been able to tell Aidan.'

'Do the crime, pay the consequences.' Darcy nudged the bowl closer. 'Besides, that's no way to feed a baby. You have a bit of Shawn's stew, and

276

for being such a sport and saving this seat for that cad Magee, I'll buy your ice cream tomorrow.'

Struggling not to pout, Jude picked up her spoon. 'Chocolate. And the cad just walked in.'

'Did he?' Pride, and not a little slice of temper, made her refuse to turn around. 'It's about bloody time. What's he doing?' Casually, she picked up Jude's bottle of water and poured it.

'He's scoping, the way men do. Hunting for you, I'd say. Ah, bull's-eye. God, the way he looks at you. It's wonderful, hot and proprietary with a little edge of aloofness. He's got a man with him, very polished and urban and attractive, who looks amused and out of place.'

Without thinking, Jude ate a spoonful of stew. 'They look like friends,' she went on. 'The one laid a hand on Trev's shoulder, buddy-like, gestured toward the bar. But Trev's shaking his head, giving it a nod in this direction. His friend's just got a load of you now, and his eyebrows went straight up, almost to hairline. I'm surprised his tongue didn't fall out.'

Impressed, Darcy angled her head. 'You're awfully good at this sort of business, aren't you?'

'Psychologist, writer. They both observe. I'm just much better, thank God, at writing about people than analyzing them. So, I'm looking forward to hearing the music tonight,' she went on, raising her voice enough to signal Darcy she could and wanted to be heard. 'I'm glad I got a table before we were overrun.'

'We'd just plant you in a chair behind the bar. Eat your stew now, before it goes cold.'

'I really don't – well, hello, Trevor.'

Prepared now, Darcy did turn, offered a friendly smile. 'Aren't you the lucky one. Jude's got a table here I'm sure she'd be glad to share with you. We're jammed tonight.' Then she shifted that same smile to the man beside Trevor and had the pleasure of seeing pure male appreciation in his eyes. 'And good evening to you.'

'Darcy Gallagher, Jude Gallagher, Nigel Kelsey. A friend of mine.'

'It's nice to meet you.'

'Trevor didn't tell me I'd be bombarded by beauties.' He took Jude's hand first, kissed it smoothly, then repeated the gesture with Darcy.

'You've brought us a charmer, Trevor. Have a seat here, and tell me what's your pleasure to drink. I've got to pick up an order at the bar that's overdue.'

'G and T for me,' Nigel ordered.

'Ice and lemon?'

'Yes, thanks.'

'Pint of Harp,' Trevor told her.

'Right away, then. And the stew's good tonight, if you're in the mood for it.'

'Or if you're not,' Jude muttered as Darcy moved off.

'So, you're the American writer who married the publican.' Nigel, in his urban black sweater, jacket, and slacks took a stool.

And looked, Jude thought, like a bohemian at a barn dance.

'I came over as an American, found out I was a writer. You're from England?' she asked, tagging his accent.

'London, born and bred. Trev was right about this place,' he added with a glance around. 'It's authentic, a movie set. Damn near perfect.'

'We like to think so.'

'Nigel doesn't mean to be patronizing.' Trevor took the seat beside Jude in the narrow booth. 'He's just an ass.'

'I meant it as a compliment. English pubs, certainly in the city, tend to be a bit more reserved than those you find in Ireland. And rarely have barmaids with faces like film stars.'

He swiveled to take another look at Darcy. 'I think I'm in love.'

'A complete ass. You're not eating,' Trevor said to Jude. 'Is Darcy wrong about tonight's stew?'

'No.' Guilty, Jude took another spoonful. 'It's wonderful. It's just I'm not really hungry. I had a late . . . mmmm.'

'Cravings?' When she flushed, Trevor laughed. 'For my sister, all three times, it was Fig Newtons for breakfast. She ate truckloads.'

'Chocolate ice cream, at teatime. Gallons.' Jude shot a wary glance toward Aidan. 'I haven't made a full confession yet. Aidan's afraid I'll waste away.' She put a hand on her belly. 'As if.'

'Here we are, now, gin and tonic and a Harp.'

Darcy set them down. 'Will you have a meal with us, then?'

'We'll have the stew,' Trevor said before Nigel could order. 'Will you sing later?'

'I might.' With a saucy wink, she sauntered off.

'I might have wanted a look at the menu,' Nigel complained.

'You're coming to the lady's rescue here. We eat the same thing, and that way we can each take a portion of her stew and save her.'

'God bless you,' Jude said with feeling and passed Trevor the basket of bread.

Their bowls had barely been served when music started. Just a fiddle and pennywhistle at first from a couple of the people crammed around the table at the front. The table itself was loaded with pints and glasses, ashtrays and packs of cigarettes.

Conversation didn't stop with the music, but it lowered. It was Darcy, Trevor noted, who worked the table, taking away the empties, the overflowing ashtrays and replacing them with fresh. An old man with a squeeze box gave her a little pat on the bottom, in much the same way an adult pats a baby, then, tapping his foot, picked up the tune and filled it out.

'That's Brian Fitzgerald on the fiddle,' Jude told them. 'We're cousins of some sort. And that's young Connor on the pennywhistle and Matt Magee, likely a cousin of yours, Trevor, on the little accordion. The young woman with the guitar is Patty Riley, and I don't know the other woman, the other fiddler. I don't think she's local or I would.'

280

Nigel nodded, sampled his stew. 'Do you get many musicians in for an informal who aren't local?'

'All the time. Gallagher's has a reputation with its sessions, formal and informal.' She looked on Trevor with warm affection when he casually spooned some of her stew into his bowl, then Nigel's. 'I'd name the baby after you for this, but Aidan would be suspicious.'

'It's not a hardship. Shawn's a genius.'

'I thought Trev was exaggerating the culinary skills of our newest artist.' Happily now, Nigel dug into the stew again. 'I should've known better. He's never wrong.'

It was the laugh that caught Nigel first. Warm, female, sexy. He glanced over, toward it, and watched as Darcy laid a hand on the old man's shoulder, counted off the time with her toe, then caught the tune with her voice.

> *As I was going over the far-famed Kerry mountains/I met with Captain Farrell and his money he was counting.*

He laid his spoon down, focused, and shut out the background noise.

> *I first produced me pistol, and then produced me rapier/Saying stand and deliver for you are my bold deceiver.*

It was a bright, jumpy song with bouncy lyrics. Nothing that put great demands on a voice but for its quickness. But it took no more than the first verse for him to know.

He looked at Trevor, nodded. 'No, you're never wrong.'

There were reels, jigs, waltzes, and ballads, with or without voices joining in. When Shawn finally came out of the kitchen, Nigel got his first look at the three Gallaghers together.

'Excellent genes there,' he murmured, and Jude beamed.

'Aren't they beautiful? And listen,' she added when they began to sing of the bold Fenian men.

Despite her enjoyment of her family, she caught the look that passed between Nigel and Trevor. These, she thought, were men who had something to say to each other, and wouldn't while she could hear. Well, she owed them. So when the song was over, she patted Trevor's arm.

'I'm going for a quiet cup of tea in the kitchen.' And then slip out the back door and home. 'Thanks for the company and the rescue. Lovely to meet you, Nigel. Enjoy your stay with us.'

She started to scoot out, couldn't manage it, then was grateful once again as Trevor somehow got her smoothly to her feet. Now, following impulse, she kissed his cheek. 'Good night.'

As the fiddlers had gone into a duel, Nigel had only to wait until Jude was two steps away before she was out of earshot. 'They're a gold mine.'

'That may be, but Aidan won't give up the pub, and neither will Shawn.' Trevor nursed his single pint. 'They'll do the performance here, and the recording. That's for family, and for Gallagher's, but the long term. No.'

'You didn't mention Darcy.'

'I'm working on her. Her loyalty's here, too, and with her brothers. But she has a taste for the rich life. I just have to convince her she can have both.' He drummed his fingers, watching as one of the fiddlers passed her the instrument instead of his empty pint. Then rose to refill it himself while she picked up the tune.

'With a face like that, a voice like that, and Christ, listen to her play, she can have anything she wants.'

'I know.' The fact that it didn't entirely please him had Trevor setting down his glass. 'And so, believe me, does she.'

'No naive Irish lass, huh? Still, I've never known you to fail when your mind's set. You'll sign her, Trev.' Nigel lit one of his dwindling pack of Players, eyed Trevor through the smoke. 'What else are you looking for from her?'

Too much for comfort, Trevor thought. Entirely too much. 'I haven't decided.'

'If you decide to keep it strictly business, I wouldn't mind—' He cut himself off when Trevor's eyes, scalpel-sharp, met his. 'I think we'll just leave that unsaid. I'll just go to the bar and order another G and T.'

283

'Good idea.'

'I think so, as we haven't snarled over a girl since first term at Oxford, and you won that one anyway.' Nigel rose, nodded toward Trevor's glass. 'Another pint?'

'No, thanks. I'll just keep my head clear. And Nigel, make this one your last, will you? You'll be driving back to the cottage on your own.'

'I see. You always were a lucky bastard.'

Luck, as far as Trevor could see, was only part of what he would need to handle Darcy Gallagher.

He waited for her, in what she liked to call her parlor. And waited restlessly among her pretty things. The scent of her seemed to be everywhere, a subtle reminder that kept him on edge.

He didn't want a reminder. He wanted her.

Everything in her rooms was feminine. Not the flouncy sort, but the sleek. Slippery pillows he had no idea she'd made herself were tossed artistically over the couch. A tall, slim vase held tall, slim flowers with bold red heads.

There was a painting on the wall of a mermaid, wild wet hair of gleaming black raining down her back and naked breasts as she surfaced in a triumphant arch of body from a blue sea.

It was stunning, sensual and somehow innocent.

It was simply and rather beautifully rendered. Anyone seeing it would note the resemblance, he was sure, in the shape of the face, the full curve of lips.

He wondered when Darcy had posed for it and immediately wanted to strangle the artist.

That, he realized, was a serious problem, every bit as serious as this unrelenting desire for her. He detested jealousy and possessiveness in relationships. They weren't just deadly, weren't just weak, they were . . . unproductive.

He needed to step back, clear himself out of this sexual haze he'd been in ever since he'd seen her at the damn window.

Then she opened the door, and that haze simply engulfed him.

'Did you send Nigel off to home all by himself, then?' She closed the door behind her, leaned back against it.

'He's a big boy.'

She reached down, flipped the lock. 'I hope you told him not to wait up.'

Trevor stepped to her. 'You've been on your feet all night.'

'That I have, and they're letting me know it.'

'Why don't I get you off them?' He scooped her up and into his arms.

Chuckling, she nuzzled his neck. 'Well, what do you know, that's better already.'

'Sweetheart, you ain't seen nothing yet.'

CHAPTER 15

'Coffee.'

A man couldn't be expected to survive on three hours' sleep without coffee. Sex might satisfy, food might fuel, love might sustain, but without coffee, what was the point?

Especially at five-thirty in the morning.

He'd showered, pulled on his jeans, but he couldn't go another step without the true blood of life.

'Coffee,' he said again, directly against Darcy's ear as she snuggled into her pillow. 'Please, tell me where it is.'

'Mm.' She shifted, turned lazily, hooked an arm around his neck. 'Too early.'

'It's never too early for coffee, or too late. Darcy, I'm begging you, just tell me where you keep it.'

She opened her eyes then, and the light was still dim enough to keep her floating on memories of the night. Which saved him from wrath. 'You need a shave.' She lifted her other hand, rubbed it over his cheek. 'Ah, you look so rough and male and dangerous. Come back to bed.'

Sex with a beautiful woman. Coffee. It was one

of life's most difficult choices. The man who could have both was a king. But first things first.

He slid his hands under the sheets, under her warm, soft body. And hauled her up out of bed. 'You can show me where it is.'

It took her a moment to realize he was carting her into the kitchen. 'Trevor! I'm bare-assed naked here.'

'Are you?' He glanced down, let his gaze roam. 'Imagine that. Coffee, Darcy, and the world is yours.'

She sniffed, huffed. 'Promises like that are kept as often as pigs fly.' She gestured to a cupboard, then squealed when he unceremoniously set her warm and naked ass down on the counter. 'Bastard.'

'I don't see it.'

'Men don't see anything that's under their noses.'

She shifted, muttering curses, and pushed a couple of tins aside. 'There. If it'd been a snake it would've bitten you between the eyes. And now I suppose you'll be wanting me to make it for you.'

It was such a lovely thought. Hopeful, he laid his palms on either side of her, nipped and nuzzled her sulky mouth. 'Would ya?'

If he hadn't been so bloody handsome, with his hair shiny and damp from his shower, his face darkened with stubble, those wonderful gray eyes so sleepy, she'd have beaned him with the can.

'Oh, move aside and let me go get my robe.'

'Why?'

She slitted her eyes instead. 'Because I'm cold.'

'Oh.' He nodded. 'Reasonable. I'll get it.' He plucked her off the counter, brushed a kiss over her forehead, then went to find her robe.

Yawning hugely, Darcy filled the kettle, got out the pot and filter. She was starting to shiver as she measured out the coffee when Trevor came back with her robe.

He studied the paraphernalia as she bundled herself into the robe. 'I'll have to buy you an automatic one.'

'I don't make coffee often enough for it to be worth-while. I start my day with tea most usually.'

'That's just . . . sick.'

'Ah, such a weakness. It's nice to find one. There. We just wait for the kettle now.' She reached up to get him a mug, and looked so pretty doing it, rising on her toes, shaking back her tumbled hair, that he was dizzy with . . .

Just dizzy, he told himself. Just dizzy from the picture she made.

'But don't think I'm making you breakfast.'

He had to touch her, just touch. So he slipped his arms around her, pressing his lips to the side of her neck as he brought her back against him. 'You're so mean.'

Her heart jumped, then beat thickly. The gesture was so simple, so warm, so full of the sweetness of intimacy that frantic sex could never achieve.

She squeezed her eyes shut and was careful, very careful, to keep her voice light.

'Well, now, aren't you affectionate of a morning?'

He wasn't, not as a rule. He'd have puzzled over it if it hadn't felt so good to just hold her. 'Any woman makes me coffee, I shower her with affection. If she makes me breakfast, I'm her slave.'

'The waitresses in New York City must fight for your table.' She laid her hands over the ones he'd linked around her waist. Just for a moment she wanted that illusion of quiet, settled love. 'Myself, I'm not in the market for a slave, but you're welcome to whatever you can forage.'

He settled for toast, since she didn't seem to have much else, and leaned against the counter while it browned and she poured boiling water over the waiting grounds.

'God.' He breathed deep. 'How does anyone live without the smell of that in the morning?' He gave her a pitying look. 'Tea.'

'You Yanks drink so much of it, you don't know it doesn't taste near as good as it smells.'

'Blasphemy. There's a deli two blocks from where I live. Now, they make coffee that brings tears of gratitude to a man's eye.'

'You miss that.' Since it did smell seductive, she got down a mug for herself. 'The delis, the hustle-bustle.' She opened the refrigerator and got out her little carton of cream. 'What else do you miss about New York?'

The toast popped. 'Bagels.'

'Bagels?' She got out butter and jam as well, then just stood holding them and staring at him. 'A man of your resources, and what you miss about New York is coffee and bagels?'

'Right at this moment, I'd pay a hundred dollars for a fresh bagel. No offense to your Irish soda bread. But, really.'

'Well, that's a wonder.'

He started to make some joke, but the glorious scent that filled the kitchen had his mind clicking in. It was, he decided, too good an opening to pass up.

'New York's got more to offer than coffee and bagels – though they shouldn't be lightly dismissed.' He put the toast on the plate she offered him. 'Restaurants, theater, art – and for the materialistic, anything and everything that can be bought. You'd love it.'

'Because I'm materialistic?'

'Because if you know what you want, it's next to impossible not to find it there. Thanks.' He accepted the mug with deep and sincere gratitude. 'It's one of the places you'd go if you signed with Celtic.'

And so, she thought, the door closes on intimacy and opens to business. There was no point in regretting it. 'And why would I go to New York?'

'The same reason you'd go to Dublin, London, Chicago, L.A., Sydney, wherever. Concerts, media, exposure.'

She added cream and sugar to her own brew.

'It's a lot to promise when you don't know how I'll record, or perform, or stand up to the kind of life that would make.'

'I do know. It's my business to know.'

'You've a lot of businesses, Trevor, and I'll wager you're good at each and every one. But it's this particular one that concerns me. I take your word on this and make this change, I change every-thing. It's a lot for me to risk because you like the sound of my voice.'

She held up a hand before he could speak. 'You'd risk as well, I understand that. You'd be making an investment in me. But that's what you do, isn't it? You make investments, and if one doesn't pay off, another does, so it's no great loss. A disap-pointment, an annoyance, but not your life.'

'Point taken,' he said after a moment. 'Get dressed.'

'I beg your pardon?'

'Get dressed. I think I have a way to settle your mind on part of this.' He glanced at the kitchen clock. 'Make it fast, will you?'

'You've your nerve, don't you? Ordering me about this way, and at six in the morning at that.'

He started to ask what the hell the time had to do with it, then wisely concluded that arguing would only force her to dig in her heels. 'Sorry. Would you come with me? It won't take long, and it does go to your point. Your very valid point.'

'Clever, aren't you? Well, I'll go because I'm up

and about anyway. But keep in mind I'm not on your payroll, and I don't jump when you snap.'

She turned and stalked back to the bedroom. Satisfied, Trevor finished his breakfast.

For the second time that morning, Trevor roused someone out of sleep. In this case, the results weren't as cozy.

'Bloody fucking hell' was Nigel's response. 'If your lady's kicked you out of bed at this godforsaken hour, take the sofa. I'm not budging, and I'm not sharing.'

'I don't want to get in the bed, I want you to get out of it. Darcy's downstairs.'

One of the eyes Nigel had firmly shut popped open. 'Does that mean *you're* sharing?'

'Remind me to punch you later. Right now, get up, get dressed, and make yourself presentable.'

'No one's presentable at . . . Jesus, six-thirty in the morning!'

'I'm pressed for time, Nigel.' Trevor turned and started out. 'Five minutes.'

'At least put the bloody coffee on,' Nigel shouted.

'I'm not making it this time,' Darcy said firmly the minute Trevor came down the steps. She had her arms folded over her breasts and a steely look in her eye. She'd already made it known, in no uncertain terms, that she hadn't appreciated Trevor rushing her along.

'No problem.' He snagged her hand and pulled

292

her with him toward the kitchen. 'Do you want some tea this time?'

'I won't be placated by a cup of tea. You barely gave me time to put on my lipstick.'

'You don't need it.'

Since he hadn't yet put the kettle on, he had to assume the hissing sound came from her and not from boiling water. 'Oh, it's ever like a man to say something so stupid and think it's a compliment.'

He got the kettle going, then turned back to her. 'You are,' he said, very deliberately, 'the most beautiful woman I've ever seen. And I've seen a considerable number of beautiful women.'

She only huffed and sat at the table. 'Flattery isn't going to help you.'

It surprised them both when he walked to her, cupped her face in his hands, lifted it. 'You take my breath away, Darcy. That's not flattery, that's fact.'

Her heart fluttered. There was no help for it, and no way to stop the emotion from swirling into her eyes. 'Trevor.' She murmured it, drawing him to her, then again with her lips against his.

And it was there, suddenly, like light. The love and the longing, the wishes yet unsaid. For an instant, for the time it takes a needy heart to beat, she felt him answer it, and her world shimmered like a jewel.

Music, she swore she heard it. The romance of harp-song, the celebration of pipes, the lusty beat of drums. The sound she made, her mouth warm on his, was a kind of song. A single note of joy.

'Sorry to interrupt,' Nigel said dryly from the doorway. 'But you did tell me to hurry it up.'

The light fractured, wavered. Trevor drew back, his hands still framing her face, his eyes still on hers. Then he stepped away, and the music died.

'Yeah.' Something was echoing in his head, in his heart, but he couldn't get hold of it. He rubbed a hand over his shirt, as beneath it the silver disk seemed abruptly hot against his heart.

Behind him the kettle shrilled, one long scream of frustration. Trevor turned and shut it off with a restrained anger that made no sense to him.

'Good morning, Darcy.' Nigel thought it was like stepping into raw nerves, but he kept his polished and pleasant expression in place. 'Can I offer you some coffee once it's done?'

'No, thanks all the same, but I've had some already. After my rude awakening this morning.'

'Ah.' Deciding to make the best of it, Nigel sat across from her at the table. 'When our Trevor gets in a mood, no one is safe. He's a tidal wave.'

'Is he, now?'

'Christ, yes.' Nigel lit his first cigarette of the day. 'You get swept along, or you drown. Of course, it's one of the ways he gets things done when he wants and as he wants.'

Enjoying herself now, Darcy leaned forward. 'Tell me more.'

'He's a single-minded individual, and detours only rarely – when he deems it worth his while.

294

Ruthless, some would say, and they wouldn't be wrong.' He paused, blew out smoke. 'But he's a boy who loves his mother.'

'Shut up, Nigel,' Trevor ordered when Darcy laughed.

'Not until I've had my coffee.'

'Oh, and dare you cross him in such a way?'

'He loves me, too.' Nigel sent Trevor a glittering look as he brooded by the stove. 'Who wouldn't?'

'I'm growing fond of you myself. And what more should I know of this ruthless individual who loves his mother?'

'He's got a brain like a blade – bright and sharp, and a loyal if stubborn heart. A generous man, Trevor, but never one to be taken advantage of. He admires efficiency, honesty, and creativity in all things. And his way with the ladies is known far and wide.'

'That'll do.' Annoyed but unruffled, Trevor set a mug in front of Nigel.

'Oh, but I'm sure he's just getting started,' Darcy protested. 'And the topic is greatly fascinating to me.'

'I've got one that should be more fascinating to you. Nigel heads up the London branch of Celtic Records. However irritating he might be on a personal level, he's unerringly astute on a professional one.'

'True.' Nigel took a sip. 'Too true.'

'You heard Darcy sing last night, in a pub, without mikes, filters, orchestration, rehearsal.

295

In what we could call the most informal of venues. What was your impression?'

'She's very good.'

'We're not negotiating here, Nigel,' Trevor said. 'Not diddling terms. Tell her what you thought, straight out.'

'All right.' Nigel replied. 'Once in a while, in my profession, you stumble across a jewel, a diamond – no, in your case we'll use sapphire because it goes with your eyes. A rare, brilliant, undiscovered jewel. That's what I heard at Gallagher's last night. I'd love to put that jewel in the proper setting.'

'I'll leave it to you to explain what that setting might be. I have to get to the site. I'm already late.' Trevor picked up his keys from the counter where Nigel had tossed them the night before. 'I'll leave the car for you.'

She could only stare blindly at the keys. 'Thanks, but I'll just walk back. It'll clear my head, and I'd prefer it.'

'Suit yourself.' But he leaned down, rested his hands on her shoulders. 'I have to go.'

'It's not a problem. Come have lunch at the pub, since you had to make do with such a skimpy breakfast.'

'If there's time.' He kissed her lightly before turning to Nigel. 'Come down and have a look at the site later. The walk will do your city legs good.'

'Thanks very much.' As Trevor left, Nigel rose to top off his coffee. 'Sure you won't have a cup, Darcy?'

'No, I'm fine, thanks.'

He poured out, sat again, smiled. 'So—'

He stopped when Darcy held up a hand. 'Please, I have a question. Would you have said what you did just now if I wasn't sleeping with Trevor? Be honest,' she continued as his eyes flickered. 'I won't tell him your answer, you have my word on that, but the truth here is important to me.'

'The truth, then. It would have been easier, and suited me more comfortably, to be able to tell you what I just did if you weren't sleeping with Trevor.'

'I'd have preferred it as well, but here we are. I hope you'll take this as truth as well. I'm not sleeping with Trevor so he'll offer me a big contract.'

'Understood.' Nigel paused, considered. 'Is having a personal relationship with him what's stopping you from agreeing to a professional one?'

'I don't know. He wouldn't make a habit of having a personal relationship with his artists, would he? It's not his style.'

'No, it's not.' Interesting, Nigel mused. No, fascinating. Unless he missed his guess, this was a woman in love. 'But I've never known him to be involved with anyone he hoped to sign for the label. I'd have to say all bets are off in this case.'

No, she thought, it was a wager still. The biggest of her life. 'If I signed with Celtic, what would be expected of me?'

Nigel's grin was all charm. 'Oh, Trevor, he expects everything. And he gets it.'

She relaxed enough to chuckle. 'Give me the high points then, and the lows as well.'

'You'll deal with directors, producers, musicians, marketing, consultants, assistants. It's not just your voice we want, but the package, and everyone will have ideas or demands for presenting that package. However, my impression is that you're a smart woman, and self-aware, so you'd know the package is already as perfect as it can get.'

'Meaning if I was toad ugly or couldn't string two coherent sentences together you'd find ways to remake the package.'

'Or use the flaws. You'd be amazed at what a clever publicity campaign can do with flaws. Regardless, the work you'll do will be hard, the hours long, and not all the choices will go your way. You'll be tired, annoyed, frustrated, baffled, stressed, and . . . are you temperamental?'

'Me?' She deliberately fluttered her lashes. 'Of course I am.'

'Add blowups, sulks, and rages, then – and that's just in the first recording session.'

Darcy rested her chin on her fist. 'I like you, Nigel.'

'That's mutual, so I'm going to tell you this – which if I didn't like you, I'd leave out. If you and Trevor continue as you are, people will talk. Not all of them kindly. Some will snipe and scratch and mutter that the only reason you got a contract is because you're shagging the boss. They'll make sure you feel that in dozens of nasty, petty ways. It won't be easy on you.'

'Or him.'

'They won't let him know, unless they're very, very stupid. And the petty and jealous are rarely stupid. You can cry on his shoulder, of course.'

Her head snapped up, her eyes kindled. 'I don't cry on any man's shoulder.'

'I bet you don't,' he said quietly. 'But if it comes down to it, Darcy, I hope you'll use mine.'

She was glad she'd chosen to walk back to the village. There were so many thoughts buzzing around in her head. How long it would take to separate them, consider each one, she didn't know. She only knew that it had to be done.

She asked herself what she would do if there was nothing between herself and Trevor but the offer. The answer came quicker than she expected. She'd take it, of course. It would be a grand adventure, and a chance for more. And if she failed, there was no shame in it. Better, if she succeeded, there was the lush life she'd always imagined.

And all because she could sing. Wasn't that astounding?

The work Nigel had spoken of didn't worry her over-much. She wasn't afraid of working hard. The travel was something she'd always dreamed of. The niggle came from the fact that she had no driving ambition to perform. But perhaps that was to the good. Without that force and need, mightn't she enjoy it more?

She'd have money to lavish on herself, her family, her friends. Oh, she'd have no problem at all with the money.

But it all circled back. There was something between herself and Trevor, and on her part it was more vital than anything had been in her life.

She had to make him love her.

It was so irritating not to know if she was making progress there. The man was much too self-contained for her peace of mind. With her mouth set in a pout, she tugged a fuchsia blossom from the hedge and tore it to pieces as she walked down the narrow road.

Why was it when it finally happened, she'd lost her heart to a man who wasn't dazzled with her? Who wasn't eager as a puppy to please? Who didn't promise her the world on a silver platter, even if those who had done that most often hadn't had the platter, much less the world, at their disposal.

She probably wouldn't have fallen in love with him if he'd been or done any of those things, but that was beside the point. She was in love with him, so why couldn't he just love her back so everything could be lovely?

Damned perverse individual.

When he'd kissed her there in the kitchen of Faerie Hill Cottage, hadn't he felt it? Hadn't he known her heart was spilling right out of her and into his hands? Oh, she hated that she couldn't stop it.

Hated more that the first time, the only time,

she'd wanted a man to see inside her, he just wasn't looking.

So, she'd have to deal with that. She tossed the remains of the tattered blossom away, watching it whip like confetti in the brisk wind on the hill. She had plenty of tools at her disposal to employ. Sooner or later, she'd box him right in.

Damned if she wouldn't.

Before she was done, she'd be rich, famous. And married.

As she came around the bend, the sun flashed into her eyes like a beacon, sharp and white and direct. She raised a hand to shield them, blinking, and saw through the glare the glint of silver.

'Good morning to you, Darcy the fair.'

Slowly, with her heart stuttering, she lowered her hand. It hadn't been the sun at all that had beamed at her. It was filtered soft through layered stacks of clouds that turned the sky the color of Trevor's eyes. It was magic that shone out at her, and the man standing on the side of the road, under the looming spear of the round tower, owned it.

'I'm told you frequent Saint Declan's Well.'

'Oh, I'm here and there, depending. And it's rare for you to wander to that hill.'

'I'm here and there as well. Depending.'

His eyes flashed with humor, as bright as the doublet he wore. 'Since here's where you are and so am I, will you walk with me?' The iron gate opened as he spoke, though he didn't touch it with his hand.

'Men are the same. Faerie or mortal, they must show off.' Pleased when he frowned, she breezed by him and through the opening. 'I wondered if you'd ever have cause to seek me out.'

'I gave you more credit than you deserved.' There, he thought when she turned her head to glare at him. Point for point. 'I was certain a woman of your talents would have conquered any man she took aim at. But you've yet to land the Magee.'

'He's not a fish. And who put the idea in his head that he was obliged to fall in love with me so he'd get his back up about it straight off?'

'Too much Yank practicality and not enough Irish romance in him, that's his problem.' Disgusted because Darcy was right about his own miscalculation, he strode over the rough ground. 'I don't understand the man. If his blood didn't leap the minute he saw you, I'm a jack-rabbit. You should've been able to bring him to the mark by this time.'

He stopped, and his eyes burned into hers. 'You want him, don't you?'

'If I didn't, he'd never have touched me.'

'And has he touched only your body? Has he reached your heart?'

She turned, looking down, to where the village lay. 'Isn't your magic strong enough to see into my heart?'

'I want the words from you. I've learned, with pain, the power of words.'

'The ones I have are for him, not for you. They'll be spoken when I choose, not when you demand.'

302

'In the name of Finn, I knew I'd have trouble with you.'

He pondered a moment, rubbing his chin. Then with a sly smile, he raised his arms high. The air shivered, rippled like water at a stone's toss. Shapes formed behind it, shadows that spread and speared up and took on color and life. The gentle voice of the sea became a roar, a thousand sounds beating against each other.

'Look now,' Carrick ordered, but she was already staring, eyes wide, at the buildings and streets and people where her village had been. 'New York City.'

'Sweet Mary.' She had already stepped back, half afraid she would stumble and fall into that vast, crowded, wonderful world. 'Such a place.'

'You could have it, the best of it. Shops full of treasures.'

Store windows, filled with glittering jewels, sleek clothes raced by in front of her eyes.

'Elegant restaurants.'

White tablecloths, exotic flowers, the shimmer of candlelight, the glint of wine in crystal.

'Luxurious quarters.'

Polished wood and thick carpets, a fluid curve of stairs, a wide, wide window that looked out over trees gone to flame with fall.

'It's Trevor's penthouse. It could be yours.' Carrick watched the awe, the pleasure, the desire, run over her face. 'He has more. His family's getaway in a place called the Hamptons, a villa in

Italy on the sea, a pretty pied-à-terre in Paris, the town house in London.'

A house of brilliant white wood and sparkling glass with the blue water close, another in soft, pale yellow with a red tile roof tucked onto a soaring cliff over yet another blue sea, the charm of old stone and iron rails over the streets of Paris, and the dignified brick home she remembered from London. They all flashed by, made her head spin.

Then they were gone, in the blink of an eye, and there was only Ardmore sitting cozily under the layered, gray-edged clouds.

'You could have it, all of it, for with some women they've only to want to have.'

'I can't think.' Giving in to her shaky legs, she sat on the ground. 'My head aches from it.'

'What do you want?' Watching her, Carrick reached for his pouch and turning it over, poured a flood of sparkling blue stones onto the ground. 'I offered them to Gwen, but she turned from them, and from me. Would you?'

She shook her head, but not in denial. In sheer confusion.

'He gave you jewels, and you wear them.'

'I . . .' She ran her fingers over the bracelet on her wrist. 'Yes, but—'

'He looked at you and found you beautiful.'

'I know it.' The brilliance of the stones made her eyes tear. It was the shine of them, she told herself. It wasn't her heart breaking. 'But beauty doesn't last. If that's all that holds him, what happens when it fades? Am I only to be wanted for what can be seen?'

It would be enough if she wasn't in love. Enough to have only that if the man was anyone but Trevor.

'He's heard your voice and promised you fame, wealth, and a kind of immortality. What more is there? What more have you ever dreamed of?'

'I don't know.' Oh, she wanted to weep. Why should she want to weep for having seen wonders?

'You have the power, you have the choice, and here is a gift for you.'

He plucked up one of the stones and taking her hand, laid it warm in the cup of her palm. 'On this you can wish. Not three wishes, as so many of the stories go, but one only. Your heart's desire is in your hand. Be it fortune, you will live in wealth. Vanity, and your beauty will fade never. Fame, and the world will know you. Love? The man you want most is yours, always and ever.'

He stepped back from her, and if her eyes had been clear, she might have seen compassion in his. 'Choose well, Darcy the fair, for what you choose you live with.'

And he was gone, and the jewels, save the one in her hand, bloomed to flowers. She saw now they covered a grave, and the name carved into the stone was 'John Magee.'

She lay her head against it and wept now for both of them.

CHAPTER 16

Darcy intended to go straight through the pub and upstairs so she could make herself presentable. But Aidan was already there, inventorying stock. He took one look at her, set down his clipboard.

'What happened?'

'Nothing. It's nothing. I had myself a little jag, is all.'

She started through, but he simply moved in front of her, put his arms around her, pressed his lips to her hair. 'There, darling, tell me what's the matter.' His greatest fear was that Trevor had hurt her in some way, and then he'd have to kill a man who'd become a friend.

'Oh, Aidan, don't start me up again.' But she held on, and held tight. 'It's just a mood.'

'You're a moody one, no question. But one thing you're not, Darcy, is a blubberer. What's made you cry?'

'Me, mostly, I think.' It felt so good to be held by one who had never let her down. 'I have so much in my head, and it seemed the only way to let some of it out was with tears.'

He braced himself for the worst. 'Magee hasn't done anything . . .'

'He hasn't, no.' And that, she thought, was part of the problem. He'd done nothing but be what he was, what she wanted. 'Aidan, tell me something. When you went traveling all those years ago, saw all those things, all those places, was it wonderful?'

'It was. Some was grand, some bloody awful, but altogether it was wonderful.' He stroked a hand through her hair, remembering. 'I guess you could say I had a lot in my head as well back then, and rambling was my way of getting some of it out.'

'But you came back.' She drew away then, studying his face. 'Of all the places you've been and seen, you came back here.'

'Here's home. The truth is . . .' He dabbed a stray tear from her cheek with his thumb. 'I didn't think I would, not when I set out. I thought, well, here's Aidan Gallagher off to see the world and find his place in it. All the while, my place was right here, where I started. But I had to go away to come back.'

'Ma and Dad, they aren't coming back.' Her eyes filled again, though she'd have sworn she had already cried herself dry. 'Sometimes I miss them so much I can hardly stand it. It's not every day or like that, but just in the once and a while it hits me that they're thousands of miles away in Boston.'

Impatient with herself, she scrubbed her hands over her face to dry it. 'I know they've come back for the weddings, and they'll come to see your baby when it's born, but it's not the same.'

'It's not. I miss them, too.'

She nodded. Hearing him say it helped. 'I know they're happy, and that's a comfort. Every time they ring or write, they're full of news and excitement about the Gallagher's Pub they've built way over in Boston.'

'We're an international franchise now,' Aidan said, and made her laugh a little.

'Next we'll be planting one in Turkey or God knows.' She let out a little sigh. 'They're happy there, and I know I'll go over and see them one day. But it makes me think that if I went away, I might not come back either. As much as I want to go, to see places and do things, Aidan, I don't want to lose what's here.'

'It's not a matter of losing, but of changing. You won't know what changes till you go. You've been needing to go since you could stand on your own feet. I was the same. It's Shawn who's planted here and never had a question about it.'

'Sometimes I wish I were like him.' She looked up sharply. 'And if you ever tell him I said such a thing, I'll swear you're a liar.'

He laughed, tugged her hair. 'There. That's better.'

'There's more.' Sliding a hand into her pocket, she fingered the stone she carried there. 'I have to decide if Trevor has it right and I should sign his contract and have him make me a singer.'

'You are a singer.'

'It's different. You know it.'

'It is. Are you asking my opinion?'

'I'd like to weigh it in.'

'You'd be brilliant. I don't say that because I'm your brother. I have traveled and in traveling had the opportunity to hear a lot of voices. Yours shines, Darcy, and always has.'

'I could do it,' she said quietly. 'I believe I could, and not make a mess of it. More, and better, I think I'd like it. Attention,' she said with a glint in her eye, 'is food and drink to me.'

'You'd have a banquet this way, wouldn't you?'

'I would. Trevor had me go up and talk to his man this morning. Nigel, from London. He didn't paint a picture that was all rose and gilt, and I appreciated that. It would be hard work.'

'You know how to work hard. And how to dance around the task when you've had enough, which is almost as important.'

Another brick of worry tumbled off her shoulder. 'I wouldn't have to dance if you weren't such a slave driver. And I have a feeling Trevor's cut from the same cloth. He'll push me, and I won't always like it.'

'It sounds as if you've decided.'

'I suppose I have.' She waited a moment, and discovered she felt relief instead of excitement. The excitement, she thought, would come. 'I haven't quite put it all in its place as yet, and I'm not ready to tell Trevor. I prefer letting him dangle a bit longer, and perhaps nudging him toward sweetening the pot.'

'There's my girl.'

'Wheeling a deal's the Gallagher way. There's more still.' Holding her breath, she took the stone from her pocket, held it out.

It wasn't surprise she saw in his eyes so much as acknowledgment, then a kind of resignation. 'I knew you'd be the third. I didn't want to think about it.'

'Why?'

He looked at her then, eye to eye. 'My girl,' he murmured.

The force of love was so fierce it nearly dropped her. 'Oh, Aidan, you'll make me cry again.'

'We can't have that.' To give them both time to compose, he got two bottles of water from under the bar. 'So, you went up to Old Maude's grave?'

'No. Tower Hill.' She took the water, drank deeply when she realized her throat was dust-dry. 'There are flowers blooming over John Magee now. I was hardly surprised to see him. Carrick, I mean. Still, my heart shook.'

She pressed her fist to it, and in the fist she held the stone. 'It's a wonder, isn't it? He looks sharp, Carrick does, and bold. But behind his eyes is sorrow. Love is such a tangle.'

'Do you love Trevor?'

Because it seemed hot against her heart, she

310

lowered the stone. 'Yes. It's not what I thought it would be. It's not soft and easy, and it sure as hell doesn't make me feel like a queen. There's been a change in me since the minute I looked out my window and saw him. There might not have been anyone else there for a space of time, and so I should have known it was already too late to stop it.'

He knew that feeling very well, and the stuttering nerves that went with it. 'And would you, if you could?'

'I think I would. Stop it or slow it or something until I could get my breath steady. Or the man could catch up with me. He keeps himself one step back. It's a cold step and a deliberate one. I understand it, as I've taken it often enough myself. He wants me.'

She said it musingly, then caught Aidan's wince. 'Oh, don't go male and brotherly on me now when you've been doing so well.'

'I am male and your brother.' He shifted, and now he drank deep as well. 'But go on.'

'There's passion, and love would be bland without it. There's a caring that stops it from being nothing but heat. But that step, the chill in it, stops it all just short of . . . trust,' she decided. 'And acceptance.'

'One of you has to take the step forward instead of back.'

'I want it to be him.'

There was a trace of her old arrogance in her

tone. It worried Aidan as much as it amused him. She opened her fingers, letting the stone rest on her palm where, like a heart, it pulsed its blue light.

'Carrick showed me things, amazing things. I could have them, he said. I've only to wish for it. Riches and excitement, fame and glory, love and beauty. To wish for it, but only one wish, one choice.'

'What do you want?'

'All of it.' She laughed, but there was something brittle in the sound that broke his heart. 'I'm selfish and greedy and want all. I want everything I can snatch up and hold, then I want to go back and get more. Why can't I want the simple and the ordinary and the quiet, Aidan? Why can't I be content with easy dreams?'

'You're so hard on yourself, *mavourneen*. Harder than anyone else can be. Some people want the simple and the ordinary and the quiet. It doesn't make those who want the complicated and extraordinary and the exciting greedy or selfish. Wanting's wanting, whatever the dream.'

Struck, she stared at him. 'What a thought,' she managed at last. 'I never looked at it that way.'

'Study on it a while.' He brushed a fingertip over the stone, then closed her hand around it. 'And don't rush your wish.'

'That I'd already concluded for myself.' She slipped it back into her pocket where it couldn't tempt her. 'Carrick may be in a fired hurry, but I'm inclined to take my time.'

She pressed a kiss to each of Aidan's cheeks. 'You were just what I needed, just when I needed you.'

She did give it time. Her talk with Aidan had settled her and made her able to enjoy the time. As the days passed into a week, she even found herself amused that neither she nor Trevor brought up the potential business end of their relationship.

He was, she thought, as canny a negotiator as she was. One of them would break first. She didn't intend for it to be her.

Work on the theater progressed in a kind of stage by stage that she found more interesting than she would ever have believed. A change was happening right outside her window. A monumental change that had its seeds in a dream and was so much more than bricks and mortar.

She wanted it for him. That, she supposed, was the nature of love. That you could want so intensely your lover's dream to come true.

Now that most of the roof was on, she missed seeing Trevor out her window. He was inside the shell of the building as often as not. As the noise was as terrible as ever, she rarely kept her windows open on the off chance of hearing his voice.

With summer, the beaches drew people to Ardmore, and so the pub. Work kept her mind occupied, and for the first time she began to see just what the theater would mean to home.

It wasn't only the villagers and the neighbors talking of it now, but those who visited.

She could stop for a moment in the crush of a lunch shift, look around at the packed tables and bar, hear the voices, and imagine what it would be like the following summer. And she could wonder where she would be.

As both she and Trevor appreciated the distance from work, most nights she went to the cottage. It became her habit to walk whenever weather allowed, though he never failed to offer his car. She liked the quiet that slid over the air after midnight, and the balm of the breeze, and rush of starlight.

Odd, but she wasn't sure she'd really appreciated it before she'd understood she wouldn't be there forever. The softness that came from the sea, and the waves that were a constant hum and lap in the night.

When the moon was bright, she liked it best, that alone time where she could see the cliffs throw shadows.

Whenever she reached Tower Hill, she stopped. If the wind was pushing the clouds, the spear of the tower seemed to sway, and the stones, old and new, beneath it stood silent and still.

Flowers bloomed yet on the grave of Johnnie Magee. But Carrick, if he was there, chose not to show himself.

She walked on. The road narrowed, and the scatter of lights in Ardmore were lost behind her.

There was the scent now of fields and grass and growing things, then the glow out of the shadowed dark that was the lights in the cottage on the faerie hill.

He was waiting for her. And that, she thought with a delicious thrill, was just how she liked it.

As always, her heart grew lighter and she had to force herself not to rush to the gate. He called out to her the minute she stepped inside.

'Back in the kitchen.'

Now wasn't that homey, she thought, amused at both of them. The little woman home from work and the man in the kitchen. It was a bit like playing house, she supposed, and tried not to worry that the house, and the game, wasn't for either of them in the long run.

He was at the stove, which amused her. He could cook, as he'd demonstrated at that first breakfast. But he wasn't one to make a habit of it.

'Want some soup?' He stirred at the little pot, sniffed. 'It's canned, but it's food. I was stuck on the phone all night and missed dinner.'

'Thanks, no. I managed to get some of Shawn's lasagna, which I can promise tasted better than that will. If you'd called, I'd have brought you some.'

'Didn't think of it.' He turned to get a bowl out of the cupboard. One look at her, and he wanted to grab her. 'You're later than usual,' he said, keeping his tone casual as she set a bag on the counter. 'I wasn't sure you'd make it tonight.'

'We were busier than usual. I shouldn't say "usual,"' she corrected and rolled the ache from her shoulders. 'We've been packed every night this week. Aidan wants Shawn to take on some help in the kitchen, and you'd think Aidan had brought his manhood into question. Such a ruckus. They were still going at it when I left.'

'Aidan's going to need another man at the bar.'

'Well, I won't be the one to say so, as he'll have the same reaction as Shawn. I'm not having my head bit off.'

She got the kettle to fill as Trevor leaned back against the counter, spooning up soup where he stood. 'I'll have some tea to keep you company. Since you're eating, you might want to have what's in the bag with your tinned soup.'

'What is it?'

She only smiled and turned on the tap. Trevor set down his bowl, peeked in the bag. When his hand darted in, like an eager boy's into a pond after a prize frog, she laughed.

'Bagels?'

'Well, we couldn't have you pining, could we?' Delighted with his reaction, she carried the kettle to the stove. 'Shawn made them, lest you think I've been baking – and believe me you're better off I haven't. He wasn't pleased with the first batch or you'd have had them a couple of days ago. But he's well satisfied with these, so I think you'll enjoy them.'

Trevor only stood there, the plastic-wrapped

bread in his hand, staring at her as she turned on the burner under the kettle. It was ridiculous, insane, but something was stirring inside him. Warm, fluid, lovely. In defense, he struggled with a joke.

'A full dozen, too. I guess I owe you twelve hundred dollars.'

She glanced back, her face blank for a moment, then it filled with humor. 'A hundred a piece. I forgot about that. Damn, I suppose I'll have to split it with Shawn.' She patted his cheek, then reached for the tea. 'Well, no charge this time. I thought you'd enjoy a little bit of home.'

'Thank you.'

His voice was so serious, she glanced back, saw his face. His mouth was serious as well, and his eyes were dark and fixed on her. Her pulse scrambled, so she covered it with a shrug. 'You're very welcome, but it's just a bit of bread after all.'

No, it wasn't. She'd thought of it. Without even realizing how much the small gesture would mean, she'd thought of him.

He set the bag down, stepped to her, turned her. And laid his mouth on hers.

Soft, lush, long and deep. That something that stirred inside him swelled.

He drew back, half believing he'd see what it was, what it meant, in her face. But her eyes were clouded. Deep blue smoke blurring whatever was behind them.

'Well.' She was sinking, sinking without meaning

to have stepped into the bog. 'I can't wait to see what happens after you taste—'

But he silenced her. Another kiss, luxurious and tender. She was trembling, he realized, and had trembled against him before. But it was different, for both of them somehow different. The crackle of power that always snapped between them was only a low humming now, steady and true. The blood that always raced ran thick, almost lazy.

'Trevor.' His name circled in her head, slipped through her lips. 'Trevor.'

He reached behind her, switched off the burner, then lifted her into his arms. 'I want to make love with you.' And saying it, he knew it would be the first time.

She pressed her lips to the side of his throat as he carried her out. It was like sliding into a dream, she thought, one she hadn't known she had pooled inside her. Being granted a wish she hadn't known slept in her heart.

She felt . . . treasured.

When he carried her up the stairs, the romance of it made her heart ache. Music drifted through her head. Harps and flutes both low and sweet. He stopped, looked at her, and she thought he must hear it as well. Such moments were made for magic.

The bedroom windows were open, so the wind danced through the curtains and brought with it all the damp and mysterious scents of night. The moon shimmered through in silver dust.

He sat her on the bed, then moved around the room to light the candles that had been set out for practicality and never used. Their flames swayed and tossed soft shadows, a softer fragrance. From the tall bottle on the table by the bed he took one of the flowers she had picked from the cottage garden and put there. He handed it to her.

Then he sat beside her, lifted her into his lap and held her. The way she curled into him as if she'd been waiting made him wonder how they had missed this step. Why they had both rushed to reach the peak, time after time, night after night, without once lingering over the journey.

This time, he promised himself. This time.

When he touched a hand to her cheek, she lifted her face, lifted her mouth to meet his. Time spun out, lost importance in this new and sumptuous mating of lips. The love hidden inside her heart poured into it without shame or fear, and still continued to rise inside her as if from a well that never ran dry.

Here was the compassion neither thought they needed, the tenderness both had shrugged aside, and all the patience they'd forgotten.

He pressed his lips to the center of her palm. Her hands were elegant, he thought, silky of texture. They might have belonged to a princess in a castle. No, there was too much strength in them for a princess. A queen, he decided, kissing her fingers one by one, who knew how to rule.

He brushed his lips over the inside of her wrist, and felt her blood beat there.

Music whispered on the wind as he laid her back on the pillows. Her arms came up, her fingers skimming over his face, into his hair, as gentle as his had been. Her eyes weren't clouded now, but clear.

'There's magic tonight,' she said, and drew him down to her.

They touched, as if it was the first time, as if there had been no others before or would be no others after. Innocence reaching for intimacy. For that night at least, she knew it was true and gave herself to it. To him.

Through the glow of candlelight and moonbeams, they gave to each other.

He tasted and she whispered. She stroked and he murmured. Sounds of pleasure twined together. Without rush, they undressed each other and savored the magic.

His skin was tones darker than hers. Had he noticed that before? Had he paid enough attention to how like silk she was, or how passion, the gradual, glorious build of it, gave that lovely white skin a flush of rose?

The taste of her, there, just at the underside of her breast. Nothing else had that delicacy of flavor. He thought he could live on that alone for the rest of his life.

And when his tongue slid over her and she shivered, he was sure of it.

Even when warmth simmered toward heat, when breaths became gasps and murmurs moans, there was no hurry. She crested on a long, gentle wave, her body flowing up to his. She felt golden, rich with sensation, each one somehow separate and shining even as they merged together.

Love made her selfless, nudged her to give back the glory. She rose over him, slid down to him, her lips warm and tender. Her hands skimmed over him, tough muscles that quivered at her lazy strokes, smooth skin that delighted her.

Now, she thought, now before greed could sneak back and steal this time from them. She clasped his hands with hers and took him into her.

Slowly and silkily, with urgency only a pulsebeat away. He filled, she surrounded.

The light danced over her skin, her hair, into her eyes, bewitching him. He remembered the painting of the mermaid with her face, that gorgeous arch of body, lovely tumble of hair. She belonged to him now, fact and fantasy. He'd have followed her, if she'd asked, into the sea. Into the heart of it.

Her eyes closed, her head tipped back, her body bowed. Nothing he'd ever seen was more beautiful than that moment when she lost herself. The shiver ran down her and into him. He swore he could feel it, feel her, in every cell.

He came up to meet her, wrapping his arms around her, pressing his lips to the hollow of her throat. And it was there, holding each other, that they let go of everything else and sank under the surface, and toward the heart, together.

In the dark, wrapped around him, her mind sliding toward sleep, Darcy closed a hand over the silver disk that lay on his heart. She assumed his Irish-loving mother had given it to him, and that he wore it touched her.

'What does it say?' she murmured, because the words were faded and unclear to her.

But when he told her she was already drifting, so his voice floated like out of a dream. *Forever love.*

Later, when they slept, he dreamed a dream of blue water shot through with sunlight like bright jewels, tipped by white waves that spewed drops like tears. Beneath the surface, where silence should have reigned, was music. A celebration of sound that quickened the pulse and fed the spirit.

He went toward it, searching shadows and light for the source. The golden sand beneath his feet was littered with gemstones, as if some carelessly generous hand had strewn them like bread crumbs.

A silver palace rose up into the blue light, its towers glinting and a banquet of flowers spread at its feet. The music swelled, seduced, became female. A woman's voice raised in song. A siren's call that was irresistible.

He found her beside the silver palace, sitting on a hill of rich blue that pulsed like a heart. There she sat and sang and smiled at him in a beckoning way.

Her hair, dark as midnight, flowed around her, teased the milky skin of her breasts. Her eyes, blue as the hill, laughed.

He wanted her more than he wanted to live. The wanting made him feel weak, and the weakness infuriated him. Still he couldn't stop himself from going to her.

'Darcy.'

'Have you come for me, then, Trevor?' Her voice wove spells, magic threads winding even when she spoke. 'What will you give me?'

'What do you want?'

She only laughed again, shook her head. 'It's for you to figure out.' She reached out a hand, coyly inviting him to join her. Jewels sparkled at her wrist, little points of brilliant fire. 'What will you give me?'

Frustration beat through his blood. 'More of these,' he said, touching the gems at her wrist. 'As many as you want, if that's what you want.'

She held her arm out, turning it so the stones shot fire. 'Well, I can't say I mind having such things, but it's not enough. What else have you got?'

'I'll take you to all the places you want to see.'

She pouted at that and picked up a glittering comb to run it through her flowing hair. 'Is that all?'

Temper snaked up, hissed in his throat. 'I'll make

you rich, famous. Put the damn world at your feet.'

Now she yawned.

'Clothes,' he snapped. 'Servants, houses. The envy and admiration of everyone who sees you. Everything you could ask for.'

'It's not enough.'

He saw that this time when she spoke, her eyes wept.

'Can't you see it's not enough?'

'What, then?' He reached for her, intending to pull her up, to make her answer, but before his hands could touch, he slipped, stumbled, and was falling.

The voice that followed him wasn't Darcy's, but Gwen's. 'Until you know and give, it won't be done. Until you do, it won't begin.'

He shot out of sleep like a man at the edge of drowning, heart thundering, breath raw. And even then, awake, aware, he heard the faintest whisper.

'Look at what you already have. Give what's only yours to give.'

'Christ.' Shaken, he got out of bed. Darcy shifted closer to the warmth he'd left, and slept on.

He started toward the bathroom, for water, then yanked on his jeans instead and went downstairs. Three A.M., he thought when he saw the clock. Perfect. He got down the bottle of whiskey and poured a stiff three fingers into a glass.

What the hell was wrong with him? But he knew, and knocked back the whiskey, hissed at the heat, set down the glass. He was in love with her. With a half laugh, he pressed his fingers to his eyes. Fell in love over bagels, he decided.

He'd been doing fire until then, he thought. Holding his own. Attraction, affection, interest, sex. Those were all safe and sound, those were all controllable.

Then she brings him a bagful of baked goods and he's gone. Joke's on you, Magee, he thought. You've been on your way since the first minute. The last slide just took you by surprise.

Hell of a slide, too.

He hadn't thought he had it in him. After Sylvia, when he'd done everything he could to be in love, had planned it, orchestrated it, and failed so miserably at it, he'd been sure he simply wasn't capable of that kind of emotion toward a woman.

It had worried him, dismayed him, angered him. Then he'd accepted it as likely for the best. If a man lacked something, it was only logical, efficient even, to compensate for it elsewhere. Work, his parents, his sister. The theater.

It had been enough, nearly enough. He'd convinced himself of it. And convinced himself that he could want Darcy, have Darcy, care for Darcy without it ever being more than that.

Now, without plan, without effort, it was . . . she was everything.

Part of him was thrilled. He wasn't incapable of love. But there was just enough fear snaking through that thrill to remind him to be cautious. Be careful.

He went to the back door, opened it to cool his head with air gone damp and misty. He needed a clear head to deal with Darcy.

Magic, she'd said. There was magic tonight. He believed that, and was beginning to accept that there had been magic all along. In her, in this place. Maybe it was fate, and maybe it was luck. He'd have to work out if that luck was good or bad. Loving Darcy wasn't going to be a smooth and easy road. Then again, he'd never really wanted the smooth and easy.

He didn't want what his grandparents had – the chill formality of their marriage with no passion, with no humor or affection. There'd never be anything like chilly formality with a woman like Darcy.

He wanted her, and would figure out how to keep her. He didn't doubt that. It was just a matter of calculating what to offer, how to offer, and when to offer what she wouldn't be able to resist.

The last echo of the dream drifted back to him. *Give what's only yours to give.*

He closed the words out, shut the door. He'd had enough of magic for one night.

CHAPTER 17

The morning was misty. Darcy woke to light gray with rolling fog, and the bed empty beside her. There was nothing new in either. The fog would burn off before long if it was meant to. And as far as she could tell, Trevor was always up before dawn.

The man was a robot when it came to such matters.

She rolled over, wishing he was there to cuddle up against and knowing that because he wasn't she wouldn't sleep for wondering what he was up to. She supposed neither of them had gotten a reasonable night's sleep since they'd become lovers. But running on sexual energy seemed to be working.

She felt wonderful.

She rose to take her robe from the hook in the closet. She had clothes in there as well and other things she deemed necessary for basic living throughout the cottage. It was a kind of living together they were doing, she knew, and had been all summer. Though neither of them mentioned it. In fact, they took great pains to avoid the subject, as if it were politics or religion.

He had a few things in her rooms over the pub, for the times he stayed there. And though it was a first for her, this having her things on a man's shelf and his on hers, it had been a casual process, this shifting of items from place to place and melding of homes and lifestyles. Casual, she thought as she walked into the bath to turn on the shower, because that's how they treated the entire business between them.

Yet there had been nothing casual in what had happened the night before. The scope of it was . . . She stepped under the spray, closing her eyes, tilting back her head. It was beyond anything she'd experienced before, anything she'd known two people could create between them.

It had to have been the same for him. He couldn't have touched that way, been touched by her that way, unless he felt something deep and something true.

Lovemaking. Dreamily, she circled soap over her wet skin while the steam rose and closed her in. She hadn't understood what that meant before Trevor. Not what it could mean. Vulnerability. She'd never realized that being vulnerable to someone else could be beautiful. Safe and warm and lovely. Just as knowing that for that stretch of time, in that soft world, he'd been vulnerable as well.

Here, at last, was a man she could open herself to completely, could promise herself to. And trust, and love, and cherish. They would spend their lives together, going wherever fate took them, grabbing hold of what life offered and making more from it. Through rushed days or quiet nights, in solitude or crowds. Making children, building homes.

She would make her mark beside him, and open all the doors she'd always longed to pass through.

It was possible to have everything after all, she thought. All you needed first was love.

He heard her singing of it when he stepped into the bedroom, of love and longing. It made him ache. He stood, while her voice slipped through the door she hadn't quite closed and twined around him. He waited until her song ended, until he saw her moving around the room through the narrow opening.

He'd spent part of his wakeful night deciding just what to do about her.

He gave the door a quick knock with his knuckle, eased it open. She'd already wrapped a towel around herself and was slathering on the cream she kept in a little white pot. He thought it smelled like warm apricots, and it never failed to whet his appetite.

Her hair was wet and curled and wild as it was in the painting she had in her room. It reminded him, uncomfortably, of his dream.

'I brought you some tea.'

'That's lovely. Thanks.' She took the cup, smiling at him. Her eyes were still dreamy from her song. 'I thought maybe you'd gone on to work already. I'm glad you didn't.'

She moved closer to touch her mouth to his. She felt soft everywhere from wishing he'd take her back to bed to make love again as they had in the night.

'I was about to come up and wake you.' Wanting her clouded his brain, just as the steam clouded the bath. So he stepped out, kept the door open. 'You beat me to it.'

She sipped the hot tea as the air in the bedroom shivered in and chilled her. 'And what did you have in mind for after you'd waked me?'

A man with a single-digit IQ and no libido would have caught the invitation. Stay on track, Trevor warned himself. 'A walk.'

'A walk?'

'Yeah.' He moved across the room to sit on the edge of the bed. He didn't intend to touch her and lose focus, but that didn't mean he couldn't watch her dress and torture himself. 'You usually walk down to the village anyway. So we'll take a walk, then I'll drive you down.'

She was pink and warm and fragrant from her shower, naked but for a towel, and the man wanted to go tramping around in the mist. A woman with less confidence, Darcy thought, would wonder if she'd misplaced her sex appeal during the night.

It didn't mean she couldn't be miffed.

'Don't you have to work?' Prepared to pout, she turned to the closet.

'I can take the morning. Mick's coming in to

keep an eye on things. Between him and Brenna I can spare a couple hours.'

The fact was, he could have spared days. Even weeks. It would have been more sensible to return to New York, handle the business he had there up front rather than long distance. But he watched Darcy slither into underwear and knew he wasn't going anywhere in the near future. Not alone.

'Mr O'Toole should be at home yet. Recuperating.'

'"I've had me fill of women fluttering around me person day and night."' Trevor's very passable mimic of Mick's disgust had a smile tugging at Darcy's lips.

'Nonetheless.'

'You want to try to keep him down? Be my guest. Me, I don't have the heart.'

'Well.' She pondered over a shirt. 'As long as he doesn't overdo. It's not that he's old, but he's not as young as he was, either. And being a man, he'll want to do more than he should.'

'Meaning men show off?'

'Of course they do.' She shot an amused and female look over her shoulder. Indulgent and insulting. 'Don't you?'

'Probably. But Brenna isn't liable to let him overdo. She doesn't flutter, she just watches him like a she-wolf watches a pup. I think he likes it. Men also like being pampered by a woman. They just have to pretend it annoys them.'

'As if having two brothers I didn't know that

already. I'll lure him into the kitchen for a hot meal and some pampering and tell him how strong and handsome he is.' She did up the buttons of the shirt. 'He likes the flattery as well.'

Holding her trousers by one finger, her shirttail skimming her thighs, she turned. 'And, as I can attest you're a man as well, wouldn't you like some of the same? I might be persuaded to fix you a meal downstairs in the cozy kitchen and tell you you're strong and handsome.'

Adam's temptation for an apple was nothing compared to Darcy's smile. But there were priorities. 'I had a bagel.' He grinned at her. 'It was great.'

'Then I'm pleased.' Baffled, but pleased. She stepped into her trousers, slipped on her shoes. 'Just let me fix my hair and face, and I'll be right with you.'

'What's wrong with your hair?'

'It's wet, for one thing.'

'It's damp out, so it won't matter.' Impatient now, he rose to take her hand. 'If I let you go into that bathroom, you won't come out for an hour.'

'Trevor.' Exasperated, she tugged to try to free her hand as he pulled her down the steps. 'I'm only half done here.'

'You look beautiful.' Moving quickly, he grabbed her jacket. 'You always do.' Then ignoring her protests, he bundled her into it.

'What's your hurry?' But she decided to be mollified with the compliment and let him have his way.

That, she liked to think, was a fine give-and-take in a relationship. Letting a man have his way when it didn't really matter one way or the other.

It wasn't particularly damp out, not to her way of thinking. The fog was thin, a lovely filter on the air that turned ordinary shapes into fanciful ones. Bright colors in the cottage garden were softly muted, the hills beyond wonderfully mysterious. Already she could see some breaks in the clouds, hopeful little patches of quiet blue among the gray.

The world was so hushed, they might have been alone in it. All the warmth and intimacy of the night before flowed back into her when he took her hand as they walked.

They went over the field, circling, and for a time she was silent, lost in the romance.

'Where are we heading?'

'Saint Declan's.'

A chill ran up her spine. Nerves, superstitions, anticipation, she couldn't be sure. 'If I'd known we were going by Old Maude's grave, I'd've brought some flowers.'

'There are always flowers on her grave.'

Magic flowers, she thought, put to grow there by powers beyond the mortal. In the distance, through the thinning fog, the stone ruin stood, like something waiting. She shivered.

'Cold?'

'No. I . . .' But she didn't mind when he released her hand to tuck his arm around her. 'It's an odd place to come on a misty morning.'

'Too early for tourists. It's a great spot. Terrific view if the fog lifts.'

'Too early for tourists,' she agreed, 'but not for faeries.' In such a place who knew what was sleeping under a hillock of grass or in the shadow of a stone? 'Are you looking for Carrick?'

'No.' Though he wondered. 'I wanted to come here with you.' He passed the well and its crosses, moved with her into the ancient, roofless church where Maude lay. The rough stones that marked ancient dead tilted up through ground and haze. In contrast, flowers swept lovingly over Maude's and thrived.

'They don't pick her flowers.'

'Hmm?'

'The people who come here,' Trevor said. 'Tourists and students and the locals who walk this way. They don't pick her flowers.'

'It would be disrespectful.'

'People don't always give respect, but they seem to here.'

'This is holy ground.'

'Yes.' He still had his arm around her, leaned down almost absently to press a kiss to her damp hair.

And the thrill moved through her, fast and bright. Alone in the world on holy ground, she realized. The morning after they'd loved each other, and in a way had discovered each other. He'd brought her here, to the cliff above sea and village, in the mist and the magic.

To tell her he loved her. She closed her eyes, trembled a little from the soaring joy of it. Of course, nothing could be more perfect. He wanted such a place to tell her his heart, to ask her to be his wife.

What could be more romantic, more dramatic? More quietly right?

'Fog's lifting,' he murmured.

Together, standing on the windy hill, they watched the veil tear gently, and the sun shimmer through, silver-edged, to touch the air with its pearly light. Far below was the village that was home, and the sea that guarded it swam slowly clear as if hands had drawn open a filmy curtain.

The beauty of it, what she saw with her eyes, what she saw with her heart, brought tears stinging. Home, she thought. Yes, Aidan was right. This would always be home, no matter where she traveled with the man beside her. Her love for it filled her as gently as the sunlight that brushed through the clouds.

'It looks perfect from here,' she said quietly. 'Like something from out of a storybook. I forget that when I'm down in it, going from day to day doing what's needed to be done.'

Swamped with emotions, she rested her head on Trevor's shoulder. 'I used to wonder why Maude chose to rest here, away from family and friends, and most of all away from her Johnnie. But this is why. This was the place for her, and she's not away from her Johnnie at all. She never was.'

'That kind of love's a miracle.' He wanted one for himself, and meant to make it happen.

'Love's always miraculous.' Tell me, tell me quickly, she thought. So I can tell you back.

'It seems to be the order of the day around here.'

Now, she thought, and wondered if a body could die of sheer happiness.

'It is beautiful, and full of charm and drama. But there are other places in the world, Darcy.'

She frowned, puzzled, then almost instantly smiled again. Of course, he thought he needed to prepare her, to explain how he had to travel for his work before he asked her to go with him.

'I've always wanted to see those other places.' She could ease the path for him. Another give-and-take, she thought, nearly giddy, in a relationship. 'To go and see and do. Just recently I came to realize that wanting that doesn't mean I don't love and appreciate what I have here. Wanting to go just means coming back.'

'You can see all those other places.' He drew her away, his hands on her shoulders, his gaze intent.

She had the sudden thought that here, now, finally, she was going to be offered her heart's desire. And the only man she'd ever loved would propose to her when her hair was wet and her face naked.

Damn.

The foolishness of it made her laugh and reach for him. He loved her just as she was, and that was a wonder. 'Oh, Trevor.'

336

'It'll be work, but exciting work. Satisfying, fulfilling. Lucrative.'

'Of course, but I . . .' The romantic haze parted, much as the fog over the sea, and let the last part of his statement swim clearly into her mind. 'Lucrative?'

'Very. The sooner you sign, the sooner we can get started on the groundwork. But you have to take the step, Darcy, make the decision.'

'The step.' She touched a hand to her temple as if dizzy, then turned away. How could she take any step when she had no balance, she thought. She had no balance at all. Who would, after being struck by such a blow?

It was the contract he spoke of, not love, not marriage, but business. Sweet God, what a fool she was, what romantic fantasies she'd woven and how completely she'd stripped herself of defenses.

And the worst of it was, he didn't even know.

'We've come here, is it, to talk of contracts?'

Step one, he thought. Get her signed, sturdily connected to him. He'd show her the world, and all the things she wanted. Once she had a taste of them, he'd offer her a feast. Anything and everything she'd ever wanted.

'I want you to have what you're looking for. I want to be a part of getting it for you. Celtic Records will nurture you, and build your career. I intend to see to it personally. See to you.'

'The package.' She tried to swallow the bitterness,

but it stuck in her throat when she looked back at him. All she'd ever wanted was standing right here, with his hair blowing in the breeze and his eyes too cool for her to reach out and touch him.

'That's how Nigel put it. So you'll see, personally, to the package?'

'And keep you happy. I can promise that.'

Cold now, she angled her head. 'How much do you judge it takes to keep me happy?'

'To start, on signing?' He named a figure that would have taken her breath away if she hadn't felt so cold, so bloody cold. Instead, she met the offer with a cynical lift of her brow.

'And how much of that, may I ask, is for the talent, and how much is because I'm sleeping with you?'

His eyes fired quickly, and went hard as stone. 'I don't pay women to sleep with me. That's insulting to both of us.'

'You're right.' Finally, the pain ate through the ice and made her weak. 'I'm sorry for that, it was badly put. Others will say it, though. Nigel warned me of that.'

He hadn't thought of it. It only showed how tangled up he was in her that he hadn't thought of it. 'You'll know better. What else matters?'

She walked away from him, back to Maude's grave, but found no comfort in the flowers or the magic or the dead. 'It's easier for you, Trevor. You have the armor of your position, and your power and your name. I'll come into this without any of that.'

'Is that what's stopping you?' He went to her, turned her back. 'Are you afraid of words spoken by jealous idiots? You're stronger than that, Darcy.'

'Not afraid, no, but aware.'

'The business is separate from our private life.' But he was merging them, knew it. 'You have a gift, and I can help you use it. What's between us otherwise is no one's concern but our own.'

'And if what's between us begins to fade, if one or the other of us should decide it's time to move on there, or away, what then?'

It would kill him. Even the thought of it stabbed his heart. 'It won't affect the business side.'

'Maybe we should have a separate contract saying so.' She meant it sarcastically, even cruelly, and was stunned when he only nodded.

'All right.'

'Well, then. Well.' She let out a shaky breath, and walked over to look down at Ardmore once again. So that was how things were done in his world. Contracts and agreements and sensible negotiations. Fine. She could handle that, would handle that.

But just let him try to walk away from her down the road. Let him try, and he'd find his legs across the room from the rest of him. He knew nothing of wrath.

'All right, Magee. Draw up your papers, ring your solicitors, strike up the band, whatever needs doing.' She didn't turn back, but whirled. And her smile glittered, hard and gorgeous. 'I'll sign my name. You'll get your voice, you'll get the whole flaming package. God help you.'

God help us both, she added silently.

Relief came to him in a wave. He had her, and was on his way to keeping her. 'You won't regret it.'

'I don't intend to.' Her eyes were sharp enough to cut glass when he took her hands again, leaned toward her. 'No, you don't. I don't seal business arrangements with kisses.'

'Point taken.' Solemnly he shook her hand. 'Business concluded?'

'For the moment.' So now he wanted a woman, a lover. Fine, then, she'd give him his money's worth there as well.

Deliberately, she ran her hands up, from hips to ribs, over chest, onto shoulders, sliding her body into his. Provocative, taunting, she nipped, retreated, nipped until she tasted frustrated desire, until she saw the flash of it heat his eyes to smoke.

Then, only then, she tipped her head back and let him take.

They feasted on each other, with none of the tender patience of the night. This was passion and passion only, with its greed and fire and demands. While her soul wept from the loss, she rejoiced.

He wanted her, would want her, again and again. This she would see to. As long as she held this power, she held him. And with it, witchlike, she would bind him.

'Touch me.' She tore her mouth from his to use her teeth in little cat bites on his neck. 'Put your hands on me.'

He hadn't meant to. The time and the place were all wrong. But heat was pumping out of her, into him, burning off control, scorching sense. His hands, rough and possessive, filled themselves with her.

But when he was on the point of losing all reason, of dragging her down to the wild grass, she pulled back. The wind caught her hair and swirled it as if in water, the sun shot into her eyes and sparkled there. For an instant, her beauty was cruel.

'Later,' she said, and lifted a hand, lover-like, to stroke his cheek. 'You can have me. As later I'll have you.'

Fury spurted into his throat, but he didn't know if it was for himself or for her. 'That's a dangerous game, Darcy.'

'And what fun are they if they're not? You'll have what you want from me, on both counts. Be content that here you've had my word on the first, and a fine taste of the second.'

He was just raw enough to risk asking, 'What do you want from me?'

Her lashes lowered, a shield against grief. 'Didn't you bring me up here because you'd figured that out for yourself already?'

'I guess I did,' he murmured.

'Well, then.' She was smiling again when she

held out a hand. 'We'd best go back, as the morning's wasting. And I never did finish my tea.' Cheerfully, she gave his hand a little squeeze as they walked. Let's just see if you can keep up with me, you blind, thickheaded bastard. 'And will you be willing to share your bagels with me?'

He ordered himself to match her mood. 'I could probably be persuaded to share.'

Neither of them looked back as they walked away, or saw the air ripple and shred.

'Fools,' Carrick muttered, scowling from his perch atop the stone well. 'Stubborn, bone-brained fools. And just my luck to be stuck with them. One step away from happiness, and they spring back as if it were bared fangs.'

He leaped off his seat, landing an inch above the ground. In the next instant he was sitting, cross-legged, by Maude's grave. 'I'm telling you, old friend, I've just no clear understanding of mortals. Maybe they are just in heat, and I'm wrong about them.'

Brooding now, he stuck his chin on his fist. 'The hell I am,' he decided, but it didn't lighten his mood. 'They're stupid in love with each other, and there, I think, lies the problem. Neither of them knows how to handle stupidity. Afraid of it is what they are. Afraid to give in to senselessness and let love rule.'

He sighed a little, then waved his wrist and took a bite of the golden apple that appeared. 'You'd say I was the same. And you'd be right enough. Magee's set on the same path I took. Promise her this, offer her that, vow to give her the world, as the world's safe when you've plenty of it to spare. But you've only one heart, after all, and giving that is a more difficult deal. I didn't look inside my Gwen, and he doesn't look inside his Darcy. He thinks it's sense, but it's nothing but fear.'

He gestured toward the headstone with the apple, as if the old woman sat there, listening. Perhaps she did. 'And she's no better when it comes to it. As different from my quiet, modest Gwen as sun from moon, but the same in this aspect. She wants him to offer his heart, but will she just bloody say so, for Finn's sake? No, she won't. Females – who can figure them?'

He sighed then, munched his bright apple, contemplated. He'd nearly lost patience, had been on the edge of springing out of the air to order them both to get on with it. They were in love, admit it and be done.

But that was beyond what was permitted. The choices, the timing, the steps of their dance together had to be theirs. His . . . contribution, Carrick decided – he didn't care for the word 'interference' – could be only minor.

He had done what he could do. Now he had to wait as he had waited three centuries already. His fate, his happiness, at times he thought his very life, depended on the hearts of these two mortals.

He'd dealt with the other pairs of them. You'd

have thought he'd have learned enough to know how to hurry these last two along. But all he'd learned was that love was a jewel with too many facets to count. Strength and weakness running side by side through it. And that no one could give or take it with any less than an open hand.

He lay back on the grass, and with his mind sketched Gwen's beloved face in the clouds. 'I ache for you. Heart, body, mind. I would give all that's in my power to give to touch you again, to breathe your scent, to hear your voice. I swear to you, when you come back to me at last, it's love I'll pour at your feet. The grandeur and humility of it. And the flowers that bloom from that will never die.'

He closed his eyes, and weary with waiting, vanished into sleep.

The effort of being cheerful and sexy and witty left Darcy near to exhaustion by the time Trevor drove her down to the pub. But determined to play it all out, she walked around the back with him so she could make happy noises about the progress of the work.

She realized that temper had her overplaying it when Trevor narrowed his eyes at her. So she beat a hasty retreat, giving him a warm but brief kiss.

She made it as far as the kitchen door when Brenna shoved in behind her. 'What's the matter?' Brenna asked immediately.

They'd known each other since birth, understood

each other's moods often better than they understood their own.

'Come upstairs, can you?' Such was the nature of their friendship that Darcy didn't have to wait for an answer. She went up fast, shedding her brightness and cheer as she might have shed clothes.

'I've a headache.' The brutal pounding sent her straight to the bathroom cupboard for aspirin. She chased it with water, drinking the whole glass down.

Their eyes met in the mirror. Brenna knew that sleek and shiny look hid some deep hurt.

'What did he do?'

How marvelous it was to have a friend who simply knew where the blame lay even before the offense was cited. 'He offered me a fortune. A small one, I suppose, by his standards, but hefty enough by mine. Enough to set me on the way to where I'm going, and in fine style.'

'And?'

'I'm taking it.' She tossed her head, and the edgy defiance worried her friend. 'I'm signing his recording contract.'

'That's grand, Darcy, truly it is, if it's what you want.'

'I've always wanted more than I have, and now I'm about to get it. I wouldn't sign if it didn't suit me. I promise you I'm doing it for me first. I haven't lost my head so much to do otherwise.'

'Then I'm pleased for you, and proud already.'

She laid a hand on Darcy's shoulder, rubbed at the tension. 'Now tell me how he hurt you.'

'I thought he was going to ask me to marry him. I thought he would tell me he loved me and wanted me to belong to him. Can you imagine that?'

'I can.' And now Brenna hurt as well. 'Perfectly.'

'Sure and his vision's not so sharp as yours. He hasn't a clue.' She gripped the sides of the sink, breathed slow and deep. 'I'm not going to cry. He won't get tears out of me.'

'Come sit down and tell me.'

When she did and when she had, Brenna held her hand. All sympathy, she said, 'Bastard!'

'Thanks for that. I hate that it's partly my fault. Oh, that's a bitter pill. But I set myself up for it, no mistake there. Spinning romantic fantasies in the shower like some fluff-brained girl.'

'Why shouldn't you? You love him.'

'I do, the cad, and I'll make him pay for it before we're done.'

'What are you going to do?'

'Trap him, of course. Blind him with lust, confuse him with my many moods, toy with him. All the things I'm best at when it comes to men.'

'I won't say you aren't skilled in that area,' Brenna said carefully. 'But if you go this way, and win, it won't be enough for you.'

'I'll make it enough. Many's the relationship that has its seeds in sex. Lust and love aren't so far apart.'

'Maybe not in the flaming dictionary. But Darcy, when one party's in lust and the other in love, they're distant as moons. And between those places is so much room to be hurt.'

'I can't hurt any more than I did this morning at Saint Declan's Well. And I survived.'

She stepped to the window. Out there, she thought, Trevor was building his dream, but he'd needed some of what was hers for it. Well, she could build her own and take some of his. Of him.

'I'll risk the rest. I can make him need me, Brenna. Need's the step between wanting and loving. It'll be enough for me.'

She shook her head before Brenna could speak, crossed back. 'I have to try.'

'Of course you do.' Hadn't she? Brenna thought. Didn't everyone who knew what love was and longing?

'But at the moment, I need to vent out this foul mood. Shawn'll be coming along shortly. I'll just go down and torment him until I feel better.'

'If that's the case, I'll get back on the job and out of harm's way.'

CHAPTER 18

Astorm hovered over the village, marching down from the northeast to camp on the border as an army digs in for a siege. The rising winds and splattering rain that were its leading edge chased people from the beaches, and brought a nasty chill. The sky, thick and bruised and ominous, had even the locals glancing upward with apprehension.

Had you ever seen that green tint to the clouds' edges before? Had you ever tasted air that had such a flavor of mean in it?

She would hit, they said, and hit hard.

Those who'd been through such things before checked their stock of candles and lamp oil and batteries. Supplies were laid in, and children ordered to stay close to home. Boats were secured in their docks as Ardmore prepared for the coming battle.

But when the door of the pub burst open, Jude's face was bright as sunbeams. 'It came.'

Excitement had her barely able to speak above a whisper that didn't carry over the voices to where Aidan was busy at the taps. It was Darcy who saw her, standing there with her bound-back hair damp with raindrops, her cheeks flushed pink. And the book clutched to her breast like a beloved child.

Darcy dumped her tray immediately, and unceremoniously, on a table where four baffled French students stared at the toasted sandwiches, piles of slaw and chips they hadn't ordered, and began consulting their phrase books.

'Is it the book? Yours?' Thrilled, Darcy tried to pry it out of Jude's grip.

'No, I have to show it to Aidan first. He has to see it first.'

'Of course he does, well, of course. Come on, then. Make way there, Jack, you're like a hulking bear. Move aside, will you, Sharon, we've business of a vital nature here.'

Snaking her way, Darcy reached the pass-through, tossed it up, then hustled Jude ahead of her behind the bar. 'Hurry,' she ordered. 'I'm dying to see it.'

'Okay, all right.' Jude exclaimed with the book pressed so tight against her she felt her heart knocking against the cover. 'Aidan.'

He served a pint at the bar, took the coin. 'Jude. Hello, darling. Can't you find a seat?'

'No, I—'

'We'll cozy you down in the snug, but I want you home and tucked in before this storm hits. Two pints Smithwick's. That's three pounds and twenty.'

'Aidan, I want to show you something.'

'I'll be with you in just a minute, darling. Eighty pence is your change.'

'A minute be damned.' Out of patience, Darcy grabbed Aidan's arm. 'Look at her, you great baboon.'

'What's the matter? Can't you see I've customers here who—' But he broke off, his grin bursting wide as he saw what was clutched in his wife's arms. 'Your book!'

'It just came. It's right off the press. It's real. It's beautiful.'

'Of course it is. Are you going to let me see?'

'Yes. I . . . I can't move.'

'Jude Frances.' The tenderness in his voice made Darcy's throat swell. 'I love you. Here, now, give it over.'

Gently he tugged it out of her grip, studying the back cover first, where her picture was printed. 'Isn't she pretty, my Jude, so solemn-eyed and lovely.'

'Oh, turn it over, Aidan.' Jude might have danced if the baby hadn't been weighing so heavy. 'That part's not important.'

'It is to me. Everyone can look at this and see what fine taste I have in wives.' But he did turn it over, and let out an *ah* of delight.

JEWELS OF THE SUN
And Other Irish Legends
Jude Frances Gallagher

The title ran across the top, and her name across the bottom of a brilliantly colored illustration depicting a man in silver and a woman with pale hair riding across a bold blue sky on a winged white horse.

'It's beautiful,' he murmured. 'Jude Frances, it's beautiful.'

'It really is, isn't it?' She didn't mind the tears that slid down her cheeks. They felt wonderful and right and well deserved. 'I can't stop looking at it, touching it. I thought I knew how much it meant. I wasn't even close.'

'I'm so proud of you.' He lowered his head to press his lips to her forehead. 'You have to give this one to me, so I can sit and read every word.'

'Start now, with the dedication.'

When he opened it, began reading the flyleaf, she turned the pages herself. 'No, you can read that later. Read this now.'

Indulging her, he began to read. Then his eyes changed, darkened, lifted to hers. The look that passed between them was strong and vibrant. This time when he kissed her, he took her mouth.

'*A ghra*' was all he said when he lifted his head, laid his cheek against her hair. My love.

'Take Jude back in the snug,' Darcy murmured. 'She shouldn't be on her feet so long. Take some time with her. I'll see to the bar here.'

'Thanks. Just let me settle her in, get her some tea.' Emotions still swirled in his eyes as he handed Darcy the book. 'Have a care with it.'

351

Ignoring customers, Darcy opened the book, and read what Aidan had.

For Aidan who showed me my own heart,
and gave me his.
With him I learned there is no magic
more potent than love.

'May I see it?'

Eyes drenched, Darcy looked across the bar at Trevor. Because she was unable to speak, she handed the book to him and immediately started the first layer on a pair of Guinnesses.

'It's gorgeous.'

'Of course it is. It's Jude's.'

Saying nothing, he walked behind the bar, set the book on a shelf out of harm's way, then took out his handkerchief.

'Thanks.' She sniffled, dried her eyes.

'Sentiment looks lovely on you.'

'It doesn't get the work done. It's Aidan's turn to be sentimental now. I'll take mine later.'

She tucked the handkerchief in her pocket – just in case. 'Isn't it *wonderful*?' She did a little step dance, then beamed at the next customer who came to the bar to order. 'My sister's a famous author, and this is her book.' She snatched it back off the shelf. 'It'll be in bookshops in just a couple of weeks now. You should buy it as soon as you can. Now what can I get you?'

'Darcy, are you ever picking up these orders, or

do I have to serve as well as cook?' Obviously put-upon, Shawn came through the kitchen door carrying a loaded tray.

'Look, you peabrain.' She turned and all but shoved the book under his nose.

'It's Jude's!' He set the tray on the bar with a clatter and made a grab for the book.

'One drop of chip fat on this, and you're a dead man.'

'I know how to be careful.' He took the book as if it were fragile china. 'Brenna has to see,' he announced, and was back out the door like a shot.

'They'll grubby it up between them, wait and see.' She turned back, a little shocked to see Trevor exchanging pints he'd drawn himself for payment. 'Well, look at himself, manning the bar.'

'I can handle it until Aidan's back, if you want to serve those lunch orders before they're cold.'

'Do you know how to build a Guinness?'

'I've watched enough of them constructed.'

'Some people watch brain surgery, doesn't mean they should be handed a knife.' But she picked up the tray. 'We're grateful for the help.'

'No problem.' It gave him a chance to watch her work. And to think.

For the last few days she'd kept him balancing on a keen and delicious edge. In bed she was a siren, and out of it a tease. She was tireless, energetic, capricious, and fascinating.

And somehow through it all, he would have said heartless.

Something had been off, he decided, between them since the night they'd made slow and gentle love. He couldn't pinpoint the change, only knew the change was there. He saw it when he caught the cold and steady gleam of calculation in her eyes.

Then again, she was a woman who made no secret of her calculations. He accepted that, and in many ways admired her lack of artifice. But the Darcy he'd just seen hadn't been calculating or capricious or self-interested. She'd been thrilled, excited, and sentimental enough to cry over Jude's accomplishment, her brother's pride.

It was odd to think that in all the weeks he'd known her he'd only seen her shed a tear over someone else's pleasure.

Where she loved she was both vulnerable and generous. He wanted that vulnerability, that generosity. He wanted that love. And, though he knew it was wrong, he wanted her to shed a tear over him.

It was time, he thought, to push her a little closer.

He waited until the shift was over, until Aidan left to take Jude home.

'She's worn out.' Darcy stood in the doorway, watching them drive off the short distance to the house. 'Such excitement. He'll persuade her to lie down a bit. Oh, the wind's kicking.'

Closing her eyes, she let it batter her, reveled in it. 'The storm will hit full before nightfall. Then we're in for it. You'd best batten down your hatches, Magee, for there's a gale coming.'

'I'm heading back to the cottage shortly, anyway. I've got work there to deal with. You're getting wet.'

'Feels good after all the crowd in here today.' But she closed the door on the wind and spitting rain, and locked it. 'I'll wager you ten pounds to your five that you'll be working by candlelight this night.'

'That's a sucker bet. I'm no sucker.'

'Pity. I can always use an extra five.' She began to gather empties from the tables. 'We'll be packed tonight. People like company when the world's wild. Come back if you can, for we'll have music to chase the jitters away.'

'I will. Can you let that go a minute? I want to talk to you.'

'Twisted me arm.' With pleasure, she sat at one of the tables, put up her feet on the chair beside her. 'Days like this you wish you had three arms and twice as many feet.'

'Looking forward to serving your last pint?'

Not as much as she'd expected, but she nodded. 'Who wouldn't be? Every time I pick up the phone and dial room service, it'll be a personal celebration.'

'You can count on doing a lot of celebrating.' He sat across from her. Time, he thought, to up the stakes and play the next card. 'They're faxing me the draft of your contract today. I expect to have it when I get back to the cottage.'

Her stomach jittered. Excitement, anticipation, nerves. 'That's quick work.'

'Most of it's standard. You'll want to look it over,

take it to your lawyer. Solicitor,' he corrected. 'Any questions, changes, we'll discuss.'

'Fair enough.'

'I have to go to New York for a couple days.'

She was grateful she was sitting down with her feet up, as her knees went soft as jelly. 'Do you? You haven't mentioned it.'

'I'm mentioning it now.' Having just decided. 'Come with me.'

Yes, a very good thing she was sitting down. She stayed stretched out as every muscle of her body tensed. 'Come with you to New York City?'

'You can sign the final papers there.' On his turf. 'We'll celebrate.' He wanted her to meet his family, see his home, his life. 'The business won't take that long. I'll show you the city.' And give her a taste of what he could offer her.

Trevor and New York. The thrill of being with him in a place she'd seen in dreams. And illusions. 'I can't think of anything I'd enjoy more. That's the truth.'

'Then I'll make the arrangements.'

'I can't, Trevor. I can't go with you now.'

'Why?'

'It's high season. You saw how it is in the pub with barely enough hands to go around. I can't leave Aidan and Shawn short that way during summer season. It's not right.'

Damn it, he didn't want her to be responsible, to be sensible now. 'You can get someone to fill in for you. It's only a few days.'

'I could, and that would ease part of the problem. But I can't leave here now, however much it appeals. Jude's due any day. She needs her family, as does Aidan. What kind of a sister would I be to go dancing off at such a moment?'

'I thought she had another week at least.'

'Men.' She mustered up a smirk. 'Babies come when they please, and first babies are the most willful, so I'm told. It's lovely to think about going off with you now, but I couldn't bear the guilt of it.'

'We'll take the Concorde. It'll cut the traveling time down to negligible.'

The Concorde. She rose, walked behind the bar for a ginger ale. Like a movie star, she thought. Jetting off wherever you pleased, whenever the mood struck, and arriving almost before you'd left.

Dear God, she'd love it. He knew she would.

'I can't. I'm sorry.'

She was right, and he knew it. Still, he wanted to push. There was an urgency inside him, to put things back on an even keel. No, that was a lie. To put things back, he thought, disgusted with himself, to his advantage.

'You're right. It's bad timing.'

'I can tell you I wish it wasn't. A trip on the Concorde and a whirl through New York City. Any other time, I'd already be packing my bag.' She would, no matter what it cost, be cheerful, be casual, be the sophisticated woman he would understand. 'So then, when do you go?'

Go? For a moment he was completely, foolishly blank. He'd never intended to go without her. Boxed yourself in, Magee, he realized, and took a swig from her bottle when she brought it back to the table. 'I'll get the draft contract to you first, and if you've got no problem with it, have my people put the final together. Couple of days. That way I can do what I have to do there and bring the papers back with me.'

'That's efficient.'

'Yeah.' He set the bottle down. It tasted foul. 'My middle name.'

'Let me know when you've made your plans.' She trailed a finger over the back of his hand. 'I'll give you a bon voyage that will hold you until your welcome back.'

She was not cooperating, Trevor decided. The woman was not following the rules here. He brooded at his office table, staring out into the storm-tossed night when he should have been working.

Why hadn't she asked him to postpone his trip a few days? Even a couple of weeks? It would have provided the perfect opportunity to give in to her, to show her he was willing to make concessions to keep her happy.

And why the hell hadn't he looked before he'd leaped? Any moron would have known she wasn't able to leave home just now. Which only proved that love made a man less than a moron. That was pathetic.

The lightning that shattered the sky in one blinding streak perfectly suited his mood. Edgy, electric.

Why hadn't he come clean with her? Well, not *clean*, Trevor mused. Just more direct. It would have been simpler, and more productive, to have told her he wanted to take her to New York. Winding business through it, certainly, but that would have put a different tone on the whole thing. He'd clutched before the first swing, he admitted, then boxed himself in when he started the whole conversation by announcing he was going.

Now he either went without her or made excuses.

He hated making excuses.

Thunder rumbled like laughter, whipped by the howling wind, and rain danced a frantic jig against his window.

The trouble was, he didn't know how to play it. And he *always* knew how to play it, how to find the most constructive route through a problem to the solution. But there were more obstacles, more wrong turns in love than he'd ever imagined. Still, he'd never come up against a wall he couldn't scale, break through, or tunnel under.

This wasn't going to be the first.

He needed to let the problem simmer, to brew a bit until the solution came to him. The best way to do that was to concentrate on something else.

He started with the faxes that had come in throughout the day. Since he'd already read over the draft of Darcy's contract, he put that in a folder. The one thing that was clear, he thought, was this angle. She was a hell of a find for Celtic Records. And Celtic would nurture her. Neither of them had to worry about this part of their relationship.

He wanted his parents to hear that voice. A tape recording. Why hadn't he thought of that before? He'd get her voice on tape before he headed back to New York. That would at least partly introduce the woman he loved to his family.

He would take the papers down to her at the pub once he'd cleaned off his desk, go over them with her, answer her questions. She was bound to have questions. Then he'd tell her he needed a tape.

Satisfied with the idea, Trevor set the folder down and turned to his other paperwork.

He thought about going downstairs and making more coffee, foraging for a meal. He didn't want to eat alone, and that annoyed him. It had never bothered him before. The fact was, he wanted to chuck even the idea of work and go down to the pub, where there were people. Where there was Darcy.

Despite the risk of the storm, he ran his E-mail instead. He knew he should shut the computer down, but he had to do *something* to keep busy, to stop himself from leaving the cottage for the pub.

It gave him perverse satisfaction to imagine her

watching the door, wondering if and when he'd come through it.

He didn't care how stupid that made him. It was the damn principle of the thing.

The business inquiries came first, as was his habit. He answered them, printed out or saved what he wanted a record of, then shifted over to personal posts.

One from his mother gave him his first smile in hours.

You don't call, you don't write. Well, not often enough. I think I've convinced your father that what we need is a nice trip. To Ireland. It's taken very little convincing, actually. He misses you as much as I do, and I think he wants to get his fingerprints on the theater. I hope it's progressing well — am sure it is, under your hand.

He's already started shuffling work and schedules though he doesn't think I know it. I'm doing the same. If all goes well, we'll come next month. Once our plans are finalized, I'll let you know all.

I assume you're well as you haven't said otherwise, and busy because you always are. I hope you're taking some time for yourself. You were working much too hard before you left, punishing yourself because of Sylvia.

I won't say any more on that, as I can see you're getting that irritated look in your eye.

No, I lied, I'll say one thing more. Give your-self a break, Trevor. No one, not even you, can live up to your standards.

There, I'm done. I love you. Prepare for an invasion.

Mom

Did he have an irritated look in his eye? He studied the faint reflection of his face in the window and decided, yes, probably. It was comforting, and disconcerting, to be understood quite that well.

He hit Reply.

Nag, nag, nag.

That, he knew, would make her laugh.

Hurry and come over so you can nag me in person. I miss that.

Yes, the theater's going well, though we had to knock off early today. Hell of a storm blowing through. I'm going to have to shut down in a minute.

I thought you'd like to know I've chosen the name for it. I'm calling it Duachais. It's Gaelic. Well, you probably know that, but I had to look up the spelling. It means the roots of a place, the traditions of it. A very clever woman told me that's what I wanted in the theater. She was right.

Of course, a name like that's going to give Publicity nightmares.

No need to worry, I'm taking time for myself. It's impossible to do otherwise here. You just have to look to be, well, sucked into looking some more.

I'm about to sign Darcy Gallagher to a recording contract with Celtic. She's an amazing talent. Wait until you hear her. Give me a year, and her voice, her name, her face will be everywhere. It's a hell of a face.

She's got ambition, talent, energy, temperament, brains, and charm. This is no shy colleen. You'll like her.

I'm in love with her. Is it supposed to make me feel like an idiot?

He stopped, stared at his last line. He hadn't meant to type that. With a shake of his head, he started to delete.

Lightning burst like a bomb, throwing hot blue light into the room. He saw the thin crack snake down the window glass, then thunder blasted in one ear-deafening roar.

And the lights went out.

'Shit.' It was his first thought once his heart stopped screaming in his ears. That one had probably fried his computer.

His own fault. He knew better.

Since the screen was as black as the rest of the world, indicating his battery backup had failed, he swore again and fumbled for the flashlight that he'd set next to the machine.

He switched it on, got nothing. What the hell was this? he wondered and gave it an irritated shake. He'd checked it before he'd started to work, and the beam had flashed on strong and bright.

More annoyed than concerned, he got up, felt his way to the spare bed, worked up to the little table beside it and the matches and candles that were always there.

The next slash of lightning had him jolting, spilling half the matches out of the box, and cursing himself. 'Get a grip,' he muttered and nearly shuddered at the sound of his own voice coming out of the dark. 'It's not your first storm, or your first blackout.'

But there was something . . . different here. Something that, if he'd wanted to be fanciful, he'd have called deliberate about the wind and rain and fierceness of it all. As if the savagery was personal.

That was so ridiculous he laughed as he struck the match. The little flame made him feel more in control. He touched it to the wick of the candle. A little breath of relief escaped as he picked up the candle, intending to carry it with him to light more.

And in the next wild spurt of lightning, he saw her.

'Carrick's temper is up.'

The candle flame shook as his hand jerked. He

had to be satisfied that he didn't drop it and set the cottage on fire.

'Storms often make people uneasy.' Gwen smiled at him gently. 'It's nothing to be ashamed of. He knows it too, you can be sure of that, and is indulging himself in a little tantrum just at the moment.'

Steadier, Trevor set the candle down. 'It seems excessive.'

'He's a dramatic sort, my Carrick. And he's suffering, Trevor. Waiting wears on the soul, and when you can nearly see the end of the waiting, it's harder still. I wonder, could I ask you a question, of a personal nature?'

He shook his head. It was all too strange, and somehow eerily ordinary, this talking to a ghost in a little cottage on a storm-ravaged night. 'Why not?'

'I hope it doesn't offend you, but I can't help wondering what it is that stops you from telling the woman you love what's in your heart.'

'It's not as simple as that.'

'I know that's your thinking.' A thread of urgency ran through her voice now, though her hands stayed quiet and still, folded together at her waist. 'I want to know why it can't be just that simple.'

'If you don't lay groundwork, you make mistakes. The more important it is, the more important not to make mistakes.'

'Groundwork?' she asked, confused. 'And that would be . . . what, exactly?'

'With Darcy, it's showing her what she can have, the kind of life she could live.'

'By that you're meaning all the grand things? The riches and wonders?'

'Yes, that's right. Once she sees—' He broke off, seriously alarmed, when the floor shook under his feet. But before he could move, Gwen held up a hand.

'I beg your pardon. I've a temper of my own.' She kept her hand up, closed her eyes. When she opened them again, they were dark and vibrant. 'And what did Carrick offer me, but the same in his way? Jewels and riches, a palace for a home, and immortality. Can you not see the mistake in that, a mistake that cost us both three times a hundred years?'

'Darcy's not like you.'

'Oh, Trevor, look closer. Why is it you can stand on the same ground and still not see each other?'

She lowered her hand. 'Well, this night's work isn't done. You'll go down to the village now. There's a need for you there.'

'Darcy?' Panic pushed him forward. 'Is she all right?'

'Oh, aye, she's fine and well. But there's a need for you. 'Tis a night for wonders, Trevor Magee. Go on, now, and be part of them.'

He didn't hesitate. She'd hardly faded away when he was snatching up the candle to light his way out of the house and into the storm.

CHAPTER 19

The air was alive, and angry. It slapped and bit. Rain, like thin needles of glass, jabbed at his clothes and stabbed at exposed skin. Nasty marbles of hail beat down on grass, battered the flowers, and turned the ground into treachery.

And still the lightning slashed, ripping open the sky so thunder could charge through in snarling bellows.

Trevor was breathless and drenched before he got to the car.

The rational part of his mind warned him it was insane to venture out on such a night. More sensible to wait out the storm than to drive into the snapping teeth of it. But he was already turning the key in the ignition.

The wind howled like a banshee, tore at the hedgerows so that bits of bloom and leaf flew past like crazed insects. He'd have sworn it had fists and fingers. His headlights made twin slashes through the wall of rain, spotlighting the full fury of it. He fought the car down the road that was rapidly turning into a ditch of mud, and when he shuddered around a bend, the sky exploded, etching the jagged burst of light on his eyes. The freight train of thunder roared after it.

Under it all, quiet as grief, was the sound of a woman's desperate weeping.

He stomped on the gas, fishtailed sickly around the next curve. In the distance, he saw a sprinkling of lights that was Ardmore.

Candle- and lamplight in the houses. Some would have generators, he realized. The pub did. Darcy was fine, tucked inside, warm, dry, safe. There was no reason to drive like a madman when there was nothing wrong.

But the sense of urgency, the brutal need to hurry stayed with him. With his hands clamped to the wheel, he skidded around the turn at Tower Hill. And his car stopped dead.

'What the hell is this?' Frantic, infuriated, he twisted the key, pumped impatiently at the gas. But all he got in return was a faint and mocking click.

Swearing, he punched open the glove compartment, snatched out the flashlight he kept there, and felt only grim satisfaction when the beam shot on.

With its next violent gust, the wind nearly swept him off his feet as he climbed out of the car. It seemed to want to. Pitting himself against it, he fought his way to the gate, muscled it open while the rain slashed and the hail pummeled. He would just cut through, save time.

The boggy ground sucked at his feet, slowed

him to a jog when he wanted, needed, to run flat out. The stones of the dead speared up like teeth out of a knee-high layer of fog that lay nowhere else.

Carrick, Trevor thought, in disgust and fury. Pulling out all the stops.

Lightning burst again, seemed to glow blue over the grave of the long-dead John Magee.

Flowers? Trevor skidded to a halt, panting, and stared down at the carpet of flowers blooming like a rainbow. The grass was bent and flattened by the force of the storm, but those fragile petals were open and perfect. The wind that shoved against him only fluttered them gently, and no cold finger of fog touched them.

Magic, he thought, then looked out, toward the sea where he could see the white-tipped walls of waves rear and crash. Magic wasn't always bright and pretty. Tonight, it was full of wrath.

He turned from the grave and rushed on.

He skidded, slithering down the hill. He rapped hard into the trunk of a tree that seemed to rise up out of nowhere. Pain pounded in his shoulder, racing to match the pounding of his heart. Every time he lost his balance, should have tumbled over the stony ground to the road below, he managed to gain it again.

Later, he would think that that alone had been a miracle.

On solid ground once more, he ran, feet pounding against the wet footpath, around yet one more turn. He could see the pub now, the warm, welcoming glow of light against the window.

Lungs burning, he focused on that. Then something drew his gaze over and up, a whisper under the wind? A weeping. He saw in the top window of the Gallagher house a woman. Pale hair glowing against the dark, green eyes watching him.

That was wrong, he thought, and she was gone as soon as he thought it. Against the glass was the faintest of light, and no movement behind it.

Wrong. Something was wrong. So he turned away from the pub and pushed through the wind to the door of the house. He shoved it open, letting in wild wind and wilder rain. Before he could call out, he saw Jude, sitting at the top of the stairs. Her face was sheet white, her hair a tangle, and the nightgown she wore damp with sweat.

'Thank God. Oh, thank God. I can't get down.' She let out a little gasp, clutched her belly. 'The baby. The baby's coming.'

Ruthlessly he shut down panic, though he took the stairs two at a time to reach her, grip her hand. She squeezed it hard enough to grind bone. 'Breathe. In and out, come on. Look at me and breathe.'

'Yes, okay, yes.' Her eyes clung to his, wide, glazed with the pain that ripped through her as the contraction crested. 'God, oh, God, it's *huge*!'

'I know. I know, honey. Keep breathing. You're coming down the other side now.'

'Yes. It's passing, but . . . I never expected . . .

It's all so fast.' Even as her breath gushed out in relief from the absence of that wicked pain, she lifted a shaky hand to push at her hair. 'I was having tea in bed. I talked to Aidan and told him I was going to bed. And then the power went out and it all started at once.'

'We'll get you to the hospital. Everything's fine.'

'Trevor, it's too late. I won't make it.'

Panic wanted to flood back, but he dammed it up before it could touch her. 'This business usually takes a while. How far apart are the contractions?'

'I haven't timed the last few. The phones are out. I couldn't call the pub or the doctor. I thought if I could get downstairs . . . but I couldn't. Before, they were close, two minutes, and now they're coming faster and harder.'

Jesus. Sweet Jesus Christ. 'Did your water break?'

'Yes. It's not supposed to happen so fast. All the classes, all the books. It should take hours. Get Aidan. Please, get . . . Oh, oh, God, here it comes!'

He helped her through it, voice calm and bracing as his mind raced. Much too close, much too hard. He'd seen the process three times and that was enough to know Jude was right. She would never make the hospital.

'Let's get you into bed. Put your arms around my neck. That's the way.'

'I need Aidan.' She wanted, badly, to weep. Just to scream out with sobs.

'I know. I'm going to go get him. You stay calm,

371

Jude. You just hold on.' He laid her in bed, glanced around quickly. She'd managed to light several candles. That would have to do. 'When the next one comes, breathe through it. I'll be right back.'

'I'll be all right.' She lay her head back where he'd propped pillows. Had to be. Everything in the world depended on it. 'Women used to do this all the time without doctors and hospitals.' She did her best to smile. 'Only, damn it, none of them were me. Hurry.'

He didn't want to think how many contractions she'd go through alone, how frightened she'd looked lying there alone in bed with only candles for light. He didn't want to think of what could go wrong.

He sprinted back into the storm. The wind had changed and was at his back, pushing him faster, shoving as if it, too, urged him to hurry. Still, it seemed he'd run miles before his hand closed over the knob of Gallagher's Pub.

He burst into the warmth, the music and laughter.

Darcy spun around, beaming. 'Well, now, look what the storm's blown in.' She got no farther than that before the look in his eye registered. 'What is it? Are you hurt?'

He shook his head, gripped her shoulder while he turned to Aidan. 'It's Jude.'

'Jude?'

Trevor had never seen the blood drain as completely, as quickly, from a man's face before.

'What is it?' Even as he asked, Aidan was throwing the pass-through up, bulleting through.

'The baby's coming. Now.'

'Ring the doctor,' Aidan shouted, and was out the door.

'Now,' Trevor repeated to Darcy. 'It's coming now. There's no time for the doctor, and the phones are out in any case.'

'Oh, Mother of God.' Then she bit back the spurt of fear. 'Let's hurry, then. Jack, Jack Brennan – man the bar. Someone tell Shawn and Brenna. Tim Riley, will you go for Mollie O'Toole? She'll know what to do.'

Leaving her jacket on the hook in her rush, she scurried out into the rain. 'How did you find her?' She was shouting, but her voice was all but swept away by the wind, drowned under the crashing of the waves against the seawall.

'I was coming down, the house was dark. I thought something might be wrong.'

'No, no, I mean how is she? Is she holding up?'

'She was alone.' Trevor would never forget the way she'd looked, or that he'd had to leave her. 'She was scared. In pain.'

Fear skidded down Darcy's spine. 'She's a tough one, our Jude Frances. She'll come through it. As for the rest of us, we'll just have to figure out what to do.'

Darcy shoved at the hair plastered to her face as she rushed into the house. 'You don't have to come up. It must be hard on a man.'

'I'm coming.'

Jude sat up in bed, her hands clutched in Aidan's as she panted. His eyes were wild, but his voice was crooning. 'That's the way, darling, that's just fine. Nearly over now. Nearly done.'

She collapsed back, her face running with sweat. 'They're getting stronger.'

'She's having it here.' Aidan got to his feet, but kept his hand gripped on Jude's. 'She says she's having it here. She can't be having a baby here. I've told her. But she won't listen.'

'Of course she can have it here.' Darcy spoke cheerfully over the sick dread in her throat. If Aidan panicked, she knew the desperate would become the impossible. 'And won't that be cozy? Such a night you've picked, Jude Frances, for bringing the next Gallagher into the world. It's a wild one.'

As she spoke, she moved to the side of the bed, dried Jude's face with a corner of the sheet. What to do? What was she supposed to do? God, she couldn't think. No, she *had* to think.

'Now, then, you went to all those classes. Why don't you tell us what we should do first to be some help in this whole business?'

'I don't know. It isn't supposed to be like this. God, I'm so thirsty.'

'I'll get you some water.'

'Ice.' Trevor took a step forward. 'She can have ice chips. Aidan, she'd probably be more comfortable if you got into bed behind her, helped support her back. She's better off sitting up a little. I was my sister's backup coach during all three of her labors.'

Of course, he thought, that had been something of a lark. All happening in a nice clean and cheerful birthing suite, with his brother-in-law manning the post and a doctor and nurse-midwife in attendance.

'There.' Darcy smiled brightly. 'A man with experience. Just what we need. I'll get you a cool, damp cloth, darling, then some of those ice chips.'

Jude let out a gasp, one hand flailing in the air, grasping for Darcy's arm. 'Now! It's coming now!'

'No, not yet.' Plan, priorities, order, Trevor told himself and bracing, flipped back the sheet. 'It's crowning.' He put everything out of his mind but what needed to be done. 'Don't push yet, Jude. Blow through it. Breathe. Aidan?'

'That's it, darling. Pant.' He wrapped an arm around her, ran his hand in circles on her rock-hard belly. 'Hold on to it now and pant, and you'll slide right over the pain.'

'Over it, my ass!' With the contraction at its vicious peak, Jude reached back, got a fistful of his hair, and had his eyes bugging out. 'What the hell do you know about it? What the bloody hell do you know, you jerk!'

'You can do better than that,' Darcy urged and wondered if Jude's fingers would dig right down to the bone on her arm. 'There's much better names to call him at such a time.'

'Idiot, moron, ape. *Bastard!*' she shouted when the pain spiked.

'All of those and more, my darling,' he murmured, still stroking. 'I'm all of those and more. There, there, it's passing. Now, if you could just let go of me hair and leave me what you haven't torn out by the roots.'

'Let's get busy.' Time, Trevor thought, was getting short. He heard the crash of the front door, the thunder of feet on the stairs and was grateful they'd have more hands.

'Shawn.' He shot out orders the minute Shawn and Brenna ran in the room. 'Get a fire going in here. We need it warm. Brenna, go down and get some ice, chip some for Jude to chew on. Find some good sharp scissors, and cord. Darcy, fresh sheets and towels.'

While they scattered, Trevor looked down at Jude. 'I'm going to wash up. My sister liked music during delivery, said it soothed her.'

'We were going to have music playing.'

Trevor nodded. 'Sing,' he ordered Aidan before he walked out of the room.

They worked smoothly together, and fast. Within ten minutes the fire was blazing, filling the room with light and heat. Outside, the storm was screaming in a kind of wild triumph, but there, in that room, voices were raised in song.

In bed, Jude leaned back against Aidan, trying to catch the breath the contractions robbed her of. Every ounce of will was focused on the child who was determined to be born. Such focus and purpose left no room for modesty. She could only be grateful that Trevor knelt at her feet, between her updrawn knees.

'I have to push. I *have* to.'

'Hold on a minute.' That was for himself, bracing room. 'You have to stop when I tell you, so I can turn the baby, the head and shoulders.' He'd watched it, he reminded himself, fascinated by the process. He could do it.

'Okay, on the next contraction, push, and when I say stop, pant and blow.' He wiped the sweat off his forehead with his forearm. He took a breath, let it out.

'It's starting. I have to—'

'Push!' he told her, just as lightning flashed, a million wild jewels of light. And to Trevor's shock, the baby shot out, a slick bullet, into his hands, and already wailing.

'Wow.' He stared foolishly at the wriggling, furious life that he held. 'She was in a hurry. It's a girl,' he managed, and looked up. But his eyes met Darcy's and watched, for the third time, as she wept.

'Jude.' Rocking, Aidan pressed his face against his wife's hair. 'Look at her. Just look. She's beautiful.'

'I want—' Words strangling in her throat, Jude held out her arms. When Trevor laid the baby over her belly, and her hands touched her for the first time, she laughed.

'She's perfect. Isn't she perfect? She already has hair. Look at her. Such lovely, dark hair.'

'And a voice to match.' Shawn came around the bed, bent to brush a kiss over Jude's cheek. 'She's your nose, Jude Frances.'

'Does she? I think you're right.' Turning her head, she met Aidan's mouth with hers. 'Thank you.'

He managed no more than her name before he laid his head on her shoulder.

'What do we call her?' Darcy turned the cloth she'd dampened again, dabbed at Jude's face. She wanted to collapse beside the bed, lay her head on it and weep and laugh. Not yet, she ordered herself. Not yet. 'What name did you finally choose for her?'

'She's Ailish.' Jude stopped counting her daughter's fingers – look how tiny! how perfect! – to look down at Trevor. 'What's your mother's name, Trevor?'

'What?' He hadn't moved, and now shook his head as if to clear it. 'My mother? She's Carolyn.'

'Her name is Ailish Carolyn Gallagher. And you'll all be her godparents.'

For a little while no one noticed the storm had gone silent.

It was the oddest sensation to find his legs weak when he went downstairs. He felt full of energy, of light, so much so that he thought he could run ten miles without being winded. But his legs were weak as water.

Brenna and Shawn were already back in the kitchen and had a glass of whiskey poured for him. Without a word, he took it, knocked it back.

'That's fine, but now you'll have to have another.' Brenna did the honors and poured with a generous hand. 'For a toast. To Ailish Carolyn Gallagher.'

They clinked glasses, and he drank again, forgetting his usual caution in the spirit of the event. 'Some night.'

'That it is.' Shawn slapped his back. 'God bless you, Trevor, you were a champion.'

'No offense to Trev, but I'll give Jude the prize tonight. I hope I'm half as sturdy when my time comes.'

Trevor raised his glass, then caught the sparkling look that ran between them. 'Are you pregnant?'

'We just announced it tonight at the pub, which is why I've tea in my glass instead of whiskey. But you needn't worry, as I'm not due till February, and we'll be done with all but the fancy work on the theater.'

'We should have ours at home as well, Brenna. It was lovely this way.'

'That's fine, we'll do just that. As soon as you figure out how to give birth.'

'Either way,' Trevor said, 'congratulations.' He touched his glass to hers again, and Shawn's. 'Just do me a favor and try not to work as fast as your sister-in-law. Managing the whole business in under two hours is just a little too nerve-wracking.'

'With the loveliest of endings. You did a fine job.'

'That you did,' Shawn agreed. 'Now we'd best get over to the pub, spread the word. If you're up for it, come and join the celebration. I can promise you won't buy another drink in Gallagher's in your lifetime.'

To Trevor's numb shock, Shawn took him by the shoulders and kissed him with great enthusiasm. 'God bless you. Let's be off, Brenna.'

Trevor stood alone in the kitchen and laughed.

'It's a happy night,' Darcy said as she stepped in.

'Shawn kissed me, right on the mouth.'

'Well, then, I can't be outdone by my own brother.' She leaped, sent him staggering back, and kissed him hard and long. 'There, now, that should do it.'

But the humor faded out of her eyes as they went soft, as she laid her hand on his cheek. 'You're a hero. No, don't shake your head at me. We might've fumbled through that without you, but I don't like thinking of it.'

'You kept your head.'

'I wanted to run screaming.'

'Me, too.'

She blinked at that, hopped down. 'Is that the truth? You looked so competent, so calm. Laying down orders, then taking charge like you delivered babies as a hobby every Saturday.'

'I was terrified.'

'Then you're even more of a hero.'

'It wasn't heroics, it was stark terror.' And now

he could admit it. 'It was nothing like my sister. All I had to do with her was be there, hold her hand, listen to her curse my brother-in-law, maybe breathe with her. And there's doctors and monitors and . . . stuff,' he said, running down. 'This was . . . Jesus. This was primitive. It was fantastic.'

He finished off the rest of his whiskey. 'Nothing was the way it should've been. The storm, the power, Jude sprinting through labor like that. Nothing was the way it should've been, yet it was all exactly right. Like it was meant.'

'All of us together this way, in this house.' She touched a hand to his arm. 'Yes, it was exactly right. I feel I was part of a miracle tonight. The baby, our Ailish, she looked healthy, didn't she?'

'She looked perfect. Don't worry.'

'You're right, of course. Bellowing like that on the way out, and already nursing. What could be better? And Jude's just glowing. So, let's have ourselves a toast to our perfect little miracle.'

He eyed the whiskey bottle. 'I've already had two, with Brenna and Shawn.'

'And your point would be?' she asked as she got another glass and poured.

'Nothing. Don't know what I was thinking. To our miracle, then. The newest Gallagher.'

'*Slainte.*' She brought the glass to her lips, tipped her head back, and swallowed in a way that made him feel obliged to do the same. 'I'm going to make the new mother some tea, then tidy up. Will you be at the pub?'

'I'll wait for you here.'

'That would be lovely.' She turned to put the kettle on, spied the pot staying warm under a cozy. 'Shawn's beat me to this as well as to kisses. Sit down and take a load off,' she suggested as she arranged cups on a tray. 'Miracles aside, delivering babies is an exhausting business.'

'You're telling me.'

He started to sit when she went out, then felt guilty. He should go up, make sure, see if anything else was needed. Besides, he couldn't sit. He was too full of that brilliant wash of energy.

Then he heard the front door open, and Darcy's voice cheerfully greeting Mollie O'Toole.

Thank you, Jesus, Trevor thought fervently, and for the first time in his life was thrilled to pass the reins of control into the hands of another. He'd wandered around the kitchen, glanced out the dark window, and was just thinking about making coffee, if he could find it, when Aidan came in, all but dancing.

'There's the man of the hour.'

This time Trevor was braced, but still didn't manage to evade the hearty kiss. 'That's three for three,' he muttered. 'I'm getting used to it. How's Jude?'

'She's glowing. Sitting up in bed, pretty as you please, and drinking tea while Darcy cuddles the baby.'

'Darcy?'

'Kicked me out of the room,' Aidan said as he

got yet another glass. 'Said I was to come down here and drink like a new father so she could start her auntie's privilege and spoil the baby.'

'Auntie?' Try as he might, he couldn't visualize Darcy as auntie.

'Mollie O'Toole's fussing around, and says she's staying the night. They've already got Ailish dressed up in a little sleeping gown with lace on it. She looks . . .'

He trailed off, just leaned forward and laid his palms on the counter. 'Christ. *Christ!* What this does to a man! My soul's shaking, I swear to you. I never knew there was more to feel than I've already felt. That I could love like this in a heartbeat's time. There she is, not an hour old, and I'd kill for her. Die for her. When I think I might have missed them if fate hadn't opened the door for me.'

Trevor said nothing, could say nothing.

'I'll owe you all of my life for this one night.'

'No.'

'I will. If one day you're blessed with a child of your own, you'll know just how much is owed.' Aidan shook himself, turned back. Any more, he thought, and he'd embarrass the man beyond redemption. 'The Irish are sentimental sorts. Let's have a drink here, so I can get my legs back under me.'

Trevor figured that if the toasting kept up at this pace, he would not only lose his legs, he'd fall on his face. But he raised his glass with Aidan to the new mother, and then to the child.

By the time Aidan went back up and Darcy came back down, he felt that he was watching a revolving door through the deep amber haze of Jameson's. And that seemed perfectly fine.

It only took one look at his face, at the cheerful and decidedly sloppy grin that was as endearing as a boy's, the tousled hair and the loose body stretched out in the chair, to clue her in.

Since the look of him had her wanting to cuddle him just as she'd cuddled her niece, she walked over and patted his cheek. 'Sure and you're on your way to being piss-faced, aren't you, darling?'

'I never drink more than two. You lose focus.'

'Of course you do, and that's a fine and upstanding rule just begging to be broken on such a night.'

'It would've been rude not to toast the baby.'

'Unforgivably.'

'Are we toasting the baby again?' There was just enough sweet hope in his tone to make her chuckle.

'I think it's time we made our way over to the pub, then we'll see about that. Let's get you to your feet. You can lean on me.'

'I can stand up.' Vaguely insulted, he pushed back from the table. The minute he was upright, the room took one slow, rather lovely spin. 'Whoa.' He put a hand out. 'I'm all right. Just finding my balance.'

'Well, let me know when you've located it.' She glanced toward the bottle, winced at the level.

She hadn't realized how much they'd gotten into the poor man between them. 'We've abused you sorely, and after all your heroics, too.' Gently, she slipped an arm around his waist. 'We'll go over and get you a meal. I bet you'd like something hot in your belly.'

'You. I've already got you there, and in my head. Every damn place. Aidan kissed me, so it's your turn.'

'We'll get to that, by and by.' With her arm around his waist and his tucked companionably around her shoulders, they staggered down the hall.

'Let's go see the baby. I'm crazy about babies.' He tried to steer toward the steps as they passed, but she kept him heading for the door.

'Are you, now?' Well, what a revelation. 'We will go see her, in the morning. Ailish is sleeping now, like an angel, and God knows, Jude needs some rest.' She managed to open the door, lead him out.

The fresh air swept over him like a wave, made him sway. 'Man, what a night.'

'I warn you, if you pass out, I'm letting you drop where you fall.' But even as she threatened, she tightened her grip.

'I'm not going to pass out. I feel great.' The stars were out. Thousands of them sparkling, winking, gleaming against a sky of black glass. There might never have been a storm.

'Listen, you can hear the music from the pub.' He stopped, bringing her closer to his side. 'What's that song? I know that one.' He concentrated, until it swam clear in his mind. Then to Darcy's surprise and delight, he began to sing.

Standing in the sea breeze and starlight, she joined him on the chorus, adding harmony.

> *Her eyes they shined like diamonds.*
> *I thought her the queen of the land,*
> *And her hair hung over her shoulders*
> *Tied up with a black velvet band.*

He grinned down at her, shifting until he could get both arms around her. 'It always makes me think of you.'

'Under the present circumstances, I'll take that as a compliment. I didn't know you could sing, Trevor Magee, and in such a fine, strong voice. What other surprises have you in store for me?'

'We'll get to that, by and by.'

So she laughed, wiggled free enough to get him walking again. 'I'll count on it.'

CHAPTER 20

Most of it was a blur. Faces, voices, movement. He lost track of how many pints had been pushed into his hands, how many times his back had been slapped. He remembered being kissed, repeatedly.

Many had shed tears. He was mortally afraid one of them had been himself.

There'd been singing – he was pretty sure he'd done a solo. Dancing – he vaguely remembered rounding the floor with his chief electrician, a burly man with a tattoo. At one point, he thought, he'd made a speech.

Sometime during the chaos, Darcy had pulled him into the kitchen, poured some soup into him. Or stuck his head in the bowl, he wasn't quite sure which.

But he recalled trying to wrestle her to the floor, which wouldn't have been such a bad idea if Shawn hadn't been in the room at the time. And if he hadn't lost the bout to a woman he outweighed by a good fifty pounds.

Jesus Christ. He'd been stinking drunk.

It wasn't that he'd never been drunk before. He'd

gone to college, for God's sake. He knew how to get drunk and party if he wanted to. The thing was, this one had snuck up on him, and he didn't enjoy being quite so hazy on the details of his behavior.

There was, however, one little item that came through clear. Waterford-crystal clear.

Darcy guiding him up to bed, him stumbling, and yes, still singing, an embarrassingly schmaltzy rendition of 'Rose of Tralee.' During which he stopped long enough to inform Darcy that his mother's aunt's cousin's daughter had been the Chicago Rose in 1980-something.

Once he was prone, he made a suggestion that was so uncharacteristically lewd, he imagined another woman would have kicked him back down the stairs. But Darcy had only laughed and remarked that men in his condition weren't nearly as good at it as they thought they were, and he should go on to sleep.

He'd obliged her, and saved himself what would have been certain humiliation, by passing out.

But he was awake now, in the full dark, with approximately half the sand of Ardmore Bay in his mouth and the full cast of Riverdance step-toeing inside his head.

He lay there, hoping for oblivion.

When his wish wasn't granted, he imagined the pleasure of sawing off his head and setting it aside to cure while the rest of him got some sleep. But to do that he'd need to find a damn saw, wouldn't he?

Deciding a bucket of aspirin was probably wiser, he eased himself up. Every inch was a punishment, but he managed to bite back a groan and keep at it until he could sit on the side of the bed.

Through bleary eyes, he stared at the glowing dial of the bedside clock. Three forty-five. Well, it just got better and better. Gingerly, he turned his head and saw that Darcy slept on, peaceful and perfect.

Bitter resentment mixed with the sand in his mouth. How could the woman just sleep when a man was dying beside her? Had she no sensibility, no compassion? No goddamn hangover?

He had to fight the urge to give her one rude shove so misery could have company.

He gained his feet, grinding his teeth when the room swam sickly. His stomach suited up, joined the other branches of his body in mutiny, and churned queasily.

Never again, he vowed. Never again would he drink himself drunk. He didn't care if he delivered triplets in a tornado. The thought of that made him want to smile, the wonder of holding that small, raging life in his hands. But all he could manage was a grimace as he hobbled toward the bathroom.

Without thinking, he switched the light on, then heard the high whine that was his own gasping scream. Blind, tortured, he slapped at the switch, came perilously close to whimpering when the blessed dark descended again.

He could only stand, his back braced against the wall, and try to get his breath back.

'Trevor?' Darcy's voice was low, her hand gentle as she laid it on his arm. 'Are you all right?'

'Oh, I'm just dandy, thanks. And you?' The words ground out of a throat currently lined with heavy-gauge sandpaper.

'Ah, poor darling. Well, if you didn't have a head after last night, you wouldn't be human. Come on, then, lie back down and let Darcy fix you up.'

Perversely, now that she was awake and prepared to soothe, annoyance added to the ugly mix brewing inside him. 'You and your horde of sadists fixed me up already.'

'Oh, it was terrible. I'm so ashamed.'

He'd have narrowed his eyes into a glare, but there was too much blood in them to risk it. 'Are you laughing?'

'Of course I am.' She tugged his arm, drawing him back into the bedroom. 'But that's neither here nor there. Here we go now, that's the way, sit yourself down.'

She was entirely too good at it, he thought. Just how many drunken men had she tucked back into bed the morning after? It was a vile thought, an unworthy thought, but even knowing that he couldn't stop it from taking root.

'Had a lot of practice at this?'

Something in his tone slapped, but she shrugged it off because he was suffering. 'You can't run a pub and not have the occasional experience with someone who's overindulged. You need a bit of the cure, is all.'

'If you think you're going to get more whiskey into me, you're crazy.'

'No, no, I've something better than hair of the dog. Just rest yourself.' She fluffed pillows behind him, gentle and efficient as a nurse. 'It'll take me a minute. I should have made some up last night, but with all the excitement I didn't think of it.'

'I just want a goddamn aspirin.' Preferably one the size of Pluto.

'I know.' She touched her lips to his throbbing head. 'I'll be right back.'

What game was this? he wondered. Why was she being so nice, so sweet? He'd awakened her at four in the morning and snarled at her. Why wasn't she snarling back? Why wasn't *she* suffering any effects of last night's celebration?

Suspicious, he forced himself to get up again, and with his jaw clenched, managed to tug on jeans. He found her in the kitchen, and once his abused eyes adjusted to the laser beam of light, saw she was mixing ingredients in a jar.

'You stayed sober.'

She stopped what she was doing, glanced back at him. Oh, the man looked as raw and rough as they came, and still managed to be handsome. 'I did, yes.'

'Why?'

'It was clear even before we got to the pub that you were going to be drunk enough for both of us. And you were entitled. Darling, why don't you sit down? There's no need to pay the piper any more than his due. Your head must be big as the moon this morning.'

'I don't make a habit of getting drunk.' He said it with some dignity, but because he felt decidedly queasy, he retreated to the living room to sit on the arm of a chair.

'I'm sure you don't.' Which was why, she supposed, he wasn't just feeling sick this morning, but insulted as well. It was adorable. 'But it was a night for exceptions, and you were having such a grand time, too. It was surely the best party we've had around here since Shawn and Brenna's wedding, and that went on all day and half the night.'

She came out, her robe flowing around her legs, carrying some dark and suspicious-looking liquid in a glass. 'We had so much to celebrate, after all. Jude and the baby, then the theater.'

'What about the theater?'

'The naming of it. Oh, that likely washed away in the beer, didn't it? You announced the naming of the theater. *Duachais*. I was never so pleased, Trevor. And those in the pub, which by the time we closed was everyone and their brother, were just as delighted. It's a fine name, the right name. And it means something to all of us here.'

It annoyed him that he couldn't get a handle on the moment, that he'd announced it when he hadn't been in control. Where was the dignity in that? 'You thought of it.'

'I told you the word. You put it in the right place. Here, now, wash the aspirin down with this, and you'll be right as rain in no time.'

'What is it?'

'Gallagher's Fix, a little potion passed down in my family. Come on, now, there's a good lad.'

He scowled at her, plucked the aspirin out of her outstretched hand, then the glass. She looked gorgeous, rested, perfect, with her hair loose and glossy, her eyes clear and amused, her lips slightly curved, in what might have been sympathy. He wanted, desperately, to lay his aching head on her lovely breasts and die quietly.

'I don't like it.'

'Oh, now, it's not such a bad taste all in all.'

'No.' With nothing else available, he drank, glared. 'I don't like the whole deal.'

This need, he thought as she patiently waited for him to drink the rest. It was too big, too sharp. Even now, when he felt as vile as a man could and still live, he was all but eaten up with need for her. It was humiliating.

'Thanks.' He shoved the glass back at her.

'You're very welcome.' A little twist of temper snaked through her, but she cut it off, reminding herself he deserved a bit of patience and pampering.

He'd brought her niece into the world, and for that she would owe him for a lifetime. He'd named his theater from a word she'd given him. That was an honor she wouldn't slight by snapping at him when he was laid low.

So she sucked it in and prepared to spoil him a bit.

'I'll tell you what you need now, and that's a good hot breakfast to set you right. And your coffee. So I'll be your loving mother and see to it for you.'

She started back toward the kitchen, stopped, shook her head. 'For heaven's sake, where's my mind? Speaking of mothers, yours called to the pub last night.'

'What? My mother?'

'It was when you were outside, serenading the Duffys on their way home. Shawn spoke with her, and she said just to give you a message.'

He'd gotten to his feet. 'Nothing's wrong?'

'No, not at all. Shawn said she sounded very pleased and happy and added a congratulations for Ailish. In any case, she said to tell you yes, of course it's supposed to, and that she couldn't be more delighted. She asked that you call her back today so you can tell her all about it.'

'Supposed to what? All about what?'

'I couldn't say.' She moved back into the kitchen, her voice carrying through the opening.

'I don't know what she's—' He broke off, staggered, and braced himself with a hand to the back of a chair.

I'm in love with her. Is it supposed to make me feel like an idiot?

But he hadn't sent that post. He'd been about to delete that part when the power had gone out,

394

the laptop had died. He had never hit Send. It wasn't possible for her to have gotten a message he'd never sent.

Then he rubbed his hands over his face. Hadn't he already learned the impossible was almost the ordinary here?

Now what? His mother was delighted that he felt like an idiot. That was good, he decided, pacing restlessly now, because he was feeling more like one every minute.

The woman in the next room was making him weak and senseless and stupid. And part of him was thrilled knowing he could be weakly and senselessly and stupidly in love. That worried him.

He stopped to stare at the painting of the mermaid and felt his temper strain. And who was he in love with? Who the hell was she really? How much of her was the siren depicted here, and how much the affectionate woman fixing breakfast? Maybe it was all a spell, some sort of self-serving magic woven over him that had taken his own emotions out of his control to satisfy someone else's – something else's needs.

Maybe she knew it.

Duachais. The lore of a place, he thought grimly. Darcy knew the lore of this place. Gwen had been offered jewels, from the sun and moon and sea. And had refused them. What had Darcy said when he'd asked her if she would trade her pride for jewels?

That she'd find a way to keep both.

He'd lay odds on it.

She had kept this painting, hadn't she? Kept it, hung it on her wall long after she'd shown the artist the door.

'I've no breakfast meats up here,' Darcy said as she came out. 'So I'll have to go down and pilfer from Shawn. Would you like bacon or sausage, or have you room for both?'

'Did you sleep with him?' It was out, stinging the air, before he could stop it.

'What?'

'The artist, the one who painted this.' Trevor turned, faced his own senseless outrage. 'Did you sleep with him?'

She took a moment to try to think over the wild beat of blood in her head. 'You're trying my patience, Trevor, and I'm not known for it to begin with. So I'll only say that's none of your concern.'

Of course it wasn't. 'The hell it isn't. Was he in love with you? Did you enjoy that, being that fantasy for him, before you sent him on his way?'

She wouldn't let it hurt. It wouldn't be permitted. So she concentrated on the bright fury in Trevor's eyes and let her own rise to meet it. 'That's a fine opinion you have of me, and not so far from the mark. I've had men, and make no excuses for it. I've taken what suited me, and so what?'

He jabbed his hands into his pockets. 'And what suits you, Darcy?'

'You did, for a time. But we seem to be at the end of that. Take yourself off, Trevor, before each

396

of us says something that makes it impossible for us to deal with one another again.'

'Deal?' She was a cool one, wasn't she? Cool and composed while he wanted to rage. 'There's always the deal, isn't there? Contracts and payments and benefits. You keep your eyes on the prize.'

She went white, her eyes a blazing blue in contrast. 'Get out. Get out of my house. I don't take a man to my bed who looks at me and sees a whore.'

Her words slapped him back, to sense and to shame. 'I never meant that. I never thought that.'

'Didn't you? Get out, you bastard.' She began to shake. 'And before you go I'll tell you this: Jude painted that for me, for my birthday.'

She whirled around, strode into the bedroom.

'Darcy, wait!' He managed to block the door before it slammed in his face. 'I'm sorry. Listen—' That was as far as he got before whatever she threw shattered against the door an inch from his face. 'Jesus!'

'I said get out of my house.'

She wasn't pale now. She was flushed with rage and already grabbing for a pretty china trinket box. He had an instant to decide – advance or retreat. An instant too long, as the box bounced smartly off his shoulder before he could reach her.

'I'm sorry,' he said again, gripping her arms before she could select the next missile. 'I was out of line, completely wrong. No excuse. Please, listen to me.'

'Let go of me, Trevor.'

'Throw anything you want. But then listen to me. Please.'

She was vibrating like a bow sharply plucked. 'Why should I?'

'No reason. Listen anyway.'

'All right, but let me go, and step back. I don't want you touching me now.'

His hands flexed on her arms, a jerk of reaction. Then he nodded, released her. He'd deserved that, he told himself. That and worse. Because he was afraid she intended to give him worse, to turn him out of her life, he was prepared to beg.

'I've never been jealous before. Believe me, I don't like it any more than you do. It's contemptible.'

'You've had women before me. Do I throw them in your face and cheapen you that way?'

'No.' He'd cut deep, he realized, and they were both bleeding. 'I had no right, and no reason. I wasn't thinking about the painting, really. My feelings for you are out of control. So I'm out of control.' Her eyes, shocked, stared back at his when he stroked her hair. 'They make me stupid.'

Her heart began to thud. 'I've thought of no man but you since we met. Is that enough for you?'

'It should be.' He dropped his hand. 'But it's not.' He paced away, back, away. Plans and schedules were out of the picture now, he decided. It was time to act. 'I need something more than that from you, and I'm willing to give you whatever you want.'

The rapid beating of her heart skipped in a quick stab of pain. 'What do you mean?'

'I want, let's say, exclusive rights. For that, for you,' he added, turning back to her. 'You can name it. I've got an apartment in New York. If it doesn't suit you, we'll find another. Personally, and through the company, I have several homes in a number of countries. If you like, I can buy property here, build a house to your specifications. Whatever traveling's required between us, I assume you'd want a base here.'

'I see.' Her voice was quiet, her eyes lowered. 'That's considerate of you. And would I also have access to bank accounts, credit cards, that sort of thing?'

His hands went back in his pockets, balled into fists. 'Of course.'

'And for all this.' She traced a finger over the bracelet she'd worn since he'd first clasped it on her wrist. That she'd loved first for its beauty, and then simply because he'd given it to her. 'I would, in turn, keep myself only for you.'

'That's one way of putting it. But I—'

He never saw it coming. The little Belleek vase smacked dead between his eyes. Through the stars wheeling in front of him, he saw her face. Pale again, rigid with outrage.

'You low-lying son-of-a-toad! What's the difference between a whore and a mistress but the type of payment?'

'Mistress?' With shock, he touched his forehead, stared at the blood on his fingers. Then he was dodging crockery. 'Who said – cut it out!'

'You miserable worm. You badger!' She sent all the pretty things she'd collected over the years crashing. 'I wouldn't have you on the silver platter you were born on. So take all your fancy houses and your bank drafts and your credit line and stuff them. Choke on them!'

Tears spoiled her aim, but the ricochets and flying debris were awesome. Trevor blocked the lamp she'd yanked out of the wall, stepped on glass, swore. 'I don't want a mistress.'

'Go to hell.' It was the best she had left, and knowing it, she snatched up a small carved box and ran out with it.

'For God's sake.' He had to sit down on the bed to pick the glass out of his feet. He had the hideous notion she might be getting a knife or some other sharp implement, then his head snapped up when he heard the door slam.

'Darcy! Damn it.' Leaping up, leaving blood smeared on the floor, he rushed after her.

He supposed he could have handled it all with less finesse. If he'd been a gibbering ape. He streaked down the stairs, swore again when he heard the boom of the pub door crashing shut. For Christ's sake, here they were, neither of them dressed, and where does she take the crisis but outside? A sensible man would run in the opposite direction.

Trevor bolted through the kitchen after her.

She let the box fly as she ran, and closed her fist tight on the stone she'd kept inside it. Wishes be damned, she thought in fury. Love be damned. Trevor be damned. She was throwing it and all it meant into the sea.

She'd have no part of it now, no part of hopes and dreams and promises. If loving meant burying everything she was for a man who had such contempt for her, she would have no part of that either.

Hair flying, she raced along the seawall under a sky softening toward dawn. She didn't hear her own sobbing over the pulse and pump of the sea, nor Trevor's call and the sudden, frantic plea in it.

She stumbled onto the beach, would have fallen if he hadn't caught her.

'Darcy, wait. Don't.' His arms shook as they wrapped around her. He'd thought she'd meant to plunge into the water.

She turned on him like a wildcat, kicking, scratching, biting. In shock as much as defense, he pulled her down to the sand where he could lie on top of her and hold her still.

A hangover, he discovered, was nothing compared to the pain inflicted by Darcy Gallagher in a temper. 'Easy.' He panted it out. 'Just take it easy.'

'I'll kill you, first chance.'

'I believe it.' He looked down at her. Her face was streaked with tears, and they continued to fall though her eyes were burning with fury. Here, he thought, was the first time he'd seen her weep for herself. And he'd caused it.

'I deserve it for fumbling this so badly. Darcy, I wasn't asking you to be my mistress – which is a ridiculous term and completely unsuitable when applied to you. I was trying to ask you to marry me.'

He knocked the breath out of her as surely as if he'd rammed his elbow into her belly. 'What?'

'I was asking you to marry me.'

'Marry, as in husband and wife, rings on our fingers, till death do us part?'

'That's the one.' He risked a smile. 'Darcy, I—'

'Will you get off me? You're hurting me.'

'Sorry.' He rolled aside, helped her up. 'If I could just start over.'

'Oh, no, let's pick up where you left off. When you were offering me houses and bank accounts. That's how you chose to propose to the likes of me?'

Her voice was like sugar, with each crystal honed like a razor. 'Ah . . .'

'You think I'd marry you for what you have, for what you can give me?' She shoved him back two full steps. 'You think you can buy me like one of your companies?'

'But you've said—'

'I don't care what I've said. Any moron would see it was just talk if they took the time to listen, to look. I'll tell you what you can do with your fine houses and your big accounts, Magee. You can burn them to the ground for all I care. I'll buy the fucking torch and light it.'

'You made it clear—'

'I made nothing clear, as nothing was clear to me. But now I will. I'd have taken you with nothing. Now I'll take you not at all.'

She turned, flung back her arm. It was blind instinct that made him grab her, pry her fingers open. 'What is this?'

'It's mine, given to me by Carrick. Sapphire.' She jerked away from him as her voice began to hitch again. 'The heart of the sea. I could wish on it, he told me. One wish only, for my heart's desire. But I didn't use it and never will. Do you know why?'

'No. Don't cry any more. I can't stand it.'

'Do you know why?' Her voice rose, thick with tears.

'No. I don't know why.'

'I wanted you to love me without it. That was my wish, so how could I use it and have it come true?'

Magic, he thought. He'd worried about magic, and she'd held it in her hand. He'd offered her things, and she'd wanted him. Enough to have thrown the fortune he'd let himself believe she desired most back into the heart of the sea.

'I did love you without it. I do.' He took her hand again, closed her fingers over the stone. 'Don't throw it away. Don't throw us away because I've been stupid. I swear to you I've never handled anything as badly as I've handled this. Let me fix it.'

'I'm tired.' She closed her eyes and turned to face the sea. 'I'm just so tired.'

'A long time ago – it seems like a long time – when I told you I couldn't fall in love, I meant it. I believed it. There was no one . . . There was never any magic with anyone else.'

She stared down at the gem in her hand. 'I didn't use it.'

'You didn't have to. You just had to be. I haven't been the same since I met you. I tried to compensate for that. Stay in control, stay focused. I didn't come here looking for you, Darcy, looking for this. That's what I told myself. I was wrong, and I knew it. Somehow I've always been looking for you, always been looking for this.'

'Do you think I'm so hard, so small of heart that I can't love where there isn't gain?'

'I think there are countless parts to you. Every time I see a new one, I'm more in love with you. I wanted you to belong to me, and it was easier to believe I could hold on to you by offering you things.'

Through the weariness was just enough shame to make her honest. 'That's what I wanted once. Before you.'

'Whatever either of us wanted once doesn't count now.'

No, nothing had to count but this. If they wished it. So she turned to him. 'Do you mean it?'

'I mean it.'

'Then so will I.'

'More than anything, right now, I want you to look at me and tell me you love me.'

She shivered in the wind, crossed her arms over her breasts, gazed out to sea. It was the moment, she thought, when her life changed, when dreams trembled, when spells were cast and broken.

'Damn it, Darcy.' His impatient voice shattered her romantic images. 'Do you want me to crawl?'

She looked at him then, the beginnings of amusement lighting eyes still damp from tears. 'Yes.'

He opened his mouth, was on the verge of dropping literally and metaphorically to his knees. And that, he decided, would just put the cap on everything else he'd suffered that morning. 'No. Damned if I will.'

Her heart simply soared. After one wild laugh, she threw herself into his arms. 'There, now. There's the arrogant bastard I love.' She pressed her lips to his, warm and welcoming. 'There's my heart's desire.'

'Say it once,' he murmured against her mouth. 'Without swearing at me.'

'I love you, just exactly as you are.' She drew back, made a sympathetic sound. 'Oh, no, look at that, you're bleeding.'

'Tell me about it.'

'Well, I'll bandage you up in a bit of a while, but I want you to ask me again, and ask me proper. Here, between the moon and the sun and the sea, before the light breaks through to morning. There's magic here, Trevor, and I want our slice of it.'

He felt it, as she did, the trembling edge of power just held in check. He had no ring to give her, no symbol to seal the moment. Then he remembered the silver disk and slipped the chain over his head, over hers.

She remembered the words that had come as in a dream. *Forever love.*

'A charm,' he said. 'A promise. Marry me, Darcy. Make a life with me. Make a home and children with me.'

'I will, and gladly. Here.' She pressed the stone into his hand. 'A charm. And a promise.'

'You humble me.'

'No, never that.' She brushed her fingers over his cheek. 'I'd take you, Trevor, prince or pauper. But, loving me, you'll understand I'm pleased you're more in line with the prince.'

'You're perfect for me.'

'I am, indeed.' She sighed, laid her head on his shoulder when he drew her close. 'Do you hear it?' she murmured. 'Over the beat of the sea.'

'Yeah, I hear it.'

Music, full of joy and celebration, the lilt of pipes, the herald of trumpets.

'Look, Darcy.' He touched her hair. 'Over the water.'

She turned her head, stayed in the circle of his arms and watched. As the sun broke through in the east, shimmered its light over the sea, turning the sky to the polished glow of seashells, the white horse flew with a flash of wing.

On his back rode Carrick, his silver doublet aglint, his dark hair swirling. In his arms, her head on his heart, rode his lady, her eyes of misty green bright with love.

Up they rose, a triumphant sweep of motion, over green hills shimmering with dew. And in their wake left a rainbow that glimmered like jewels.

'They're together at last,' Darcy whispered. 'And happily now, ever after. The spell's broken.'

'That one is. This one . . .' He turned her face back to his. 'It's just getting started. Can you handle ever after, Darcy?'

'That I can, Trevor Magee.' She kissed him, sealed the vow. 'I can handle it, and you.'

While the sun strengthened, they walked away from the sea. The music drifted into the hush of dawn, under a rainbow that arched from beginnings to ever afters.